"PROFOUNDLY MOVING, WONDERFULLY CRAFTED . . .

One Perfect Rose is Mary Jo Putney in top form. . . . Brimming with details of the era. . . . A feast for the heart and mind. Mary Jo Putney has created a meaningful novel. . . . A definite 'keeper.' "

—*Romantic Times*

"With a beautiful underlying theme of love, forgiveness, redemption, and the possibility of life after death . . . *One Perfect Rose* is one perfect book."

—*Baton Rouge Advocate*

"Brilliant . . . *One Perfect Rose* may be the best Regency romance to come along in several years. . . . The metamorphosis of Stephen is real and will be deeply felt by readers. . . . [A] great novel that will require readers to purchase multiple copies because the book will be read so often, the pages will be ruined."

—www.amazon.com

"Get out your handkerchiefs. . . . *One Perfect Rose* will have you turning the pages while you wipe that annoying wetness from your eyes so you can keep reading. Putney always does tortured heroes well, but this time she's surpassed herself in the gentle story of Stephen and Rosalind."

—*CompuServe Romance Reviews*

*Please turn the page
for more rave reviews. . . .*

"AN EXTRAORDINARY STORY

that will tug at the heartstrings of all readers. Mary Jo Putney brings to life a cast of characters the readers will adore. She weaves an incredible tale of love, pride, betrayal, and family devotion. Readers will not want to put this book down."

—America Online Review

"Wonderful . . . It's like finding a Pot O' Gold at the end of the rainbow. . . . An endearing story of how love overcomes everything. . . . The reader wishes it would last much longer. Read it!"

—*The News-Chief* (Florida)

"*One Perfect Rose* will go on my keeper shelf along with most of Putney's other books. I know I will want to reread it because it is such a compelling story."

—*The Romance Reader* (online)

"BREATHTAKINGLY BEAUTIFUL!

It was riveting from page one; you just can't stand for this to end. . . . You will love their story; get the book, clear some time, and enjoy the magic."
—*Bell, Book, and Candle* (newsletter)

"Mary Jo Putney has no peers when it comes to attacking modern society's problems by adeptly placing the issue in an historical context. Her range is mind-boggling: death, alcohol, and physical and mental abuse. . . . *One Perfect Rose* is one perfect Regency romance."
—*Affaire de Coeur*

"In her superb, inimitable style, Putney takes a pair of magnetic, beautifully matched protagonists, places them in a dark, impossible situation, and makes it work."
—*Library Journal*

BOOKS BY MARY JO PUTNEY

Fallen Angels Series
Thunder and Roses ✓ Nick
Petals in the Storm ✓
Dancing on the Wind ✓
Angel Rogue ✓
Shattered Rainbows ✓
River of Fire ✓ Kenneth
One Perfect Rose* ✓ Stephen

Silk Trilogy
✗ *Silk and Shadows*
Silk and Secrets ✓
Veils of Silk ✓

Other Historicals
Dearly Beloved ✓
The Rake and the Reformer ✓
Uncommon Vows ✓

Regencies
✗ *Carousel of Hearts*
The Diabolical Baron ✓
✗ *The Would-Be Widow* —
✗ *Lady of Fortune* —

**Published by Fawcett Books*

ONE PERFECT ROSE

Mary Jo Putney

FAWCETT GOLD MEDAL · NEW YORK

To Pat Rice: friend, ally, co-conspirator

I'd like to give a special acknowledgment to Michael Miller
for his wonderful insights about what it's like to look into the
abyss and return. And to his wife, Laurie Grant Miller, for the
other half of the story.

A Fawcett Gold Medal Book
Published by The Ballantine Publishing Group
Copyright © 1997 by Mary Jo Putney

http://www.randomhouse.com

Library of Congress Catalog Card Number: 98-96114

ISBN 0-449-00018-4

Manufactured in the United States of America

First Hardcover Edition: July 1997
First Mass Market Edition: June 1998

10 9 8 7 6 5

*I believe as I did as a child, that life has
meaning, direction and value;
that no suffering is lost; that each drop
of blood and every tear counts;
and that the secret of the world is to be found in
St. John's "Deus Caritas est"—"God is love."*

—FRANÇOIS MAURIAC

PROLOGUE

London, 1794

Silent as a mouse, the child stood in the alley, her gaze riveted on the young couple sauntering down the shabby waterfront street. The two were different from those who lived in the neighborhood, their clothing clean and their voices full of laughter.

And they were eating meat pies. The little girl sniffed the savory scent longingly.

The tall gentleman made a sweeping gesture with one hand, and a sizable chunk of his pie fell to the dirty street. He didn't even notice.

The child waited with the patience bred of fear for the couple to move on a safe distance. But she daren't wait too long because a dog or maybe a rat would get her prize. When she judged it safe, she darted forward to grab the scrap and stuff it into her mouth. It was still warm, the best-tasting food she'd had in forever.

Then the lady glanced back over her shoulder. The child froze, hoping not to be noticed. She'd learned quickly that it was better not to be seen. Bad Boys threw stones, and there had been the Bad Man who'd lured her close with the offer of a sausage, then picked her up and run his hot hands over her. He'd wanted to eat her, she thought, but he let her go quick enough when she bit his tongue.

Then he'd chased her, screaming bad words until she squeezed under a sagging fence and hid in a pile of trash. She'd eaten the sausage there, and ever since she watched out for the Bad Man, and for any other men who might get that queer look in their eyes.

The pretty dark-haired lady raised her brows and said with a smile, "There's a wee scavenger alongside us, Thomas."

The smile was nice, but even so, the child started to retreat toward the alley.

The lady crouched so that her blue eyes were at the same level as the child's. "No need to run, sweetheart. There's enough to share." She held out the rest of her meat pie temptingly.

The child hesitated, remembering the Bad Man, who had also lured her with food. But this was a lady, and the pie smelled so *good*.

She skipped forward and snatched the morsel from the lady's hand. Then she backed up a few steps and ate, keeping her wary gaze on her benefactors.

"Poor mite," the man named Thomas said in a deep voice that rolled across the street. "Her parents should be whipped for letting her roam the streets like this."

A rusty voice spoke from the shadows. "The brat ain't got no parents. She's been livin' alone in the streets hereabouts for a couple of months."

The child recognized the voice as that of the grizzled old woman who spent every day watching from a shadowed doorway, a clay pipe clamped in her toothless gums. The old woman had once traded some food, and she'd thrown no stones. She was safe.

The pretty lady frowned. "The child has been abandoned?"

"Orphaned, more like," the old woman said with a shrug. "I hear she came off a ship with some female who up and died in the middle of the quay soon as they landed. A watchman tried to catch the brat so's she could be sent to an orphanage, but she hid. She's been scrounging around here like a seagull ever since."

The pretty lady looked horrified. "Oh, Thomas, we can't leave her here. She's just a baby—she can't be much more than three years old."

"We can't carry her off like a kitten, Maria," the gentleman said. But his gaze went consideringly to the child's face.

"Why not? No one else seems to want her. The good Lord must have sent us down this street to find her. We haven't had a babe of our own yet, and heaven knows it's not for lack of trying." The pretty lady looked sad for a moment. Then she turned back to the child and extended her hand slowly. "Come here, sweetheart. We won't hurt you."

The child hesitated. She had learned the hard way to be wary. But Maria reminded her of a different lady from that other life before hunger and rags and filthy streets. Before . . . before . . .

Her mind veered away, unable to name the unbearable. Instead, she looked at the blue eyes. There was kindness, and something more. A promise?

The child began to inch forward, her gaze flicking back and forth between the lady and the gentleman. If he'd moved, she would've run, because men weren't always safe, but he stayed very still. His eyes were just as blue, and just as kind, as his wife's.

When she came within reach, the lady tenderly stroked her head. "Your hair is blond, isn't it? I didn't realize what was under the dirt. Very nice with those big brown eyes. Would you like a new mama and papa, sweetheart?"

Mama. Papa. Those were words from the distant, golden past. The child weighed the chance of danger against her desperate longing. Suddenly hope over-powered fear. The child ran the last two steps and flung herself into the lady's arms.

Maria swooped her up in a hug. Her arms were warm and soft, like that other lady's in the past. Warm and soft and *safe*.

"Don't worry, sweetheart," she crooned. "Thomas and I may not be respectable by some standards, but you'll never lack for food or love." The child saw with wonder that there were tears in the lady's blue eyes when she glanced at her husband. "Don't look at me like that, you big Irish fraud. Your heart is just as soft as mine."

" 'Tis not our hearts that are soft, but our heads," Thomas said wryly. "But you're right; we can't leave her here, and the sooner we get her into a soapy tub the better." He took the child's hand in his great warm grasp. "What's your name, darlin'?"

Embarrassed by his attention, the child buried her face against the lady's neck. She smelled clean and sweet, like flowers after rain.

"I guess we'll have to name her ourselves." Maria stroked the child's back tenderly. "Pretty as a rose, but so brave. Imagine, surviving on the streets for weeks when she's such a tiny thing."

"Then let's name her after Rosalind, the most intrepid of heroines," Thomas suggested. He squeezed the child's hand gently. "This is your lucky day, little rose."

"No, Thomas." Maria pressed a warm kiss to the child's temple. "The luck is ours."

CHAPTER 1

Ashburton Abbey, 1818

"Mortally ill."

The physician's words hung in the air, stark and lethal as scorpions. Stephen Edward Kenyon, fifth Duke of Ashburton, seventh Marquess of Benfield, and half a dozen other titles too trivial to mention, went still as he donned his shirt after the medical exam. Mentally he repeated the phrase, as if study would somehow alter its significance.

Mortally ill. He had known that something was wrong, but he had not expected . . . this. The doctor must have made a mistake. True, in the last few weeks the pain in Stephen's belly had gone from mild discomfort to attacks of wrenching agony. But surely that meant only an ulceration—painful but not life threatening.

Grateful for his skill in controlling his expression, he resumed buttoning his shirt. "That's a surprisingly definite statement for a physician. I thought you and your colleagues preferred to avoid dismal predictions."

"You have always been known as a man who appreciates honesty, Your Grace." Dr. George Blackmer concentrated on meticulously replacing equipment in his medical case. "I thought I would do you no favor to conceal the truth. A man in your position needs time to . . . put his affairs in order."

Stephen realized, with jarring force, that the physician

was quite serious. "Surely that won't be necessary. Apart from occasional stomach pains, I feel fine."

"I've been concerned about your condition ever since the pains began, but hoped my early suspicions were wrong. However, the truth can no longer be denied." The physician glanced up, his gray-green eyes troubled. "You are suffering from a tumefaction of the stomach and liver—the same condition that afflicted your gamekeeper, Mr. Nixon."

It was another blow. Nixon had deteriorated from a bluff outdoorsman to a pain-wracked wraith in a matter of months. And his death had been a difficult one.

Not ready to face himself in the mirror, Stephen tied his cravat by touch, going numbly through the usual motions. "There is no treatment?"

"I'm afraid not."

Stephen pulled on his dark blue coat and smoothed the wrinkles from the sleeves. "How precise is your estimate of six months?"

Blackmer hesitated. "It's hard to predict the course of a disease. I would say that you would have no less than three months, but six months would be . . . optimistic."

In other words, if the physician's diagnosis was correct, Stephen would be dead by Christmas. Probably well before then.

What if Blackmer was wrong? It was certainly possible, but the man was a respected and conscientious physician. A foundling raised by the parish, he'd been so promising that the old duke, Stephen's father, had sent him to study medicine. In return, Blackmer had provided the Kenyon family with excellent care. It was unlikely he would give the son of his former patron a death sentence unless he was absolutely sure.

Stephen forced his numb mind to consider what other questions to ask. "Should I continue taking the pills you gave me on your last visit, or is there no point?"

"Keep taking them. In fact, I've compounded more." Blackmer reached into his case and drew out a corked jar. "They're mostly opium to dull the pain, with some herbs to cleanse the blood. Take at least one a day. More if you feel discomfort."

Like habit, manners were a convenient crutch. As he accepted the jar, Stephen said politely, "Thank you, Dr. Blackmer. I appreciate your honesty."

"Not all of my colleagues would agree, but I believe that when the end is inevitable, a man should have time to prepare himself." The doctor closed his case with a snap, then hesitated, his expression deeply troubled. "Do you have any other questions, Your Grace?"

Next to a death sentence, no other question mattered. "No. I bid you good day, Doctor." Stephen reached for the bell cord.

"I can find my own way." His gaze intense and unreadable, Blackmer lifted his case and went toward the door. "I shall call again in a fortnight."

"Why?" Stephen asked, no longer able to keep the edge from his voice. "By your own admission you can do nothing, so I see no reason to suffer more prodding."

Blackmer's face tightened. "Nonetheless, I shall call. Just continue taking your medicine, and send for me if you feel the need." Then, shoulders bowed, the tall man left the duke's private sitting room.

Stephen stood quite still in the middle of the floor, trying to absorb the reality of the doctor's words. Death in a matter of months. It seemed impossible. He was only thirty-six, for God's sake. Not young, perhaps, but not old, and in excellent condition. Except for the mild asthma he'd had as a boy, he'd always enjoyed robust good health.

A tendril of anger began to twine through his numbness. He should know perfectly well that age had nothing to do with it. His wife, Louisa, hadn't even been thirty when she had died of a fever. Her death had been a shock, but at least it had been mercifully swift.

His gaze fell on the gilt-framed mirror above the mantel. His reflection looked no different than it had an hour earlier: a tall, lean figure, chestnut hair, the strong-boned Kenyon face that was so well suited to arrogance. But an hour ago he had been a duke in the prime of life, a man who had just put off mourning clothes for his wife and who had begun to think of new beginnings.

Now he was a dead man walking.

Anger flared again, as intense as the time when he was fifteen and his father had announced that a suitable marriage had been arranged. Lady Louisa Hayward was only a child, but pretty and exquisitely mannered. The old duke had said that she would grow up to be a perfect wife and duchess.

Furiously Stephen had protested that a decision so important to his future should not be made without his knowledge. His brief rebellion had quickly withered in the face of his father's anger and scorn. By the time he left the study, he had accepted his duty.

Looking back, he had to give his father credit: the old duke had been half right. Louisa had grown up to be a perfect duchess, if not a perfect wife.

He crossed to the door that connected his rooms with the duchess's suite. He had not set foot there since Louisa's death over a year ago. And not often before, if the truth be told.

The bedroom and dressing room were immaculately clean and empty, with no lingering traces of Louisa except for the samples of her exquisite needlework. Beautifully embroidered pillows, chair seats too pretty to sit on. Whenever he thought of his wife, it was with her head bent over an embroidery frame. She had passed through life lightly, guided by the dictum that a lady's name appeared in the newspapers only three times: on her birth, her marriage, and her death.

Stephen closed the door and turned back to his sitting room. A picture of Louisa hung across from him. It had been painted by Sir Anthony Seaton, the finest portrait artist in England. Seaton had done a good job of capturing Louisa's porcelain beauty, and the hint of sadness behind her enigmatic gaze.

Stephen wondered for the thousandth time if somewhere behind his wife's flawless facade there had been strong emotions. Passion, anger, love, hate—anything. But if deep feelings existed, he had never found them. In all the years of their marriage, they had never exchanged a harsh word. Anger required emotion.

It was true that she had regretted not bearing a child, but her regret had been for what she saw as her failure to do her duty. Unlike Stephen, she had not regretted the lack of children for their own sake. But she had been unflagging in her duty, urging him to visit her bed regularly even though their couplings had been joyless.

Would Louisa be waiting for him when he died? Or was that reserved for people who had loved each other? They had been, at best, friends. At worst, strangers who sometimes shared a bed.

He went to the window and gazed out over the vast, rolling acres of Ashburton Abbey. The small lake shimmered like a silver mirror. He could not remember ever being told that someday the abbey would be his; the knowledge had always been part of him. The greatest satisfactions of his life had come from this land.

If Blackmer was right, soon his younger brother, Michael, would be the master of the estate. Stephen had long accepted that his brother or his brother's son would probably be the next duke, but he had thought that would be years in the future. Decades.

His brother would make a just and capable duke because he also knew his duty. But Michael hated Ashburton Abbey. Always had. Given what he had suffered here as the family scapegoat, Stephen couldn't blame him, but it meant that Michael would surely continue to live at his much loved Welsh estate. The abbey would be silent and empty, waiting for some future generation to take pleasure in the ancient stones, in the magnificent great hall and the peaceful cloister garden.

His anger again erupted into rage. All of his life, Stephen had done his duty, striving to master his responsibilities, to be worthy of his position. He had excelled in both athletics and academics at Harrow and Cambridge. He had consciously tempered the arrogance his father considered suitable to a Kenyon, for his own belief was that a true gentleman had no need of arrogance or boasting. He had treated his wife with consideration and respect, never reproaching her for what she was incapable of giving.

He had always played by the rules—and for what? *For what?*

Violently he swept his arm across a graceful side table, sending china ornaments and fresh flowers crashing to the floor. He had lived the life ordained for him, and it had been no life at all. Now that he was finally in a position to reach for a richer existence, his time had run out. It wasn't fair. *It bloody wasn't fair.*

With the long wars over, he'd been planning to travel, to see Vienna and Florence and Greece. He had wanted to do foolish things for no other reason than because they gave him pleasure. He'd wanted to learn if he was capable of passion, and perhaps take another wife who would be a companion instead of merely a perfect duchess.

He swung about, half suffocated by his anger. Though he had no intention of discussing his condition, such news would not stay secret for long. Soon there would be curiosity in people's eyes as they studied him, wondering how much longer he would last. Worse, there would be pity. His neighbors would whisper when he entered a room. His valet, Hubble, would go around with tears in his eyes, making a bad situation worse.

For the first time in his life, Stephen yearned to escape Ashburton Abbey and everything it represented. He paced across the room. Though he was surrounded by people, there was no one to whom he could unburden his soul. At Ashburton he was "the duke," always calm and detached. But now he felt a desperate desire to be someplace where he was a stranger while he came to terms with Blackmer's crushing diagnosis. He wanted to be anonymous and *free,* even if it was only for a few weeks.

Well, why not? He stopped pacing and thought about it. Nothing was stopping him from leaving. He could go anywhere he chose, at any speed he wished. He could stop at village fairs and admire the pretty girls. Stay at inns that his servants would consider beneath their dignity. And August was a lovely time to ride through England.

This might be his last summer.

Gut twisting, he went into his bedroom and jerked open a drawer, yanking out a couple of changes of linen. Since he would go on horseback, he must travel light. How did ordinary people get their laundry done? It would be interesting to find out.

The door opened and his valet entered. "I heard something break, Your Grace." Hubble halted, his eyes widening at the disarray. "Your Grace?"

Stephen straightened from the pile accumulating on the bed. Since Hubble was here, he might as well be put to work. Stephen could be on his way that much sooner. "I'm going on holiday," he said with private irony. "Pack my saddlebags."

Hubble regarded the clothing doubtfully. "Yes, sir. Where are we going?"

"*We* are not going anywhere. I am going alone." Stephen added a well-worn volume of his favorite Shakespeare to the growing pile.

The valet looked baffled. He was a competent and good-natured man, but he'd never understood Stephen's antic streak. "But who will take care of your clothing, sir?"

"I guess I'll have to do it myself." Stephen unlocked a desk drawer and took out a fistful of money, enough for several weeks. "It will be quite educational."

Hubble visibly winced at the thought of how badly his master would be turned out. Forestalling the inevitable protest, Stephen said sharply, "No arguments, no comments. Just pack the blasted saddlebags."

The valet swallowed. "Very good, sir. What sort of clothing will you require?"

Stephen shrugged. "Keep it simple. I don't intend to go to any grand balls." He lifted his gold card case from his desk drawer, then dropped it in again. Since he wouldn't be traveling as the Duke of Ashburton, there was no need for calling cards.

Then he sat down and wrote brief notes to his secretary and steward, telling them to proceed as usual. He considered writing his brother and sister but decided against it. There would be time enough for that later.

As the duke wrote, Hubble packed the saddlebags. When he finished, he asked in a subdued voice, "Where shall I send urgent messages, Your Grace?"

Stephen sealed the last note. "Nowhere. I don't want to receive any messages."

"But, sir . . ." Hubble started to protest, then quieted when his master gave him a gimlet stare. He settled for saying, "How long will you be gone, Your Grace?"

"I have no idea," Stephen said tersely. "I'll come back when I'm ready, and not a moment before."

Beginning to look frantic, Hubble said, "Sir, you can't just run off like this!"

"I'm the most noble Duke of Ashburton," Stephen said, a bitter edge on his voice. "I can do any damned thing I want." Except live.

He slid his arm under the bulging saddlebags and lifted them before remembering something else that must go. There was just enough room to add Blackmer's jar of pills.

Then he spun on his heel and headed for the door. He didn't know how much time he had left, but he intended to enjoy every minute of it.

CHAPTER 2

"Rose!" Maria Fitzgerald cried. "My left wing is falling off!"

"Just a moment, Mama," Rosalind replied. Swiftly she pinned the end of a long swath of shimmering blue-gray fabric onto the rough boards of the barn wall. The generous folds of material had done duty as royal hangings and misty seas, and they made quite a decent magical cave. She attached the other end of the fabric twenty feet away, studied the effect, then went to help her mother.

The barn was bustling as the Fitzgerald Theater Troupe prepared for the performance that would begin in a few minutes. Even though they were staging *The Tempest* in an isolated market town and half the people in the cast weren't really actors, the members of the company took their work seriously.

Sure enough, one of Maria's silvery wings was drooping. Rosalind retrieved needle and thread from her kit, then ordered, "Turn around."

Obediently her mother pivoted so Rosalind could make repairs. Maria Fitzgerald's lush womanly curves were not what Shakespeare had in mind when he described the delicate sprite Ariel. However, the gauzy, floating layers of her costume would win approval from male members of the audience, and her acting skill allowed her to make any role her own.

Rosalind anchored the sagging wing to her mother's

bodice with a dozen swift stitches. "There you are, as good as new. Just don't go flying into any trees."

While her mother chuckled, a clear soprano voice wailed, "Rose, I need you most *desperately*! I can't find Miranda's necklace."

Rosalind rolled her eyes as she responded to her younger sister's plea. Jessica, a blood-and-bone daughter of Thomas and Maria Fitzgerald, had inherited her parents' beauty and expressive nature. Her dark lashes sweeping upward, she said dramatically, "If I don't have my glittering sea creatures around my neck, everyone will watch Edmund instead of me. It will quite upset the balance of the play."

Rosalind made a rude noise. "You know very well that the men who aren't staring at Mama will be staring at you. As to your necklace, I think it's in that box."

Jessica dug into the chest that doubled as furniture in Prospero's sea cave. A moment later she pulled out a nine-foot-long silken rope with gilded shells, starfish, and sea horses dangling from it. "Yes! How do you keep everything straight?"

"Organizational skill is the boring gift of the untalented," Rosalind said as she draped the long rope of ornaments around her sister's slim figure.

Jessica laughed. "Nonsense. You've all sorts of talents. The company would fall apart without you." She surveyed her sister's tall form. "And if it weren't for that awful costume, the men would stare at you as well."

"I can live without that pleasure." Rosalind pinned the trailing necklace to her sister's costume. It wouldn't do for her to trip over a dangling starfish, as she had that time in Leominster. She'd fallen right into the mayor's lap, not that he'd minded. "Besides, I rather like my awful costume. You must admit that Caliban is a perfect role for me. Very little acting required."

Jessica looked stricken. Since acting was her life, she had never really grasped that her adoptive sister didn't feel the same way. "You're quite a good actress," she said loyally. "You do well at all sorts of roles."

"Meaning that I speak my lines clearly and don't fall over my feet on the stage," Rosalind said cheerfully. "That doesn't make me an actress, love."

"Rosalind!" A rich baritone voice boomed across the barn, sending pigeons flapping from the rafters. "Help me with the lights."

"Coming, Papa." She crossed the improvised stage to where Thomas Fitzgerald, in full magician's robes for his role as Prospero, was setting the footlights. Gingerly she lifted one of the reflectored oil lamps and set it a foot to the left, then moved another a bit farther to the right. "There, that should light the corners better."

"Right as always, darlin'," Thomas said with a fond smile. He gestured toward the door. "Brian says there's a good crowd gathering outside."

"Of course—we're the most exciting thing to happen in Fletchfield this summer."

As her father moved away, Rosalind scanned the straw-strewn stage. The simple set was decorated, all the actors costumed. Outside Calvin was selling tickets in a staccato cockney voice. All was in order for the performance.

How many such scenes had she surveyed—hundreds? Thousands? She suppressed a sigh. She had spent most of her life in similar places, creating evenings of magic for the entertainment of the locals before packing up and moving on to the next town. Perhaps at twenty-eight she was getting too old for the life, though age hadn't dimmed the zeal of her adoptive parents. But they were actors. Rosalind Jordan, foundling, widow, and de facto stage manager, was not. Sometimes she thought wistfully of how nice it would be to have a home to call her own.

But everyone she loved was under this roof, and that made up for the more tiresome aspects of life on the road. She raised her voice and called, "Places, please."

The members of the cast darted behind the flimsy panels that acted as stage wings. When Rosalind had taken her own place, she signaled to her young brother, Brian, to open the doors and admit the waiting audience.

Let the magic begin.

Day Eighty-three

A week of aimless traveling had taken the edge off Stephen's first furious reaction to the news of his impending demise. His mood had ranged from anger to fear to a fervent hope that Blackmer was wrong, though two agonizing attacks of gastric pain made the diagnosis seem increasingly plausible. Luckily both seizures had been at night, in the privacy of a rented room. He hoped to God that he wouldn't have one in public, though it would probably happen sooner or later. He tried not to think about that.

With bitter humor he had decided to count down the days of his life. Assuming that he would have at least three months, he'd started the count at ninety. He would go down to zero. Then, if he still lived, he would begin counting up because every day after that would be a bonus.

With doom's own clock ticking in the back of his head, he had wandered north from Ashburton Abbey through the Marches, the ancient borderlands where the Welsh and English had skirmished for centuries. When he crossed the old Roman road that ran west into Wales along the southern coast, he had reined in his horse and considered going to visit his brother. Michael had been a soldier, and had more than his share of firsthand knowledge of how to face inevitable death.

But Stephen was not yet ready to reveal his grim news to his brother. Perhaps it was because he was the elder. Though they'd become friends in the last year and a half, he did not want to go to Michael as a fearful supplicant. Which proved, he supposed, that he might have renounced arrogance but pride was still very much a part of him.

His pace leisurely, he had continued north into Herefordshire, then angled east, enjoying the scents and sights of late summer. It had been interesting to book rooms at inns for himself, to negotiate the cost of a bed or a meal. As a gentleman he was always treated politely, but without the awed deference that was usual. He enjoyed the change. Being a duke could be a flat bore sometimes.

But his journey was a lonely one. He'd always been detached from the turbulent, often childish emotions that controlled most of humankind. Now he felt sometimes that he was already a ghost, watching the activities of mortal men but not participating. It was time to turn his horse for home and become the duke again. He must fulfill his responsibilities: update his will, notify those who had a right to know of his condition, decide what actions he wanted accomplished before the estate passed to his brother.

He must also visit his elder sister, Claudia. In recent years they had not been close, but he would like to see her again before he died. Perhaps they might find common ground before it was too late.

Storm clouds were gathering as he rode into the small town of Fletchfield. Since there was no good reason to continue riding and get soaked, he scanned the facades of the two inns on opposite sides of the high street, choosing the Red Lion because of its flower-filled window boxes.

Stephen engaged a room and was about to go upstairs when he noticed a playbill posted on the wall. The "Renowned Fitzgerald Theater Troupe" was going to present Shakespeare's *The Tempest; or, The Enchanted Island* that very evening. Stephen had always enjoyed the theater, and the tale of the magician duke who lived in island exile with his young daughter was a particular favorite. Heaven only knew what a cast of fourth-rate actors would do to the play, though.

Glancing at the innkeeper, he asked, "Is this company any good?"

"Well, I don't know what a gentleman such as yourself would think," the innkeeper said cautiously, "but we like 'em. They come through every summer. Always put on a rousing good show. Action, excitement." He grinned. "And some very attractive ladies givin' a glimpse of their ankles, and sometimes a bit more."

It didn't sound like great art, but it would be a diversion. After Stephen had rested and dined, he went out to the high street. The air was heavy with August heat, but a distant rumble of thunder gave promise of cooling rain.

The temporary playhouse on the outskirts of town was easy to find, since a good part of the population of Fletchfield was going in the same direction. A few glanced curiously at the stranger, but most were too excited by the prospect of the play.

Outside the barn where the performance was to be held, fifty or sixty people were milling about while a foxy little man with a cockney accent sold tickets. A shilling bought a wooden disk stamped with an *F* that would be collected when the doors opened. No nonsense about box seats versus the pit here.

Stephen was waiting in line to buy his ticket when he saw two elderly ladies, clearly sisters. Their clothing was shabby but almost painfully clean. The smaller one said briskly, " 'Twould be fun and no denying, but we simply can't afford two shillings."

Her sister, tall and sweet faced, said wistfully, "I know, Fanny, I know. 'Tis better to eat than watch a play. But *Romeo and Juliet* was ever so lovely that time five years ago when the hens were laying well and we had a bit of money to spare."

"No use thinking about it." Clearly the leader, Fanny took her sister's arm and started to lead her away. "Let's go home and have a nice cup of raspberry leaf tea."

It was Stephen's turn to buy a ticket. On impulse he handed the seller three shillings and received three disks. Then he circled around and made his way through the crowd to the elderly sisters. Bowing politely, he said, "Excuse me, ladies, but could you do a service for a stranger?"

Fanny surveyed him skeptically. "Are you in need of directions?"

He shook his head. "I was to meet two friends here to see the play, but I've just learned that they will be unable to come. Would you take these?" He held out two disks.

The tall sister's eyes lit up. "Oh, Fanny."

Her sister said gruffly, "Can't you return them?"

"The chap selling the tickets looks like a stubborn sort to me," Stephen said earnestly. "I'd rather not get into an argument with him."

As Fanny debated the morality of accepting his offer, her gaze went from Stephen to her sister's hopeful face. Understanding flickered in her eyes. "Thank you, sir. You are most kind." She put out her hand. Though she might not accept charity for herself, she would not deny her sister the pleasure of the play.

"It is you who are kind, ma'am." He handed over the tokens, then bowed and moved away, feeling a warm glow. Each year he gave literally thousands of pounds to the local parish and charities for everything from supporting military widows to establishing schools for the children of laborers. But those things were done from a distance; he didn't even write the bank drafts himself. Spending two shillings from his pocket to give a treat to a pair of elderly ladies brought him more satisfaction than all of the money he had given away in the past. Perhaps he should become more involved with the results of his philanthropy.

His pleasure dimmed when he recalled that there was not much time to change his habits. Still, there were a few months ahead of him. He resolved to spend part of that time making sure that his charitable bequests would achieve the best results. He might visit some widows and schools, not to receive gratitude for doing what was his duty, but to appreciate the humanity of those he helped.

The doors swung open, propelled by a lively boy of ten or eleven from inside the barn. "Ladies and gentlemen, step inside," the cockney ticket seller shouted. "*The Tempest* is about to begin!"

The approaching storm produced a timely rumble of

thunder. Amid general laughter, the crowd moved into
the barn, each receiving a playbill in return for hand-
ing over a disk. A pungent atmosphere gave evidence
that cows were usually stabled within. Crude wooden
benches were set in rows facing the improvised stage,
which ran across the far end of the building. Light came
from narrow clerestory windows and a half-dozen footlights that separated the audience from the actors.

The barn filled quickly, the elderly sisters managing
to secure seats in the first row. Since there were not
enough benches for everyone, Stephen took a position
by the right wall. Not only was there a cool draft, but
he would be able to leave quietly if the play was
unwatchable.

Gradually the audience settled down, buoyant with
anticipation. Stephen found that he shared the feeling.
There was something magical about the theater, even
under these crude conditions. Though he had a box at
every important playhouse in London, it had been
years since he'd looked forward to a performance this
much. He mentally crossed his fingers that the actors
were halfway decent.

A metallic boom of artificial thunder filled the barn,
causing several nervous feminine squeals. Then, as
flashes of false lightning illuminated the shadowy corners of the barn, two sailors staggered from the left
wing and started talking loudly about the storm and the
likelihood that their ship would sink.

The sailors were soon joined by their noble passengers, all of them bewailing their imminent drowning.
After they left the stage, there was a long moment of
stillness before the magician Prospero and his lovely
young daughter Miranda emerged from the flimsily
curtained right wing. Both players had dark hair and

striking blue eyes, and were clearly blood kin. Stephen glanced at his playbill. Thomas and Jessica Fitzgerald.

Prospero had such a commanding presence that it took a moment for Stephen to really see Miranda. His first look was followed by another, for the girl was a beauty. The audience greeted her with applause and whistles of appreciation. Miranda gave her admirers a saucy smile and waited for quiet. When she had everyone's attention, she began to speak in a crystalline voice that carried easily throughout the barn.

Prospero replied, his rich baritone explaining that he was really the Duke of Milan and she was a princess. Stephen straightened from his lounging position, attention riveted. Fitzgerald and his daughter were splendid, with a natural style that suited the intimacy of the improvised theater perfectly. Stephen had never seen the scene played better.

Next to enter was the sprite Ariel, accompanied by more whistles and claps from the rowdier men in the audience. Stephen didn't blame them; Ariel was a voluptuous woman of mature years named Maria Fitzgerald, surely wife to Prospero and mother to Miranda in real life. She could also act. Her rich voice brought poignance to the role of the invisible spirit who served the magician faithfully yet yearned for freedom.

Stephen crossed his arms over his chest and relaxed against the wall, more than willing to surrender to the illusions of the play. Nature helped by contributing a genuine tempest and drumming rain to counterpoint the story. Within the darkened barn, it was easy to believe in a distant island of mist and magic.

Though the other actors weren't as talented as the three Fitzgeralds, all were competent. The monster Caliban drew laughter when he appeared in a shaggy ape suit that completely disguised the age and appearance of the actor. Cheerfully unsubtle, the monster's stomping about the stage was received with great approval. The handsome young man who played Ferdinand, the yearning lover, wasn't much of an actor, but his appearances brought happy sighs from females in the audience.

The Tempest wasn't noted for a strong plot. However, Stephen particularly liked the story because of the way Prospero forgave his brother Antonio for the latter's murder attempt a dozen years before. The world needed more forgiveness, which was why Stephen had taken such efforts to reconcile with his own brother. He had been rewarded many times over for reaching out across years of anger and misunderstanding.

By the time the lovers had been united, Ariel had been joyfully released from the magician's service, and Prospero had drowned his magic book, Stephen felt better than he had in days. The Fitzgerald company was an unexpected gem. He joined the enthusiastic applause after Prospero's final speech.

One by one the other actors emerged from the wings to take their bows. Dropping her sprite's playfulness, Maria Fitzgerald was regal, while her daughter Jessica was a charming coquette.

Then Caliban strode out onto the stage and swept off the shaggy headdress to reveal the tawny hair and pleasant features of an attractive young female. Though she was not so beautiful as Jessica Fitzgerald, there was something about the young woman's laughing expression that appealed to Stephen. She seemed like someone he would enjoy knowing.

She glanced in his direction, and he saw that her eyes were dark brown, a striking contrast to her light hair. She was older than Jessica, perhaps in her mid-to-late twenties. A woman, not a girl.

He looked down at the playbill and saw that Caliban was played by Mrs. Rosalind Jordan. No Mr. Jordan was listed in the cast. He raised his eyes as the players departed from the stage. For a moment he indulged himself in the fantasy that this was London and he was a well man so that he could go to the greenroom and meet that laughing, tawny lady. Discover if she was as winsome as she seemed, and what sort of figure was concealed beneath that enveloping costume.

But this was not London, and he was not a well man. It was hard to be interested in amorous play when concerned about survival. Good-bye, Lady Caliban.

The performance was to conclude with a one-act afterpiece, but Stephen decided he'd had enough of the smoke and smell of the improvised theater. He edged his way to the door and went outside. The storm had passed, leaving a light misting rain and refreshing coolness. The days were long in August, and the lingering, cloudy twilight turned Fletchfield into a hazy fairyland.

Stephen walked along the empty high street, enjoying the scents of wet earth and growing things, of wildflowers and the faint, delectable aroma of baking bread. He liked the feel of moisture on his face and the otherworldly beauty the misty droplets lent to the landscape. Rain was one of many things he appreciated as never before. The only positive effect of Blackmer's pronouncement was that, in an odd way, Stephen felt more alive than he ever had.

His reaction to Rosalind Jordan had reminded him that although he was dying, he wasn't dead yet. What was the right course of action for a man in his circumstances? He'd intended to look for a new wife until he heard Blackmer's death sentence. Of course, there were some who would say it was his duty to remarry swiftly in the hopes of fathering an heir. His brother Michael would be delighted if that happened.

But years of dutiful marriage had produced no children before, and Stephen was not convinced that the fault had lain with Louisa. It was as likely that he was the one incapable of creating new life. Or perhaps the emptiness of their marriage had made it impossible to produce something as full of vitality as a baby.

The thought of marrying in cold blood for dynastic reasons made his mouth tighten to a thin line. He'd made one dutiful marriage, and he'd be damned if he would do it again. So he would not seek a wife.

What about an affair? In London there were beautiful women who would give a convincing illusion of passion to a man who could pay the price.

But would he want even that? The loneliest times of his life had been in Louisa's bed, where their bodies joined but nothing he did could call forth a single spark of response from his wife. A purchased pretense of love might be equally bleak, especially now, when passion was not in the forefront of his mind.

No, if he was dying, he would do it as he had lived—alone. Many men, and women, too, had done that with dignity. Surely he could do the same.

The rain was becoming heavier. He raised his face to the sky and closed his eyes, letting the cool liquid trickle over his face as he thought of some lines from the play he had just seen: "Full fathom five thy father lies; of his bones are coral made." Or perhaps he should be pondering the words from the funeral service: "Ashes to ashes, dust to dust."

In this case it would be Ashburton to ashes.

Expression grim, he lowered his gaze from the heavens and continued down the street in the lovely, lonely rain.

CHAPTER 3

Thomas Fitzgerald frowned out the window of the private parlor at the steadily falling rain. "Performing *The Tempest* during a real tempest was all very well, but the roads are in terrible shape this morning."

Rosalind glanced up from the costume she was mending. "True, but the rain should stop soon, and it's only eight or nine miles to Redminster."

"It will take all day to cover them," Thomas said gloomily.

Maria leaned across the breakfast table and poured the last of the tea into her husband's cup. "And what else would we be doing with the time, my lord and master?"

Thomas leered wickedly at his wife. "We could stay tucked up in this snug inn while I remind you what's best to do on a rainy day. Instead, I'll be spending my time pulling wagons out of the mud."

Maria batted her long dark lashes demurely. "There's still time to go back to our room for a quick reminder, since the young ones haven't had breakfast yet."

"Behave yourself, you two," Rosalind ordered as she slipped half a piece of toast to Aloysius, the family wolfhound, who was lazing beneath the table. "With the weather like this, we need to be off as soon as possible. If you're planning to spend the day in mud, Papa, be sure to change into your oldest clothes."

"Not a romantic bone in her body," her father grumbled.

"And a good thing, too." Rosalind was knotting her thread when Jessica floated into the private parlor.

"Good morning," her sister said with a languid sigh. "Are The Parents treating us to another show of embarrassing marital devotion?"

"I'm afraid so." Rosalind snipped her thread and put all the sewing tools back into her box. "Who are you this morning—Juliet?"

Jessica draped herself gracefully across a chair. "Yes. I think I shall die of love. Did you see that absolutely splendid gentleman in the audience last night? He was standing against the left wall. Such an air! Such presence! Such a tailor! He must be a lord. We shall have an affair."

"You will *not*!" her mother said firmly. "You're not too big to be spanked, young lady."

Not missing a beat, Jessica continued, "His lordship will admire me extravagantly, but I shall spurn his advances. Consumed by love, he will offer marriage despite my humble station, but I shall say I can never leave the stage for the boring life of a society matron. He will sink into a decline and die of unrequited passion."

Rosalind had also seen the man, for he was the kind a woman noticed—tall, confident, handsome. Well worth a few fantasies. But there was no time for fantasy this morning. "The fellow is more likely a lawyer than a lord," she said briskly. "Or perhaps a successful corn broker. Eat your eggs before Brian arrives and devours everything that isn't nailed down."

Her sister chuckled and got to her feet, her affected manner vanishing as she served herself a hearty breakfast. "I'll bet Juliet was never told to eat her eggs before her little brother got to them."

"She would if Brian had been her brother." Rosalind folded the garment she had mended and packed it into the costume trunk. "And speak of the devil . . ."

Clattering feet could be heard racing down the stairs outside the parlor. They ended abruptly in a crash. Rosalind frowned. As she was getting up, her little brother entered the parlor. He was pure Fitzgerald, with dark hair and bright blue eyes, but now his face was pale and his left hand curled protectively around his right wrist. "I just fell and broke my wrist, I think."

In the Fitzgerald family, it was very hard to tell real problems from imaginary ones, but Rosalind, her parents, and Aloysius all converged on Brian just in case his injury was serious. The boy gave a genuine yelp when Rosalind carefully examined his right wrist. "It looks like a mild sprain," she said when she was done. "I'll bandage it, and you'll be fine in a day or two. Next time, don't run on the stairs."

"I shall not be able to do my mathematics today," her brother said hopefully.

"You can and you shall," Thomas said sternly. "One does mathematics with one's head, not one's hands."

"Not true. Brian needs his fingers to count on," Jessica said with deliberate provocation.

"I do not!" her brother said indignantly. "You're the one who never got through algebra." Using his left hand, he spooned the last of the eggs onto a plate while Aloysius watched with keen canine interest.

Jessica tossed her head. She was extremely good at it. "A goddess of the stage does not need algebra. It's quite enough that I can estimate the box office receipts after a single glance at the theater."

Rosalind rolled her eyes. "I'll get my medical kit while you two squabble." She headed for the door.

Since Brian had a ten-year-old boy's talent for damaging himself, she always packed the kit last, so she could find it quickly. But before she left the parlor, she paused for a moment to glance at each member of her family.

Her heart swelled with love. Once again she gave thanks for the fate that had sent Thomas and Maria along a shabby waterfront street, and the generosity that had caused them to take in a beggar child. Rosalind had only a few vague, nightmarish memories of her time on the streets, but she remembered meeting the Fitzgeralds with absolute clarity. If she lived to be a hundred, she would never forget the kindness in Maria's eyes.

She noticed with a pang the signs of age in her parents. Both were handsome still, but they were nearing fifty, with silver threads in their dark hair. Life with a traveling theater troupe was hard. How much longer would they be able to continue? And what would happen when the long hours and constant moving became too much? They lived with modest comfort, but there was little put by. Salaries and costumes and wagons cost money.

Not that Thomas worried; he had faith that the Lord would provide. Unfortunately Rosalind lacked his belief that the Lord took a personal interest in the Fitzgerald finances.

She left the parlor, closing the door gently behind her. Perhaps Jessica would decide to try the London stage and become so wildly popular that she could afford to support her parents in their old age. She had the talent, and the ambition. Or perhaps Brian would be a great success, since he also showed signs of significant acting ability. The two of them were the family's best hope for prosperity, for Rosalind's talents were modest. One might almost say nonexistent.

With a sigh she climbed the stairs to the small room she had shared with her sister. There was change coming; she could feel it in her bones. Of course she'd always known that the family could not stay together forever. Jessica might joke about falling in love with handsome strangers, but it was a sign that she was ripe for the real thing. Someday soon she would find a husband and leave the troupe.

Rosalind only hoped that when her beautiful young sister married, she would show better judgment than she herself had.

Day Eighty-two

By the time Stephen finished a leisurely breakfast, the rain had stopped, so he set off on the long ride home to Ashburton Abbey. The violent gastric pains he'd suffered during the night had made it clear that it was time to end this self-indulgent escapade and become the duke again. There was much to be done at the abbey, and in London.

As he left Fletchfield, he crossed an arching stone bridge. Underneath ran the river that roughly paralleled the road that had brought him into town the day before. He'd thought the river placid and pretty. This morning, though, the waters had been swollen to a torrent by the night's heavy rain. Since he was taking the same route south again, he thought a moment, trying to remember if there had been a ford. No, the river and road had not crossed, which was fortunate because the floodwaters would make fording very dangerous today.

As the morning advanced, the sun emerged from

behind the clouds. He halted to admire the view from the crest of the highest hill in the area. That was part of a promise he'd made to himself: for whatever time he had left, he would never be too busy to admire a landscape or sniff a flower. He saw beauty in things he'd scarcely ever noticed before, and found a bittersweet pleasure in that.

This view was well worth admiring. Miles of lush English countryside spread out before him, the multicolored fields and copses divided by blooming hedgerows. To his right, the swollen river cut a wicked path through the green fields. The channel was narrower and the current even more turbulent than downstream at Fletchfield.

His gaze went along the road below him. A half mile ahead, a carriage and four wagons had pulled over to the side of the road because the last wagon had become mired in a muddy wallow. As Stephen watched, two men went to unfasten the team from the middle wagon to help pull the trapped vehicle free.

There was something familiar about the figures that milled around the wagons. He studied them and realized that it was the Fitzgerald Theater Troupe. The company must have gotten an early start that morning. Thomas Fitzgerald himself was giving the orders for freeing the wagon. A young boy wandered toward the river, while the ladies of the troupe began to stroll along the edge of the road, a lanky dog providing escort.

Except for one lady. Stephen smiled when he saw the tawny, bonnetless head of Rosalind Jordan. It was still hard to be sure of her figure, for she had a large shawl swathed about her. However, it was going to take time to free the wagon. Long enough for him to reach the travelers, make a polite offer of aid, and see Lady Caliban at close quarters. He set his horse, Jupiter, trotting down the hill.

The place where the road leveled out was only about a hundred yards from the flooding river. He glanced at the swift current, then frowned. The dark-haired young boy from the troupe was climbing a willow tree that overhung the swift waters. The child's parents should keep a closer watch, not that watching was easy with a lad that age.

Stephen was turning his attention away when he heard a cracking sound and a startled cry. He whipped his gaze back to the river in time to see the branch that held the boy angle downward in horrifying slow motion. Finally it broke entirely, sending the small figure into the raging waters.

A shout of alarm rose from the group around the wagons. As Stephen urged his horse toward the river, he saw from the corner of his eye a rush of movement as the members of the troupe raced toward the water.

But they would be too late. The torrent was sweeping the boy toward Stephen at the speed of a cantering horse. The small dark head disappeared from sight under the muddy waters for long, frightening moments. Either he couldn't swim, or he hadn't the strength to fight the surging river.

Stephen reached the embankment and catapulted from his horse, his mind racing. He was the only one who might be able help, but how? There were no fallen branches to extend because the river was cutting through a grain field here. Jupiter was a fine horse, but he'd always been a little water shy. It would be impossible to persuade him into the river quickly enough to save the boy.

Even before his mind reached the logical conclusion, Stephen was stripping off his coat. Then he looked at

the torrent and froze. It was fierce enough to overpower
a full-grown man, even one who was a strong swim-
mer. He was no hero. If he went in after the boy, the
odds were better than even that he would drown. It
would not be death four or five months hence, but
now, in broad daylight watched by a dozen strangers.

He wasn't ready yet. He stared at the deluge, rigid with
fear, and could not make himself move forward.

Then the raging waters lifted the boy's head above
the surface. For an instant their gazes met. The terror
and despair on the child's face ended Stephen's paralysis. He took two steps forward and made a long, flat
dive into the turbulent river. The muddy water was
shockingly cold after the warm summer day. Blinking
silt from his eyes, he struck across the current. It pum-
meled him fiercely as he fought his way toward the
center of the river. But he was making progress. He
should intersect the boy's course in a dozen or so
strokes.

As he neared his quarry, the boy submerged again.
Stephen dived below the surface, stretching as far forward as he could. His fingers found a yielding object
and he grabbed, catching the boy's wrist. He pulled the
small body toward him to get a better grip, at the same
time kicking hard to propel them upward.

The boy was gulping for air when the pair emerged
into the sunshine, but he had the wits to cooperate, not
fighting or grabbing at his rescuer. Stephen looped an
arm around the narrow chest and started toward shore.

With only one arm free for swimming, progress
against the rushing river was slow. Stephen almost lost
hold of the boy when a swirling branch slammed into
his throat. He choked, inhaled water, and went under.
By the time he got himself and his charge above the
surface again, he was exhausted. But the riverbank was

only a few feet away. He was reaching toward it wearily when he heard a cry of warning.

It was already too late. Something smashed into Stephen with numbing force, and he knew no more.

CHAPTER 4

Panting with effort, Rosalind managed to keep up with the men of the company, who were cutting across the field to the river where Brian had fallen. But they would not be in time. Unless a miracle occurred, her little brother would drown right in front of their eyes. She had no breath to spare, so her prayer was silent. *Please God, oh, dear God, please don't let him die. . . .*

Then she saw a horseman turn from the road to the river below them. The rider vaulted from his mount when he reached the bank and peeled off his coat. After an intense study of the river, he plunged into the torrent, his powerful body cleaving the waters and propelling him toward Brian.

Beside her, Calvin Ames, the Fitzgerald driver, ticket seller, and man of all work, swore as Brian and the man both disappeared. "Damned fool. They'll both drown."

"No!" Thomas said, agonized. His breathing was ragged and his face flushed, but he did not slow as he raced along the bank. "We'll get there in time. We *must.*"

The stranger resurfaced, one arm locked around Brian. "Look!" Rosalind cried, giving passionate thanks as the man began struggling toward shore. But the churning waters were fierce. Could even a strong man reach safety with only one arm free for swimming? Yet he was making headway, hard-fought foot by hard-fought foot.

Then renewed fear stabbed through her. A tree trunk was sweeping down on the pair. Barely visible, it was moving with the force of a runaway coach. Rosalind cried a warning, though the man could not avoid the hazard even if he saw it.

The log struck, and both dark heads disappeared.

A long, long minute passed. Then Rosalind saw the man rise again, Brian still secure in his grasp. And finally luck was on their side. The current had carried the pair from the fields into a wooded area. Ahead another willow leaned out over the river, the lower branches submerged. The current carried the two right into it. The man wrapped his free arm about a branch and clung, his other arm supporting Brian. He made no move toward shore, apparently too battered for further efforts.

A moment later the members of the troupe reached the trembling willow. Rosalind realized with alarm that half the earth around its roots had been swept away by the flood. Getting the man and boy to shore would be hazardous.

Summing up the situation in a glance, Calvin said tersely, "I'll go. I'm smallest."

A thick branch extended toward the unmoving figures, a foot or so above the choppy surface of the river. Calvin climbed on and carefully inched his way forward. The narrow willow leaves shivered and the branch creaked dangerously under his weight. When he was within reach, he called, "Brian, lad, can you take my hand?"

Brian raised his head. His eyes were glassy, but he reached up and grasped Calvin's hand firmly. He had to pry himself loose from the stranger's clasp. When he was free, Calvin towed him back to the bank.

Tears rolling down his face, Thomas dragged his son from the water into a fierce embrace. "Damn you, if you ever do anything so foolish again, I'll drown you myself!"

Shaking violently, Brian burrowed into his father's arms.

Thankfully Rosalind turned her attention to her brother's rescuer as Calvin called, "You, sir, do you need help?"

There was no answer. The stranger still clung tenaciously to the branch, his body swaying in the current, but there was no sign of life. Rosalind frowned. "I don't think he can hear. He must be dazed from being hit by the log."

Her gown had a sash, so she pulled it off and handed it to Calvin. "Tie this around him so that if something happens, he won't be swept away."

Calvin nodded and crept out on the branch again to tie the sash, keeping the other end looped around his arm. When the stranger was secure, Calvin said, "Jeremiah, can you help me? He's a big fellow."

Jeremiah Jones nodded. A large, calm man, he played character roles and took care of the horses. He gingerly moved out onto the branch. The tree groaned and dipped toward the water, but mercifully held. Working together, the two men managed to loose the stranger's grip and pull him to the bank. It took the help of two more men to lift him from the water and lay him out on his back.

Rosalind dropped to her knees to examine the stranger as the other women of the troupe arrived,

Aloysius loping beside them. Maria and the wolf–hound almost smothered the shaken boy, Maria simultaneously thanking God and scolding her son.

Rosalind smiled a little, but most of her attention was on the man who lay unconscious before her. Releasing Brian into Maria's embrace, Thomas came over and frowned down at the stranger. "Surely the brave devil hasn't drowned, has he?"

She shook her head. "His pulse and breathing are strong. He took quite a blow from that log, though."

Her fingers slid through his silky wet hair. Dry, it would be a dark chestnut, she thought. He was going to have quite a lump there. After careful probing she said, "I don't think his injury is too serious, but we should get him to a doctor. Redminster is closest. We can make up a bed in one of the wagons and take him into the town while you're getting the other wagon out of the mud. Does Brian need to see a doctor, too?"

"I'm all right," her brother said unsteadily. "T-take good care of that gentleman, Rosie. I thought I was gone for good."

"Aye," Thomas said forcefully. "If not for him . . ." His voice broke for a moment. "Calvin, get the man's horse. Jeremiah, bring the lead wagon as near as you can. Rose, you go along and take care of him. We'll see you at the Three Crowns in Redminster."

As Calvin and Jeremiah left to obey, Jessica came to Rosalind's side and looked down at the stranger. "Good heavens!" she exclaimed. "It's the man I noticed at the show last night—the handsome one."

For the first time Rosalind looked at the man as a whole rather than as a casualty to be examined. "I believe you're right. Keep your hands off the poor fellow until he's conscious and able to defend himself, Jess."

Jessica gave a contemptuous sniff as she knelt beside her sister. "He might not be a lord, but he's certainly brave."

Rosalind nodded in silent agreement as she studied his face. Handsome, certainly, but also stern. There was passion in that sensual mouth, and lines of strict control around it. He was a man used to being obeyed, she guessed. Not surprising since the cut and quality of his clothing clearly stated that he was a gentleman. Yet, paradoxically, his hard hands and lean, fit body showed that he was not a stranger to physical exertion.

"Should we see if he's carrying anything that has his name and address?" Jessica asked. "There must be someone we should notify."

Rosalind hesitated, then shook her head. "I'd rather not look through his things unless we have to. He can tell us himself when he wakes."

"That will ruin the mystery," Jessica said with regret. "He'll probably turn out to be sober and pompous, with a wife and eight children."

Perhaps. But as Rosalind gently tucked her shawl around his wide shoulders, she knew that none of that would matter. To her he would always be a hero.

Stephen returned to consciousness gradually. He was swaying. A ship, perhaps? No, a carriage of some sort. He was lying on his back with very little room to move. And he ached in a variety of places.

Christ, what if he had been wrongly declared dead and was in a coffin? There were ghoulish tales of those who had been prematurely buried. His eyes snapped open. To his relief, he saw that he was in a canvas-topped wagon. His movement was restricted because he was surrounded by chests and boxes, but he lay on a comfortable pallet, and a soft quilt had been tucked around him.

His head ached. He raised an unsteady hand to it, only to have his wrist gently caught in midair. "Better leave the bandage alone," a husky contralto voice said. "You took quite a knock on the head."

He glanced to his right, then blinked. Kneeling beside him was Lady Caliban. Or rather, Mrs. Rosalind Jordan. As she laid his hand down, a stray shaft of sunlight transformed her tawny hair into burnished bronze and gold and amber. All of the colors of autumn, though the unimaginative might call it light brown. Her expression had the humor and intelligence he had seen when she was onstage.

What he had not expected was the profound warmth in her dark brown eyes. He stared into the chocolate depths, mesmerized by the fact that all that kindness and concern were focused on him.

"How are you feeling?" she asked. If her eyes were chocolate, her voice was like the finest brandy, where rich smoothness concealed a powerful punch. And he mustn't forget the cream of her complexion. She reminded him of every delicious thing he'd ever tasted in his life.

She was also going to think him an imbecile. He tried to say "Fine," but the word emerged from his dry throat as a croak.

She reached for a jug beside her. "It sounds ironic after what you've been through, but would you like some water?"

When he nodded, Mrs. Jordan lifted the jug and poured water into a tin cup. Then she held the vessel to his lips so he could drink. When he was done, she sat back on her heels. "Do you remember what happened? The river?"

He thought back, then shuddered at the vivid memory of the water dragging him down. "Is the boy all right?"

"Brian is fine. Rather better than you, actually. He's my little brother. We're getting you to a physician, to make sure that you took no serious injury."

"Thank you," he murmured, his voice still almost inaudible.

"It's you who needs thanking. My whole family will be eternally grateful for what you did." She frowned. "Do you live in Fletchfield? Perhaps we should have taken you there, but Redminster is closer."

He shook his head. "Live in . . . the West Country," he managed.

"Then we'll take care of you until you're well enough to travel home." She laid her hand over his. "I'm Rosalind Jordan. I'm afraid I don't even know your name."

"Ash . . ." His throat dried before he could finish saying Ashburton.

Mrs. Jordan cocked her head to one side. "Mr. Ashe?"

He tried to correct her, but the wagon lurched into a deep rut, pitching him against a trunk of some sort. As he slipped into unconsciousness again, he was glad that Lady Caliban still held his hand.

He was running through a field of flowers, pursuing a laughing woman. Her hair streamed behind her with all the colors of autumn, and her figure was sumptuously female. He caught her by the edge of the meadow and swung her around for a kiss. She tasted of wild strawberries. Her hands ran through his hair, stroking and teasing as her breathing quickened. In the way of dreams, suddenly they were lying down together, and she was responding to his caresses with an eagerness that matched his own.

He pulled her close and kissed her again. Wild, sweet strawberries. She yielded utterly, kissing him back with frantic ardor.

Then suddenly she was pushing against his chest, saying breathlessly, "You're obviously feeling better."

His dream faded, and he realized that he was looking into startled chocolate eyes that were only inches away. He was lying on his side, this time in a real bed, in a dark, candlelit room. And Rosalind Jordan lay within the circle of his arm, hair disheveled, mouth lusciously kissable, and her expression between laughter and dismay.

He wanted to kiss her again. Instead, feeling as if her mouth and body had imprinted his like a brand, he reluctantly bid good-bye to the field of flowers and moved away. "Good God, I'm sorry, Mrs. Jordan. What . . . what has happened? Where am I?"

She propped herself up on one arm and pushed a wisp of hair behind her ear. She was fully clothed and lying on top of the covers. "A fine nurse I am," she said wryly. "I'm the one who should apologize for not doing my job better. You seemed to be doing well, so I lay down to get a bit of rest and promptly fell asleep."

She covered her mouth and gave a delicate yawn. "Sorry. It's been a long day. We're at the Three Crowns in Redminster. A physician has examined you. He said you'll have a headache and will need a day or two of rest, but your adventure caused no real harm. How are you feeling?"

Hoping his voice sounded normal, he replied, "The doctor was right about the headache, but otherwise I'm well enough, Mrs. Jordan."

"Call me Rosalind. Everyone does. Except when

they call me Rose." She gave him a wonderful, sunny smile. "After that kiss, formality would seem out of place."

As he flushed and muttered another apology, she yawned again, then swung her feet to the floor on the opposite side of the bed. "Would you like some soup? The landlady sent up a jug in a straw-packed basket, so it should still be warm. There's a pitcher of milk, too, in case that would settle better."

Though food had not always agreed with him lately, he realized that tonight he was famished. "Soup would be very welcome."

Cautiously he pushed himself upright and leaned back against the headboard. A wave of dizziness went over him but quickly subsided. He wondered who had put his nightshirt on him. "Is it my imagination, or is this situation very improper?"

She laughed. "I suppose it's improper, but we theater people are an unconventional lot." She hesitated, her expression growing wary. "Perhaps I should have warned you. My father is owner and manager of the Fitzgerald Theater Troupe."

Clearly she'd been snubbed in the past because of the family business. Wanting to restore her smile, he said, "I know. I saw *The Tempest* in Fletchfield. The performance was outstanding."

Her wariness vanished. "I think it's an excellent production, too. Prospero is one of Papa's finest roles. When he speaks of breaking his staff and drowning his book of magic, it sends chills down my spine every time."

"It had the same effect on me. He captured the essence of renunciation, when a man must give up what has been his life." Stephen hesitated, afraid his voice might give away too much, before continuing in a lighter tone, "Everyone was good, particularly Miranda and Ariel. And you're the most unusual Caliban I've ever seen."

She stood and crossed the room. Her tall, delectably rounded figure was every bit as fine as in his dream. "In the ape costume, anyone can play that role. In fact, Calvin, our ticket collector, is doing it tonight." She ladled soup into a deep bowl. "We didn't want to leave you to the care of a stranger."

"You're all so kind," he said, wishing for stronger words.

"It's no more than you deserve." She handed him the bowl and a spoon. "After all, you saved Brian's life and very nearly lost your own in the process. You're a hero."

He took a spoonful of the soup. Beef and vegetable, very tasty. "Not at all. When I got a good look at the river, I almost turned around and got back on my horse."

"But you didn't," she said, her great dark eyes glowing with warmth. "To be afraid and risk your life anyhow makes you even more of a hero in my eyes."

He shifted uncomfortably, knowing that her admiration was misplaced. It had been no great thing to risk a life that might be measured in months.

She poured some soup into a cup and took a chair near the bed. "By the way, your horse is stabled here at the inn." Her expressive eyes sparkled with humor. "Every man who sees the beast admires your taste in horseflesh. Your baggage is over in the corner. I'm afraid your boots will never be the same, but Jeremiah, our expert on leather, is drying them out. He says they'll be quite wearable by tomorrow."

Stephen shrugged. Since he'd always been able to buy anything he wanted, belongings meant very little to him—except for his horse. Jupiter was a friend, not a possession.

"Is there anyone you would like us to notify about your accident, Mr. Ashe?" Rosalind's glance went to her steaming cup of soup. "Surely your wife and family are worried about you."

He thought of his staff at Ashburton Abbey. A single note that he had been injured would bring a dozen worried people down on his head. He could summon family or friends with equal ease. But there was no one who would really *miss* him. "Thank you, but I'm not expected home at any particular time. And I'm not Mr. Ashe."

"I'm sorry," she said contritely. "What should I call you?"

He started to answer, then closed his mouth. The moment he identified himself as the Duke of Ashburton, this friendly intimacy would be over. If Rosalind Jordan was venal, she'd try to crawl into his bed again in the hope of gaining some advantage by seducing a duke. If she was the sunny, straightforward woman she seemed, she would probably be intimidated by his rank. She would become very formal, perhaps leave in confusion.

He looked at her warm eyes and could not bear for that to happen. "My Christian name is Stephen," he said. "After all, you said I should call you Rosalind."

"Very well." She cocked her head to one side. "Stephen Ashe?"

He considering telling the truth, that his family name was Kenyon, but then he would have to explain the "Ash" that he had mumbled, and the monogrammed *A*s on some of his possessions. Easier simply to nod and change the subject. "So you're a Fitzgerald daughter. Is Mr. Jordan part of the company?"

She sighed, some of her brightness fading. "He was once, but that was a long time ago. He's been dead for years."

"I'm so sorry," Stephen said, trying to sound sincere when his real reaction was pleasure. So Lady Caliban was a widow. A lovely, unconventional widow who wasn't the least upset at lying down by a stranger and wakening to his kiss.

Mention of her husband brought Rosalind to her feet. "I should be letting you rest. Since you're doing so well, I'll go to my own room. Do you need anything before I leave?"

Suppressing the improper answer that came to mind, he asked, "Will the company be leaving Redminster tomorrow?"

"No, the town is larger than Fletchfield. We'll stay for several days." She smiled. "We even have a fairly decent theater in the assembly room of the Royal George."

"Why don't you stay at the Royal George? Would playgoers pester members of the company?"

"Perhaps, but the real reason is that we can't afford the rates there," she said cheerfully as she left the room. "I'll see you in the morning, Stephen."

After the door closed, he got cautiously to his feet. More dizziness, but it passed quickly. He went to his luggage across the room, feeling every bruise he'd acquired in the river, and dug out Blackmer's jar of pills. He'd been taking the medication faithfully, despite its limited usefulness. At least tonight opium would help his throbbing head. He tipped two pills into his hand and washed them down with water.

Then he returned to his bed, shaky enough to appreciate lying down again. Yet he drifted toward sleep in a surprisingly good mood.

After seeing *The Tempest*, he had decided that he didn't want either a wife or the synthetic passion of a courtesan. That was easy to say when desire was dormant. But now it had returned in full flood. Perhaps it would be possible to bed a warm, attractive woman who was worldly and unconventional enough to take a love affair lightly. Was Rosalind Jordan such a woman? He wanted to think so.

God, how he wanted to think so.

Rosalind was grateful to return to her room and find that her sister hadn't yet returned from the performance. She sank onto the bed, her hand pressing to her mouth.

As she and Jessica had both noticed even during a performance, Stephen Ashe was . . . very attractive. And not only because he was tall and strong and handsome. She'd been right to see passion in his features when he was unconscious. In fact, she would be willing to wager that under his facade of light, ironic detachment was a character of Shakespearean complexity. Passion and hidden fires. Dark, compelling currents that contained—what? Anger, sorrow, desire? A decisive Hamlet, a man of natural authority. Yet at the same time, he had a gentle courtesy that she found immensely appealing.

Plus, of course, he kissed very well. Part of her wished they had stayed longer in that hazy, unreal state between waking and sleeping. In his arms she had felt warm. Secure. Desired. And just a little bit alarmed.

Firmly she told herself that she was letting her imagination run away with her. She and Mr. Ashe were strangers to each other, and she found him intriguing mostly because he was different from anyone else she'd ever met.

Her vagabond life meant that she knew mostly actors and other volatile sorts. Not that she didn't adore her father and many of the other actors she'd met over the years, but she'd sworn never to marry such a man again. Charles Jordan had been blindingly handsome and, when he chose, utterly charming. He had also been dishonest and unreliable, and he had overrated his acting ability.

She chuckled at the last thought and lay back across the bed. Obviously she was enough of a Fitzgerald to rate bad acting as a character flaw.

Yet she was different from the other Fitzgeralds. The mysterious parents she could not remember had left their mark on her, both physically and mentally. The rest of her adoptive family seemed content with their nomadic existence, but Rosalind often looked at the homes she passed and wondered what it would be like to live in one for always. She talked to men like Stephen Ashe and realized how refreshing it was not to have to deal with an artistic temperament. Sometimes she daydreamed about being married to a good-natured country squire and creating a home and family.

She released her breath in a sigh. Though her dreams were not outrageous, she might as well be wishing for a castle on the moon and a knight in shining armor. The harsh truth was that she was probably incapable of having children, and she never stayed in one place long enough to form a relationship with the sort of man who attracted her.

Besides, if she ever *did* meet a solid, respectable gentleman like that, he'd think her a wicked actress. The thought made her laugh, since she was neither wicked nor much of an actress. Nor was Stephen Ashe a jolly country squire by any stretch of the imagination.

Laughter was better than the knowledge that the most interesting man she'd ever met would be gone in a day or two, and she'd never have a chance to know him.

Chapter 5

Day Eighty-one

Stephen was almost asleep when the first pains seared through his stomach. He came to full wakefulness instantly, dreading what would come next. The heat flared into paralyzing agony as he stumbled from bed. Luckily Rosalind had left a candle burning.

He made it to the chamber pot just before a violent, prolonged attack of retching purged his stomach and left him panting on the floor, skin clammy and heart pounding. Christ, how could he have been thinking about initiating an affair with a woman when he couldn't trust his own body?

He pushed himself to a sitting position and wiped his sweaty face with a nightshirted forearm as he grimly forced himself to face the truth. Until now he had not fully accepted that he was dying. Deep inside he'd believed that there must be some kind of mistake. He was the Duke of Ashburton and in the prime of life. Surely he could not be mortally ill. But after tonight's attack, he could no longer believe that. He was dying. There would be no special exceptions made for him.

Death be not proud, though some have called thee mighty and dreadful. He smiled bitterly as he thought of Donne's words. He hated knowing that eventually he would surely suffer one of these humiliating episodes in public. The Duke of Ashburton would show himself as a spewing, pathetic wreck of a man. Interesting how illness had brought him face-to-face with his particular sin of pride.

Though he'd never felt the need to flaunt his wealth and lineage, he was learning that he despised showing weakness. The fact that his illness would soon be visible to the world would doubtless give him a valuable lesson in humility, but he was in no hurry to learn it. The longer he could delay the inevitable, the better. He'd return to the abbey as soon as he was strong enough to ride. There the sight of his failing body would be limited to his servants. As few of them as possible.

He lurched to his feet, gut burning and far dizzier than he had been earlier. It would be futile to take more opium pills—he'd never be able to keep them down. But he needed something for his terrible thirst. Thankfully he remembered the milk sent by the landlady. It came cool and fresh from a small pitcher. He sipped slowly at first, drinking more deeply when the milk began to settle his ravaged stomach. He'd always had an unfashionable taste for milk, and his consumption had trebled since his illness set in.

After emptying the pitcher, he lay down and dragged the covers over his shivering body. This time when he drifted into restless sleep, there were no pleasant dreams.

* * *

Stephen awoke to morning sunshine and gray resignation. His thoughts about Rosalind Jordan the previous night had been more than a little fevered. The most she could ever be to him was a fantasy. He had too much consideration and—admit it—pride, to become involved with a woman when his future consisted of decay and death.

He wearily got out of bed, weak and dizzy and head aching. Yet overall he didn't feel really wretched. Tomorrow or the next day he'd be ready to go home.

He glanced into the mirror over the washbasin and winced at the sight of his face. Between beard, bandage, and bruises, he looked like a ruffian. He went to his luggage for his razor. After shaving, he removed the bandage and examined the gash in his scalp. The doctor had shaved the area around it and neatly stitched the wound up. Since there was no sign of bleeding or infection, Stephen applied a piece of sticking plaster and combed his hair over the bare spot. The change in hairstyle made him look faintly rakish, but at least it disguised his injury.

Then he dressed. As Rosalind had said, his boots were quite wearable, though his valet would have thrown them out immediately. But Stephen Ashe was not a duke and had no need to maintain impeccable standards. The knowledge was rather liberating.

The routine of washing and dressing improved his mood. Since his stomach was feeling reasonably steady, he went downstairs in search of breakfast. The Three Crowns was the sort of modest, clean establishment he'd become acquainted with on this journey. At the bottom of the steps he paused. Thomas Fitzgerald's resonant voice could be heard behind a door on the right. The family must be breakfasting in a private parlor.

He could eat alone, of course, but he was tired of being alone and didn't feel that another attack was imminent. He tapped on the door and entered when Maria called permission. All five Fitzgeralds were seated around the breakfast table. They were an attractive family, though it was interesting how different Rosalind looked from all her dark-haired, blue-eyed kin.

Stephen's entrance was met by a moment of utter silence. Then pandemonium broke out as everyone but Rosalind rose and converged on the newcomer. Even the lanky wolfhound emerged from under the table and loped forward.

Maria Fitzgerald reached Stephen first. Clasping his hand to her bountiful bosom, she said in a rich, emotional voice, "Rosalind has told us all about you, Mr. Ashe. Bless you for saving my baby's life. I vow before God that from now on, my life is yours to do with as you choose."

Stephen stared at the tears trembling in her great blue eyes, bemused by two simultaneous thoughts. One was that Maria was surely a very fine tragic actress. The other was that under her dramatic manner, she was completely sincere. If he said that he wanted to take her life, she would have handed him a pistol.

Gently he disengaged his hand. "I did only what any man might, Mrs. Fitzgerald. And I can think of no better use of your life than the one to which you are putting it."

That elicited a booming laugh from Thomas Fitzgerald, who took hold of Stephen's newly freed hand and pumped it energetically. "Well said, Mr. Ashe. But I must tell you that I share my wife's sentiments completely." He gave an affectionate glance at his son, who stood beside him. "Brian here is a rare scamp, but we would have missed him sadly."

Jessica Fitzgerald rumpled her brother's hair. "That we would. I quite enjoy chasing him about with my hairbrush when he's impossible." As Miranda in the play, she had been a stunner; as an affectionate sister, she was completely endearing.

Flushing a little, Brian bowed and said very formally, "I am eternally indebted to you, sir. I recognize that my thoughtlessness endangered your life, and I give thanks that you took no permanent harm."

More than a little overwhelmed, Stephen was wondering what to say when Rosalind's teasing voice interjected, "You're embarrassing the poor man to death when surely what he wants most is his breakfast. A cup of tea, Mr. Ashe?"

Gratefully he moved around her effusive family and accepted the steaming cup Rosalind held out. After a bracing swallow, he said, "Truly, you make too much of what I did. I'm glad to have been of service. Let us speak no more about it."

But the Fitzgeralds were not ready to drop the subject of the rescue. As Stephen served himself modest amounts of toast and coddled eggs and took a seat by Rosalind, the family began to relive the previous day's adventure. Every reaction of shock, horror, and relief was detailed with flare and gusto.

Though self-conscious about his prominent role in the drama, Stephen was also fascinated. A scene more different from his own childhood meals would be hard to imagine. The Fitzgeralds were a *family,* not merely a collection of people connected by blood and fortune. Every member was secure in the knowledge of being loved and accepted; in return, they rendered respect and affection to the others.

The only person who didn't join in the cheerful babble was Rosalind. Quietly she made sure everyone was well served, even the dog. Stephen sensed that if each Fitzgerald had a role in the family, she was the bright, still center.

He also received other, more subtle impressions, like the faint scent of rosewater that perfumed the air when she turned her head. And the almost inaudible rustle of her skirts when she got up to ring for a fresh pot of tea. Though he tried not to look at her, he could not recollect when he had been so acutely aware of a woman's presence.

When Rosalind returned to her seat, she paused a moment to examine the wound on his head. The touch of her fingertips when she brushed back his hair was subtly erotic. "This is healing well, Mr. Ashe," she remarked, "but you look rather drawn. I hope you'll stay in Redminster at least another day. Travel might aggravate your injury."

"The name is Stephen, if you'll recall. And yes, I intend to stay at least until tomorrow."

She smiled with a warmth that struck to his heart. "Very good, Stephen."

"You are my guest for as long as you are at the Three Crowns," Thomas said emphatically. "Feel free to fill a hip bath with champagne if you wish."

Stephen felt a twinge of guilt at accepting the hospitality of a man who could probably ill afford it when he himself could buy the inn from pocket change. But he must allow the older man to express his gratitude. He had learned that from observing the effects of his father's sometimes oppressive charity. "That would be a criminal waste of champagne. Perhaps later I shall order drinks for everyone in the taproom instead."

"By all means," the older man said. "I shall take the opportunity to propose a toast to your long life and good health."

The words brought a sharp jolt of reality. No toast would provide Stephen with either life or health. Appetite gone, he got to his feet. "I think I'll go to the stables to see how Jupiter is faring."

"I'll go with you," Brian volunteered.

"You have lessons to do, young man," his mother said firmly. "And Thomas, you and Jessica are due at the theater for rehearsal. Rose, why don't you take Mr. Ashe to the stables, then bring him to the Royal George later?" Maria halted, adding a little shyly, "That is, if you'd like to see our theater troupe at close hand."

"There is nothing I'd like better," Stephen said truthfully. He'd been backstage at several regular theaters but had no experience of strolling players. Visiting this troupe would be a pleasant distraction.

Rosalind stood, and they went outside into the sunny courtyard together. As they crossed to the stables, she said with a humorous glint in her eyes, "I hope you didn't find a Fitzgerald breakfast too overwhelming."

He smiled, as much for the sight of sunshine on her tawny hair as for her question. "It was an experience. But not an unpleasant one."

They reached the stables, and he opened the door for her. Giving in to curiosity, he commented, "You certainly don't resemble anyone else in your family. Were you a fairy changling, perhaps, found amidst the cowslips and strawberries?"

"Nothing so poetic." Her expression became opaque. "I was adopted. The Fitzgeralds found me scavenging near the London waterfront when I was three or four. Apparently I'd come ashore with my real mother, who died immediately. Heaven knows what would have happened if the Fitzgeralds hadn't happened by."

He stared at her, chilled by the knowledge of all

the horrific things that might befall a lost girl child. Especially a pretty one. "That's an incredible story to relate so casually. Did the Fitzgeralds try to learn more about your origins?"

"They didn't have much time because they had to leave London for an engagement in Colchester. Mama says my clothing had been well made and I spoke with a good accent, so my family was probably not impoverished." She shrugged. "That is the extent of my knowledge about my history."

Jupiter stuck his head out of a loose box and gave a peremptory snort. Stephen stroked the velvety nose. "Do you ever think about your original family?"

Rosalind hesitated before saying, "Yes, though I wouldn't let Mama and Papa know for the world. They'd be hurt by the implication that they hadn't done enough, when no one could have raised me with more love or kindness."

"Yet still, it is natural to be curious," he said quietly.

"You understand, don't you?" Her eyes devoid of their usual laughter, she began stroking Jupiter's sleek neck. "Quite possibly I have relatives somewhere. I used to study the audiences for people who looked like me. I wonder sometimes what my real name is, and if someone was waiting for me and my mother in London. It's been almost twenty-five years now. Does anyone anywhere remember that little girl who was lost?" She glanced at him, her gaze wistful.

Her hand had stilled on Jupiter's neck, so he touched it in a gesture of comfort. Their fingers met, and he felt a small shock, almost like static electricity in the winter. But this was . . . different. Dropping his hand, he asked, "You recollect nothing of the time before the Fitzgeralds?"

"A few scattered images. Being hugged, though perhaps that was Maria. A stone house that seemed large, but probably wasn't except in a child's mind."

"You don't even remember your own name?"

There was a flash of something dark and terrible in her eyes before she looked away. "Not even that."

It was time to change the subject. "It must be strange to know nothing about one's ancestors." Stephen gave a wry smile. "In some ways, that's a blessing. I think many children would like to believe that they were born to royalty, stolen by gypsies, then left by accident with the peculiar people who claim to be their parents."

Rosalind smiled, all trace of darkness gone. "That's true, isn't it? Human nature is the most foolish thing. We always long for what we can't have." Her casual words struck her ears with unexpected force. Like a horse yearning for the grass on the other side of the fence, she yearned for the outside world, the one that had nothing to do with the theater or the Fitzgerald troupe. That was probably why she was so intrigued by Stephen, who was from that outside world, as well as kind and attractive.

Very attractive, actually. He'd combed his hair into a more informal style, and it suited him. But he was not for her. He was a gentleman. She was a strolling player, and not even a very good one. At least she could act well enough to say lightly, "The next time I regret my lost family, I shall remind myself that I am also free of dreadful aunts and drunken cousins."

"If you feel the lack, I have droves of appalling kinsmen I can lend you," he said, his expression sober, but his eyes glimmering with amusement. "Little old ladies who put brandy in their tea, then curse like sailors. Distant connections who have lost everything gambling and come around looking for handouts.

Pious hypocrites who preach virtue and secretly practice vice—I have them all."

"I wouldn't dream of depriving you of such delights," she said generously. "I do hope you have some nicer relatives as well."

"A few. My older sister is rather rigid, but she has a good heart and her children are delightful." Stephen pulled an irregular chunk of sugar from his pocket and offered it to Jupiter. The horse delicately lapped up the treat. "And I have a younger brother who was a soldier. We had our differences growing up, but we've become much closer since he left the army. I guess we both learned a little wisdom over the years."

Rosalind noted that he made no mention of a spouse, though that didn't mean he wasn't married. Perhaps he'd had a fight with his wife, which was why he was rambling around England alone. Reminding herself that his marital status was no concern of hers, she said, "Since Jupiter is content, perhaps we should see how the troupe is faring."

Stephen agreed and offered his arm. Together they strolled out of the stables and into the Redminster high street. Rosalind enjoyed the solid feel of his forearm under her palm, and the envious glances other women gave her after looking over her handsome escort. In fact, she was enjoying this walk entirely too much. Reminding herself they were together by chance alone, she resumed their earlier conversation. "Are you and your brother much alike?"

"Only superficially—Michael is far more intense than I," Stephen said reflectively. "Even now that he has married and settled down, he has what I've heard called a thousand-yard stare—a constant awareness of his surroundings that comes from having lived with danger. I suppose that's how he survived so many years of war."

"A thousand-yard stare," Rosalind repeated. "I'll remember that. The concept could be useful to an actor who wanted to portray that kind of character."

"Is that what it is like to be an actress—constantly observing the world to learn how to best perform your roles?"

She laughed. "I'm no actress. I fill in where needed—even breeches parts if necessary, because I'm tall for a woman. But Jess is the one with the talent. My real value is as stage manager and prompter. I keep track of costumes and scenery and scripts, and anything else that helps the company run smoothly."

"Does the troupe travel continuously?"

She shook her head. "Not quite. In the coldest months of winter, we take lodgings in Birmingham and perform at various places in the area. Come spring, we're off again." She nodded at the inn ahead. "If we're lucky, in a place like the Royal George. If not, in a courtyard or barn."

"It sounds beastly uncomfortable," Stephen said frankly. "Do you wander through the countryside as the spirit moves you?"

"No, we have a regular circuit through the West Midlands. People expect us, and we know what facilities are available in each town." They had reached the inn, so she led him under the coaching arch into the courtyard. "Strolling players are at the bottom of the theatrical barrel. The London playhouses are the most important, of course. Then come the major provincial circuits like Bath and the one based in York. People like us go to the towns too small for anyone else to bother with."

"Yet your parents are extremely talented. Surely

they could have succeeded in one of the more important theaters."

Rosalind gave him a quick, rueful smile. "Talent isn't all. My father can play everything from Lear to Falstaff, and my mother can make grown men weep when she does a tragedy like *Isabella*. That was noticed, and when I was little, John Philip Kemble engaged them both for a trial period at Drury Lane. It only lasted a month. Family legend says that Kemble was jealous of Papa's notices, and there may be some truth to that. But it's also true that my father likes to do things his own way. Theater managers are an arrogant lot and won't tolerate anyone who is equally obstinate."

"Particularly an actor who hadn't been in London long enough to develop the sort of following that would have made Kemble willing to tolerate artistic temperament."

She nodded. "The only solution was for my father to be his own manager. The Fitzgerald Troupe may not be famous, but Papa can do exactly as he wishes."

She led Stephen toward the large hall that had been added to the inn for assemblies and other entertainments. As they climbed the steps, a handsome young man with a dandyish air came out the door in front of them. Stephen recognized him as Edmund Chesterfield, the actor who had played Ferdinand to Jessica's Miranda.

Chesterfield gave Rosalind a broad smile. "And how are you this morning, my magnificent rose?"

"Neither yours nor magnificent," she said with the casualness of long habit. "Edmund, this is Mr. Ashe, who rescued Brian from the river."

Chesterfield's gaze sharpened. Stephen guessed that the young actor constantly evaluated other men as possible rivals or potential sources of patronage. Apparently dismissing Stephen as neither, he said, "You're a brave man to risk your neck for such a brat, Ashe. Now, if it had been the luscious Jessica, I'd have gone into the river myself."

"And ruin your coat? Somehow, I doubt it," Rosalind said sweetly.

"Alas, fair Rosalind, you know my weaknesses." Chesterfield gave an elaborate bow. "Until tonight, cruel mistress."

Rosalind said with surprise, "Is the rehearsal over already?"

"I've done as much as I need to." The actor grimaced. "Other theater managers don't demand constant rehearsals. I think the old boy enjoys tormenting us."

"He enjoys seeing the plays performed as well as possible," Rosalind pointed out crisply. "Your own skills have improved markedly since you joined us."

"Perhaps," Chesterfield admitted. "But that was a year ago. I hardly see the need to waste a lovely sunny day when I have my role down word perfect and there are pretty milkmaids to charm." After a farewell nod, he proceeded down the stairs.

Stephen said in an undertone, "Delightful fellow. Is one of his roles Duncan in the Scottish play? If so, the mock dagger could be replaced by a real one."

Rosalind smiled involuntarily. "Edmund may be vain and lazy, but he doesn't really deserve to be stabbed to death by Macbeth."

"You're right. Better he should play Antigonus and be eaten by a bear."

"You know your Shakespeare," she said with approval.

"I've always enjoyed the theater, Shakespeare most of all. I've even taken part in amateur productions of his plays." He opened the door to the hall for her.

"Long after a performance is over, the Bard's words linger in the mind like the taste of fine brandy." A few of those words suddenly danced through his head: *"She's beautiful, and therefore to be woo'd. She is a woman, therefore to be won."* Good lord, where had that come from? *Henry I, Part I,* if he recalled correctly, and from Rosalind's enchanting smile.

He took a deep breath, then followed her from the foyer into the main hall. At the far end was a raised area that could be used either as a stage or a musicians' dais. A number of people bustled about the platform, several working on the set while others rehearsed under Thomas's direction. Stephen asked, "How large is your company?"

"Eighteen. About ten of us do real acting—the others, like Calvin Ames and Ben Brady over there, are musicians or stage crew and act only in minor parts." Rosalind frowned. "It looks as if Ben is having trouble. I'd better go see."

Stephen followed her toward the stage, where the actors were hurling accusations of betrayal and jealousy at each other. "What play is being rehearsed?"

"*The Ghost Speaks.* We're performing it tomorrow." She gave a mischievous smile. "The play isn't much, but it does allow us to take advantage of the Royal George's nice trapdoor. Whenever we perform here, we do at least one play with ghosts."

"It would be a pity to waste such a fine opportunity," he agreed. "What is tonight's show?"

"*A Midsummer Night's Dream.* One of my favorites. I play first Hippolyta, then Titania's chief attendant. It makes for a busy evening."

"Are the costume changes difficult?"

"Not really. In this play, everyone wears flowing, medieval sorts of robes, so a change in mantles and perhaps a hair ornament is usually all that is required." She had a shawl draped over her shoulders, so she stopped and turned toward Stephen, flipping the shawl over her head like a medieval cowl. " 'Tis clothing that makes the woman, you know," she said in a dark, conspiratorial voice.

"You're a better actress than you give yourself credit for," he said, impressed.

"Oh, I know the tricks of the trade." She returned her shawl to its usual position. "Mama and Papa have seen to that. But I lack the inner fire."

Perhaps she didn't have an actor's fire, but he suspected that she was capable of more intimate fires. That lush, beautiful figure was made for passion.

Knowing he'd better change the direction of his thoughts, he glanced at the materials stacked against one wall. "I suppose all the sets and costumes are used in many different ways."

She nodded, then climbed onto the stage and circled around the actors, who were too absorbed in their roles to notice distractions. "That painted tree Ben is holding has shaded Macbeth and his witches, concealed Bonnie Prince Charlie, and lashed in many a stormy gale."

The tree, however, had definitely seen better days. In fact, two of the flat spreading branches had broken off. Rosalind asked the wiry man examining the pieces, "What happened, Ben?"

"That clumsy assistant of mine dropped it," he said dourly. "First all the excitement yesterday put us behind schedule today, and now my tree is broken."

Rosalind frowned. "What needs to be done?"

Ben rattled off a list of tasks, ending gloomily, "Most of which won't get done if I take the time to repair this properly, so I suppose we'll have to do without the tree."

"I can help with the scenery," Stephen volunteered. "Though I don't know anything about carpentry, I can fetch and carry."

Rosalind hesitated. "But you're recovering from an injury."

"I promise I won't carry anything on my head," he said gravely.

Before Rosalind could protest further, Ben said, "Take him up on the offer, Rosie. We need every pair of hands if we've going to put this play on properly."

"Very well—but if you feel tired, Stephen, please rest."

"I will." Under Ben's direction, Stephen went out the stage door to the wagons and brought in an armful of shimmering blue-green draperies that would be hung along the back wall. He recognized the fabric as having been used in Prospero's cave. It made an equally effective backdrop for a magical forest.

For the next several hours, he fetched, carried, stacked, and erected sets under Ben's direction, all the while marveling that such simple materials could create such grand illusions. He also enjoyed the controlled chaos of the theater, with actors coming and going and dramatic scenes being declaimed over his head.

Dusty and a little tired, he was admiring the finished set when Maria Fitzgerald exclaimed behind him, "Mr. Ashe is the duke, Thomas!"

Dismayed, Stephen swung around, wondering how she knew. Perhaps he had been pointed out to her somewhere, and she only now had remembered his real identity.

Maria's exclamation had stopped everyone in their tasks, and all eyes were on Stephen. His period of blessed anonymity was over.

The keenest gaze belonged to Thomas Fitzgerald,

who said thoughtfully, "He certainly has the countenance of a duke, my love, and it would save me two costume changes, but perhaps Mr. Ashe has no desire to tread the boards with us."

Stephen blinked in confusion. "I beg your pardon?"

Maria gave him a brilliant smile. "You would make a most impressive Duke of Athens, Mr. Ashe. Since Rosalind says that you've had some amateur acting experience, would you like to take the role of Theseus in tonight's play?"

His relief that he had not been identified was quickly followed by shock. The Duke of Ashburton, appear in a play performed in a common tavern? He stared at Maria. Acting with a professional company, even in a minor role, was quite a different matter from performing in a country house with friends.

"Not everyone fancies standing up in front of an audience, Mama," Rosalind said. "Most people would consider it a penance, not a pleasure."

"And Mr. Ashe is convalescing," Jessica added.

Maria's face fell. "Of course. I wasn't thinking."

Her crushed expression gave Stephen a sudden insight into why she had made the suggestion. For Maria, acting was delight. Like a cat presenting a favored human with a dead mouse, she had impulsively offered the man who had saved her son the chance to act because it was the greatest treat she could imagine.

The idea was absurd, of course. Yet after his surprise wore off, he found the prospect of behaving so outrageously rather appealing. "I will surely regret this, but I'd like to try it anyhow," he said with a slow smile. "As long as you're sure I wouldn't ruin the performance."

Maria's face brightened and Thomas said with a

rumbling laugh, "Splendid! Don't worry about hurting the play. It's not a large part, and with a bit of coaching from me no one will realize you're a novice."

Jessica clapped her hands together gleefully, and Rosalind gave him a warm smile. "Welcome to the Fitzgerald Theater Troupe, Stephen."

"It's just for a night," he pointed out. Yet as Thomas led him aside to begin work, Stephen found that he was very pleased with himself.

CHAPTER 6

Rosalind stayed close to Stephen as they waited in the wings before the play began, and not only because they would make their entrances together. Even the most experienced actors felt tension before a performance. Though her protégé hid his nerves behind an impassive face, she sensed that he was ready to jump out of his skin.

Garbed as Oberon, the fairy king, her father peered out at the audience. "A full house," he said with satisfaction as he turned to the other actors. "I'll go tell the musicians to start the march." He slipped away to perform the task.

Stephen gave Rosalind a rueful glance. "Is it too late to change my mind about playing Theseus?"

"I'm afraid so, but don't worry," she said soothingly. "You'll be fine. Mama was right—you make a wonderful duke."

"Easier to be a duke than an actor, I think."

"Nonsense. You have the lines down perfectly, and you did very well when Papa put you through your scenes earlier." She surveyed him from head to foot. In a flowing purple robe and wearing gold chains and crown, Stephen had a natural aristocratic dignity that made him a convincing royal hero. He should be almost as effective in the role as her father was. "Remember, all you have to do is say your lines clearly and don't fall down. And you have to convey only two emotions—your authority as ruler of Athens, and your love for the woman you are about to marry."

"You make it sound suspiciously easy, Hippolyta," he said dryly.

"It will be easy, once you've said your first lines," she assured him. "If you make any errors, I can gloss them over so the audience will scarcely notice."

The musicians ended the overture and struck up the stirring march that signaled the entrance of Theseus, Duke of Athens, and his affianced wife, Hippolyta, Queen of the Amazons. Feeling the tingle of excitement that always came when she was about to go onstage, Rosalind took Stephen's hand. "Courage, my sweet duke. This is only Redminster, and if you do badly, who will know?"

"The Bard may rise from his grave and smite me," he said darkly.

"Don't flatter yourself," she said briskly. "He's slept through centuries of performances that have mauled his work in every way imaginable. You can't possibly be as dreadful as some of the actors I've seen."

He gave her a ghost of smile, but she suspected that he would rather be almost anywhere than about to go onstage. Luckily their musical cue sounded before his nerves could get any worse. She raised their joined hands to shoulder height, and together they swept grandly onto the stage.

Covertly watching her partner, Rosalind saw the instant when he felt the impact of all the watching eyes. His face tightened into a mask.

She squeezed his hand hard. "Say the words, and don't fall over your feet," she breathed in a tone that barely reached his ears.

He closed his eyes for an instant, collecting himself. Then he turned to her and said with a powerful authority that filled the hall, "Now, fair Hippolyta, our nuptial hour draws on apace."

Rosalind caught her breath, shaken by the warmth in Stephen's eyes. Perhaps because he was not a trained actor, he had none of the mannerisms of the professional. Instead, he radiated a sincerity that for a moment was more real than the stage around them. He was a ruler and a hero, a man among men. He was her beloved, come to claim her for all time. She wanted to lift her face for a kiss and press her body to his. . . .

A cough in the audience brought her back to her senses before she missed her cue to answer him. Calling on her decades of professional experience, she smiled seductively at Theseus—not Stephen, *Theseus*—and told him in Shakespeare's lush words how quickly the days would pass until they wed.

As the scene progressed, Rosalind began to feel excitement. A competent troupe would always produce a decent show, but sometimes everything came together and a kind of magic was created. She sensed that this was going to be one of those nights. Though Stephen was not a trained actor, he had an air of command and a compelling masculine presence that brought out the best in her own acting. It was easy to believe she was the warrior queen who had been "woo'd by the sword" and was now about to marry her warrior lover with "pomp and triumph and reveling."

The rapt silence of the audience told her that they were totally caught up in the illusion of the play. For the rest of the night, their hearts would belong to the Fitzgerald Theater Troupe.

Tormented lovers and parents arrived on the stage to ask the duke for royal justice. Catching the magic, Jessica and Edmund and Jeremiah and the others *became* their characters in an utterly convincing way.

Soon Rosalind and Stephen's part in the scene was over and they made their exit. Maria was waiting in the wings, dressed in the silvery gown of Titania, the fairy queen. She hugged Stephen exuberantly. Rosalind envied her mother the easy affection of that hug. She herself was too aware of Stephen to give so casual an embrace.

"You were splendid!" Maria said, voice quiet but vibrant. "Wasn't it wonderful?"

"My Amazon queen saved me from making a fool of myself." Stephen's warm gaze met Rosalind's over her mother's head. "Thank you for allowing me to act with you. It was an opportunity that few men get."

Pleased and relieved that he had found the experience rewarding, Rosalind went down to the tiny women's dressing room to change into a different gown. Getting into another costume was easy.

Becoming a fairy instead of Stephen's intended bride was harder.

Since his character had only three scenes, at the beginning and end of the play, Stephen spent most of the evening watching from the wings. Jessica sparkled as pretty, perplexed Hermia, Thomas and Maria were fey and charming as the estranged fairy king and queen, and Brian made a delightfully impish Puck. Stephen had never seen the play performed better. Thomas Fitzgerald had created a company to be proud of. Stephen wondered if the playgoers of the West Midlands circuit realized how lucky they were.

He felt a surprising sense of satisfaction at being part of the evening's entertainment. Not because he was essential; the troupe had managed perfectly well without him in the past. But tonight, in a small way, he had contributed to the dramatic tapestry that held the audience in thrall. There was a power in that very different from the power of wealth and position he wielded as a duke.

As he watched the performance, his mind occasionally drifted back to the pleasure he'd felt in speaking to Rosalind as if she were his intended bride. In those moments he had forgotten his grim fate in the enchantment of a midsummer dream. No wonder theaters and storytellers had flourished since the dawn of time. A compelling, well-told tale brought peace and joy, at least for a while.

Theseus and Hippolyta always appeared together, and eventually it was time for them to take the stage again. Rosalind had flitted about the stage as Titania's servant, her admirable figure set off to perfection by gauzy fairy veils. Now she reappeared in the splendid gown of Hippolyta, as regal as a queen—or a duchess.

She gave Stephen a swift smile. "You no longer look terrified."

He cocked a disdainful brow. "Do you think these peasants would dare show disrespect to the ruler of Athens?"

Her smile became a grin. "You make an alarmingly impressive duke."

If only she knew . . .

Hunting horns sounded their cue, and they went onstage. Stephen was startled when he and Rosalind were greeted with a spattering of applause. She said under her breath, "They like you, my lord."

Absurd, of course, but he enjoyed the moment anyhow.

In his last two scenes, he made his speeches with more confidence. He did stumble once on his lines but recovered quickly after Rosalind silently mouthed the right words. He left the stage for the last time with a giddy sense of relief and triumph. The Duke of Ashburton had risked making a complete fool of himself, and survived.

After Puck's closing speech, the audience exploded into applause. The actors came out to take their bows in reverse order of their importance. When their turn arrived, Stephen took Rosalind's hand again. It was beginning to seem natural.

They strode onto the stage and were greeted with enthusiasm. Stephen was amused when a balled-up scrap of fabric fell at his feet and opened into a lacy feminine handkerchief. Under cover of the applause, Rosalind said laughingly, "You've made a conquest, Stephen."

"Gad, I hope not." Yet he felt a heady pleasure in the applause. Still holding hands, he bowed while Rosalind made a sweeping curtsy that would have done her credit at the royal court. Then they stood aside as the other actors came out for their moment of glory.

When everyone was finally onstage, all the members of the cast joined hands for a bow. Stephen had Jessica on his left and Rosalind on his right. He thought irreverently that his friends would deem him mad if they saw him now, but they would also envy him his lovely companions.

Then it was over. The audience stood and began to leave the hall. Backstage, Thomas threw an arm around Stephen's shoulders. "Well done, sir. As good a Duke of Athens as ever I've seen."

"I have an aptitude for arrogance, I think," Stephen said modestly.

Face flushed with excitement, Maria laughed, then said, "Time to return to the Three Crowns. We'll have supper and celebrate your debut on the boards."

Stephen agreed, glad he would have a chance to enjoy the company for an evening before returning home. Then he went down to the crowded men's dressing room. He'd worn his own shirt and boots and breeches under his purple robe.

He was almost ready to leave when Edmund Chesterfield entered and said waspishly, "So you think you're an actor now, Ashe?"

Jeremiah Jones rolled his eyes. Stephen gathered that Chesterfield was not popular with his colleagues. "Hardly an actor," he said peaceably. "Merely an amateur who was given an evening of adventure by a troupe of gracious professionals." He began to tie his cravat. "By the way, your Demetrius was very fine."

Mollified, Chesterfield said, "I *was* good, wasn't I? Demetrius is a far more interesting character than Lysander."

Stephen suppressed a smile as he left the dressing room. Clearly a well-chosen compliment went a long way toward disarming an actor's envy.

He was going to miss these people. He really would.

● ● ●

Everyone in the Fitzgerald Theater Troupe loved a party, and honoring Stephen Ashe gave them a good excuse. After eating the supper prepared by the inn and downing several toasts to Stephen, all were in a mellow mood. The company musicians gathered in a corner and played their instruments for their own amusement, while other members broke into small conversational groups.

Rosalind always enjoyed such evenings. Her father bore the cost, which was one reason why he would never be rich, but the troupe had a warm, familial atmosphere that was rare among theater groups.

Her gaze went across the crowded private parlor to where Stephen was talking to Jane and Will Landers, a young couple who played secondary leads. She asked Jessica, who sat next to her, "Do you still want to cast Stephen as the aristocratic hero of your little tragedy, with him dying of unrequited love for your lowborn self?"

Her sister laughed and swallowed her last bite of pork pie. "He's far too formidable for me to imagine him pining away."

Rosalind ate a small spice cake and washed it down with champagne. "He fits in with our lot very well for a gentleman. I think he's on first-name terms with everyone in the company."

"That's because he really is a gentleman," Jessica said thoughtfully. "The genuine ones don't have to make a show of their superiority."

Across the room Stephen laughed at some comment of Jane's, his habitual seriousness gone. In fact, Rosalind realized as she studied his face, the underlying darkness she had sensed in him was also gone, at least for the time being. She was glad that they had been able to give him that in return for what he'd done. At the same time, she felt an ache at the knowledge that he would leave in the morning. She would never see him again.

The thought emboldened her. "Since Stephen is part of the company, if only for tonight, we should initiate him."

Jessica laughed, her blue eyes dancing. "A splendid idea! I wonder if his aplomb will survive."

"It will," Rosalind said thoughtfully. "He has the kind of bone-deep dignity that will be with him even on his deathbed."

Jessica got a glint in her eyes as she memorized that thought for future use; then she gave the quick nod that meant she had absorbed it. "I'll declare the initiation now." She set down her glass and swept to the middle of the room, raising her arms in a commanding gesture.

"Hear ye, hear ye, hear ye!" she cried out, her trained voice cutting through the talk and laughter. "Since Stephen Ashe has successfully trod the boards with us, it is time to initiate him into the ranks of the Fitzgerald Theater Troupe!"

There was a rumble of laughter through the room, except from Edmund Chesterfield, who scowled. He resented anyone besides himself being the center of attention, which meant that he spent much of his time in a bad mood.

Stephen said warily, "What form does this initiation take, fair Hermia? A ducking in the nearest horse trough?"

"New members of the company must kiss every member of the troupe of the opposite sex," Thomas explained with a grin.

Jeremiah chuckled. " 'Tis no great burden, Stephen."

"And I shall be the first," Jessica announced. She bounced over to Stephen and put her arms around his neck, tilting her head back in a lavish gesture that she'd taken from one of her stage roles. She and Stephen made a striking pair. For the first time in her life, Rosalind found herself envious of her sister's beauty. What man could resist having such a vivacious creature in his arms? Rosalind felt a moment of unworthy satisfaction that his kiss was merely friendly.

The other women of the company lined up for their turn, giggling like schoolgirls, even old Nan, who played crones and acted as wardrobe mistress. Stephen entered into the game good-naturedly, kissing the ladies with dramatic flourish.

Rosalind stayed in her seat. She should not have impulsively suggested the initiation as a way to get a kiss for herself. This wasn't what she wanted. She wanted . . .

It was better not to think it.

Maria was the last in line. She gave Stephen a smacking buss straight out of *The Merry Wives of Windsor*. Then she turned and beckoned to Rosalind. "Your turn, my dear. One last kiss, and Stephen will be one of us forever."

The onlookers applauded. Reluctantly Rosalind rose and crossed the room. When she stood in front of Stephen, she lifted her head and saw stillness in his eyes. He, too, was uncomfortable with the situation. She'd been a fool to start this, for it would cheapen the subtle but real bond she'd felt between them.

He reached out his hand. "Come, my Hippolyta."

Invoking her stage role made it easier. She was an Amazon queen who went to her lover with pride. Taking his hand, she dropped into a curtsy. "My dearest duke."

He raised her from her curtsy, and she saw rueful humor in his eyes as he bent for the kiss. His lips were warm, the pressure light, yet she felt an emotional impact through her entire body. Yes, there was something between them, a connection that in another time or place might have blossomed into something deeper. But they would not be so lucky.

Then the kiss was over. Holding his gaze, she murmured, "Thank you, Stephen."

He said with matching softness, "The pleasure was mine, Rosalind."

The room broke into applause, and Thomas came over with more champagne for Stephen's glass. Rosalind turned away, oddly content. She no longer regretted the fact that she had instigated the initiation ceremony. Even a public kiss was better than none.

Stephen's stomach had been uneasy, so he'd avoided the food and slipped up to his room for a pill. The champagne seemed to settle his digestion though, so he had sipped it throughout the evening. The conversation had certainly been different from anything he'd hear in a London drawing room. Ben Brady, for example, had explained how to do explosions onstage without burning the building down. Then Brady's wife, Nan, had raucously confided that she adored tales of virtuous maidens taming wicked rakes, even though she'd lost her own virginity before George III had lost the American colonies. There wasn't a bore in the whole company, except for Edmund Chesterfield.

After the initiation ceremony, Stephen sat by Thomas and Maria, who lounged in an oak settle telling wickedly amusing tales about their years in the theater. He envied their closeness, and the way their hands automatically linked together.

The sight sent a shaft of loneliness through him.

Firmly he repressed it. He'd been lucky in other ways; he had no right to self-pity.

His thoughts were interrupted when Thomas glanced at his pocket watch, then beckoned to Brian. "Midnight. Past time you were in bed, my lad."

Caught in the middle of a yawn, the boy gave a sheepish smile. "I haven't translated my Latin lines yet."

"You can do them in the morning," Maria said. "As long as you're finished by noon. And don't forget to do your sums for me, either."

After Brian gave his mother a good-night kiss and left, Stephen said, "Latin?"

Thomas nodded. "My Greek is too rusty to teach, but I have the Latin still. The lad's well into Caesar now."

Stephen's brows arched. "He's lucky to have such a good education."

Eyes twinkling with amusement at Stephen's surprise, Thomas explained, "I went to Trinity College in Dublin. Ah, I was quite the likely lad then. The church, my parents thought, or maybe the law." He shook his head with mock regret. "Then I met this wanton lassie here. Saw her play Juliet in Dublin, and threw all my prospects away to lay my heart at her feet."

Maria gave a ladylike snort. "Don't you believe it, Stephen. It's true that Thomas came of the gentry, but he was born to be hanged." She gave her husband an intimate smile. "I had my work cut out for me, keeping him out of trouble. Wild to be an actor, he was, so he used his Irish blarney to convince me of his undying devotion. In my innocence, I didn't suspect that all he really wanted was a wife from a fine old theatrical family like mine to teach him how to act."

"She's a hard woman," Thomas said sadly. "Keeps

me under the cat's paw, she does." Before he'd finished the words, his wife laid her hand on his thigh in a most improper way. He grinned and put an arm around her shoulders, drawing her across the oak settle so that she was tight against his side.

Jessica floated by. "Don't mind The Parents, Stephen," she said airily. "They have no sense of propriety. They quite put me to the blush."

Stephen chuckled at the reversal of roles between the generations. A pity his own parents hadn't had a tenth of the mutual affection that the Fitzgeralds did.

A slow, unpleasant burn began in his stomach. Experienced in the subtleties of pain, he doubted that it would develop into a full-fledged attack, but he would take no chances. He emptied his glass and set it aside. "I'm for bed. It's been a tiring day."

He got to his feet, and swayed, almost falling. Damnation! He hadn't drunk enough champagne for such a reaction. He put a hand to his head, which was aching, and prayed that he would not break down in a roomful of people.

Instantly Rosalind was by his side. "Lord, we've all forgotten that yesterday you were thumped by a tree." She slipped her arm around his waist. "I'll help you to your room, since I'm ready to retire myself."

He'd half forgotten the head injury, but it made a convenient excuse. Using Rosalind for balance, he crossed the room, saying his good-nights.

It was a relief to reach the cool hallway. He felt better immediately but was in no hurry to let go of Rosalind. She was delightfully soft, and such a convenient height. With Louisa he'd always felt like a looming giant.

Arms around each other, they made their way up the stairs to Stephen's room. When they were in front of the door, Rosalind glanced up, concern in her dark eyes. "Will you be all right?"

He nodded. "It was just a moment of dizziness. As you said, my head was thumped by a tree only yesterday. It seems much longer."

She brushed back his hair from the stitched wound. "No sign of infection. Still . . . perhaps you shouldn't leave tomorrow. Not if you're still feeling dizzy."

He seized on the excuse. "You're right. I need at least another day."

It was time to move apart, but neither of them did. They simply stared at each other. She was still within the circle of his arm, warm and womanly and enticing. He wanted to stroke the tawny silk of her hair, kiss those full lips as he had the night before when he awoke and Rosalind had been beside him. . . .

Without conscious thought, he drew her closer and kissed her. She gave a soft sigh and slid her arms around his neck. She tasted of champagne and spice. He caressed her ripely curving hips as desire flared into pure fire. The embrace was nothing like the awkward public kiss earlier in the evening. It was deep and intimate and right.

Wrong.

He raised his head, feeling dizzy for reasons that had nothing to do with being hit by a tree. Rosalind blinked at him, her eyes as dazed as his own must be.

"I'm sorry," he said unsteadily, shocked and shamed by his lack of control.

"You have the most dreadful ability to make me forget that I'm a prim, respectable widow." She removed her arms from around his neck without haste and stepped back. "It's very bad of me, but I thoroughly enjoyed that kiss."

"So did I. You are the most irresistibly kissable

woman I've ever met, though it's no credit to me I gave in to temptation." He hesitated, wanting to say more. "It isn't just that you are lovely. You . . . move me."

She raised her hands to his cheek, her fingers gliding lightly over the planes of his face. "There is something special between us, isn't there?" she asked softly. "A fragile blossom that will never bear fruit. But not without value." She pressed the lightest of kisses to his lips. "Never that."

She turned and walked down the hall toward her bedchamber, her tall figure swaying with unconscious provocation. He watched her go, feeling a raw hunger that was partly desire, but also something much deeper.

It took all his will to keep himself from following.

He went into his room and closed the door, leaning back against it as he knotted his hands into fists. Being a duke was a lonely business. He was flattered to his face and probably cursed behind his back. Except with a handful of friends, he had always felt set apart from the normal run of mankind.

But tonight, for a few hours, he had been a part of a friendly, tolerant group that had accepted him exactly as he was. The warmth of that was like a goose down quilt protecting him against the bitter cold of eternity.

He gazed across the dark room at the pale curtains stirring lazily in the breeze from the open window. He had not known how much he craved community until tonight, when he had briefly become part of one. How could he bear to leave these people who made him feel happier than he could ever remember being?

If it had been only Rosalind or only the companionship of the troupe, it would not be so hard to return to the abbey. But the combination was dangerously potent. That was part of the reason he knew he should leave. It was wrong, unsafe to want something so much. Particularly now, when his future was cruelly limited.

But when he thought it through, there was no real need to leave yet. His health was still good enough that he should be able to conceal his condition. He doubted that anyone in the troupe would tell him to leave, especially if he made himself useful. Yes, he would stay on for several days more. Perhaps a week.

His rush of relief at the decision was so strong that he almost changed his mind again. But what the devil, a condemned man was entitled to some pleasure. A lifetime of discipline should keep him from behaving badly with Rosalind again. He'd avoid champagne, and being alone with her, too.

Feeling more at peace, he stripped off his clothing in the dark and crawled into bed. But as he lay back against the pillows, he was struck by a vivid, tactile memory of holding Rosalind in his arms here the night before. He rolled to his side, aching with emptiness. *Damn* the illness that cast a black shadow over everything.

He closed his eyes, all too aware that he had not behaved well. Yet however ill-advised it had been to kiss her, he would carry the memory of her embrace until that not-too-distant day when he would die.

CHAPTER 7

George Blackmer climbed from his chaise and ascended the massive stone steps of Ashburton Abbey. When his knock gained him admittance, he said, "Inform the duke that I'm here to see him."

The usually impassive butler, Owens, could not conceal a tightening of expression. "His grace is . . . unavailable."

Blackmer stripped off his gloves. "I'll wait. When do you expect him back?" When Owens didn't answer, the physician said impatiently, "Come, come, man, I'm the duke's doctor, not an importunate beggar. He'll see me."

Owens hesitated a moment longer, as if weighing whether he should speak, then said in a rush, "His grace is not in residence. He left suddenly, without a word as to his plans, and he went alone. I . . . we are somewhat concerned."

Blackmer's brows arched. "Alone?"

The butler nodded. "By horseback, without taking even his valet. It happened immediately after your last visit."

"You've had no word from him for a fortnight?" the physician said incredulously.

"None at all."

"Have you informed anyone of the duke's absence?"

"Who would we tell? After all, his grace has every right to leave voluntarily, as he did. Yet"–Owens swallowed hard–"such behavior is most unusual."

Unusual, indeed; Blackmer had observed Stephen Kenyon closely for many years, and doubted the man had ever done anything so unpredictable in his life. But of course, a sentence of death might unbalance anyone. Tersely he said, "If he returns, or you hear news of him, tell me at once. It's important that I know."

Then he left the abbey, swearing under his breath. His blasted patient could be anywhere in Britain. God only knew what might be happening to him. His overall health was probably still fairly good, but that might change at any time.

Blackmer reached his home and went into his study, pacing restlessly as he considered what the devil he should do. Obviously Ashburton's staff was reluctant to take any action that might displease their master, but someone must do something, and only Blackmer understood the ramifications of the duke's absence.

Ashburton's brother in Wales was the logical person to write—in fact, there was a fair chance that the duke was visiting there, seeking comfort and preparing his heir to succeed to the title and estates. Blackmer had only the slightest acquaintance with Lord Michael Kenyon—just enough to know that he was a hard and dangerous man, and notifying him would unleash unpredictable forces. Lord Michael might rejoice in the prospect of inheriting. Or he might become furious and blame the messenger, in this case the duke's physician. He might . . . the possibilities were numerous and alarming.

Yet what other choice was there? The physician swore again. Then he sat down and composed a letter to Lord Michael Kenyon, choosing his words with painstaking care.

CHAPTER 8

Rosalind scanned the dozen or so people milling about the small theater until she caught Stephen's eye. "Could you give me a hand with these sets, Stephen?"

"Of course." He joined Rosalind, then lifted a false-framed window from the floor. "Where would you like it?"

"Here, please. Right where Aloysius is sleeping. He has a genius for choosing the spot where he'll be most in the way."

While Stephen persuaded the wolfhound to move, Rosalind watched with a private smile. She had once heard an Arab proverb that if the nose of a camel entered a tent, the rest of the camel would soon follow. While it was unfair to compare Stephen's aristocratic nose with that of a camel, he had certainly slid into the tent very deftly in the past week, the tent in this case being the Fitzgerald Theater Troupe. He'd helped with the hard physical work of moving sets and scenery, driven a wagon when they traveled, played small walk-on parts, and tutored Brian in Latin when Thomas was too busy.

Since his head injury had healed, she guessed that he stayed simply because he was having a good time. Certainly his spirits seemed much lighter than when he had first joined them.

She thought, often and wistfully, of that lovely, heart-pounding kiss they had shared. But they had tacitly avoided being alone again. Instead, they gravitated together when part of a group, talking of anything and everything while studiously ignoring the intense physical awareness that pulsed between them.

As he placed the last set piece where she indicated, she wondered how much longer he would stay. But she did not ask. She had a superstitious fear that if the subject was brought into the open, he might feel obligated to return to his normal life. That day would surely come, and soon. But she would not encourage it to happen.

Stephen turned to her, "Is anything else needed, Madame Stage Manager?"

She surveyed their surroundings, mentally ticking off every aspect of the seating, lighting, and sets. "All seems in order. This is one of the easier theaters to prepare."

He ruffled Aloysius's ears. "What is tonight's play?"

"*Isabella; or, The Fatal Marriage*. It's a wildly emotional tragedy of innocence betrayed and cruel death." Rosalind chuckled. "One of my mother's best roles—she chews up the scenery and spits it out, leaving every woman in the audience wailing with grief. The first time I saw her play Isabella was right here in Whitcombe. I was four or five, and I ran screaming onto the stage when she did the death scene because I thought it was real. The audience loved it. We always play *Isabella* here by popular demand."

His dark brows rose. "You tell it as a joke, but surely that must have been upsetting to a small child."

She stiffened as his words triggered an unexpected stab of emotion. Feeling chilled, she pressed her hand to the center of her chest as she remembered those moments when her adored foster mother lay dying. Anguish and terror beyond bearing . . .

Stephen caught her arm, his expression concerned. "Are you all right?"

Drawn back to the present, she gave an embarrassed laugh. "How strange. For some reason, your words brought back the experience as if it were happening right now. Foolish of me."

"Not foolish at all," he said quietly. "You had already lost your natural mother. To see your adoptive mother apparently dead must have been terrifying. Like the end of the world."

"That was it exactly." Something dark and horrifying stirred in the depths of her mind. Her mother's death. The end of the world.

She shivered and forced the unformed thought back into the shadows. Odd that Stephen had recognized the connection instantly when she herself never had. But then, she tried not to think of her life before the Fitzgeralds had adopted her.

He squeezed her hand comfortingly. "Do you ever try to remember what your natural mother was like?"

"Sometimes. With no success. But Maria says she must have been a good mother, because I had very nice manners for a small child." Disquieted by the conversation, Rosalind glanced around the theater. "Edmund isn't here, is he? We were supposed to rehearse the afterpiece because it's one we haven't done recently."

Stephen dropped his hand, accepting the change of subject. "What is it called?"

"*The False Lover*. It's a foolish bedroom farce. A nice change of pace after the melodrama of *Isabella*." She frowned as she saw her father pacing around the entrance to the theater. "Papa is not happy that Edmund is missing."

Sure enough, a moment later Thomas slapped his palm with the sheaf of papers he held, then pivoted and came to the stage. "Stephen, I need you to fill in as the villainous lover in the afterpiece. Very little dialogue—mostly a matter of looking noble and wicked and bedding the wrong woman."

"I beg your pardon?" Stephen said, startled.

Rosalind laughed, her good humor restored at his expression. "You're Claudio, the wicked duke who lusts after Annabelle, a virtuous maiden played by Jessica. You threaten to execute her father unless she lies with you. Annabelle agrees on the condition that you come to her in the dark to preserve her modesty. Then she and her beloved Anton, played by Will Landers, cleverly decide to ask her less-innocent friend Ethel—that's me—to take her place. I'm the duke's abandoned mistress who still yearns for him, so I agree to take part in the deception."

His brows arched. "Apparently I can make a modest career out of playing dukes."

"You have the right look," Rosalind and Thomas said simultaneously. The three of them exchanged glances, then broke into laughter.

"Condemned to dukeliness," Stephen said wryly. "Is that the script there?"

Thomas handed it over. "The dialogue isn't particularly witty, so it's all right to improvise a bit if you can't remember the exact words. The important thing is to act broadly. Larger than life. Naughty but not vulgar."

Stephen nodded and began scanning his part while Thomas collected the other players who would be in the farce. By the time they were ready to run through the piece, Stephen had most of the dialogue down, not always word for word but well enough to fake his way through his scenes. Mostly he had to look arrogant and demanding, which he did with intimidating ease. He also showed unexpected comic talent when he leered at

Jessica. As Annabelle, she cowered with a fine Gothic flare.

The rehearsal went smoothly, punctuated by several occasions when Thomas stopped the action to ask for a different way of speaking or moving. Rosalind enjoyed herself so much that she overlooked the dangers of the big deception scene that was the climax of the farce. Then Stephen tiptoed into what was supposed to be a darkened bower, calling, "Where are you, my dearest darling dove?"

Rosalind caroled, "Here, Claudio! Here! Here!" She was on the verge of embracing him when she recognized the implications of the fact that this was Stephen, not Edmund. With Edmund an embrace was merely acting. But with Stephen . . .

He felt the same way, for he halted a yard away, his expression changing from exaggerated lust to consternation.

"What are you waiting for?" Thomas said impatiently. "Kiss her."

Stephen took a deep breath and dropped out of the character of the villainous duke. "Sorry. I've never performed a public theatrical kiss, much less with a woman in front of her own father. I trust you haven't a horsewhip handy?"

Thomas laughed. "Hadn't thought of that, but I can understand your misgivings." He turned and beckoned to his wife, who was chatting with several other women in the back row of seats. "Come here, my sweet, and we'll show this earnest young man how it's done."

"I fly to you, my hero!" Maria cried grandly.

As her mother climbed to the stage, Rosalind moved aside, trying to decide whether she was more amused or alarmed. It would be awkward if that intense physical attraction struck while she and Stephen were in the middle of a stage. But it was also true that the situation was as farcical as the little play they were rehearsing.

When Maria was in place, Thomas minced onstage, trilling, "Where are you, my dearest darling dove?"

"Here, Claudio!" Maria threw herself into his arms. "Here! Here!"

The kiss that followed was dramatic in the extreme, punctuated by Claudio's comments about her beauty and how he felt as if he had known her always, which was surely a sign from heaven that they were meant to be together. Maria played up to him outrageously, reducing all the onlookers to helpless laughter.

When the demonstration was over, Jessica said in a penetrating stage whisper, "The Parents are at it again!"

After another burst of hilarity, it was time for Rosalind and Stephen to play the scene. When they were face-to-face, she gave him a wink and murmured, "Since we have no choice, we might as well enjoy it."

His eyes lit with wicked amusement. Then he swept Rosalind into his embrace, flamboyantly tipping her over backward at a precarious angle.

She clutched at him instinctively, barely remembering to use the exaggerated movements of comedy. Yet once she got over the initial shock, she took a heady pleasure in his embrace. Nothing untoward would happen in front of an audience. And since the characters they played were supposed to be in total darkness, as an actress she was justified in running her hands over his broad shoulders and taut muscles. She could gaze up into the smoky depths of his gray-green eyes and caress the stern, handsome planes of his face. She skimmed his lips with her fingertips, as a woman might do in the darkness, and said throatily, "You cannot know how I have longed for this moment, beloved."

He responded, "I have dreamed of you, my dearest dove." His eyes burned with desire. "I have yearned for you in the lonely silence of the night."

His voice died away, leaving an expression of longing that made her heart tighten with a wish that his words were real.

As they traded florid dialogue, Stephen slowly raised her to an upright position, at the same time shifting so that the audience could see her face clearly. Wryly Rosalind recognized that if Edmund had been playing the role, he would have arranged matters so that his noble profile was visible and her back was to the audience. But Stephen did not have an actor's hunger for attention.

Tenderly she rubbed her cheek against his, with no idea how much was acting and how much was real. "Promise you will not forget me, beloved."

"How could I forget such sweetness, such fire?" He kissed her, his lips warm and compelling on hers.

As she responded, Thomas roared, "Unhand that woman, thou dastard duke!"

Rosalind and Stephen both jumped as if ice water had been poured over them, and it was only partly acting. Rosalind felt her partner in crime tense, then relax as he looked up to see Thomas sweep onstage, followed by two servants whose torches were supposed to bring light to the dark bower. Stephen exclaimed, aghast, " 'Tis the archbishop!"

His gaze went to the woman in his arms. "And Ethel!" He leaped away as if she had turned into a serpent. "Trollop! How dare you deceive me! What have you done with my adored Annabelle?"

At the cue, Jessica and Will Landers entered hand in

hand, looking vastly smug. The archbishop thundered that he had just married the young couple and that because of his wickedness, the duke was to be deposed and executed by the church.

Rosalind dropped to her knees in front of Thomas and raised her clasped hands dramatically. "Please, Your Excellency, spare the life of my beloved! It is true that he has sinned, but his heart is not wicked. He only suffers from too much wealth and power!"

That line always got a laugh from the audience, most of whom would welcome the opportunity to suffer from too much wealth and power. Then Rosalind turned to her faithless paramour. "I cannot make you love me—but dearest duke, when you thought I was another, did you not find my kisses sweet?"

Stephen shuddered dramatically and raised his eyes to the heavens. After a long, pregnant moment, he said huskily, "They were sweet indeed, dear Ethel."

He took her hand and brought her to her feet, his expression a study in remorse. "Forgive me, faithful mistress, for the way I have wronged you. Remember me when I have gone to the doom I deserve."

Then he kissed her hand, a very effective bit of stage business that he had thought of himself. At least, Rosalind found it effective. She tingled all the way to her toes.

Satisfied with the duke's repentance, the archbishop granted pardon and married him to Ethel on the spot. Jessica was about to sing the naughty closing song when a man snarled, "Damnation!"

Everyone turned to look as Edmund Chesterfield slammed the door, then stalked down the center aisle toward the stage. "How dare you give my role to that— that useless dilettante. You had no right!" He gave Stephen a venomous glare.

Thomas said dryly, "It's traditional to allow actors to keep their accustomed roles, but only when they fulfill their responsibilities. You have forfeited this part by missing one rehearsal too many."

Rosalind guessed that her father would have reconsidered if Edmund had apologized for his tardiness. Instead, the younger man exploded, "You—you vain, pathetic old tyrant! Because you can barely remember your lines, you demand rehearsals as a way of abusing better actors. You're jealous of me because you're a failure who had to start your own company or you'd never have worked at all!"

Thomas and Maria paled while the other members of the troupe gasped and Jessica's expression turned homicidal. Rosalind took an instinctive step toward her father, knowing he would be deeply wounded by the cruel taunts.

Then Stephen said icily, "You have the manners of a pup in need of housebreaking, Chesterfield. Thomas Fitzgerald is as fine an actor as Britain has ever seen. If you won't respect his authority, you must at least acknowledge his talent if you have a shred of honesty in your soul."

It was Edmund's turn to pale. "You peacocking parasite! I've seen how you've wriggled your way into this troupe, wanting to be something you'll never be. And I've seen you sniffing around Jessica, too. Well, she's never going to drop her handkerchief for an aging lecher like you!"

Rosalind clenched her fists, feeling an instinctive desire to attack. How *dare* Edmund say something so vicious and untrue!

But Stephen was not a temperamental actor, and he was not disturbed by the insults. He actually smiled faintly. "I've been despised by experts, Mr. Chesterfield. I'm afraid you really can't say anything that will upset me. I have no desire to be an actor, nor have I been, as you so vulgarly put it, 'sniffing' around Jessica." He shot a swift ironic glance at Rosalind. "And I am certainly aging. All of us are." His mouth twisted. "It's better than the alternative, don't you think?"

Enraged beyond recovery, Edmund spat out, "That does it! I'm leaving today. The manager of the Theater Royal in Bath has been begging for me to join him, but I stayed with this hopeless lot of strolling players from loyalty." Voice trembling, he spun on his heel and stalked up the aisle. "Be damned to the lot of you."

He progressed a dozen steps before Stephen broke the strained silence by saying dryly, "One can't deny that he makes a rather decent exit."

The tension shattered as everyone in the troupe began to laugh. Edmund gave one last furious glare, then stormed out of the theater.

When the laughter died down, Thomas said, "I won't be sorry to see the last of him, and that's the Lord's own truth. The lad has some talent, but no discipline."

Jessica sniffed. "Plus the manners of a pup in need of housebreaking."

Thomas sighed, his amusement fading to reveal a concerned theatrical manager. "Still, losing him is awkward." His brows drew together for a moment. Then he shot Stephen a glance. "Join me for a pint at the inn. I'd like to talk to you."

Expression a little wary, Stephen agreed and the two men left the theater. Rosalind watched with a frown and wondered what her father had to say.

CHAPTER 9

Day Sixty-nine

Thomas Fitzgerald collected brimming pints of ale, then chose a private corner of the taproom. The inn was quiet at midafternoon, so they would not be disturbed.

Stephen's stomach was uneasy, but he sipped at his ale anyhow as he wondered what Fitzgerald wanted. Might the older man object to seeing his daughter embraced rather too enthusiastically during rehearsal? Stephen had done his best to be an actor rather than a man with a wonderfully desirable woman in his arms, but he was uneasily aware that he had not quite succeeded.

Trying a different topic to deflect justified criticism, he said, "Sorry I spoke as I did to Chesterfield. If I hadn't goaded him, he might have calmed down and apologized."

"I doubt it." Thomas shrugged. "If the truth be known, I'd considered discharging him myself more than once. He was grateful for the work in the beginning, but gradually he started thinking he was God's own gift to the theater. Too many adoring milkmaids, I suppose." The actor shook his leonine head. "However, he had a contract. It's not easy to replace someone in the middle of the season, so I would have kept him on until the end of the year. Now I'll have to find someone else."

"Until then, can you perform plays that require smaller casts?"

"We may have to, but it would be a great complication. More rehearsals, changes in sets and costumes." The older man paused, then said craftily, "It would simplify things greatly if you took Chesterfield's place."

Stephen choked on his ale. "Surely you're joking."

"Not at all." The older man made an expansive gesture. "I know you haven't the passion to perform that makes a serious actor, but you're a very decent second lead and character actor. You have considerable stage presence, you're an extremely quick study—very useful under these circumstances—and your voice has excellent power and range. It's almost as good as mine. Surprising for an amateur."

Not surprising at all—there were a fair number of similarities between acting and addressing the House of Lords, Stephen reflected. But the troupe's season would go on for months. Heaven only knew how much longer his health would hold up. He'd noticed a slight but unmistakable deterioration in the three weeks since Blackmer had given him the news. "Sorry. It's rather flattering, but I really can't accept."

Thomas sighed. "I didn't think so, you being a gentleman and all. Still, it was worth asking since you seem to be enjoying yourself with us. You have the great advantage of not having a damned actor's temperament."

Stephen smiled. "That's because I'm not a damned actor."

Thomas chuckled, then said seriously, "It's asking a great deal, but could you fill in until I replace Chesterfield? That shouldn't take long. By chance I just got a letter from a friend in northern England extolling a young fellow called Simon Kent. Bates says the lad has great potential and is in dire need of a position. I'll write today and hire him for the rest of the season. But until he arrives, I'll be shorthanded. You know how little slack there is in the troupe—the loss of a single member will be felt."

Stephen nodded. That was why his own modest skills had been useful. Ironically Thomas was offering the perfect excuse for Stephen to do what he wanted. Instead of returning home as he ought, he could stay with the pious excuse that he was helping his friends. "I must leave in a fortnight or so, but I'd be pleased to help out until then."

"Good, good." Beaming, Thomas downed the rest of his ale. "Just mind you don't seduce my daughter."

Stephen stiffened. "Surely you don't think I've been 'sniffing around' Jessica."

"Of course not. It's clear to anyone with eyes in his head that it's Rosalind who takes your fancy. I commend your taste—any man can appreciate a beauty like Maria or Jessica, but it takes more discernment to realize that Rosalind is every bit as lovely in her way." His expression became satiric. "I must also thank you for your restraint. My little Rose may be a woman grown, but that doesn't mean her heart couldn't be broken again."

At least he was being given credit for restraint, Stephen thought gloomily. Embarrassing to realize just how much Thomas, and surely his wife as well, had observed. "Believe me, I have no desire to hurt Rosalind. She and I are both aware that it would not be wise to become involved."

"Because the adopted daughter of a pair of strolling players is beneath a gentleman's touch?" Thomas asked tartly.

Stephen clamped down on his surge of temper. It was a fair question, for many men of his class would consider an actress fair game for seduction, and nothing more. As if the label "actress" could even begin to describe a woman like Rosalind. "You were a gentleman, yet you married Maria, a common actress."

"There was nothing common about Maria!" Thomas retorted. Then he stopped, realizing he had been baited. "Sorry. It was unfair of me to suggest that you're no better than a London rake. A father's feelings aren't always reasonable."

Perhaps being with actors was loosening his sense of propriety, for even though it was none of his business, Stephen found himself asking, "Is there any difference between how you feel about your adopted daughter as compared to your two natural children?"

"When you've watched a child grow and laugh and wake up sobbing in the night, she's yours, never mind what man fathered her. If there's a difference, it's maybe an extra bit of protectiveness, for she was such a tiny mite." Thomas absently traced a Tudor rose in a few drops of spilled ale. "And so good. Rosalind was a perfect child—almost unnaturally so. I sometimes think that if we hadn't given her a home, God might not have given us Jessica and Brian later. And that would have been a great tragedy, for having a child to raise is what turns a boy into a man." He stopped, embarrassment on his face. "There's no denying that we Irish are a sentimental lot."

Stephen lifted his glass in an impromptu toast. "Perhaps, but Rosalind was blessed the day you and Maria found her." His voice became bleak. "I only wish that I were in a position to pursue a . . . a serious relationship."

Thomas exhaled roughly. "So you've a wife. I suspected as much. See that you remember that."

Better the other man think him married than know

the truth. "Believe me, I will not forget my situation," Stephen said without inflection.

Though they'd concluded their business, he was in no hurry to leave. This was the first time he had talked to Fitzgerald at length, and he was enjoying the experience. He signaled for the landlord to refill his companion's empty mug. As that was done, he asked, "Do you think that Chesterfield really had an offer from the Theater Royal in Bath? It's one of the best playhouses in England."

The older man shrugged. "If they wanted him, it was for very minor roles, not substantial ones like he had with me. More likely he was lying. After all, what is an actor but a man who lives a lie? Or rather, a whole series of lies. No wonder players have always been viewed with suspicion."

It was quite a jump from the life of a gentleman to a disreputable player. Curious about Fitzgerald's motives, Stephen said, "You said you were considered a 'likely lad' when you were at university. Did you ever regret giving that up for a life in the theater?"

"Not for a moment," the older man said instantly. "But I do regret holding Maria back. She could have been one of the great tragediennes—the equal of Sarah Siddons. Marrying me meant exile from the great playhouses because I'm incapable of getting along with theater managers who are damned fools." He smiled self-mockingly. "Which is to say, all of 'em excepting my own fine self."

Stephen smiled a little but shook his head. "Your talent is the equal of hers. Did you ever try to compromise in order to achieve the fame you deserve?"

Thomas sighed. "Oh, I tried a time or two, but within a few days I was always at daggers drawn with whoever hired me. Perhaps if my father hadn't been such a tyrant, theater managers wouldn't make me so stubborn. But if he were a reasonable man, I probably wouldn't have gone on the stage and gotten myself disinherited."

In a few words, the actor had revealed a great deal about what and who he was. As the son of another tyrannical father, Stephen understood stubbornness very well. But he had chosen the path of detachment and obedience rather than rebellion. Did that make him wiser than Thomas, or more of a coward? If he'd had a burning passion to act, would he have run away for a life on the boards? Or would the immense wealth and responsibility of Ashburton have held him hostage?

Almost certainly yes, for responsibility had been drilled into him from the day he was born. Yet he felt a deep grief that his gaze had been so firmly fixed on the obvious path that he'd never seen the myriad other routes he might have taken. His brother had rebelled, and found his way to happiness. But not Stephen. He'd lacked the courage, or the imagination, to know that he had choices. Perhaps there would have been ways to balance responsibility with other interests, if he'd looked hard enough.

But now he was dying, and the knowledge that he had done his duty was thin gruel compared to the rich banquet of Fitzgerald's life. He sipped more ale and wondered if it was his imagination that it tasted of ashes. "Starting your own company must have been difficult, but you have a freedom that very few men achieve."

"Aye." Thomas smiled a little, his eyes distant. "I used to dream of someday having a little theater of my own in a city like Bristol or Birmingham. A snug house and enough money to buy my wife and children a few luxuries. I could try all my theories about realistic acting and historical costumes and . . ." He broke off. "But I'll never have the money for that, and in another ten years I'll be too old to play any of the great roles except Lear. Like Edmund said, I'll be a pathetic old wreck, sitting by the fire and thinking of my failures."

His expression was so theatrically woebegone that Stephen had to laugh. "You exaggerate—which is, after all, your business."

Thomas grinned. "There's none like the Irish for self-pity, lad. I've had a good life, speaking great words, bringing pleasure to many people, and with the finest woman in the world at my side. Many of the players I've trained have gone on to successful careers in famous theaters, so there must be something in my methods. I'm leaving that, plus three children who would make any man proud. Not a bad monument, eh?"

The grief Stephen had been feeling intensified to dagger sharpness. If children were a man's best monument, he'd failed there, too. He should have adopted a child, but it had never occurred to him to try because only a son of his own blood could inherit Ashburton, and he'd thought more about the succession than the state of his soul. Now it was too late. Quietly he said, "You're leaving a legacy to be proud of."

Then he got to his feet, knowing that otherwise he would end up demonstrating that the English could match the Irish for self-pity. "I'd best go back to the theater to see about a costume for the dastardly duke."

Thomas drained his mug. Then, seeing that Stephen had left some of his ale, he drained that mug as well. "Pity to waste it," he explained as he stood. "I'm off to write Mr. Simon Kent. Pray that he's half as good as my friend Bates says."

Stephen nodded and left the inn. But it wasn't a costume that he wanted, it was Rosalind. Her warmth and sunny nature would cure his gray mood.

As he headed down the high street toward the theater, he would not let himself think about how powerfully he craved her.

Rehearsal over and everything ready for the performance, Rosalind left the theater. She was closing the door when Stephen appeared, coming toward her with his long, loose-limbed stride. Lord, he was good-looking, with his broad shoulders and the sun finding russet highlights in his hair. But he'd lost weight in the two weeks since he'd saved Brian. The planes of his face were more sharply defined, revealing the strength of the underlying bones. They must be working him too hard.

Or perhaps she was simply looking at him more closely. She gave him a wide smile, wishing fervently that she weren't dusty and disheveled from her work. Ah, well, she usually was, so there was no point in regret.

Stephen came to a stop in front of her, his admiring gaze indicating that he didn't mind a bit of dust. "Rosalind, has anyone ever mentioned that when you smile, it's like seeing the sun rise?"

She laughed, pleased even though she didn't take his words seriously. "Consorting with actors is gilding your tongue, Mr. Ashe. What did Papa want?"

Stephen made a sweeping, theatrical bow. "You are looking, Madame Caliban, at the company's newest actor—at least until your father gets a proper replacement for Chesterfield. He's hiring someone recommended by a friend."

"Wonderful!" That meant Stephen would stay for

another week or two. "Since you're so quick at learning dialogue, you'll do splendidly."

"I thought I should see about a costume for tonight. Do we need to go through the wardrobe to see what will suit?"

Even though she already knew the answer, she spent several moments studying his tall frame for the pleasure of it before saying, "You'll have to wear the same robe you wore as Theseus. We haven't much for a man your height, and that costume is the only one splendid enough for Duke Claudio."

"Oh." He looked disappointed.

She was disappointed, too, because that meant they had no excuse to spend time together. Well, who needed an excuse? They were adults; they could be together without pouncing on each other. Probably.

"Would you care to go for a walk?" she asked recklessly. "There's a footpath along the river that I use whenever we come to Whitcombe."

He gave a warm, slow smile and offered his arm. "I'd like that very much."

As they strolled toward the river, he said, "Perhaps your smile isn't exactly like a sunrise, but you do have a sunny nature. "

"Why shouldn't I when I'm both lucky and happy? I've a wonderful family, interesting work." She grinned. "The satisfying knowledge that if it weren't for my organizational skills, the company would be in chaos."

"You could take the facts of your life and create a tragedy," he pointed out. "An orphan, adopted by itinerant parents who have to struggle for a living, widowed very young, forced to work in the family business, an uncertain future."

She gave a peal of laughter. "I suppose you're right, but I prefer my version of my life. All futures are uncertain, so why cast myself as a tragedy queen? It sounds deucedly uncomfortable."

"The older I get, the more I appreciate how great a blessing it is to be born with a happy disposition," he said reflectively. "Just as it is a great curse to be always gloomy even when one has been lucky in life."

"You're right—apart from life's normal problems, I've always been happy, and I can't take any credit for it. Mama says that even when I was a grubby little brat, I was always smiling." She gave him a slanting glance. "How would you describe your native temperament? You're not the gloomy sort, are you?"

"No, but certainly trained to sobriety. A man of affairs must be responsible and reliable." He gave a self-mocking smile. "He must also be rather boring."

She laughed, her hand tightening on his arm. "You are never that. I'm sure you've been exercising that dry humor since you were in the nursery."

"True. Luckily, few people recognize my subversive streak."

She chuckled again. They'd reached the pathway that wound among the trees lining the riverbank. The shady track was a cool refuge from the afternoon sun. She inhaled deeply. "Mm-m, smell the trees and flowers and grasses. I love the lush days of late summer."

Stephen picked up a dry fallen leaf and tossed it into the river. It spun lazily in the current as it drifted slowly downstream. "The harvest season is beginning. After the corn is gathered, autumn will come. All too soon it will be winter."

Hearing an undertone of bleakness his voice, she said, "Then spring will come, and the world will be young again."

He was silent for a moment. Then, his gaze on the water, he quoted softly, " 'To every thing, there is a

season, and a time to every purpose under heaven.
A time to be born, and a time to die, a time to mourn,
and a time to dance.' " Turning to her, he said with
quiet intensity, "And now it's high summer, and time
to live."

She realized with unnerving clarity how dangerously
close she was to losing her head over him. It would be
so easy for something—the warmth of his smile, the
honesty of his words—to push her over the precipice to
emotional disaster. Luckily she was not a young girl, or
she might have jumped off that cliff herself.

Yet though she could not let herself love him, she
was starkly aware of the passing time. Soon he would
be gone, leaving her world safer but less alive. Reckless
again, she let go of his arm and took his hand in hers. It
was large and warm and strong.

He threaded his fingers between hers. Then, hand in
hand, they followed the path along the river. She still
enjoyed the loveliness of the day, but that had become
a background to her acute awareness of Stephen. It was
remarkable, really, how much could be said without
words.

A mile or so down the river, they reached a grassy
glade where a willow tree spread strong, gentle arms.
By unspoken consent they sat on a thick branch that
formed a natural bench. The water flowed lazily, lap-
ping among the reeds. Rosalind said, "It's hard to
believe that this is the same river that almost drowned
Brian."

"Is it really? Here it's placid as a pond." Stephen
squeezed her hand, then released it as he said ruefully,
"We've been discovered. Your father didn't only talk
about me helping out until he gets a new actor. He's
seen how I look at you, and knows that it isn't Jessica
who needs to fear my wicked ways."

She made a face. "I should have known he and Mama would notice. They're both fearsomely observant. But probably it was the way I looked at you, not the reverse."

He bent forward and picked a golden rockrose, rolling the stem between his thumb and forefinger. "I had the vague, superstitious hope that as long as nothing was said aloud, we were . . . safe."

She nodded, knowing exactly what he meant. "But there could be no future, so there had better not be a present. Correct?"

"Correct." He swallowed, his throat tightening. "I wish it were otherwise."

So did she. For a moment she considered asking him outright if he was married, but decided she'd rather not know. There were other possible reasons why there could be no future for them. Perhaps he could not afford a penniless wife, or perhaps he would not lower himself to marry a woman of unknown ancestry and low station. Or maybe what he felt for her was mostly lust, and his conscience would not permit him to seduce her.

Since none of the reasons she could imagine were comfortable, it was better to leave the subject alone. Lightly she said, "Wrong time, wrong place."

"And the wrong man." He turned to her, his gaze burning. "But you, Rosalind, are a perfect rose." He tucked the golden rockrose behind her ear.

His hand hovered in midair by her head. Then, his motions jerky, as if they were against his will, he caressed her cheek. There was a faint, erotic roughness in the pads of his fingers as he brushed back a strand of her hair and skimmed the edge of her ear.

He cupped her chin. She became absolutely still, sure that a single movement would shatter her. The beat of the blood in her throat was hard against the heel of his hand, and she did not know if she was more afraid that she would surrender or that she would run away.

Desire palpable in his eyes, he said huskily, "You send all my good intentions straight to Hades, Rosalind."

He bent for a kiss, his mouth demanding. Her eyes closed and her lips opened under his. Passion scorched through her body, sharpening her senses to preternatural acuteness. She loved his scent, a male tang that underlay the country fragrances. All around them narrow willow leaves rustled in the breeze, weaving a hypnotic song. She stroked his head, and the soft waves curled silkily around her fingers.

His breathing roughened and he drew her closer, lifting her onto his lap. She twisted so that they were pressed breast to breast. Her thigh slipped between his and she straddled his leg, finding heat and hardness and intimate closeness.

His hand cradled her left breast, and his thumb stroked her nipple through the thin muslin of her gown. She gasped as hot, spiky sensations jolted through her body. Her pelvis began rocking in an instinctive plea for greater closeness.

He groaned and his hands slid to her hips, pulling her hard against him. She felt his body throbbing, shockingly intimate. Then in one smooth movement, he lifted her from his lap and laid her on the velvety grass, coming down beside her. He kissed her throat and the sensitive hollow below as his hands caressed her everywhere. His touch was flame, and she vibrated with a longing to be consumed. It had been years, too many years, since she'd known a man's touch, and never had she felt such fierce desire.

A tug at her bodice, then cool air flowed over her

breast. "So beautiful," he whispered. His tongue touched her nipple lightly, teasing and licking, before his mouth closed around the taut flesh. She went rigid with pleasure, her breathing ragged and her hands mindlessly kneading his shoulders.

Then he caressed her thigh, his palm warm on her bare flesh, and she realized how close they were to the point of no return. Her body was on fire with wanting, but she knew with sudden terror that if they joined together, her defenses would crumble and she would be irrevocably in love with him. It would be hard enough to lose Stephen as matters were now. If they became lovers, it would tear her into pieces when he left.

As his hand slipped between her thighs, she gasped, "No. Please, no." Yet she made no move to stop him, and knew with treacherous certainty that if he continued, she would accept him with mindless hunger.

But he stopped. After pulling her gown down again, he moved away, swearing with an intensity that was all the more scalding for the softness of his tone. He rolled onto his stomach and braced his elbows on the green turf, burying his face in his hands.

Shaking with reaction, Rosalind whispered, "I'm sorry."

He fell silent, and she saw the iron tension in his shoulders. After a long, long moment, he looked up with a crooked smile. "It's not you I'm angry with, Lady Caliban, but myself. I'd sworn I wouldn't do anything like that. And though you might not believe it, in general my self-control is very good."

She did believe it, and supposed she should be flattered that he was so susceptible to her. She *would* be flattered, and delighted, if there was any future for them.

But there wasn't. She sat up and ran her fingers

through her hair, which had fallen about her shoulders.
"Good sense is the very devil, isn't it?"

"It certainly is." His wry smile deepened. "It's the
great tragedy of my life that all my devils are so blasted
respectable."

She smiled, releasing her breath in a sigh of relief as
she saw the rueful warmth in his gaze. They could
never be lovers, but at least they were still friends.

CHAPTER 10

Still shaken by the tempest of interrupted passion,
Stephen sat up and leaned against the trunk of the
willow tree. Rosalind was watching him with sumptuously loosened hair and fathomless regret in her brown
eyes. She looked altogether entrancing, and he wanted,
more than anything in the world, to reach for her again.

Touching her would be madness, of course. He
looked away and breathed slowly as he mastered his
desire. It was harder to control his thoughts. He wanted
to maintain their closeness by engaging her mind and
spirit. He wanted to know what made her the woman
she was. Discarding manners, he asked bluntly, "What
was your husband like?"

"Charles?" Unoffended by the question, she slowly
finger-combed her tawny hair as she considered her
answer. "He was an actor. Rather like Edmund
Chesterfield, actually, though more talented. Handsome, often quite charming. I was eighteen, a suscep-

tible age, when he joined the company. Naturally I fancied myself madly in love. My parents weren't wild about the match but couldn't think of a good reason to forbid it. We were married within a year."

She shifted to straighten her gown. The movement put her into a shaft of sunshine that filtered through the willow leaves, burnishing her hair into a halo of gold and amber and sandalwood. She did not look like a woman who was still mourning; she looked like a pagan goddess of the harvest, her bountiful curves a promise of fertility and life. Stephen swallowed, hard. "Was Jordan unkind to you?"

"Well, he never beat me, but he was a chronic womanizer. I was shocked the first time. I thought all men were like my father, who never looked at a woman other than Maria. But Charles looked, and a good deal more." She grimaced. "At least he cured me of romantic illusions, which was no bad thing."

Stephen imagined Rosalind as a radiant young bride. She would have given herself, body and soul, with complete generosity. And that greatest of gifts had been wasted on a selfish swine. "What a fool Jordan was, not to realize what he had."

"Frankly, I thought that myself," she said with tart humor. She twisted her glowing tresses into a knot at her nape and stabbed a hairpin into the middle. "However, Charles didn't think with his mind, but with . . . a lower portion of his anatomy."

Stephen smiled wryly. "Men often do, I fear. How did he die?"

Her gaze went to a brilliant blue kingfisher as it dived into the water with a splash that sounded loud in the stillness. "We'd been married for three years when he was offered a contract at a theater in Dublin. He said it was a great opportunity, and went to Ireland immediately. He was supposed to send for me after he settled in, but he kept delaying. Six months later he was shot by the husband of a woman he'd seduced."

Stephen winced. "Good Lord, how theatrical. And not decent drama, but farce."

A smile tugged at Rosalind's lips. "Too true. I grieved for Charles, but I've never been quite able to forgive his sheer bad taste for dying in such a vulgar way."

Their gazes met, and they both began to laugh. In the past two weeks, Stephen had carefully preserved a hundred mental images of her, but this was how he would remember her best: laughing with the rueful compassion of a woman who had seen much of the world and learned that laughter was the best antidote for life's trials.

Damning the fate that had brought them together too late, he stood and held out his hand. "Time to go home, Lady Caliban. Is there a quicker way than along the river?"

She took his hand and came lightly to her feet, a graceful goddess. "If we cut across that field, we'll come to a lane that leads directly into town."

He tucked her arm in the crook of his elbow because it was less provocative than walking hand in hand. Not that it mattered. Every breath Rosalind drew was pure provocation.

By the time they reached the quiet lane, Rosalind had regained her self-control and they were chatting idly about the upcoming performance. Still, beneath her surface ease was sharp regret that the golden afternoon was spilling away like the sands of an hourglass. There could be no more such intimate occasions. It would be too risky.

They rounded a curve and found an open wagon

halted in the lane while the driver argued with a wiry man on horseback. Rosalind frowned at the angry voices. "They sound ready to do murder. I wonder what the argument is about."

Then a woman's cry sliced through the air, coming from the bed of the wagon.

"What the devil!" Stephen broke away from Rosalind and strode to the wagon. "Has someone been injured?"

The driver, a burly man with harsh features, shrugged. "The wench says she's in labor." He turned and barked over his shoulder, "See that you don't whelp yet, girl. Not till I have you out of Cowley Parish."

The man on horseback exclaimed, "I told you that you'll not bring her any farther, by God! The citizens of Whitcombe won't pay for her bastard."

Stephen's face darkened, and he muttered an oath under his breath. Rosalind caught up with him and asked quietly, "What's happening?"

"According to the poor law, place of birth determines what parish pays to support a pauper child," he explained grimly. "Which means that some parishes try to move a pregnant pauper girl to save the cost of supporting her and her baby."

Another sound came from the wagon, this time a despairing whimper that broke Rosalind's heart. She looked up at the arguing men and said fiercely, "Have you no decency? While you're squabbling, that girl is suffering."

The men broke off, and the one on horseback shifted uneasily in his saddle. "Not my fault. I'm Joseph Brown, an alderman of Whitcombe. It's sheer chance that I came along this way and discovered that Cowley Parish is trying to unload this girl on us. The Cowley vestry is notorious for sloughing off their responsibilities." He scowled at his opponent. "Crain here is the overseer who does the dirty work."

The overseer gave a hoarse chuckle. "And I'm bloody good at it. Soon as I pass that elm tree, the girl and her brat are yours." He cracked his whip to start the team moving, ignoring Brown's angry protest.

Face like granite, Stephen leaped in front of the wagon and caught the bridles of both horses. When his weight had dragged the team to a halt, he ordered, "Rosalind, get in the wagon and see how the woman is doing."

Crain bellowed, "Damn you, mind your own business! I'm taking this whore into Whitcombe Parish!" He raised his whip and slashed furiously at Stephen.

Stephen jerked his arm up to protect his face. The lash curled around his forearm with a vicious crack. Quick as a cat, he grabbed the thong with both hands and yanked the whip from Crain's grasp. The black leather sailed through the air like a furious snake.

Effortlessly Stephen reached up and caught the handle in his right hand. Then he lowered the whip and coiled it with menacing calm. "You'll shut your mouth and stay put, or you will rue the day you were born," he told Crain in a voice that could have cut glass. "I promise it."

Crain paled and Brown swallowed hard, clearly glad that Stephen's fury was not directed at him. Rosalind gaped at Stephen's transformation into a man of terrifying authority. It would take a brave person to disobey him.

A moan spurred her into action. She scrambled up the back wheel and into the wagon. Lying in a bed of hay was a terrified girl no more than seventeen or eighteen years old. Normally she might be pretty, but now her swollen body was writhing with pain, and her soft brown hair was plastered to her skull with sweat.

"Don't worry," Rosalind said soothingly as she dropped into the hay by the girl and took one clenched hand. "You're not alone."

"But . . . the baby's coming right now." The girl's hazel eyes were dazed with fear, and the skirt of her shabby gray dress was soaked. "I . . . I'm so afraid."

Rosalind squeezed her hand. She wanted to offer comfort, but she was alarmed by the fact that birth was clearly imminent. If there were any complications, the girl and her baby could be dead in minutes.

Stephen came to the edge of the wagon and briefly laid a hand on her shoulder as he looked inside. "Brown, bring a midwife or physician immediately."

Responding to the commanding voice, the alderman turned his horse to obey. Then he hesitated. "Promise you won't move the wagon beyond the elm."

"I assure you that this wagon isn't going anywhere." Stephen turned to Crain. "Unless you know how to deliver a baby, I suggest you get yourself out of the way."

The overseer sputtered, "That little slut can't drop her bastard in my wagon!"

"Then you shouldn't have put her in it," Stephen retorted. "Now *move!*"

Crain opened his mouth for another protest, then wilted under the force of Stephen's gaze. The overseer scrambled from his seat and withdrew to a point where he could watch what was happening.

Stephen swung into the wagon and knelt on the other side of the girl. Rosalind gave a sigh of relief. Having him near made it seem as if everything would be all right.

"What's your name, my dear?" he said in a voice

that was startlingly gentle after the way he'd dealt with the men.

"Ellie, sir." She squinted up at him. "Ellie Warden."

"Well, Ellie, it appears that you're going become a mother any minute. Is this your first baby?"

She nodded.

"Then you're bound to be nervous, but don't worry. Women have been having babies from the dawn of time." He pulled out a handkerchief and wiped the perspiration from her face. "We know what to do, so you have nothing to fear."

Rosalind glanced up and gave a horrified shake of her head to indicate her ignorance. Stephen saw, and responded with a faint nod that told her not to worry.

Ellie's hand clamped onto Rosalind's, and she cried out again.

"The pains are very close. It won't be long now," Stephen said calmly. He handed Rosalind his handkerchief and silently mouthed the words "Keep her attention." Then he began gently adjusting the girl's body and clothing to prepare for the birth.

Rosalind wiped the sweaty face again. "Have you always lived in Cowley?"

"I was born in Norfolk, and my pa brought us here ten years ago," Ellie replied, seeming grateful for the distraction. "He was a carpenter and he had a good job. Bought us a little cottage and fixed it up ever so nice, but after he died three years ago, there was no money. We've no family here, so my ma had to ask for parish relief to keep us from starving." Another pain struck. She closed her eyes, and her hand clamped fiercely on Rosalind's, but she did not cry out.

When she could speak again, she continued, bitterness in her voice, "The vestry men said everything of value we had must be sold to pay back the parish funds. When my mother was dying, they took the feather bed from underneath her and sold it. Then when she was gone, they took the cottage away from me. And now they're throwing me and my baby away as well."

How could men calling themselves good Christians behave so vilely? Thomas Fitzgerald, who'd never set foot in a church in Rosalind's memory, was a thousand times better a man than the vestry council. Clamping down on her anger in favor of more practical matters, Rosalind asked, "Can your child's father help you, Ellie?"

The girl's face twisted. "Danny and I were going to be married, but there were no jobs here, so he went into Wales to work at a slate quarry. He . . . he was killed in an accident the day before coming home to be wed." She drew a shuddering breath. "We . . . we only did it once. He never knew he was going to be a father."

"You've been unlucky, but that's over now," Stephen said soothingly. "Soon you'll be holding your baby in your arms."

For a moment Ellie relaxed. Then another pain convulsed her. "Jesus help me, I'm dying!"

"No, you aren't," Stephen said firmly. "This may hurt like the devil, but that's normal. You're doing very well. The baby's coming quickly now, and everything will be all right. I promise it."

The next painful minutes blurred together for Rosalind. She held Ellie's hand and made encouraging remarks. Her gaze avoided Stephen and the progress of the birth. Though she'd treated fevers and bruises in the troupe, that was very different from midwifery, and she didn't want to risk fainting or anything equally foolish.

Ellie gave a last wrenching cry. Then silence, until a

thin, indignant wail sliced the air. Stephen said triumphantly, "Well done, Ellie! You have a handsome little boy."

Rosalind glanced up and saw that Stephen was cradling a red-faced, kicking infant. The baby looked small in his large hands. He used handfuls of hay to carefully wipe the tiny body clean. By the time he'd finished that task and cut the cord, the afterbirth had been delivered. He said with a smile, "You did a swift, efficient job, Ellie. You obviously have a talent for making babies."

Ellie gave a crooked smile and reached out. "I want to hold him."

Stephen laid the infant in his mother's arms. He stopped crying immediately. Wonder spread over the girl's face. "He is beautiful, isn't he?"

"He is indeed," Rosalind said warmly. Surreptitiously she flexed her numb right hand, trying to restore sensation after the effect of Ellie's paralyzing grip.

Travelers were approaching. She looked up and saw a small, sturdy woman driving a pony cart at a fast clip with Mr. Brown trotting behind. The woman halted her cart by the wagon. "Are you the girl . . . ? Ah, I see you are."

She leaned forward for a closer look. "And what a fine healthy boy you have there! I'm Mrs. Holt, the midwife. Didn't want to wait, did you, my dear?" She gave a deep chuckle. "But I wager you'll want some help learning how to care for him. I'll take you both to my house. You can stay until you're stronger."

Stephen climbed from the wagon and said quietly, "I'll take care of her expenses, Mrs. Holt. See that the girl gets some new clothing for herself and the child."

The midwife nodded. "Can you move them into my cart?"

Stephen opened the end of the wagon and slid his arms under the new mother, ignoring the fact that Ellie and her gown were a filthy, bloody mess. Effortlessly he lifted mother and baby together and transferred them to the cart, which was padded with old quilts. Rosalind followed with Ellie's pathetically small bag of possessions.

Mrs. Holt swiveled in her seat and took the infant, wrapping him in a worn, clean towel while she crooned nonsense talk. Then she returned him to his mother. Rosalind smiled wearily, glad Ellie would be under the care of a woman who clearly loved her work and her patients.

Mr. Brown said nervously, "The fact that Mrs. Holt is taking the girl into Whitcombe doesn't mean this parish is responsible for her."

"Don't worry," Stephen said dryly. "Mrs. Jordan and I will bear witness to the fact that the baby was born in Cowley Parish." He turned to Crain, who had come to reclaim his wagon. "I shall call on the chief man of your vestry council tomorrow with some suggestions as to how they may best support Ellie Warden and her son."

" 'Tis none of your affair," Crain growled. "And she made a mess of my wagon."

Stephen simply repeated coolly, "I shall call tomorrow."

Belligerence gone, the overseer climbed into his wagon and turned to head back toward his own town. After a quick businesslike exchange between Stephen and Mrs. Holt, the alderman and the midwife took Ellie and her baby away.

As soon as they were out of sight, Stephen sank

down by the edge of the road, braced his elbows on his knees, and buried his head in his hands. "Thank God it was a simple, uncomplicated birth. Heaven knows what would have happened otherwise."

Rosalind gave a shaky laugh and dropped down beside him. Now that the crisis was past, she felt weak all over. "You were wonderful! Are you a physician?"

He looked up, "Not at all. Merely a farmer who's delivered his share of foals and calves and lambs."

Rosalind stared. "Good heavens, all your confidence was false?"

He cocked a brow with mock disdain. "I may not be much of an actor, but I can play the role of a doctor."

Rosalind collapsed against the grassy bank and began to laugh helplessly. "Wretched man! I thought one of us knew what to do."

"I knew the principle for humans is the same as for livestock," he said mildly.

"So that's why you cleaned the poor infant with hay!" She laughed even harder, and Stephen joined in. She felt very close to him, and more than a little awed. He was no physician, yet he could deliver a baby. He was a gentleman, yet he cared about the fate of a desperate girl who had been rejected by her own community. And though he claimed to be merely a farmer, he was used to being obeyed, which implied ownership of an estate.

Nonetheless, he was here, and his presence had been a godsend. She studied his face fondly. "You're very brave. Most men would bolt when confronted by a strange woman in labor."

"Someone had to do something, and it was clear that I was the best qualified." He smiled reminiscently. "My head groom once treated me to a detailed description of how he had delivered his daughter when his wife went into labor too quickly to get the midwife. At the time, I rather wished he had kept the subject to himself, but what he said came in handy today. His daughter is a lively little thing of five, and God willing, Ellie's baby will do equally well."

His expression was wistful. She realized that he liked children and probably had none of his own. A great pity—and a lack that she could identify with all too easily.

Her exhilaration faded and she relaxed, her gaze on the summer sky. "We have less than an hour to get back to Whitcombe, clean up, and prepare for tonight's performance."

He groaned. "I'd forgotten all about that."

"Which proves you're not really an actor." Rosalind got to her feet and offered a hand to help him up as he had done with her earlier in the afternoon. Sternly she said, "The show must go on, Duke Claudio."

Stephen smiled and accepted her help in rising. "Since the role involves me kissing you, I believe I shall be able to manage."

Rosalind blushed a little but said primly, "It was very conscientious of you to take me off for private practice."

He gave a shout of laughter. Then they resumed their walk to Whitcombe. Hand in hand.

CHAPTER 11

Lord Michael Kenyon pulled his horse to a halt in front of Dr. George Blackmer's house, then swung wearily from the saddle. He hoped the blasted man would be in because Michael had ridden a long way to find answers and was in no mood to wait.

The elderly servant ushered Michael into the doctor's dispensary, where Blackmer was using a mortar and pestle to grind some chalky substance. Michael had met the man only once before, at the funeral of the Duchess of Ashburton, his sister-in-law. The circumstances had not been such as to give him much faith in the physician's abilities.

Blackmer glanced up, then scrambled to his feet. "Ashburton! I'm glad to see that you've returned. I've been concerned."

"Look again." Michael removed his hat so the physician could see his face more clearly. "Not Ashburton, but Ashburton's brother."

Blackmer stopped in his tracks. "I see. Sorry. You do look much like him."

Since Michael had been hearing that all his life, it was not news that interested him. "I was away from home and didn't receive your letter until yesterday. I came at once, of course, but when I stopped at the abbey, I was told that my brother left over three weeks ago, and they haven't heard a word from him since then. What the devil is going on?"

Blackmer sighed. "So the duke has not been visiting you in Wales. I had hoped that he might be there."

"No, nor is he in London, because I was there until a few days ago," Michael said impatiently. "Your letter said that my brother is seriously ill. What is wrong?"

Blackmer hesitated, as if wondering how to break the news. "He has a tumefaction, a deadly internal disease that is destroying his stomach and liver. He will almost certainly be dead in a matter of months."

Michael went rigid. Blackmer's carefully worded letter hadn't led him to expect such bad news. Stephen was almost never ill. He'd visited Michael and Catherine in Wales only a couple of months earlier and had been in the best of health. How could he suddenly be dying? Tightly Michael said, "There is nothing that can be done?"

Blackmer looked away uncomfortably. "Prayer, perhaps."

Michael had to fight off an impulse to strike the man. There was no point in killing the messenger. Another unpleasant thought occurred to him. "Might Stephen have left because the illness has affected his mind?"

"Certainly not," the physician said, startled by the suggestion. "My guess is that the duke wanted some privacy to come to terms with his affliction."

Michael could see Stephen doing that. Still . . . "Three weeks' absence seems excessive. Might his illness have worsened suddenly, so that he is lying ill somewhere?"

Blackmer shook his head. "Possible, I suppose, but very unlikely."

Michael weighed what to do next. Stephen had spoken well of Blackmer's skill, but for a country physician that meant dosing fevers and setting broken bones.

The man hadn't saved Louisa, and he obviously hadn't the vaguest idea what to do for Stephen.

Perhaps Ian Kinlock could help. A surgeon friend of Catherine's, he'd saved Michael's life after Waterloo with a daring experimental procedure. Kinlock was now at St. Bartholomew's Hospital in London, working at the frontiers of medical knowledge. If anyone could help Stephen, it would be Ian. All Michael had to do was locate his brother and get him to London.

Intensely relieved at the prospect of positive action, Michael said, "Thank you for your information, Doctor. Good-bye." He spun on his heel and headed toward the door.

"What are you going to do?" Blackmer asked.

"Find my brother, of course," Michael flung over his shoulder.

"Wait! I want to come with you."

Michael paused, saying impatiently, "Why the devil would you want to do that?"

Blackmer looked down and absently touched the stone mortar on the table in front of him. "He's my patient. If you can find him, I should be there."

Michael frowned, on the verge of flatly refusing to allow the other man to come. He didn't want the company of a stranger, and he really couldn't tell Blackmer that his goal was to find Stephen and take him to a different doctor. Still, Michael had to admire the man's conscientiousness. He compromised by saying, "I suppose you can come if you wish, but you'd better be a good rider. I won't slow down for you."

"I'll manage," Blackmer said tersely. "But I'll need a little time to make arrangements and ask another physician to look after my patients. It's late in the day now. Can we start in the morning?"

Michael glanced out the window and saw how low

the sun was in the sky. "I suppose so," he said reluctantly. "I need to question the abbey servants and write some letters. Until tomorrow, Dr. Blackmer. Meet me at the abbey at dawn." Then he left, telling himself that surely Ian Kinlock could help Stephen if anyone could.

He refused to believe that his only brother might be beyond help.

After his visitor left, Blackmer sank back into his chair, shaken. Like his late father, Lord Michael had his full share of Kenyon abrasiveness, with the addition of an army officer's formidable air of command. Traveling with him would not be easy, and not only because Kenyon had years of experience with hard campaigning.

Blackmer had met Lord Michael only once and had been left with the impression of a man who looked much like Ashburton but with ramrod posture and piercing green eyes. He had not expected to see such unmistakable pain at the news that his older brother was critically ill. Most men would secretly rejoice at the news that a dukedom would fall into their hands in a matter of months.

The physician stared at the unlit fire. As he had feared, notifying Lord Michael had stirred up a hornet's nest. Ashburton could be anywhere in Britain, and the chances of locating him were slim. It was far more likely that the duke would return on his own than that he would be found. But if Lord Michael managed to find his brother, the duke's physician should be there as well.

Blackmer stared at his cold hearth and wondered with deep foreboding what he had let himself in for.

CHAPTER 12

Rosalind awoke late to a sunny morning. Jessica had already gotten up, dressed, and gone down for breakfast. But then, Jessica had not taken a long walk by the river nor had she helped deliver a baby.

Rosalind rolled over and stretched luxuriously. The high drama of the previous day had ended with a very successful performance at the local theater. Maria's wildly emotional role in *Isabella* had reduced the audience to happy sobs. The farcical afterpiece had been well received, and she and Stephen had reached the point where they could kiss with pleasure and no danger—at least when they were in front of an audience.

She thought of that kiss, and the others earlier in the day by the willow tree, and heat flooded her limbs. For a few moments she allowed herself to imagine what would have happened if they had continued. It would have been a rare and wonderful thing to share such passion with a man she cared for deeply.

But caring for him too much was the problem. She sighed and swung her feet from the bed. Stopping before it was too late had been the right thing to do. And not stopping sooner had left her with lovely memories. Better than nothing, she supposed.

After washing and dressing, she went downstairs. To her disappointment, Stephen had already gone out. In fact, he did not appear until after luncheon. Rosalind had finished a lunch of bread, cheese, and ale in the private parlor, and was making lists in her notebook. Seeing Stephen go down the hall, she waved for him to join her.

He changed course and entered the parlor. "What mischief are you up to?"

"Nothing very exciting." She indicated her lists. "In a couple of days we'll be doing a private performance at an estate near here. A very prestigious engagement, so I'm taking extra care to make sure we have everything we need. Unfortunately, the one thing we need most, good weather, I can't arrange."

"An outdoor stage?"

She nodded. "There's a lovely little Greek-style amphitheater, perfect for performing *A Midsummer Night's Dream*. If the weather is awful, we can move indoors, but it won't be anywhere near as nice." She set aside her notebook. "Have you eaten?"

Stephen shrugged off the question, as he often did his food, and unconsciously rubbed his stomach. She surveyed him critically. He was definitely getting thin, and she realized that she had seen that gesture before. Perhaps he suffered from indigestion, or even an ulcerated stomach.

Before she could decide whether it would be impertinent to ask about his health, he said, "Would you like to visit Ellie Warden?"

She smiled, forgetting about his lack of appetite. "I'd love to." She went and got her bonnet, and together they left the inn.

As they walked toward the far end of Whitcombe, he said, "In case you're wondering, I went to Cowley this morning."

"Ah, of course," she said, enlightened. "Were you able to talk to the head of the vestry council about Ellie's future?"

"Yes," he said, but volunteered no more. Nobly Rosalind refrained from further questions. She'd find out soon enough.

Mrs. Holt lived in a pleasant cottage surrounded by the brilliant, heavy-headed flowers of late summer. A perfect place for the cheery midwife. Mrs. Holt herself opened the door after Stephen's knock. "Ah, here are the good angels!" She stood back so they could enter. "Ellie and her boy are doing just fine."

"I'm so glad to hear that," Rosalind said warmly. "Can we see them?"

"Right this way." Mrs. Holt led them up a narrow stairway to a sunny bedroom at the back of the house. Ellie was sitting in an upholstered chair by the window, her baby sleeping in her arms. As Rosalind had expected, cleaned up and in a nice robe, she was a very pretty girl, with soft brown curls and a sweet face.

She lit up when she saw her visitors. "I'm so glad to have the chance to thank you properly. I don't know what I would have done without you."

Rosalind's heart melted at the sight of the sleeping infant. He had a full head of silky dark hair. "May I hold him?"

"Of course." Ellie passed her son over carefully.

Rosalind cradled the warm, malleable form and felt a terrible urge to run away and keep the baby for herself. She had expected to have children, and babies would have done much to compensate for the shortcomings of her marriage. But she was barren, and would never hold a child of her own in her arms. Huskily she said, "He's lovely."

"So small and perfect." Stephen touched a tiny hand gingerly, as if fearing that he'd damage it. "Will you name him for his father?"

"Aye. And . . ." Ellie ducked her head shyly. "I never did learn your name, sir."

"Stephen Ashe." His gaze never left the baby. Rosalind felt in him, as clearly as spoken words, the same hunger for a child that she had.

"Then I'd like to call him Daniel Stephen, if you don't mind, sir."

Stephen looked up with an expression of startled delight. "I'd be honored." His gaze dropped to the baby again. "I've several godchildren," he said softly, "but this is special."

Rosalind silently blessed the girl for giving Stephen a gift greater than she knew. Then she regretfully returned the infant to his mother.

Stephen touched the baby's petal-soft cheek. "Sleep well, Daniel Stephen." He looked up, his expression businesslike. "Do you have any plans for the future, Ellie?"

The girl's happiness dimmed. "I'll try to find a position where I can keep him with me. It won't be easy, but I'm not afraid to work."

"This morning I spoke to the Cowley vestry council," Stephen said. "They agreed that the amount of parish relief that went to you and your mother was much less than the value of your cottage, so you will receive two hundred pounds in compensation."

Ellie gasped. "Two hundred pounds! It's a fortune!"

"Not a fortune, but a good cushion against disaster," he agreed. "I believe that I know of a suitable position as well. A friend of mine has an estate in Norfolk, and the place could use another maid. The housekeeper is a good-natured widow who likes babies." He smiled. "A woman rather like Mrs. Holt. And perhaps you'll find some relatives in the area."

Ellie stared, stunned, tears forming in her hazel eyes.

"That would be perfect, sir. You and your wife have been so good to me. I shall never forget you."

Rosalind and Stephen exchanged startled glances. "We're not married. Just . . . friends," she said, knowing the words were inadequate.

Ellie blushed. "I'm so sorry. I thought . . . the way you two are with each other . . ."

"An easy mistake to make, because we're very *good* friends," Stephen said with a smile in his eyes. "Incidentally, when you go to Norfolk, if you wish to call yourself Mrs., with your Danny's last name, no one need ever know differently. After all, you were married in your hearts, if not in the church."

This time she did start to cry. "So no one will ever call my baby bastard. Oh, sir, it's . . . it's like a miracle."

Looking embarrassed, Stephen said, "You've had your share of ill fortune. It's time for a change." He glanced at Rosalind. "And it's time for us to be off."

She nodded, then bent to give Daniel Stephen a feather-light kiss on the cheek. His eyes opened, and he regarded her gravely. Knowing that she also would be crying if she stayed any longer, she squeezed Ellie's hand and wished her well. Then they went downstairs. Stephen explained Ellie's prospects to Mrs. Holt, who agreed to keep the girl until she was strong enough to take a coach to Norfolk. There was a discreet clinking of coins as he paid for Ellie's expenses.

Rosalind waited until they were well away before asking, "How on earth did you get the Cowley vestry to give Ellie money from the sale of the family property?"

"Threats," he said cheerfully. "I've some knowledge of the law, so I pointed out their misdeeds and said I'd get the lord lieutenant of the shire on them. In fact, I'll do that anyhow. Ellie is not the only one they have abused."

Rosalind remembered how he had looked the day before when dealing with Crain, and she had no trouble believing that he had intimidated the vestry into fulfilling their responsibilities. He probably hadn't even had to raise his voice. "Was the cottage really worth two hundred pounds?"

He hesitated. "Half that, after they had deducted every penny that had ever been spent on her family, plus interest. I doubled the amount to give her some security."

"So you're giving her a hundred pounds, plus expenses at Mrs. Holt's. That's incredibly generous."

"It's only a hundred pounds," he said, embarrassed. "Not a great amount."

If she'd had any doubts about his station in life, they were now resolved. "A small fortune by most people's standards," she said wryly. "Certainly to a Fitzgerald."

When he glanced at her, expression troubled, she said, "We come from different worlds, Stephen. Even more different than you realize, I think."

He turned and laid his hand over hers, where it rested on his arm. "But haven't we built a bridge between those worlds?"

"Yes," she said quietly. "A frail one that will dissolve as soon as you leave."

His face tightened, and there was bitter regret in his eyes when he said, "Why do things have to be this way?"

"They just are. You're a gentleman, and I'm an actress. Most of the time, the only way people like us meet are behind closed doors." She smiled at him. "And we've been lucky enough to have a little holiday from the usual way of the world."

He released his breath in a sigh. "You're right. As always."

She resumed walking, keeping her hand tucked in his arm as she said aloud what she had sensed. "You're running away from something, aren't you?"

He slanted a glance at her. "Am I that transparent?"

"I'm enough of an actress that I watch people closely." And because she cared about Stephen, she watched him very closely indeed.

"Nothing illegal," he said after a long silence. "I've been running from . . . life, I suppose. It's time to go home and take up my responsibilities again. As soon as Edmund Chesterfield's replacement arrives."

It was suddenly very important for her not to let him know how much she would miss him. Lightly she said, "It's been a lovely flirtation."

He glanced at her, an indefinable blend of emotions in his eyes. "So it has." He caught her hand and lifted it to his mouth for a brief kiss. Then, using a deliberately theatrical voice, "I shall remember you all of the days of my life, Lady Caliban."

As she would remember him. And someday, in a year or two or three, she would probably be able to think of him and it wouldn't hurt.

CHAPTER 13

Day Sixty-two

Stephen didn't recognize impending disaster until the eleventh hour. The troupe was on the way to stage the private performance that Rosalind had mentioned. Most of the players were in the carriages and lead wagon, while Stephen followed, driving the wagon that contained the costumes and sets.

The horses were nothing like his own highbred teams, which meant he could pay attention to his passenger. Rosalind had tossed her bonnet into the wagon and rode bareheaded, her face and hair full of sunlight. The warmth of her autumn-colored tresses made him realize that the first nip of autumn was also in the air. Time was passing by.

Preferring to forget that, he asked idly, "By the way, where are we going?"

"Bourne Castle, the seat of the Duke of Candover. I'm surprised that you haven't heard Papa mention it. He's immensely proud of the fact that for the last four years we've performed there at the duke's personal request."

Bourne Castle? Christ have mercy! Stephen's hands tensed involuntarily, and the horses whinnied in complaint. Automatically he loosened the reins, hoping Rosalind hadn't noticed his shock.

Rafe Whitbourne, the Duke of Candover, was one of Michael's closest friends, and he and Stephen had known each other for years. Certainly they were well enough acquainted that Candover would recognize his fellow duke instantly. Stephen felt a powerful urge to hand the reins to Rosalind and bolt.

For weeks he had been traveling with the Fitzgeralds in a magical world that was completely separate from his normal life. Now those worlds were about to collide. He might be able to escape detection if he were working behind the scenes, but tonight he was to play the Duke of Athens again. He and Rosalind would be the first people to step onto the damned stage. There was no way he could avoid identification.

Keeping his voice rigorously even, he asked, "Is the performance just for the duke's household?"

"Oh, no. It's quite a grand occasion," she said serenely. Aloysius was traveling on their wagon, and he chose this moment to push his head between them. She stroked the dog's shaggy head. "The duke and duchess invite all the gentry for miles around. Before the performance they feed everyone dinner, and even send the same dishes to us humble players. Excellent food and an appreciative audience. It's the high point of our annual tour."

Wonderful. Stephen would know half the people there. He was probably godfather to some of their children. Dourly he asked, "How did this event begin?"

"The duke and some of his grand friends came to see us perform in Whitcombe. I suspect they came to scoff, but they stayed to admire. It was *The Tempest* that night." She smiled reminiscently. "Afterward Candover came backstage—he's *very* handsome—flirted elegantly with every lady in the troupe, including old Nan, and asked if we were available for a private performance in his outdoor theater."

"Naturally, the answer was yes," Stephen said hollowly. It wasn't too late to run, but he couldn't, not when the company was already shorthanded. Leaving Thomas without a Theseus would be unconscionable.

"Hold on," he warned as he maneuvered the wagon around a massive rut, wondering why the thought of discovery was so upsetting. After all, he was the Duke of Ashburton and could do pretty well what he pleased. People might laugh at his eccentric behavior, or they might scoff, but it certainly wouldn't be to his face.

Was he ashamed of performing onstage? Not at all. He was proud of his modest skill, and he greatly enjoyed being part of an ensemble.

Then why was he concerned?

The problem, he realized, lay in that collision of worlds. The last weeks had been a special time—a secret pleasure that would help sustain him in the difficult months ahead. Having his adventure become common knowledge among his peers would tarnish what had been rare and wonderful.

Worse, the vulgar would assume that he was sleeping with one or more of the actresses. He could not bear for Rosalind and her family to be demeaned by ignorant gossips. But how the devil could he avoid being recognized?

A possibility occurred to him. "I've been thinking that I'd like to play Theseus with a wig and beard, so I'd look less modern. That can be arranged, can't it?"

"Yes, but why would you want to wear a beard?" she said with surprise. "They itch—I've worn them myself when playing a man. And they cover so much of the face that it's hard to project emotion."

He gave her a slanting glance. "The first time I played this part, you said yourself that all I had to do was convey authority, and love for my intended bride."

"And you can convey authority even with a sack

over your head," she said with a laugh. "Very well, indulge yourself with some false whiskers."

He relaxed a little. With a disguise and some alteration of his voice, he should be able to escape unscathed. It wasn't as if anyone would expect the Duke of Ashburton to be part of a traveling theater troupe.

The lead vehicles were turning between a pair of towering gateposts. After Stephen followed, Rosalind said, "Look. Isn't it wildly romantic?"

Towered and turreted and crowning a hill, Bourne Castle was indeed dramatic, though Stephen thought Ashburton Abbey more beautiful. As they started up the long drive, he pulled his hat down on his face and slouched lower in his seat. Luckily several weeks of living out of a pair of saddlebags had removed most of his aristocratic polish.

Their route took them past the sprawling stables. Behind were parked a dozen magnificent carriages, many with noble crests on the doors. Rosalind gestured toward the vehicles. "Splendid, aren't they?" She gave Stephen a teasing glance. "Though I suspect that for you, there is nothing special about such a sight."

She was right; he had not thought twice about the collection of expensive equipages. "Do you ever wish that you had that kind of wealth?" he asked seriously. "Gowns and jewels and carriages at your command?"

She looked surprised. "Not particularly. I already have all of life's necessities, a few luxuries, good health, and wonderful family and friends. I don't need more baubles." Her thoughtful gaze went to the castle. "Oh, I wouldn't mind having a nice house, but wealth doesn't make for happiness, and I suspect such riches carry many burdens."

Her words struck to his heart. Comfort, health,

warm companionship. When all was said and done, what else was there? Riches, titles, and power were just another form of bauble. Quietly he said, "You're a wise woman, Rosalind."

As he steered his wagon to the left, they passed a second row of carriages parked behind the first. His gaze went over them. The one on the end had a crest that looked familiar. Where . . . ?

Oh, God. He almost groaned aloud. It was the Herrington crest—and his older sister, Claudia, was Countess of Herrington. She and her husband were probably staying in the area with friends, and naturally such distinguished visitors would be invited to the evening's entertainment.

If he made a list of those he wanted to hide from, Claudia's name would be at the top. They had always gotten on well, but she had very firm ideas about the natural order of things. If she discovered that her noble brother was larking about on a stage, she'd give him holy hell. Once more he considered flight.

But the troupe needed him. From what Rosalind said, tonight's performance was very important to her family, especially her father. Leaving them in the lurch would be a wretched return for their generosity.

It was going to be a long, tense evening. As Stephen pulled to a stop beside the other troupe wagons, he uttered a brief prayer to Hermes, the Greek god of tricksters.

He would welcome help from anywhere he could get it.

Jessica carefully pressed down the left edge of the false beard, then stepped back. "What do you think, Rose?"

Rosalind studied their victim, then nodded. "He'll do very well."

Stephen said dryly, "Will I be permitted to see my own face?"

Rosalind gave him a wicked smile. "With that thicket in place, you won't see your own face even with a mirror."

Jessica's dark brows drew together. "I think he looks quite impressive. Like one of the medieval kings. An Edward, perhaps."

Unwilling to wait while the sisters decided exactly which king he resembled most, Stephen took a hand mirror from the makeup chest and surveyed their handiwork. Then he gave a sigh of relief. They'd given him a long, dark wig that fell to his shoulders in masculine waves, with a luxuriant matching beard. No one would think the hairy accessories were really his, but his appearance was effectively disguised, and that was what mattered. "I think I look more like an Old Testament prophet. One who's been in the desert a bit too long."

Rosalind laughed as she lifted the Duke of Athens's royal diadem—an iron circlet with cheap gilding—and placed it on Stephen's flowing locks. "I have to admit that your idea was a good one. You positively reek with royal authority."

"That's not authority, that's the lavender sachets used to keep moths out of the hairpieces," Jessica said irrepressibly, sliding away with a laugh before her sister could swat her with a blond braid from the costume chest.

Stephen stood and straightened his purple robes. Rosalind had been right about the beard; it itched. "It must be almost time to begin."

Costumed as Oberon, Thomas Fitzgerald rushed by.

He was in his element, bustling around and giving sometimes contradictory orders. Luckily Rosalind had done her usual fine job of organizing, so sets, actors, and costumes were in good order. Even the weather had cooperated.

The greenroom and dressing rooms were actually underneath the amphitheater. Stephen went to a small window and peered out. Shaped like three-quarters of a circle, the theater was set into the hillside, with the stage at the bottom and concentric circles of seating rising at a steep angle so that everyone in the audience would have a clear view. Huge old trees loomed behind the stage, literally within touching distance of the actors. That was one reason why *A Midsummer Night's Dream* had been chosen—the trees could be used as part of the set.

Earlier Stephen had helped the stage crew string ropes from the trees. When the company had done a quick walk-through of the play to adjust their movements to the stage, all of the actors playing fairies had swung merrily about. Stephen had cringed when Rosalind sailed down to the stage on a rope, but she'd had a wonderful time. Even Maria, in her role of Titania, had joined in the fun.

Now dusk was falling, converting the stage and the towering trees into the mysterious forest of Shakespeare's imagination. A nightingale caroled plaintively in the woods as the human guests gathered for the performance. Beautifully gowned women and elegant men drifted through the twilight, laughing and talking as they chose seats. Stephen looked for his sister but couldn't see her from his limited view. With luck, she had a headache and had decided to skip the play.

He didn't expect to be so lucky.

Then he smelled roses, and an instant later Rosalind

joined him at the window. She was lovely in the regal robes of the Queen of Amazons, her hair swept up and secured beneath a golden diadem. Her stage makeup emphasized the fullness of her lips, and her darkened lashes were seductively long. She looked ripe and luscious and utterly desirable.

He wanted to draw her into an embrace, but reason prevailed. He settled for sliding his left arm under her mantle and around her warm, supple waist, knowing that her garment would conceal the gesture from the others in the greenroom.

Their bodies came together from the curve of her hip to the softness of one breast. His blood began pulsing through his veins in quick, hard beats. He opened his left hand and caressed her midriff, moving his palm in slow, sensual circles as he murmured, "Are you ready for our coming nuptials, my Hippolyta?"

She looked up, her eyes heavy-lidded with desire as she said huskily, "Yes, my dearest duke. I'm ready." Ever so slightly she rubbed against him.

Heat blazed through him. For an instant he let his imagination run riot. They were an immortal king and queen, lovers safely caught in the words of a play where they and their passion would never die. He would woo her with wine and roses, and they would mate in the enchanted forest, forever young and strong.

Then his stomach gave a familiar twinge of pain, pulling him back to reality. Damnation, he was like a moth flying too close to the flame of Rosalind's bewitching loveliness. Why was he torturing them both this way?

Because the pain of unrequited desire was far sweeter than the cold comfort of logic. Nonetheless, he dropped his arm and moved a step away. "Have you done *As You Like It* here? This amphitheater would be perfect for the Forest of Arden."

She went completely still at the abrupt shift from sensuality to mundane reality. After a moment she said, "Just last year. I played my namesake, Rosalind."

He would have liked to see that. Her tall, splendid figure was ideal for a breeches part. There were a thousand ways he would like to see her—most of all between satin sheets clothed only in her glorious tawny hair.

He almost leaned forward to kiss the elegant ear partially revealed by her upswept hair. Instead he looked outside again and saw the Duke and Duchess of Candover crossing the stage and headed directly toward him.

His heart seemed to jump straight up in the air. Reminding himself that they couldn't possibly know of his presence, he said in a slightly constricted voice, "Are these our employers coming toward the greenroom? They look ducal."

"The duke and duchess always come in person to welcome the company and see if we're ready to begin," Rosalind explained. "Isn't she beautiful? They've been married several years, and they still act as if they're on their honeymoon."

The duchess, Margot, was indeed beautiful, almost as beautiful as Michael's wife, Catherine. Almost as desirable as Rosalind . . .

Cursing his single-mindedness, Stephen beat a hasty retreat to the farthest corner of the greenroom before the Candovers entered. They greeted Thomas and Maria with familiar ease, then turned to the other long-term players with friendly words. Stephen studied Candover with clinical interest. A few weeks ago, he himself had moved with that same expectation of deference and near-arrogant authority.

As the Candovers took their leave, the duchess looked around the room with a smile for the other members of the troupe. Her gaze lingered for an instant on Stephen, but probably that was because of his whiskers. He inclined his head deferentially, and her gaze moved on. Then she and her husband left the greenroom.

After the door had closed, Thomas raised both arms in a commanding gesture. "There has never been a stage better suited to this play, and the night is full of magic. Shall we go forth and make this a performance that no one will ever forget?"

There was a chorus of agreement from the players. Brian, costumed as Puck, said, "Oh, yes, *sir!*", then blushed when his voice rang out above the others.

His father grinned, then gestured for Stephen and Rosalind and their attendants. Heralded by a trumpet fanfare, they made their entrance into the glamorous kingdom of the imagination. It was almost full dark, and the stage was lit by tall, flickering torches. High above, in the trees, tiny lamps sparkled like fairy stars.

They swept to the middle of the open stage. As Stephen majestically turned to address his Amazon bride, he saw his sister in the second row.

Despite her stern, uncompromising expression, Claudia was a handsome woman, with the chestnut hair and strong features of the Kenyons. Her hands were clasped primly in her lap, and her quiet husband sat beside her. Stephen wondered what their marriage was like. Did Claudia and Herrington really care for each other, or had they made a mere aristocratic accommodation as strangers sharing a roof? If he were a better brother, he would know. He made a private vow that he *would* know before he died.

It was time to speak. Stephen pitched his voice more

deeply than usual, effortlessly filling the amphitheater. He was Theseus, who had fought great battles and done heroic deeds, and now he had come home to join with the love of his life.

Regal and brave, his Amazon queen replied in Rosalind's voice, her words liquid with the sweet eagerness of a woman who could scarcely wait to wed her beloved. Stephen gazed into her chocolate eyes and answered with the unnamed emotions of his heart, letting the Duke of Athens say what the Duke of Ashburton could not.

Then it was time for Theseus and Hippolyta to leave the stage to the young lovers. Rosalind raced off to change to the costume of a fairy attendant, but Stephen was free to watch from the shadows.

As the play progressed, it became clear that Thomas Fitzgerald would get his wish. In his lifetime Stephen had seen *A Midsummer Night's Dream* performed perhaps a dozen times. He had taken part on three of those occasions. But never had he seen a finer performance than on this night.

The setting was pure enchantment, giving the members of the fairy court an unearthly beauty as they watched the strange antics of the humans. Thomas and Maria played the estranged fairy rulers with the snap and bite of a couple who had been together for eons and still had the passion to fight. All of the actors were at their best, with Jessica especially poignant as confused Hermia, whose lover turned against her.

The comedy of errors progressed until it was time for Stephen to go onstage with Rosalind again. He no longer worried about being identified. Many members of the audience knew the Duke of Ashburton, but tonight he was Stephen Ashe, a man freed of the tyranny of rank, and he gave the best performance of his life.

There was a hush after Brian delivered Puck's final speech. Then the audience rose to its feet, clapping and shouting with an enthusiasm that sounded more like working-class London than the usually jaded nobility.

The cast began to take their bows. Stephen and Rosalind made their appearance together, and it was like being struck by a wall of sound. He drank in the clamorous approval, knowing that he had earned his share, and found that it was the headiest of brews. No wonder actors became addicted to this . . . this rapture. This intoxicating sense of power and achievement.

He made a sweeping bow, Rosalind's hand in his, profoundly grateful that he had been given the chance to taste this life that was so different from his own.

After the performance the audience came down to the stage to mingle with the actors. Several women, Stephen saw, were heading purposefully toward him, so he slipped away and retreated to the farthest corner of the men's dressing room. Earlier Rosalind had told him that the cast, still in costume, would go up to the castle for a reception with the duke's guests. After an hour or two, Thomas and Maria would collect their crew and they would drive back to Whitcombe by moonlight.

Stephen waited until he could hear no more voices before he removed his wig, beard, and costume. There would not be another performance of *A Midsummer Night's Dream* in his last few days with the company, so he said a nostalgic good-bye to Theseus as he packed his royal robes and hairpieces away.

Then he picked up the costume chest and carried it outside. Since he was the only member of the troupe not at the reception, he might as well make himself useful.

He set the chest in the back of a wagon. Aloysius was sleeping underneath. The dog raised its head, then whined and thumped his tail. A whiff of tobacco smoke came to Stephen. He spun around and saw the glowing tip of a cigar a dozen feet away.

An amused voice drawled, "So it really is you, Ashburton."

Hell and damnation. Stephen sighed and leaned back against the tail of the wagon, crossing his arms over his chest. The moonlight was bright enough to show the other man's tall, dark figure and the general cast of the hawklike features. Stephen had been caught red-handed by the Duke of Candover.

"Good evening, Candover," Stephen said with resignation. "How did you identify me? I thought I'd disguised myself rather well."

"Margot recognized your voice," the other man explained. "When she said you were playing Theseus, I thought my darling bride had drunk too much claret with dinner. Then I saw that the playbill listed the Duke of Athens as Stephen Ashe, which seemed suspiciously similar to your name. I decided to see for myself when you didn't come to the reception. I should have known Margot was right. She's uncannily good with voices and accents." The end of his cigar flared as he drew in on it. "One of the unexpected benefits of marrying a lady spy."

Luckily another advantage of a lady spy was that she was capable of being discreet. Stephen asked, "Does anyone else know?"

Candover shook his head. "Only the two of us. Care for a cigar, by the way?"

"Thank you." Though Stephen seldom smoked, he

welcomed having something to fidget with. He accepted a cigar and light from the other man.

Candover tapped a glowing ash from his cigar. "The Fitzgerald Troupe is remarkably fine for a company of strolling players, but still an unlikely place to find you. Dare I ask why you're here, or is it none of my business?"

Deciding that a degree of honesty would be best, Stephen said, "Do you ever get tired of the obligations of rank?"

"Sometimes. Not often, but sometimes," Candover said thoughtfully. "So you're taking a holiday from dukedom."

"Precisely. One I would just as soon keep private."

Wicked amusement in his voice, Candover said, "You're really quite a decent actor, but I suppose your family might not approve of your new career."

"Michael would probably laugh after he recovered from the shock, but my sister, Claudia, would have palpitations," Stephen said frankly. "And by the time she finished scolding me, *I'd* be having palpitations."

The other man laughed aloud. "I take your point—your sister is a formidable woman. I won't reveal your presence. I'm surprised Fitzgerald hasn't let the cat out of the bag, though. He must be elated to have you in his troupe."

"He doesn't know. No one in the company does."

"You certainly believe in anonymity." The duke dropped his cigar and crushed the butt under his heel. "Sure you don't want to come up to the castle? You could put that shrubbery back on your face, and no one would ever know."

"Why borrow trouble?" Stephen released a mouthful of pale smoke. "Besides, I'm enjoying the night. It's peaceful."

"Very well." Candover offered his hand. "Good to see you again. You must visit us sometime in your proper persona. Or will you stay on the boards?"

"No danger of that. I'll be leaving the troupe in another week or so." Stephen shook the other man's hand. "Please give my regards to your clever duchess."

He drew another mouthful of smoke from the cigar, exhaling slowly as he watched Candover's tall figure disappear into the shadows. He'd gotten off lightly. There were men who would not be able to resist brandishing such an irresistible bit of gossip, but Candover was not one of them.

A stab of pain sliced through him. He pressed his hand to his stomach, giving a slow sigh of relief when he recognized that this would not degenerate into a full-scale attack. It would merely be a ratlike gnawing in his internal organs.

Wearily he settled onto the grass and leaned back against the wagon wheel. Pain had become a chronic presence, to be ignored unless it became especially bad. Then the opium pills provided some relief, though they dulled his wits more than he liked.

How long had it been since he'd felt really well? Three months or so, he calculated. A dish of bad fish had given him and several other members of the household food poisoning. Dr. Blackmer had been summoned and efficiently dispensed treatment. Everyone had recovered, but from then on, Stephen had suffered increasing gastric pains.

He smiled without humor. Was he dying because of a bad fish? When he saw Blackmer again, he'd mention it. Perhaps that bit of information would contribute to the advance of medical knowledge.

He rubbed his belly. The disease was progressing rapidly; he wouldn't last the six months Blackmer had tentatively predicted. Three would probably be more like it, and one of those was already gone. A good thing he was leaving the troupe in another week.

It would have been pleasant to take Candover up on his invitation, but Stephen would probably never see the duke or his wife again. He might never sit like this on the grass at night, entirely alone except for the stars. The sense of loss was piercing.

Everything he did, everyone he saw, was another good-bye. How could he bear to leave Rosalind? If he could have her with him for the last weeks of his life, he'd die happy—or at least happier. Not so alone.

The vision was so tempting that he seriously considered it for a moment. Though she didn't crave riches, she might appreciate the chance to give her family security. All it would cost would be a few weeks or months of her time.

A few very harrowing months while she watched him rot away. Better to say good-bye now, before it became obvious how much his health was failing.

Aloysius rolled over and laid his head on Stephen's lap. Stephen scratched the dog's ears. He'd miss the beast.

He'd miss everything about the Fitzgerald Theatrical Troupe.

When Rosalind realized that Stephen was not at the reception, she asked a servant for a basket and packed some food and drink. Then she made her way through the park to the amphitheater. The cool night was a welcome change after the heated gaiety of the reception. There was an ancient tradition of players and aristocrats mingling that went back to the medieval courts, and that tradition was alive and well at Bourne Castle.

Still, it had been a tiring day, and she'd had enough of crowds. It would be much more pleasant to tempt her willpower by being alone with Stephen.

By the time she reached the troupe wagons, her eyes had adjusted to the moonlight, and she easily spotted the shadowed shape of a man sitting against a wagon wheel. "Hello," she said cheerfully as she folded gracefully onto the grass beside him, Hippolyta's robes rippling in all directions. "I thought you might be hungry. Or thirsty. Care for some champagne?"

After a hesitation he said, "I'd like that."

There was a dark note in his voice, perhaps a sense of letdown after the exciting performance. Well, champagne should brighten his mood. The bottle was already open, so she pulled the cork and poured them each a glassful. "To a very successful evening." They clinked their glasses together and drank.

Rosalind felt the strain of the day ebb away. She gazed up at the dark bulk of the castle looming against the night sky. "Bourne Castle is probably drafty, but there's no denying that it's picturesque."

"Would you like a castle?" he asked seriously. "Or perhaps an abbey?"

She pretended to consider. "An abbey would be very nice, but only if the cloisters were intact so I could walk there on rainy days and think deep thoughts."

"Duly noted. Shall I give you an abbey with cloisters?"

"Never mind. I shouldn't know what to do with an abbey. I'm really not very good at deep thoughts." Her humor faded as she remembered the news she'd just heard. "Papa said tonight that he just received a letter from Simon Kent. The fellow is very eager. He'll join us in four days."

"So soon." Stephen was silent for a minute. "I'll go the day after he arrives."

She shivered, only partly because of the cool night. His arm came around her. She relaxed against him, her head pillowed against his shoulder. She fit there very nicely. "You won't have to leave because of Kent," she said wistfully. "There will still be roles to play. Scenes to set. Wagons to drive."

"It's time, Rose," he said quietly.

She burrowed closer. He was so warm and solid, so *present*. It was hard to accept that soon he would be gone. "I'll miss you," she whispered.

"And I'll miss you." He kissed the top of her head.

She raised her face and suddenly they were kissing with fierce intensity. The velvet night was heavy with the scents of champagne and flowers, with sensual secrets that shunned the light of day. Their arms locked around each other, and they sprawled back onto the grass, bodies twined full length. She loved the feel of his hard, commanding body, and the knowledge that she could stir such desire.

He cupped her breast, then stroked down the worn silk of the Amazon queen's gown. She inhaled sharply when his hand came to rest at the juncture of her thighs. Her pulse drummed throughout her body, and she wanted to yield utterly. But somewhere in the back of her mind, she felt the fear of looming love, as she had once before. Passion would bring such brief satisfaction, and cause such lasting grief.

He hesitated, sensing her withdrawal. Then Aloysius whimpered and shoved his cold nose between them.

When he gave Rosalind's cheek a wet lick, she began to laugh helplessly. "Oh, dear. This is turning from romance to farce."

Stephen rolled away. "That dog has more sense than either of us," he panted.

He got to his feet, caught her hand, and pulled her up. His hands brushed over her swiftly, smoothing her costume and soothing her jangled nerves.

Then he lifted her chin and gave her a swift, hard kiss. "Go back to the reception, and don't return until you're surrounded by members of the troupe. Otherwise, I may do something we'll both regret."

He was right, of course. Leaving him the champagne and basket of food, she made her way rather dizzily back to the castle.

Yet she could not help wondering: if something *had* happened, would she truly have regretted it?

CHAPTER 14

Haverford was more a village than a town, but the Fitzgerald Troupe had always done good business there, and the Green Man Inn was pleasant. Rosalind took her belongings to her tiny attic room. Then she came downstairs with tea on her mind. As she headed toward the private parlor, she saw her father talking to the landlord, Mr. Williamson. Frowning, her father gestured for her to join them.

"Williamson says that the tithe barn we've always used burned down recently. He has two suggestions of other places that might do." Thomas handed her a slip of paper with directions written on it. "I'll check one, and you go look at the other."

"The owners are willing to have us?"

"Aye, Mrs. Jordan," the landlord said. "Farmer Brown and his family are busy bringing in the harvest, but until they do, the threshing hall will be available. He said to just go and take a look on your own, since everyone will be out in the fields."

Rosalind scanned the directions, making a mental note to leave performance tokens for the farmer and his family even if the troupe chose the other barn. It was good of them to be willing to have players in, for the fee paid wouldn't be much compared to the nuisance.

Thomas said jovially, "Take Stephen, in case you get attacked by a lamb, or whatever lives in barns."

She nodded. Any excuse to be with Stephen would do. The four days until Simon Kent would arrive had dwindled to only one. Tomorrow Kent would come, and the next day Stephen would go. The knowledge was a cold weight on her heart.

Putting on a determinedly cheerful expression, she went into the private parlor, where Stephen was tutoring her little brother. "May I borrow your teacher, Brian? Papa wants us to look at a barn."

"Take him," her brother said swiftly. "The needs of the troupe come first."

"What you mean is that you haven't translated your Latin lines," Stephen said dryly. "Be sure they're finished by the time I return."

Brian gave a persecuted sigh and bent his head to his task. Stephen grinned and brushed the boy's hair lightly with his fingertips. "Just think of how you can use this suffering to enhance your acting."

Brian brightened and started to pantomime a death scene, clutching his throat. Rosalind laughed as she took Stephen's arm and led him from the private parlor.

As they walked toward the front door of the inn, she saw his expression tighten. "Wait a moment while I get a drink of water," he said.

He went into the taproom and talked to the landlady, who instantly complied. Rosalind thought dryly that women were always happy to indulge Stephen's requests.

Her eyes narrowed when she saw that he was using the water to wash down a pill. When Stephen rejoined her, she said, "Not feeling well?"

His face shuttered, and he gave a shrug. "Just a touch of indigestion."

He so obviously didn't wish to discuss the matter that she said nothing more. They went out into the sunny street. It was a glorious day, autumn rather than summer. The first dry leaves were rattling crisply in the breeze.

Not speaking much, they followed the high street until it turned into a country road again. Their destination was just outside the village. There was no answer to a knock on the door; as Williamson had predicted, the family and servants must all be in the fields, taking advantage of the fine weather to bring in the harvest.

Rosalind glanced around the farmyard, which was enclosed by weathered brick buildings on three sides. "Where would we find the threshing hall?"

"On the left, I think," Stephen said. "Next to the granary and opposite the byre."

More proof that he knew his way around a farm. They entered the threshing hall through a pair of doors high enough to admit a loaded wagon.

Rosalind slowly turned, surveying the space with a calculating eye. Ancient gnarled trusses supported the roof, and high windows let in a fair amount of light. A hayloft stretched across the left end of the area. "We could perform under the loft, but there isn't really an area that could be used for the wings."

"There's a door to the granary in the corner. Entrances can be made from there."

They paced around, discussing how the space could be used. Finally Rosalind said, "It's a bit small, but it will do if Papa's barn isn't better." Then she heard a high squeak and cocked her head. "What was that?"

"Probably a mouse being caught by an owl."

The cry came again. "It's from the hayloft," she said. "I'll go up and see."

A sturdy ladder led to the loft. She climbed up cautiously, knowing, and not sorry, that she was showing an indecent amount of ankle. Stephen steadied the ladder for her, then climbed up himself.

The loft was sunny and fragrant with the distinctive grassy scent of fresh hay. If Rosalind were a child, she would have loved to play here. For that matter, adults could play here, too, though they would choose a very different game.

The cry came again, this time as a soprano chorus. She scanned the piles of hay looking for the source, then said with delight, "Look—kittens!"

She crossed the loft and knelt near the round depression that held four plump multicolored kittens and a wary tabby mother. "Don't worry, darling," she said softly. "I won't hurt your babies. May I hold one?"

The mother cat did not look convinced by the sweet talk, but a black-and-orange kitten bounced toward Rosalind, barely able to move over the thick, springy hay. She laughed and put her hand in the kitten's path. It walked right onto her palm. "Look, Stephen, isn't he adorable? He just fits into my hand." She stroked the kitten with a forefinger and was rewarded with a high, barely audible purr.

"She. Tortoiseshell cats are always female," Stephen said in a tight voice.

She glanced up, surprised by his tone, and saw that his face was rigid.

"I'll wait for you below," he said abruptly.

She frowned with concern as he turned to go down the ladder. He took two steps and staggered. She saw him fighting to retain his balance. Then his hands went to his abdomen, and he slowly folded into the hay with an agonized gasp.

Rosalind set down the kitten and darted across the loft. Stephen had curled into a tight ball, arms wrapped around his middle and his face glazed with sweat.

Horrified, she gasped, "Stephen, what's wrong?"

He shook his head and tried to speak but couldn't get any words out.

Hands shaking, she loosened his cravat so he could breathe better. His skin was cold and clammy. Jumping to her feet, she said, "I'll go for a doctor."

"No!" he said, voice a thin rasp. "I'll . . . be fine."

She had seldom seen anyone who looked less fine. "Can I do anything?"

He closed his eyes. "Water," he panted. "Please."

Rosalind bolted down the ladder and went outside. Where was the well house? There, at the far end of the farmyard. She raced to it. Inside was a windlass and a bucket. Hands shaking, she dropped the bucket into the well, then laboriously turned the crank to bring it up again. It seemed to take forever.

A large tin dipper hung from a nail on the opposite wall. She scooped it full of water, then returned to the threshing hall, wanting to run but having to walk to avoid spilling the dipper.

Though climbing the ladder was tricky, she managed it with only minor water loss. To her relief, Stephen was no longer knotted in that terrifying ball. He had straightened out and was lying on his back in the deep hay, one hand pressed to his abdomen. His eyes were closed, and illness was written on his painfully drawn face. How could she have missed seeing it before?

She knelt beside him and held the dipper to his lips. "Here. Drink."

He raised his head, using one hand to steady the dipper. At first he sipped. Then he swallowed more deeply until the dipper was empty. "Thank you," he said hoarsely.

"Shall I get more?"

He shook his head. "I'm all right now. Just give me . . . another minute. Then we can leave."

Suddenly angry, she snapped, "Liar. There have been other signs of illness, but you've always shrugged them off, and I've been stupid enough to allow it. I should have dragged you to a doctor earlier. What's wrong?"

He looked directly at her. All of the green had been leached from his eyes, leaving them a pale, lightless gray. There was a long, long silence. She sensed that he was considering what lie would best mollify her.

She took his cold hand and gripped it hard as she stared into his eyes, willing him to tell her the truth. Her fierce need to know clashed against his exhausted resistance until finally, the words seeming wrenched against his volition, he said in a raw whisper, "There's nothing you or anyone can do."

Her heart seemed to stop. "What do you mean?"

His eyes drifted shut. In a barely audible voice, he said, "I'm dying."

It was the worst of all possible news, so horrifying that she could not get her mind around it. Dying? Impossible. He was too strong, too vital. Too alive.

Yet his flat words could not be doubted.

She pressed her free hand to her heart. The magnitude of her anguish revealed just how deeply she cared for him. She had denied that, even to herself, to mitigate the pain of inevitable loss.

But the pain of separation had been a mere shadow compared to this. She had known from the beginning that eventually he would return to his family and friends. Secretly she had hoped he would think of her now and then with affection, but she had genuinely wanted him to be happy. Not lying in the cold, cold ground.

So many things came clear. The darkness she'd sensed in him. The distance he'd maintained when passion and harmony of mind kept drawing them together. His insistence that he must leave. His loss of weight and the deepening lines in his face.

Her mind raced. The one thing she must avoid was burdening him with her terrible grief. Concentrating on keeping her voice steady, she said, "I don't approve. Your death will be a beastly, horrible waste."

His eyes opened, and she saw that his pupils were enlarged. Probably there had been opium in that pill he took, which might explain why he had finally revealed what he had so carefully hidden.

"I think it's rather a waste myself." His mouth twisted with ironic humor. "Still, we all must die someday. I am merely doing it sooner than expected."

It was one thing to know that death comes for everyone. It was quite another to look across the table and see that the Grim Reaper had arrived for tea. Rosalind tried to imagine how she would feel if facing imminent death, and failed. Her grip on his hand tightened. "Is this why you were running away from your usual life?"

He nodded wearily. "After the doctor's diagnosis, I felt a powerful need to get away while I came to terms with the news."

"Doctors can be wrong."

The lines in his face deepened. "True, but the body doesn't lie. Every day I feel the disease advancing. It's just a matter of time—and not much of it."

"What is your illness?"

"The physician called it a tumefaction of the stomach and liver," he said tersely.

"And I thought that you might only be on holiday from a difficult marriage," she said, hating herself for her lack of perception.

"I was married." His gaze shifted to the wooden truss above their heads. "Louisa died a little over a year ago."

The starkness in his voice implied that he had loved her very much. Softly Rosalind asked, "What was she like?"

He searched for words. "Beautiful," he said at last. "A perfect lady always."

No one would call Rosalind a lady, and she certainly wasn't perfect. But Stephen desired her, which meant that it might be within her power to give them a few brief moments of joy. And she might as well, because nothing they did together could make her hurt more than she did now.

She must take exactly the right tone, or he would retreat into his rigid self-control again. After a moment's thought, she said lightly, "It occurs to me that you have been very nobly keeping your distance for fear I would become all hysterical and difficult if I learned of your illness."

His eyes snapped open and he stared at her. Then his mouth curved in a wry smile. "I didn't use quite those terms, but that's essentially accurate."

"What a proud, foolish man you are." She leaned forward and kissed his cool lips, hoping that he was not too drained by the attack to feel desire.

Lifting her head only a fraction of an inch, she murmured, "I'm not the least bit hysterical, or prone to unseemly emotion." She buried her pain, thought of pleasurable things, and managed to create a teasing smile. "Since you will be leaving tomorrow, I would dearly like to give you a good-bye to remember. For both our sakes."

For the space of ten heartbeats, there was silence as he gazed at her with piercing intensity. The green tone had returned to his eyes. It was so quiet that Rosalind could hear the mother cat's tongue as she washed her kittens.

Then Stephen slipped his arms around her waist and pulled her down into another kiss. It started where hers had ended, swiftly growing deeper and more demanding. She literally felt his temperature rising from coolness to normality, then to fever heat.

There had been a powerful attraction between them from the beginning despite their best attempts to deny it. Now his revelation had shattered their painstakingly erected barriers. They had been building to this moment since they met; every touch, every private glance, every theatrical kiss, and every real one had laid a stick of kindling on the fire. Now she had tossed on the match, and they both burned.

Their bodies molded together, her breasts crushing into his chest as he kneaded her back and hips. Her legs opened and slipped outside his, bringing their pelvises together with stunning intimacy. She gasped, shocked by her own unbridled response. There had been passion between her and Charles, at least at the beginning, but not like this Not even close to this.

She and Stephen kissed each other breathless. Then, in a cloud of sweet herbal scents, he caught her in his arms and rolled them over so that he was above, his body pressing hers into the deep hay. "I want to make love to you, Rosalind," he said hoarsely. "If you have any doubts, act on them now."

The loft glowed with honey-gold light, haloing his broad shoulders and chestnut hair. Like an angel?

Like a lover. She lifted her hand and caressed his cheek with the back of it. "I have no doubts, Stephen. Only regrets that we didn't do this sooner."

He enfolded her with his body, kissing her throat as he deftly untied the drawstring that secured the gathered neckline of her gown. Then he slid his hand behind her back, loosening her stays so he could pull them and her shift down from her shoulders. His mouth followed the swelling curves, leaving a scalding trail. When her breasts were bared, he cupped them in both hands, kissing the tender skin with an ardor that left flagrant marks of possession.

She stiffened when his tongue lapped her nipple. When it had been teased erect, his mouth descended, tugging with an intensity that found the ravishing point just short of pain. Sensation flooded her, driving out all thoughts and leaving only desire.

She slid her hands below his coat and yanked his shirt free, then laid her palms on his bare flesh. The long, taut muscles jerked convulsively at her touch. She caressed the smooth skin of his back before she slid one hand between them, seeking and finding the hard ridge of flesh that strained against his clothing.

He groaned, his whole body going rigid as she squeezed him. Then he shifted his weight to one side, kissing her throat as he stroked the length of her body like a skim of fire. Catching her skirts in one hand, he raised the crumpled fabric to her hips. Then he slipped his hand between her inner thighs.

She gave a suffocated cry when he touched her intimately. As his long fingers probed the sensitive folds to find moist, hot readiness, her legs separated and her back arched involuntarily. She was brazen, a wanton, to feel such arousal. "Please," she said hoarsely, "please, now . . ."

There was a pause that seemed to last forever while he wrenched at his clothing. She ached with emptiness, not only for the weeks she had known him but for all the years that she hadn't. Then he settled against her, hot and heavy. Her hands gripped his buttocks, rough with impatience, as she pulled him closer.

"Oh, God," he groaned as he buried himself in her welcoming warmth. She felt a spasm of discomfort because it had been so long since she had lain with a man. It passed in an instant, overwhelmed by a firestorm of desire.

He began driving into her again and again. She responded with her whole being, panting and straining and clawing as they found a savage rhythm together. Heaven and hell, bliss and frantic need.

The climax was a mutual shattering, a vortex of sensation where her fierce contractions triggered his own shuddering response. She felt as if she were being flayed alive–yet in the same instant she found balm, and sweet release.

Then the storm passed, leaving her weak and utterly

spent. She gulped for breath, her whole body trembling as she clung to him. The wildness of what had just passed between them was almost frightening. Yet she knew with every fiber of her being that nothing could ever make her regret what she had just done.

Day Fifty-nine

His awareness returned in fractured pieces. No longer could he wonder if he was capable of passion. He had not dreamed that desire could be so violent, so swift and heedless. He would have been shamed by his blind selfishness, except that she had shared his madness, and his fulfillment.

For the first time, he understood why sexual congress was sometimes called the little death. He had been annihilated, yet still he lived, suspended in a time where there was no past or future, only an eternal present. And he had never felt more profoundly alive. He was almost painfully conscious of the perfumed softness of the hay, of the fevered pounding of his heart, of Rosalind's yielding body trapped below his.

He rolled to his side and drew her into his arms, cradling her against his chest. Her breath tickled his throat, and her skin was salty when he kissed her temple. Their clothing and limbs were tangled with profound intimacy.

He experienced a sudden, vivid memory of the dream he'd had the night after rescuing Brian from the river. He had pursued a laughing woman—Rosalind—through a field of sunlit flowers that glowed with the colors of autumn. When he had caught her, she had swung around into his arms, giving herself with an eagerness that had matched his. They had tumbled to the ground and made love deliriously.

Today the dream had become reality, and the only cause for regret was that it was over so quickly. That, and the bitterly ironic fact he had discovered passion too late.

No, not quite too late. He could not—*would* not—let her go.

He'd done his best to stay detached, to admire and flirt without entanglement. He had tried to behave honorably and avoid a situation that might cause harm.

But honor be damned. He wanted her, and his ruthless Kenyon blood said that he must have her for as long as there was breath in his lungs.

He considered what that meant, and saw that the price would be steep. She would cost him his pride, for he would be unable to conceal his increasing weakness from her. The stunning pleasure they had just shared would not last until the end. No matter how intense the passion that bound them, the day would come when his body would no longer be capable, and that would be bitter. And his need for her would become greater and greater as his weakness increased, and that was the most bitter thought of all.

Even at such a price, she was worth it. Unconsciously he had been treating her like a glasshouse flower, a fragile blossom that could not bear a harsh breeze. Like Louisa. But Rosalind was strong. She had survived the waterfront slums when scarcely more than an infant. She had adjusted to the demanding life of the theater, becoming the heart and soul of her family and their troupe. Her wisdom, good sense, and optimistic nature had carried her through more than her share of life's vicissitudes. And luckily her coarse fool of a husband had cured her of romantic illusions.

There was friendship and passion between them. That would be enough. Though she didn't love him, Stephen thought she would find it no great burden to share his life and bed for a few weeks. Not when security for her family would be the reward.

Tenderly he stroked her nape, feeling the dampness of the curling tawny hair as he considered the best way to speak. He didn't want to overlook anything, for there was no time to waste in courtship.

At length he decided it would be best simply to ask. She was intelligent enough to see the advantages of an arrangement. And tenderhearted enough, perhaps, to stay with him from pity . . .

He winced at the thought but knew that even that would be acceptable, as long as she stayed.

"Rosalind," he murmured.

She opened her eyes and gazed up at him with a dreamy smile. "Yes?"

He felt like melting. Reminding himself to keep to the point, he said coolly, "I have a proposition to make. Would you consider marrying me?"

CHAPTER 15

Marriage? Startled almost speechless, Rosalind said stupidly, "Surely an offer of matrimony is a proposal, not a proposition."

He smiled without humor. "Usually, but under these circumstances, 'proposition' is a more accurate term. We would not be husband and wife long enough to really settle into marriage, and there is no love between us. However, there is friendship." His gaze went to her half-uncovered breasts. "And most certainly desire."

Embarrassed at the reminder of her brazen behavior, she sat up and restored herself to respectability while she tried to collect her thoughts. "This is . . . unexpected."

His smile widened and became real. "I believe that the correct line is, 'Sir, this is *so* unexpected.' "

She laughed, and some of her shock faded. "Well, it is a surprise." She began combing hay from her hair with her fingers. "You truly want to wed?"

His face sobered. "I realize that there can be little attractive about marrying a dying man. However, there will be compensations. I'll be out of your way in a few months. I will not ask you to be with me at the distasteful end. In fact, I shall insist that you leave." He hesitated. "Also, I'm a wealthy man. I'm prepared to make a financial settlement to ensure the future of you and your family."

She lowered her hands from her hair and simply stared at him in astonishment. Even lying on his side with hay scattered over him and his clothing in disarray, he was a powerful presence. A gentleman and, by his own admission, wealthy.

Also, obviously, out of his wits. Did he seriously think she was so venal that the only way she would marry him would be for money? That she would welcome a swift widowhood? That if they married, she would allow him to send her away when he was on his deathbed? If he believed those things, why on earth would he want her for a wife?

A reason occurred to her. "If you are hoping for an

heir, I am unlikely to be able to give you one," she said bluntly. "I'm probably barren."

His expression tightened. "That doesn't matter. My marriage lasted for many years and was childless. The fault for that is as likely to lie with me as with my wife."

It was to his credit that he did not blame his wife for "failing," but Rosalind was left puzzled. The tortoise-shell kitten that had come to her earlier suddenly appeared, moving through the hay with strenuous hops. Mechanically she picked the little creature up and cuddled it on her lap. "If you have no hope of an heir, then why offer marriage? As an actress, I am better suited to be a mistress than a wife. It would be foolish for you to let a . . . a passionate interlude cloud your sense of what is appropriate."

He made a swift gesture of irritation. "Imminent death has a way of making worldly considerations seem like utter nonsense. I am asking a great deal of you. I want your time, your companionship, your patience, and your passion. The least I can give in return is respect." He pushed himself to a sitting position. "Besides, I must spend time in London arranging my affairs. It will be simpler to keep you with me if we are married."

"But your brother and sister and other family," she protested. "Surely they will object to such a mésalliance."

His brows arched. "I am the head of the family. It is not for them to judge my actions. If they disapprove, they may all go to the devil."

His aristocratic hauteur was so profound that she almost laughed. No wonder her father kept casting Stephen as a nobleman. But . . . "What if you don't die? Doctors are often wrong. Will you regret marrying beneath you?"

"It would take a miracle to save my life, and I don't

believe in miracles." He gave her a level look. "But if that happens, I will not regret my choice. Will you?"

"No, I would not," she said quietly. Yet she was still unsure how to answer him. His businesslike manner had nothing to do with the hot, fierce passion they had shared. Still less did it involve love.

Then she gazed into his eyes, and understood. If he were in good health, they would never have met, and he certainly would not have offered marriage, even if he had by some strange chance fallen in love with her. But now he was facing death, lonely and afraid and far too proud to admit it. She guessed that he would literally rather die than say that he needed her, or anyone. But need her he did.

With brutal clarity she recognized what marrying him would mean. There would be some joy, and a far greater amount of sorrow. She would have to watch him wither away without letting him know how much his pain distressed her, because such knowledge would increase his burdens. She would have to enter his world and be strong, without the comfort of her family around her. Even with Stephen's support, she would be despised by most of his family and friends.

A wise woman would decline with thanks. A proud woman would feel insulted by the cold-blooded manner of his proposal.

She looked down at the kitten, stroking its tiny throat with her forefinger. Obviously she was not proud, and certainly not wise. She lifted her head and extended one hand, saying quietly, "Yes, I'll marry you."

He clasped her hand and squeezed it tightly. "I'm very glad. I shall do my best to see that you do not regret your decision."

The vivid relief on his face was proof that she had

made the right choice. She cared for him deeply, and the thought of his death was agonizing. But if they spent his remaining time together, at least she would have some happy memories. And she'd be a liar if she didn't admit that she would welcome financial security for her parents.

Turning to more practical matters, she said, "As a strolling player, I have no parish of my own, so I suppose we must go to your home to be married."

"That won't be necessary. I shall send to London for a special license. That should take no longer than"—he thought—"three days. Say four to be on the safe side. Shall we marry on Wednesday?"

She blinked, a little startled by such speed. But there was no reason to wait, and every reason to hurry. "Very well."

He frowned as he retied his cravat. "Will you be able to leave the troupe right away, or will it be necessary to wait while your father finds a replacement?"

She considered the company's repertory. "There will be a couple of plays that will have to be set aside until another actress is found, but my departure won't cause insurmountable problems. There are fewer parts for women than men."

"Good. I'd like time for a brief honeymoon before going to London." He brushed the hay from his dark coat. "I've been neglecting my duties by staying with the troupe for so long. I didn't want to go home."

She smiled at him. "I'm glad you neglected your duty for once. We've all enjoyed your company." Her gaze went to the window and the angle of the sun. "Heavens, we must return to the inn. Papa will think we've been eaten by wild lambs."

Stephen stood and helped her up. The kitten skittered to her shoulder and clung, its tiny claws stabbing

like needles. Carefully he disentangled the little creature and returned it to its mother. Then he drew Rosalind into his arms. The embrace was quite unlike the
fevered kisses they had exchanged earlier. Instead, it
was calm and possessive. He murmured, "I'm being
horribly selfish, and I can't even bring myself to feel
guilty."

She tilted her head back and gazed into his face. The
loss of weight emphasized his good, strong bones.
"Why is it selfish to take a mate? Each of us will give,
and each of us will take. It's the most natural thing in
the world."

He sighed and traced the edge of her ear with one
fingertip. "I hope you're right."

She rested her head on his shoulder, thinking how
little she knew of him. She'd met none of his family,
never seen his home, knew nothing of his life except
that he was "a farmer." But she knew he was kind and
honest. That was enough.

She indulged herself in the luxury of his embrace for
a little longer. He made her feel so safe. At peace. For
the time being, there was an emotional balance between
them. How long would that last? Soon their roles
would shift, and he would need her strength more than
she needed his. He would hate that, and perhaps he
would come to hate her.

So be it. If she had wanted her life to be easy, she
could have turned him down.

She stepped away and began to tidy herself. "I look
like a milkmaid who has been well and truly tumbled in
the hay," she said ruefully.

He surveyed her with warmth in his eyes. "You
have far too much natural elegance to resemble a
milkmaid."

She laughed. "But I do look tumbled. Can you brush the hay from my back?"

He did, his hands gentle as they skimmed over her body to straighten her clothing and remove stray stalks. He took rather longer than necessary, but she didn't mind.

A few minutes of work returned them both to relative respectability. As Stephen collected the tin dipper to return to the well house, Rosalind stepped onto the ladder. She cast a last glance over the hayloft. Such a humble place to have been the site of such passion and drama.

She felt a combination of happiness and melancholy that she feared would never leave her again.

Once more disdaining what people thought, Stephen held Rosalind's hand as they walked back to the Green Man. He was . . . happy. It was good to have something joyful to look forward to. And even under ordinary circumstances, what more could a man ask in a wife than a friend who was also a passionate bedmate?

His mind buzzed with plans. They were still near Bourne Castle, so he'd ask the Duke of Candover to send a trusted man to London; his brother's friend would be happy to oblige. The agent could procure a license at Doctors' Commons and take a draft to the family bankers, since Stephen was running low on money. He could also take Jupiter to the Ashburton House stables and collect some clothing while he was there. Stephen was heartily sick of the few garments he'd brought on this trip.

Apart from that, he needed only Rosalind. He watched her from the corner of his eye, marveling at how lucky he was. She gave him a sidelong glance, her smile warm and intimate. He was tempted to take her back to the hayloft. Ah, well, soon she'd be his and they could share a bed whenever they wished. Or a hayloft.

A jolt of pain brought him back to reality. He had considered, and rejected, the idea of telling Rosalind his true name and rank. She'd have to know, of course, but better to wait until after the wedding. She already had doubts about their different stations in life. If she knew how wide the gap really was, she might change her mind.

He thought briefly about what his father's reaction would have been to the knowledge that his son and heir was marrying an actress. If the old boy weren't already dead, the news would kill him. Stephen mentally shrugged; no matter how hard he'd tried to please his father, he'd never succeeded. Eventually he'd stopped trying.

His father would also have loathed the fact that Michael would be the next duke. A pity that he would never know, Stephen thought dryly. The old duke had been a harsh and difficult man, but in most ways he'd been just. However, he had hated his own younger brother, and as a kind of vengeance, he'd done his best to alienate Stephen and Michael. It was the one act that Stephen could not forgive.

Claudia would also be horrified, and that was more of a problem. With luck, Stephen would be able to reconcile her to his new wife. If not . . . He shrugged again.

The Green Man came into view. As they approached, a cart dropped off a travel-worn young man and woman and their baggage. When the couple went into the inn, Rosalind said thoughtfully, "I wonder if that could be Simon Kent. I didn't know that he had a wife, but that fellow did look as if he might be an actor."

"He isn't very prepossessing. But then, neither is Edmund Kean."

Rosalind glanced at him. "You've seen Kean?" When Stephen nodded, she asked eagerly, "Is he as good as his reputation?"

"He's superb. I saw him on the night of his famous London debut, when he played Shylock in *The Merchant of Venice*."

Her eyes widened. "I've heard that Drury Lane was two-thirds empty when he began, and that his performance was so powerful that people rushed out on the streets at the first interval and told other people to come in. Did that really happen?"

"It did indeed." Stephen smiled reminiscently. "Even though it was January and the weather was vile, I went to a nearby eating house and dragged three friends back to my box. By the end of the play, the theater was full. It was quite extraordinary."

"I should like to have been there," she said wistfully.

He squeezed her hand. "I'll take you to Drury Lane when we go to London. The season will be starting in another week or so."

She chuckled. "And you have a box. I'll be very grand!"

Grander than she realized, or would be comfortable with, he feared. Preferring to change the subject, he said, "Kean is outstanding—but I think your father is his equal."

He was rewarded by Rosalind's blazing smile. And his words were honest. If Thomas Fitzgerald had been able to get along with theater managers, he and Maria would be as famous as Kean and Sarah Siddons. It was sad but true that talent alone was not enough to produce great success.

They reached the inn and followed the sound of

voices to the private parlor. Half of the Fitzgerald troupe was gathered around the two shabbily dressed newcomers. The young man had removed his hat and was talking to Thomas.

As Stephen and Rosalind entered, Thomas glanced over at them. "Rosalind, Stephen, this is Simon Kent, a day ahead of schedule. And his sister, Mary Kent."

As the introductions were completed, Stephen surveyed his replacement. Kent was barely middle height and his fair, shaggy hair needed cutting. Not handsome. In fact, barely presentable. But his dark gray eyes were compelling.

Rosalind said, "The threshing hall we looked at would do, but it's a little small."

Thomas nodded. "That's all right. The barn I went to was quite suitable. I made arrangements for us to perform there tonight." He turned back to Kent. "Let's see how you act. What role would you like to show me?"

Kent's jaw dropped. "Now?"

"Now." Thomas's voice was jovial, but his eyes were dead serious. Stephen suspected that this was a deliberate test of the young actor's mettle.

Taking pity on the newcomer, Jessica stepped forward, a touch of mischief in her eyes. "You listed Romeo as one of your roles, Mr. Kent. Shall we run through the balcony scene together?"

"That would be very helpful," he said gratefully.

The onlookers stepped back a little, leaving the two actors some space. Mary Kent, a small, fair girl who resembled her brother, looked on nervously.

Jessica climbed onto a sturdy chair and struck a pose in the air, as if she were leaning on her window frame and gazing out into the night. She sighed, elaborately unaware of the young man admiring her from below.

Simon Kent cleared his throat, then began, "But soft! What light through yonder window breaks? It is the east, and Juliet is the sun!"

His voice was uncertain for the first lines, but he swiftly gained strength and power. Before Stephen's fascinated gaze, the actor was transformed into a yearning lover. Kent was not merely a competent actor; he had the fire to be one of the great ones.

As he spoke, Jessica's levity dropped away. Her gaze caught Kent's, and when she made her first speech, it was with the sweet blossoming desire of Juliet. The dialogue rippled back and forth with the easy rhythm of natural speech, emphasizing the almost unbearable excitement of young love. It was a riveting performance.

Stephen felt the hair prickling at the back of his neck. This was more than a scene between two very talented performers—the attraction between Simon Kent and Jessica was palpable. Or was he imagining that because of his own romantic mood?

When Jessica delivered her last lines in a throaty whisper, she poignantly extended her hand to her admirer, wanting to touch him. He reached out also, their fingers failing to meet by mere inches.

"Good night, good night! Parting is such sweet sorrow that I shall say good night till it be morrow." She exited by climbing from the chair, but not before casting a last longing glance at the man who had captured her heart and would be her doom.

Kent delivered Romeo's last lines with the passion of a man who had found the love of his life. Then he turned and withdrew several steps to signal the end of the scene.

There was a hushed silence. Then the onlookers burst into spontaneous applause.

"Well done, sir!" Face rosy with pleasure, Jessica

offered her hand to Simon. They took a bow together, as if they were onstage.

Applauding, Stephen whispered to Rosalind, "How much of that was acting?"

She was staring at her sister. "Not all of it, I'll wager."

On the other side of the room, Maria was regarding Kent with a speculative air. Probably evaluating him as a prospective son-in-law. Kent himself was looking happy and relieved. He'd forgotten to release Jessica's hand.

Stephen found Thomas's expression the most interesting. On his face was excitement and approval, but also the wistful regret of an old lion who sees the young lion who will someday replace him.

To his credit, he stepped forward and clapped Kent on the shoulder. "You'll do very well, my boy. But would you mind unhanding my daughter?"

Kent turned scarlet and dropped Jessica's hand. The young lion was still a long way from being king of this particular jungle.

Stephen put an arm around the waist of his fiancée. "This seems like a good time to announce that Rosalind has done me the honor of consenting to be my wife. I do hope that we shall have her family's blessing as well."

All the Fitzgeralds whipped around to stare at the newly betrothed couple. Maria said, "How wonderful! But . . . a bit sudden? You've known each other only a month."

Rosalind glanced up at Stephen and smiled affectionately. "Long enough."

"Ah, you sound like me when I met Thomas." Maria crossed the room and gave a hug first to Rosalind, then to Stephen. "I always wanted another son, and who better than the man who saved my baby from drowning?"

Stephen hugged her back, trying to remember if his mother had ever embraced him with such enthusiasm. If so, he had forgotten the occasion.

Thomas's eyes narrowed, and Stephen wondered if they'd missed a telltale stalk of hay. With an expression that said "Engaged, and not a moment too soon!" he shook Stephen's hand and gave his daughter a long hug. The other members of the troupe crowded around to offer their congratulations, the men pumping his hand and the women hugging him exuberantly.

Stephen was acutely aware of the extent to which one married not just an individual but a family. He'd been less conscious of that when he married Louisa, probably because her parents, the Earl and Countess of Rotham, were very like his own parents. But now he was becoming part of the Fitzgerald family, and they were part of his. He grinned at the realization that Brian would be his brother-in-law.

After Jessica hugged her sister, she asked, "When will the wedding be?"

"Wednesday," Rosalind said imperturbably.

That created another startled silence. Then Jessica exclaimed, "We've got a lot of work to do!" Seizing her sister's hand, she hauled her away upstairs. Rosalind cast a laughing look over her shoulder at Stephen just before she vanished.

"I had thought you had a wife," Thomas said to Stephen in a low, controlled voice that was not quite accusing but which demanded an explanation.

"I'm a widower. No children," Stephen said succinctly. "There were . . . other reasons why I hesitated to propose, but I decided to explain my situation to Rosalind and let her choose for herself."

The older man nodded, looking relieved. "My girl has a level head. If she thinks you're decent husband material, that's good enough for me."

"I have been honest with her, and I'm very grateful for the choice she made." Stephen paused, then added, "Rosalind said that her leaving would not cause problems for the company. Is that true, or should we stay with you until you can replace her?"

"You're taking her away from us," Thomas said sadly.

Stephen nodded. "But not forever. She'll want to see her family often."

Thomas frowned and turned to survey the room. His gaze fell on Mary Kent. "You, girl," he said in his booming voice. "Can you act?"

She jumped visibly at the unexpected notice. After swallowing hard she said, "Yes, sir. I'm not so good as Simon, but I've had several years' experience in small roles." She smiled unexpectedly. "I'll make a fine maid to Miss Jessica's heroines."

Thomas laughed. "Very well. Will you work for me for two pounds a week?"

"Oh, yes, *sir*!" she said fervently. Stephen guessed that her brother would be making three or four pounds for larger roles. Between them, they'd be comfortable.

Everything was working out with amazing smoothness. He wondered how long such good luck could last.

Chattering with excitement, Jessica flopped on the bed in the small room the sisters shared. "What shall you wear for the wedding—that pretty blue gown you wore when you married Charles?"

Rosalind made a face as she unbuttoned her rumpled dress. "Definitely not. I was considering the

Ophelia gown in the costume chest. What do you think?"

"Perfect! You've always looked wonderful in that." Jessica grinned. "The way it laces up the back really shows off your figure. Stephen will be blinded by your beauty. I'll go get it now so we can decide what accessories you'll need."

Rosalind nodded and pulled off her gown. As soon as she laid it aside, she realized that Jessica was staring at her. Rosalind looked down and saw bruiselike marks on the exposed upper curves of her breasts. Her face flamed and she made a futile effort to cover the love bites.

Before she could decide what to say, Jessica said with horror, "Did he hurt you? I swear, if he did—"

"Oh no! Not at all."

Remembering that despite Jessica's apparent worldliness, her sister was still a virgin, she sat on the sagging bed and said evenly, "I'm sorry—I should have been more careful, but you and I have been sharing a room so long that I simply didn't think. Believe me, Stephen did not hurt me. We behaved very badly, and it was . . . quite wonderful." Her voice took on a warning note. "Remember, I'm a widow of mature years, and allowed a little license. You are *not* to copy my behavior, no matter how romantic your Romeo!"

It was Jessica's turn to blush. "He's not my Romeo. But Mr. Kent is a very fine actor, isn't he?"

"Yes. I'm sure that you'll enjoy initiating him into the troupe," Rosalind said teasingly. "You can find out if you like his kiss as much as his talent." She thought of the shimmering sense of wonder between her sister and the new actor, and suddenly, to her complete shock, she began to cry.

As she buried her face in her hands, her sister's arms

came around her. "Rose, what's wrong?" Jessica said worriedly. "These don't look like tears of happiness."

Rosalind wept even harder. She had a desperate need to tell someone the full story, and Jessica was her closest friend. Together they had shared a thousand late-night confidences; her sister could be trusted with this one as well. "Stephen is very ill," she said unsteadily. "He . . . he probably will not survive more than a few months."

"Dear God." Jessica's arms tightened. "Oh, Rose, I'm so sorry. Is that why he was slow to propose, even though he was obviously smitten with you?"

Rosalind nodded. "He had intended to leave without speaking, but he had a horrible attack and I made him tell me the truth, and . . . and one thing led to another and now we're getting married in four days."

She turned into her sister's embrace, her body shaking with sobs. Jessica held her quietly, patting her back until Rosalind had run out of tears. She would not be able to cry like this in front of Stephen. With him she must be calm and controlled.

Making an effort to collect herself, she straightened and dug out her handkerchief. "Don't tell Mama and Papa. I don't want them to be upset any sooner than necessary."

"Very well," Jessica said gravely. "But . . . are you sure you want to marry him? I like Stephen immensely, but he had no right to ask you to do something so painful."

"He had every right." Rosalind clasped her hands tightly in her lap. Her voice dropped so that she was speaking more to herself than her sister. "And there is nothing on earth I want more than to be Stephen's wife—for however long I can be."

CHAPTER 16

A cold, penetrating autumn rain had been falling since dawn, knocking yellow leaves from the trees and turning the roads to mud. Lord Michael Kenyon was tired and thoroughly exasperated. After a fortnight of seeking his missing brother, he'd learned very little except that tracing a man on horseback was far more difficult than following a carriage would have been.

Despite Dr. Blackmer's repeated assurances that Stephen was unlikely to be lying ill somewhere, it was a relief every time Michael found someone who could say definitely that his brother had passed that way. When there had been no sighting for too long, they would painstakingly retrace their way and try other roads until they found the trail again.

It didn't help that Stephen's route seemed entirely random.

On the meandering way north, Michael stopped at the estate of his friend Lucien, Earl of Strathmore and spymaster extraordinare, to enlist help. Luce had offered several good suggestions and promised to see what he could learn through his own vast network of informants. Nonetheless, the search still came down to stopping at half the taverns and villages in the West Midlands to ask if anyone had seen Stephen. Luckily the duke had been riding Jupiter, one of the superlative horses bred by Michael's friend Lord Aberdare. Men remembered the horse, if not always the rider.

Jupiter had been Michael's birthday present to

Stephen the year before. The memory produced a twisting in his gut. At heart, Michael could not believe that Stephen was really mortally ill. Physicians were often wrong, and Stephen had been in fine shape the last time the brothers had met.

And yet—men and women died at all ages and from many causes. Perhaps Stephen's time had come. Michael acknowledged that in his head, though it seemed bitterly unfair that he might lose his only brother so soon after they had become friends.

It was remarkable that Stephen had turned out so well even though, as heir, he'd borne the full weight of the old duke's critical eye and meanness of spirit. Michael had spent as little time as possible at the abbey; that distance had saved him from emotional destruction. Stephen, however, was made of tougher stuff. He had survived and grown both strong and just. His strength and usually even disposition were what made this disappearance so strange.

Michael glanced at his companion, who was hunched morosely against the rain. Though he knew the feeling was irrational, he wanted to blame Blackmer for his brother's illness. The physician should have broken the news to Stephen better, or not spoken at all. Michael knew from his own experience of critically ill soldiers that state of mind had much to do with recovery. Telling a man he was dying could go a long way to making the prediction come true. For a doctor, honesty might not always be the best policy.

The saturnine physician was something of an enigma. Even after a fortnight during which the two men had spent virtually every waking hour together, Michael had no sense of what lay behind Blackmer's unreadable eyes, except that he was obviously deeply concerned about Stephen's welfare. Or was he merely worried that losing his most prominent patient would be bad for business?

A weary voice interrupted Michael's thoughts. "Will we be stopping for dinner?"

"I thought the next town. Redminster, I believe," Michael replied. "The horses could use an hour or so of rest. Then we can continue until dark."

Blackmer lapsed into silence until they rode into Redminster in late afternoon. The rain had stopped, and pale sunshine was gleaming on the puddles. Just before they reached an inn called the Three Crowns, Michael had to swerve his horse abruptly to avoid a little girl of four or five who raced into the road after a ball. The child's pretty, dark-haired mother darted from the yard of her cottage to retrieve her wandering offspring. She offered Michael a smile of apology, then carried her daughter inside.

Tiredly he turned his horse into the Three Crowns. Feeling a little guilty at how he was pushing a man who had not been hardened by years of campaigning, Michael said to his companion, "I'll take the horses back. You go and order us something to eat."

Blackmer nodded gratefully, then dismounted and went inside. Michael led the horses into the stables. An ostler with a clay pipe was at work cleaning a harness.

Michael was about to speak when the man glanced up, then smiled. "Good to see you again, sir. 'Tis a terrible day for travel and no mistake."

Michael became alert. "You've the wrong man. I've never been here before, but has someone who resembles me?"

The ostler squinted for a closer look, then made an apologetic gesture with his pipe. "Oh, yes indeed. You and your horse are very like a guest we had a few weeks back."

"Actually, I'm trying to locate my brother, who was riding a horse sired by the same stallion as this one."

The ostler gave a satisfied nod of his head. "Ah, so you're another Mr. Ashe. That would explain it, for 'tis too strong a likeness to be chance. Will you be leaving your horses here for the night, sir?"

Mr. Ashe? Stephen must be traveling incognito; it wasn't likely that there were two men with Michael's face and a similar horse roaming the Midlands.

"My companion and I are stopping only to dine. I'd be grateful if you'll take care of the beasts for an hour or so." Michael took off his hat and ran a weary hand through his damp hair. "Do you happen to know where my brother was going from here?"

The ostler frowned with concentration. "I believe the Fitzgerald Theater Troupe was heading toward Whitcombe next."

Michael's brows drew together. "Theater troupe?"

"Aye, your brother went off with 'em," the ostler explained. "Saved Fitzgerald's young son from drowning and got injured in the process. Quite the hero he was."

"Injured?" Michael asked swiftly.

"Not badly," the ostler assured him. "Mr. Ashe seemed in fine fettle by the time he left here. In fact, they say he acted in one of the plays." The ostler winked. "Myself, I think he went with the troupe because of the actresses. Fitzgerald has several very pretty fillies, and—well, actresses, you know."

Michael listened with a combination of shock and hope. Would Stephen have really gone onstage with a company of strolling players? Granted, he'd always enjoyed the theater and had acted quite capably in amateur productions with friends, but that was a very different matter. And would he have a fling with a common actress? He'd always been a sober sort. But then, who the devil knew what a man would do when told his days were numbered? Stephen was no longer married, so there was no good reason not to indulge himself with a bit of muslin if he chose.

If he was with this theater troupe, it should be easy to find him because actors must travel slowly, and they would leave a clear trail. Feeling elated, Michael thanked the ostler and went into the inn. Over a dinner of beef and boiled potatoes, he relayed what he'd heard. Blackmer seemed equally surprised to hear that the duke may have taken to the boards, but characteristically he didn't comment. Instead, he silently got to his feet when the meal was done and prepared to continue on to Whitcombe.

Outside, the temporary lull in the rain had been followed by ominous looking thunderclouds. As the two men stepped into the courtyard, there was a flash of lightning, quickly followed by a long, rumbling thunder roll. Rain began to fall hard.

As more lightning flared across the sky, Blackmer said in a neutral voice, "Not the best travel conditions."

It was the closest the physician had come to asking for respite. Michael hesitated. The fact that he was an old campaigner didn't mean he enjoyed being wet and cold and exhausted. Still, the new information from the ostler made him eager to press on. "Thunderstorms usually blow over quickly. We should be able to reach Whitcombe before dark."

Blackmer sighed faintly but did not protest.

They were just outside the stables when an immense bolt of lightning flashed across the sky, filling the courtyard with searing blue-white light. The booming thunderclap was instantaneous.

Michael ducked reflexively, as if he were caught in a French artillery barrage. As he straightened, a long, echoing crash reverberated through the rain-filled air.

"Good God, what was that?" Blackmer exclaimed.

Michael swung around, trying to locate the source of the crash. "At a guess, that lightning bolt brought a tree down."

A woman's piercing scream issued from nearby. Recognizing the sound of disaster, Michael pivoted, then ran across the courtyard and into the street. The cause of both crash and scream was instantly visible. A huge elm had been shattered by the lightning and crashed onto the cottage of the pretty dark-haired woman who had retrieved her small child from the road earlier. The timber-framed house was made of the woven lath and clay material called wattle and daub, and the elm had crushed it like an eggshell.

Grimly Michael went to investigate. Smoke curled from the blackened wood of the elm, but at least the heavy rain was preventing a fire. When he reached the house, he found the dark-haired woman clawing at the wreckage.

"Are you hurt?" Michael yelled over the sound of rain and storm.

She swung around, water streaming down her face and her eyes glazed with shock. "I . . . I came outside to pick herbs for supper and wasn't touched, b-but my husband and little girl are in there, in the back." She caught Michael's arm with trembling hands. "Please, help them!"

His mouth tightened when he looked at the devastation. The chances were that anyone in the building was dead or severely injured.

Blackmer arrived on the scene, panting from the run. "There are people in there?"

"This woman's husband and child." Michael surveyed the crushed house with the experienced eyes of a mine owner. Clumsy rescue work could shift the cracked timbers and crumbling walls, dooming anyone inside who might still be alive. But at least this rescue was not taking place five hundred feet below the surface, as when his Welsh coal mine had exploded. "The best bet is to lift the tree straight upward to minimize further damage."

By this time a dozen neighbors had arrived. One of them cried, "Dear God, look at the Wyman house!" Another, probably the woman's brother, based on the similarity of their features, gasped, "Emma, are Jack and Lissie inside?"

When Emma nodded, shaking, he enfolded her in his arms, his face ashen.

Michael had long since learned that it was better to concentrate on what needed to be done than to worry uselessly about the injured. Since no one else was taking charge, he began rattling off orders. Once an officer, always an officer, he thought dryly as he sent men running for lumber, block and tackle, and a team of oxen.

Then a child's cry came from the wreckage. Emma broke away from her brother and ran closer. "Lissie! Are you all right?"

The child wailed, "Yes, b-but Papa's bleeding, and I can't wake him up."

Michael scanned the wreckage. The little girl was only a few feet away, apparently on the other side of what had been the wall of the kitchen. Perhaps it would be possible to free her before the tree was removed. He gripped a slab of wattle and daub and tried to shift it, working carefully so as not to precipitate a collapse.

Blackmer took hold of the other end of the slab. It always surprised Michael when he noticed that he and the physician were the same size; the other man's self-effacing personality made him seem smaller. Between them, they were able to move the crumbling material safely. A dark, irregular hole was revealed at ground level.

Lissie called out excitedly, "I see light, Mama!"

Emma wiped the rain from her tense face. "Can you crawl toward the light and come outside, sweeting?" she said with forced calm.

There was a pause. Then Lissie quavered, "I can't get there from here, Mama. Papa and pieces of house are in the way."

Blackmer examined the hole. "I'll try to crawl in from this side. If Wyman is between here and the child, maybe I can help him."

"You can't do that," Michael said immediately.

Blackmer looked at him with contempt. "If you're in such a rush, go on to Whitcombe alone. I'll catch up with you tomorrow."

Usually the physician's expression was an impervious mask, so Michael was startled to see a complex blend of emotions visible in the gray-green eyes. Resentment, certainly, and irritation.

Irritated himself, Michael snapped, "Don't be a damned fool. I'm concerned because of the danger. The rest of the house could come down at any time."

"I'm a doctor. I must try to help." Blackmer lay down on the muddy ground and began inching into the hole while the onlookers held their breath. Michael tensed when there was a rattle inside the wreckage, but it stopped quickly.

After a long two minutes, Blackmer called, "Wyman

is alive. His heart is strong, but he's unconscious and bleeding from a torn artery."

Emma said reverently, "God be thanked!"

Knowing enough of wounds to understand the danger, Michael said, "Can you stop the bleeding with a tourniquet?"

"No—there's a blasted beam in the way," the physician growled. "I can hold the wound for now, but get that damned tree out of here quickly."

The equipment had arrived, so Michael supervised the attachment of block and tackle. When they were ready to begin, he called, "Blackmer, we're ready to lift. Better come out now."

"Can't," the physician said tersely. "Wyman's lost quite enough blood."

An older man said urgently, "But the doctor will die if the walls collapse!"

"He knows that." Michael grimly gave the signal to begin.

With a creaking of harness, the oxen began to move. The ropes squealed with protest at the weight. Michael held his breath as they stretched. If they broke, a slower, more dangerous rescue method would have to be attempted—assuming that a failure didn't kill all three people within the structure.

Cheers went up as the massive elm slowly rose from the ruined cottage. There was a rattle of shifting debris, but no major collapse. Eager hands helped swing the shattered tree to one side. Just as the trunk cleared the house, one of the ropes snapped. The other two followed immediately, and the trunk crashed with a force that caused the wet earth to shake. It barely missed an onlooker, but miraculously no one was hurt.

As Michael had hoped, the removal of the tree revealed a gaping hole in the roof and made it possible to enter the house directly. Working with painstaking care, the rescuers soon reached the little girl. The first was Emma's brother.

Lissie cried, "Uncle John!"

A moment later her uncle emerged from the wreckage with the child clinging to him. Emma swooped Lissie into her arms, holding her daughter as if she would never let go. Tears of thanks mingled with the raindrops on her face.

Not wasting time on observing the reunion, Michael turned back to the wreckage. Working carefully, he and a burly, taciturn blacksmith were able to clear the way to the injured man. Wyman lay on his back, his shirt saturated with blood. Luckily the beam that had blocked access from the other side had also protected Wyman from more serious injury, except for the long gash in his arm.

All that was visible of Blackmer were his right wrist and hand where they emerged from a hole in the rubble and clamped around Wyman's upper arm. Working entirely by touch, the physician had located the wound and stopped the lethal bleeding.

Michael pulled out his handkerchief and tied it tightly above the wound. "You can get out now, Blackmer. We'll take him from this side."

Michael and the blacksmith lifted the injured man free and passed him to waiting hands outside the wreckage. As soon as Wyman was laid on the ground, Emma dropped to her knees beside him, one arm around her daughter and her other hand clasping her husband's. "Thank God," she whispered. "And thank you all."

Wearily Michael climbed from the wreckage. The older man who had spoken to him earlier said, "I'm William Johnson, mayor of Redminster. We're all grateful for what you and your friend have done, especially you being strangers."

"I've owed my life to strangers," Michael said with a faint smile, "and I always pay my debts." Then he circled to the other side of the cottage to see if Blackmer needed help. The rain had stopped and it was nearly dark.

The physician was backing out of the narrow tunnel. He was almost out when the wreckage began shifting with a horrific groan. Michael grabbed Blackmer around the waist and yanked him clear just as the tunnel collapsed. A fragment of hardened clay struck the physician's cheek, but he was otherwise unhurt.

Silently giving thanks that luck had been on their side, Michael helped the other man to his feet. "Wyman looks as if he'll be all right. How are you?"

Blackmer wiped at the scratch on his face, smearing blood across his cheek. "Uninjured. I guess divine retribution has other plans for me."

As the physician started to turn away, Michael stopped him with a hand on one arm. "That was well done," he said soberly.

Blackmer flinched, looking at Michael's hand as if it were a scorpion before he said in his usual sardonic manner, "Does that mean it's time to leave for Whitcombe?"

Michael gave a lopsided smile. "I think we could both use a bath, a couple of glasses of brandy, and a good night's sleep at the Three Crowns."

The physician expelled his breath in a ragged sigh as he let his fatigue show. "An excellent idea." Then he went to check on Wyman.

Michael watched him go. He still didn't understand

Blackmer—or particularly like him—but by God, the man had courage.

CHAPTER 17

"Hold still, Rose, or you'll go to your wedding with half your hair down," Jessica said in a threatening tone.

Rosalind obediently settled onto her chair again and locked her hands in her lap. She hadn't entirely adjusted to the shock of marrying so quickly. She didn't know quite how he had managed it, but Stephen had procured a special license from London. Since the license specified that the ceremony could be held at any convenient time and place, Maria had suggested that as the weather was good, they could use a pretty woodland glade outside Bury St. James, the troupe's latest stop.

It was a crisply sunny autumn day, and in an hour Rosalind would be wed.

Jessica pinned her sister's tawny hair into an elaborate chignon, then carefully arranged small bronze chrysanthemums around it. "You look splendid. Can you stay out of trouble while I go and dress myself?"

"I think I can manage," Rosalind said with a wry smile. "I've been through this before, you know."

"Yes—but you didn't look quite so dazed then," Jessica said tartly before she left the room. Rosalind leaned back with a sigh, grateful for a few minutes of quiet.

The fact that it was a second wedding did not mean that she was free of tension.

How was this different from her first wedding?

Then she had been full of dreams and excitement, driven more by youthful passions than love for Charles Jordan. She had been a girl. Now she was a woman, and what she felt for Stephen went far deeper than what she had been capable of feeling before.

And this time she knew what awaited her in the marriage bed. Her face heated at the thought, but she could not stop from smiling with anticipation. There had been no opportunity to be alone together since that magic hour in the loft. Ridiculous how desperately she wanted Stephen when it had been only four days. Thank heaven that in a few hours they would be together. Legally.

A knock sounded on the door. Then the voice of her betrothed called, "Will the heavens fall if I come in?"

Rosalind rose and went to open the door with relief. "Am I glad to see you! We should have run off to Gretna Green. How can one mother and sister create so much chaos in four days?"

With a laugh, Stephen set a medium-size wooden box on the table and drew her into his arms. "I'm glad for it. You deserve to have a special day." He stepped back, letting his hands rest on her shoulders. "You look truly beautiful, Rosalind," he said quietly. "I'm a lucky, lucky man."

The Ophelia gown did look rather nice. Rosalind's gaze traveled over her intended. He'd procured some new clothing—again, she had no idea how. Though he was a little thin, the excellent tailoring made the most of his tall, broad-shouldered figure. "You look so distinguished that I'm almost afraid to marry you," she said, only partly joking.

"There are good reasons not to marry me, but looking too distinguished isn't one of them." He hesitated before continuing, "I came to warn you so you won't be surprised during the ceremony. My family name is actually Kenyon, not Ashe."

She blinked. "Why on earth did you use Ashe?"

He smiled wryly. "You misunderstood what I said when half-conscious. Letting the error stand seemed a convenient way to lose myself for a few days."

She could understand that, but she asked warily, "Are you still Stephen? If not, we may have to call this off."

"Luckily I was christened Stephen Edward Kenyon." He leaned forward and kissed her, his lips warm and firm.

"Mrs. Stephen Kenyon. That will do very nicely." She relaxed into his embrace with a sigh of pleasure. For today, at least, she would try to suppress the thought of how terribly little time they would have. Nonetheless, it was at the back of her mind. She tightened her arms instinctively.

He stroked her neck beneath her upswept hair with a delicacy that sent tingles through her whole body. "There's something else I need to tell you."

She tilted her head and looked at him through lazy-lidded eyes. "You are full of surprises, Mr. Kenyon. Are you going to reveal that you're a highwayman escaped from Newgate Prison?"

He smiled faintly. "Almost as bad."

Before he could continue, a squeaky cry came from the box he had brought. Rosalind glanced over and saw that the box had a brass carrying handle and a number of holes drilled through the wood. "What on earth . . . ?"

"Your wedding present." He lifted the lid. Inside the

box was a fuzzy little blanket, a small tray of sand—and the tortoiseshell kitten from the barn loft. It reared up on its hind legs and braced its paws on the side of the box, the huge green eyes bright with curiosity.

"At first I had trouble deciding between diamonds and a worthless barn cat," he explained. "Being a miserly sort, naturally I settled on the kitten."

"Oh, Stephen!" Delightedly Rosalind scooped up the tortoiseshell. The tiny face was mostly black, but with a dashing orange swash across the forehead and a white patch on the chin. Rosalind allowed the kitten to scramble up to her shoulder, blithely ignoring the trail of black fur left on the ivory fabric. She gazed at her future husband, eyes shining. "This is a better present than all the diamonds in England."

He touched her cheek tenderly. "I'm glad to have pleased you."

Her heart ached at the knowledge that one reason he'd chosen the kitten was to give her a source of uncomplicated pleasure in the difficult months ahead. He was so good. So dangerously lovable.

Dropping her gaze so that Stephen would not see her feelings in her eyes, Rosalind took the kitten from her shoulder and set her on her bed. The kitten bounded vigorously across the counterpane, the short, plump tail pointed straight in the air.

The door opened and Maria entered, magnificent in the blue gown she wore when she played a queen. Aloysius loped amiably at her side. As soon as he scented the kitten, his ears stiffened with excitement. He covered the distance to the bed in one leap and thrust his nose at the newcomer.

"Don't you dare!" Rosalind exclaimed, diving toward the bed to prevent her new pet from being swallowed whole.

Stephen also moved to intervene, but their efforts were not needed. Completely unafraid, the kitten looked up at the looming canine head and panting mouth. Then, with casual precision, she lifted her tiny paw and smartly spatted Aloysius's nose.

The dog yelped and jumped. The kitten took two steps toward the dog and stared with the ferocity of a Siberian tiger. There was a long, tense silence, broken only by a high-pitched feline hiss. Aloysius's nerve broke first. He bounded behind Maria.

Rosalind's mother laughed. "What on earth is going on here? Poor Aloysius may never recover from the humiliation."

Rosalind picked up the kitten and scratched her head. "Portia is Stephen's wedding present to me."

"Portia?" he said with amusement.

"A good name for a cat," Maria decreed. Then she swung around with Lady Macbeth's theatrical grandeur. "But you, treacherous man, are trespassing! Have you never heard that it's bad luck for the groom to see the bride before the wedding?"

"I wanted to talk to Rosalind," he said meekly.

"You have a lifetime for that," Maria said firmly as she shooed him from the room. "Out, out, out!"

He gave Rosalind a rueful glance and withdrew in defeat. For a moment she wondered what else he had wanted to say. Then she shrugged. It would keep. Next to the grim reality of his illness, all else was trivial. What did it matter that he was named Kenyon instead of Ashe?

Maria said, "Let me look at you." She circled her daughter with a critical eye before giving a nod of approval. "You look as a bride should look, my dear."

"Surely a bit long in the tooth," Rosalind suggested.

"Beauty is timeless and ageless." Her mother settled

on the bed. Portia promptly came and rubbed against Maria's hand for attention.

As Maria started petting the kitten, Rosalind said softly, "All defenseless little creatures come to you trustingly. I did."

"It seems like only yesterday that Thomas and I found you in that horrible stew," Maria said with a nostalgic smile. "How did you turn into a woman so quickly?"

"Oh, Mama." Tears in her eyes, Rosalind sank onto the bed and hugged Maria. "I can't imagine what my life would have been like if not for you and Papa. You have given and given and given. I owe you more than I can ever repay."

"Taking you home was the best day's work we ever did." Maria took hold of her daughter's hand and squeezed tightly. "Sometimes I think it's a blessing that we never joined one of the famous companies. Success on such a scale would have brought many temptations and distractions to both of us. The family would have suffered, and when all is said and done, family matters most." She smiled suddenly. "Not that I would have minded acting *Isabella* at Covent Garden when Sarah Siddons was playing the same role at Drury Lane. I don't think the audiences that saw me would have felt ill-used."

"You would have been better than Mrs. Siddons, Mama," Rosalind said loyally.

"Perhaps, perhaps not." Maria shrugged. "It doesn't matter that I never had the chance to play before grand audiences. I played the roles grandly, and that's enough." She rubbed noses with Portia. "We have a few minutes. Should I give you a mother's lecture on the facts of life and love?"

Rosalind laughed. "I think I know most of them,

Mama. After all, I was married for three years." She frowned as she saw her mother wipe her eyes. "What's wrong? You don't object to me marrying Stephen, do you? I thought you liked him."

"I do like him, enormously. He's a very special man." Maria pulled out a handkerchief and blew her nose. "It's just that after today, life will never be the same. You didn't leave us when you married Charles, but Stephen will take you away into another world. Soon there will be other changes. You've seen how Jessica and Simon Kent look at each other. It won't be long till they're headed to the altar, too, particularly if your father catches them kissing over the costume chest. They'll go off to join a grander company. That will leave us with just Brian, and him a growing lad."

Rosalind swallowed the lump that was forming again in her throat. "If . . . if, God forbid, something should happen to Stephen, you'd let me come back, wouldn't you?"

"Of course, but losing your husband is no topic for your wedding day," Maria said, scandalized.

The remark made Rosalind glad she hadn't told her parents about Stephen's illness. There would be time enough for that later, when she needed to come home. Jessica hadn't spoken of the matter, though sometimes she had studied her sister and Stephen with sorrowful eyes.

Enough. Rosalind got to her feet and picked up the bouquet she was to carry. It was made of autumn blossoms in gold and orange and amber. "It's time, Mama."

As she and her mother descended the stairs, she remembered Stephen saying gravely, "It's time, Rosalind."

Time was her enemy.

Day Fifty-five

Despite calming comments by the elderly vicar, Stephen paced restlessly around the sunny glade where the ceremony was to be held. It was a splendid setting for a wedding, with the trees at the brilliant height of their autumn glory. All members of the troupe except the wedding party were present, and other women besides Rosalind had robbed the costume chest in order to look their best for the occasion.

Also present were some citizens of Bury St. James who had become family friends over the years, including the theater-loving squire who owned the glade. As the company musicians played Handel, guests hovered hungrily around the heavily laden tables at the edge of the clearing. Stephen was providing an al fresco wedding breakfast, and the local innkeeper had provided an impressive spread of cold meats, made dishes, and a haunch of beef roasting over an open fire. Old Nan stood guard over the food, giving her best imitation of a Shakespearean witch when anyone tried to steal a premature bite.

Stephen paced, praying to the God he didn't believe in that he would not suffer from one of the convulsive pain attacks. This was one day that he wanted to be perfect.

Jeremiah Jones, who was acting as groomsman, said soothingly, "You're going to wear a hole in the turf with your pacing, Stephen. Never fear, Rose will be here." He chuckled at his unintended rhyme. "Jane Landers and Mary Kent will do well enough with the acting roles, but we're going to miss having Rosalind as stage manager, and no mistake. The next few weeks of performances will be chaotic."

But *would* Rose be here? Perhaps she had suffered a

last-minute change of heart. Stephen still could not understand why she was willing to marry him despite his condition. It wasn't for the financial security he'd promised her, since no Fitzgerald seemed to care much about money. She must have accepted him from pity.

Gad, if that was true, don't let her run out of pity now. He continued to pace.

Then the music stopped. He turned and saw that the wedding party had arrived at the opposite end of the clearing. Rosalind was so lovely that it hurt to look at her. The Ophelia gown was designed with stark elegance, the ivory silk flowing to the ground in sumptuous folds. The simplicity suited Rosalind, as did the bronze flowers in her hair and the back lacing that caused the fabric to cling seductively to her splendid figure. She was far more appealing than any Ophelia he'd ever seen onstage. Hamlet's lady had been a weak creature, while Rosalind radiated warm, womanly strength.

Stephen took his position by the altar, Jeremiah beside him. The musicians began to play a solemn march. Since there was no aisle, the bride advanced gracefully across the grass with her father and Brian on one side and Maria and Jessica on the other. The whole Fitzgerald family was giving her away.

Stephen's throat tightened. He had no right to take her from the family she loved—but he could not regret his selfishness.

When the Fitzgeralds reached him, Thomas said in a stage whisper that filled the glade, "Mind you take care of her well, lad, or you'll rue the day."

"I'll do my best, sir." Smiling, Stephen took Rosalind's hand. This was the most unusual wedding he'd ever seen. And the best.

She returned his clasp firmly, her dark eyes glowing.

He had to restrain himself from kissing her immediately. They both turned to the vicar while her family withdrew to join the other guests.

In a deep voice that compared favorably with that of Thomas Fitzgerald, the vicar began the wedding ceremony. Stephen heard the familiar words as never before, perhaps because his first marriage had not been of his own choosing.

There was a faint puzzled stirring when the vicar said the name Kenyon, but no one reacted. For Stephen the difficult moment came when the cleric first asked the question ". . . so long as ye both shall live?"

Rosalind's gaze involuntarily went to his, and he saw in her eyes a reflection of his own bittersweet emotions. "I will," he said firmly. His hand tightened on hers, and she gave him a tremulous smile.

When her time came, she said, "I will," in a clear, stage-trained voice that contained no hint of doubt.

Jeremiah produced the ring with the flourish of a man who knew how to make the best of his moment at center stage. Stephen slid it onto Rosalind's finger and said gravely, "With this ring I thee wed, with my body I thee worship, and with all my worldly goods I thee endow."

She smiled, her hand closing over the ring without looking. He wondered when she would notice that the band was embedded with small, exquisite diamonds. Because, after all, he'd wanted to give her both jewels and barn cats. He wanted to give everything in his power in return for the miraculous gift she was making of herself.

"I pronounce that they be man and wife together."

The ceremony was over, and Stephen could kiss his radiant bride. Their lips touched only lightly, but he pulled her close in his arms, feeling her heart beating against his. Rosalind. His wife. His perfect rose.

Then they were surrounded by well-wishers, men clapping Stephen's back and shaking his hand, the bride getting hugged by everyone. The informality of the setting brought a joyous abandon to the congratulations.

When the excitement died down, Stephen put an arm around his new wife. "Shall we proceed to the wedding breakfast?"

Frowning, Thomas said, "A moment. The vicar said your name is Kenyon?"

"Stephen told me about that this morning," Rosalind gave her new husband an affectionate glance. "I misunderstood his name the first time he said it, and he was such a gentleman that he never corrected me."

Several people chuckled, but Thomas's frown deepened. "Seems damned irregular to me." Then his eyes widened with shock. "Kenyon. Ashe. *Ashburton.* Isn't the Duke of Ashburton named Stephen Kenyon?"

Stephen braced himself. This wasn't the way he would have chosen to break the news, but Maria had interrupted him when he had tried to tell Rosalind earlier.

He looked down at his wife, his arm tightening around her waist. "Yes. And the Duchess of Ashburton's name is Rosalind Fitzgerald Kenyon."

CHAPTER 18

There was stunned silence. Rosalind stared at her new husband. Surely he was joking. But there was no teasing in his eyes, only wary resignation.

Stephen was Ashburton, one of the wealthiest noblemen in the country? She said feebly, "If that isn't a joke, no wonder Papa kept casting you as a duke."

Stephen's mouth twisted. "It's no joke, Rosalind."

Thomas Fitzgerald exploded. "Damn you, Ashburton, what kind of mockery is this? Did you get a false marriage license so that you could have a pretend marriage?"

"Of course not," Stephen said in a level voice. "The marriage is entirely legal. Everything I said about myself was true, except for my last name."

Thomas opened his mouth to reply, but Maria forestalled him with a hand on his arm. "Control that Irish temper of yours, my dear."

Her husband growled, "He lied, and there's no excuse for it."

"No?" Maria gave Stephen a piercing glance. "Thomas, my love, you and I can play any role we wish onstage, then walk away. It's harder for a man to walk away from the role of duke."

"Exactly. I've never had the chance to be less than a lord." Stephen cast an ironic gaze around the circle of wedding guests. "Given the way everyone is stepping back as if I've suddenly developed leprosy, perhaps you can understand why I enjoyed the anonymity of being plain Mr. Ashe."

Jessica came forward. "Well, I, for one, think it's positively splendid. I long to tell people, 'I just dined with my brother-in-law, the Duke of Ashburton.' Or perhaps, 'You like my shawl? It was a gift from my dear sister, the Duchess of Ashburton.' I shall flaunt your title *shamelessly*." She gave Stephen an energetic hug. "And I like you very well even if you are hopelessly noble."

Silently blessing her sister for breaking the ice, Rosalind said, "He did try to tell me, Papa, but Mama shooed him away before he could."

Yet even though she instinctively tried to smooth over the awkwardness, she was struggling with her own shock. She looked up at her new husband, unable to comprehend the implications of her new status. A duchess? Rosalind Fitzgerald Jordan, foundling, actress, and widow?

Her gaze fell to her wedding ring. It sparkled with a fortune in brilliant gems. Her mouth tightened. Even the ring was vivid proof that they came from different worlds.

She would think about that later. Right now, she sensed, Stephen needed her to accept that he was still the man he was before. Lightly she said, "I'm going to want a diamond-studded collar for my kitten, my dear."

His expression eased. "If that's what you want, Portia shall have it."

Thomas still looked dissatisfied. Rosalind suspected that while much of his anger was because he'd been deceived, a small part was a father's ambivalent feelings about the men who took their daughters away. His anger would pass soon; it always did.

Before Thomas could speak again, Brian said in his most Puckish voice, "Good sirs and madames, may I respectfully suggest that it is time to begin the wedding breakfast?" He gave the bride and groom a mischievous glance. "Surely even dukes and duchesses must eat."

His comment occasioned general laughter, and people began to move toward the banquet tables. Stephen's arm stayed around Rosalind as they crossed the glade. She found it comforting. Yet she could not stop wondering what this news would mean.

The wedding feast was a great success, though Rosalind's nerves were too tightly strung for her to fully enjoy it. She laughed and talked and silently cooperated with Maria in keeping Thomas and Stephen apart.

Lavish amounts of food and drink eliminated the wariness the troupe members had briefly experienced upon learning that they'd been asking a duke to carry scenery. Stephen was at his most charming and unpretentious; by the time the bridal couple was ready to leave, almost everyone was inclined to treat the matter as a great joke.

Rosalind hugged everyone at least once—family members twice—then accepted Stephen's help into the elegant carriage he had hired. At least she thought he'd hired it; perhaps he'd bought it from pocket change. Then, Portia's travel box in hand, he climbed in and closed the door, taking the rear-facing seat opposite Rosalind.

She waved and smiled when the carriage pulled away, continuing until she could no longer see her family. Then, as they began to move at the speed that could only be achieved with first-rate horseflesh, she leaned back against the velvet seat and contemplated her new husband. Oddly, now that the original shock was past, she was not really surprised to learn that he was a peer of the realm. It had been clear that he was a gentleman, and he'd always had an unmistakable air of authority. He had silenced the bullying poor law over-seer, Crain, with a single glance. She had tended to overlook that side of Stephen's nature because he was so easygoing with her and her friends.

But he was one of the most powerful men in England. If he spoke, the Prince Regent would listen. She closed her eyes and rubbed her temples.

"You have a headache?" Stephen asked with concern.

"A bit of one. Jessica pulled my hair too tightly when she styled it." Rosalind took out her hairpins and the wilted chrysanthemums, exhaling with relief as her hair fell around her shoulders. "Plus, of course, I feel as if I've wandered into the tale of King Cophetua and the beggar maid."

His face darkened. "I am no king, and you are no beggar maid."

"Close enough." She began combing her fingers through her hair to loosen it. "A gentleman marrying an actress of dubious origin is scandalous enough—for a duke to do that is outrageous. I'll be universally seen as a fortune hunter, and you a fool."

"There is nothing outrageous about our marriage," he said sharply. "You were raised in the household of a gentleman, albeit one who decided to go on the stage. You are a lady in speech and manner and refinement—no one who knows you could think otherwise. And any man who meets you will be envious, not judge me a fool."

Was he being naive? Or was he so used to deference that he couldn't see that it would not be extended to her when he was not by her side? With black humor, she thought that it was just as well their marriage would be a short one, because she would never be accepted in his world.

But that really didn't matter. When he was gone, she would return to her own kind. In the meantime . . . "What do you want of me, Stephen? What are the social obligations of a duchess?"

He looked surprised. "I want you to be my wife, Rosalind. My friend. My companion. My mistress. Your social duties can be as much or as little as you wish. If you want to be presented at court, I shall arrange it. If you prefer never to set foot in a fashionable drawing room, that's all right, too. The choice is yours."

It sounded easy, but she didn't believe that. "Your rank makes you a public person with responsibilities. There must be many men with strong claims on you."

"Why do you think I ran away?" he said with unmistakable bitterness.

"Is it so dreadful to be a duke?"

Curbing his flash of emotion, he said, "Actually, in the two years since I succeeded to the title, I've found that it's far more pleasant to be a duke than it was being the heir. Now I can do very nearly anything I please— even become a commoner, at least for a while."

"You enjoyed being Mr. Ashe?"

He hesitated, then said quietly, "I've never felt more like myself than I have for the past month. No one had any preconceptions as to what I should be like, what I should do or say. I felt like a falcon that had escaped my jesses."

Sensing that the subject was one that should be explored, she asked, "You said that being the heir was worse than being a duke. Why?"

His face hardened. "I was the Marquess of Benfield from the instant I first drew breath. My whole life was preparation for the exalted rank I would someday bear. A boy who will be a duke does not cry for any reason— not for sentiment, and certainly not when he is beaten. Which he is, often. He does not indulge in undignified activities, such as playing with children of common rank. He must excel at his studies and sports. He does not complain when older boys torment him at school, or for any other reason. He never shirks his duty, nor apologizes to his inferiors, which include almost everyone. He honors his sovereign, even if the king is merely a jumped-up Hanoverian with vulgar tastes. He chooses his companions only from among those who are worthy of his regard. He marries—" Stephen stopped abruptly.

She stared at him, appalled. "That sounds dreadful."

He began unconsciously rubbing the area just below his rib cage, a sure sign of pain. "You'll have noticed that not all of my training took. It enraged my father that I never set a high enough value on my rank. He considered me soft. Lacking in dignity." He smiled with ironic humor. "By his standards, I was, and am."

But much of that training *had* taken. No wonder Stephen was so good at concealing pain. If not for his innate decency and sense of justice, he would have become the kind of monster his father seemed to have been. "Did the ducal code allow any room for love?" she asked quietly.

He shifted his gaze to the window. "Love was . . . not part of the curriculum. Lust was quite acceptable— both of my parents had notorious affairs. But love was a foreign language." A muscle jumped in his jaw. "I think that, like languages, the ability to love must be learned when one is young. Otherwise one will never have the ear for it."

So even if he loved his wife, he might not have been able to say the words, Rosalind thought compassionately. She hoped that the previous duchess had been good at hearing what was unsaid. "You make me very glad I'm a commoner. But you turned out rather well despite everything."

"So you don't regret having married me?"

The words were light, but she saw in his eyes that the question was in dead earnest. Lord, when time was so limited, why were they even talking about things like social rank? "Of course not—I'm congratulating myself on my brilliant instincts. Here I thought you were merely a delightful, sinfully attractive man. Now I find that I pulled off the marital coup of the year without even knowing it," she said in a teasing voice. "My only regret at the moment is that you're too far away."

"That's easily remedied." He unfolded himself from his seat, stepped over Portia's box, and settled next to Rosalind. In the tight confines of the carriage, that meant they were touching from shoulder to thigh.

"Where are we going and when we will get there?" She took his hand, sliding her fingers between his. "Things have been in such a turmoil that I forgot to ask."

"I have a small house by the sea not far from Chester. It's pretty and private, with only a married couple for servants. We should arrive about sunset."

"How many houses do you own?" she asked curiously.

He thought a moment. "Six. Remember when I asked if you'd like a cloistered abbey? The family seat, Ashburton Abbey, has a cloister garden. It's very lovely."

So she'd gone from not having a roof of her own to being mistress of six houses. She shook her head, bemused, then found herself yawning. As she covered her mouth with one hand, she said apologetically, "Sorry. I didn't get much sleep last night."

He put his right arm around her. "Use me for a pillow."

She curled up against him, her head on his shoulder. They fitted together so nicely. Be damned to the difference in their ranks, this was *right*. This was what she wanted of a husband, this sense of peace—and this burn of anticipation.

She drifted into a dreamless sleep, her lips curving into a smile.

As they rolled across the parklike hills of the Cheshire Plain, Stephen savored the soft, trusting form of his new wife. He felt . . . contented. More so, perhaps, than ever before in his life. In the last weeks he'd learned to live in the moment, and this one could hardly be improved on.

Then a blaze of pain scorched down his esophagus and through his belly. He stiffened, fighting the urge to double up convulsively. Not now. Not today.

His arm had tightened around Rosalind, and she made a small sound. He forced himself to hold still so that he would not wake her. Though how could she not feel the vicious scarlet pain that burned a few inches away from her softly curved cheek? Or the chill clamminess of his right hand, where it rested on her waist?

But she shifted slightly and slept on, sweet and calming by her very presence. Carefully he used his left hand to dig an opium pill from an inside pocket. He'd taken one just before leaving the wedding breakfast, and would have preferred not to take another so soon. He disliked wasting any of his remaining time in a haze, though perhaps, at the end, cowardice would overcome his qualms. Many people's fondest wish was for "a good death," with massive doses of opium to shield them from the pain.

If another pill meant keeping Rosalind from learning of this attack, it was worth taking it. He swallowed the medication with some difficulty, then closed his eyes and waited. Gradually the tide of pain ebbed, leaving numbness in its wake. He supposed that he must consider himself lucky that he hadn't vomited uncontrollably or suffered some of the other unpleasant symptoms that sometimes accompanied an attack.

Lucky. *Hell.*

A gentle hand caressed Rosalind's arm. "Time to wake up, Lady Caliban. We're almost there."

"Mm-m-m." She lazed a little longer, enjoying being so close to Stephen. Then, just as the carriage stopped moving, something cool and moist touched her cheek. She opened her eyes and saw that Portia was nose to nose with her. "Am I dreaming, or do I have a cat on my chest?"

"I let her out. After she exhausted herself playing ricochet, she decided that you look soft and comfortable." His eyes sparkled with humor. "I couldn't agree more."

Blushing a little, she sat up and stretched her cramped muscles. "Have we really arrived already?"

"Indeed." Stephen captured Portia and returned her to the travel box. "You have a great talent for sleeping. You hardly stirred through two changes of horses."

"Being able to nap anywhere is very useful for a strolling player." She glanced out the window. Well-kept parkland rolled away in front of her, gradually dropping to shimmering sands. And on the horizon, a blood-red sun was dropping toward the sea, the molten rays transforming clouds into drifts of hot coral and deepest indigo. "How beautiful! What is this place?"

"Kirby Manor. You're looking across the estuary of the River Dee to the Irish Sea." He unlatched the carriage door and helped her out. "The house is behind us."

He started to turn, but she caught his hand. "The house can wait."

Silently they watched the sun slide into the sea, the sky and clouds darkening. The day passed so swiftly at the end. She thought of Stephen's approaching demise and felt the tightness of regret in her throat.

She turned to the house. Kirby Manor was half-timbered in the local style, a sprawling, magpie building with crooked beams and diamond-paned windows that glowed orange-gold in the last light of the day. It, too, was beautiful. She studied the elaborate herringbone timber patterns with fascination. "It's wonderful, but certainly not my idea of a small house."

"The smallest residence I own. Only five bedrooms."

A man and woman who had apparently been waiting for the ducal attention came forward. "Welcome to Kirby Manor, Your Grace." The man bobbed his head and the woman curtsied. "I hope you find things to your satisfaction. If we'd had more time . . ." His voice trailed off nervously.

"As long as the main rooms are clean and you have some good Cheshire food, we'll do very well." Stephen drew Rosalind forward. "Rosalind, here are Mr. and Mrs. Nyland. Allow me to present the Duchess of Ashburton."

She almost winced when Mrs. Nyland curtsied again and her husband made an awkward bow. Rosalind wasn't a duchess, for heaven's sake; she was an actress with her hair around her ears like a schoolgirl.

But apparently she *was* a duchess, and she must act like one for Stephen's sake if not her own.

The solution came in a flash: play the part of duchess as if it were a stage role. She inclined her head and smiled, gracious but not overly familiar. "It's good of you to be ready on such short notice. When you take the baggage in, please use special care with my kitten's box. Portia travels very well, but I expect she's ready for some supper."

The Nylands collected Portia and the other luggage and went inside. As the coachman drove off toward the stables, Rosalind and Stephen climbed the front steps arm in arm. He opened the front door, then unexpectedly bent and swept her up in his arms. As she laughed and clutched him for balance, he explained, "Though it isn't Ashburton Abbey, it is my threshold."

"Will this happen at all six of your houses?" she asked as he carried her inside.

"If you like, but I shouldn't think you'd want to set foot in the hunting box. All dark wainscoting and stuffed animal heads."

And there would not be time to get to all of his houses. "You're right—it sounds dreadfully dismal," she said in a more subdued voice.

He carried her down a dim passage and into a sizable hall. She had an impression of carved oak and softly muted carpets. Then he lowered her to the floor, letting her slide slowly down his body. She was breathless by the time she was on her feet again.

Laughter died away. His expression was somber, as if he was memorizing her face in this moment. Then he kissed her with aching tenderness. Her mouth opened under his, and carnal shivers danced over her skin.

The four days since they had made love seemed like forever.

When he'd reduced her to the pliancy of wax, he raised his head and said huskily, "After we've refreshed ourselves and eaten, may I come to your room?"

She stared at him in astonishment for a moment, then laughed aloud. "Stephen, my dearest husband, nothing more clearly illustrates the difference in our rank. Among my kind, there is never a question of whether or not a couple share a room and a bed. I suspect that it helps people make up their quarrels more quickly." She brushed his hair back from his forehead, wishing she could say words of love. "You will always be welcome in my bed. In fact, I shall feel offended if you sleep elsewhere."

His gaze intensified. "So I can assume that your answer is yes."

"It most certainly is." She touched her tongue to her lips. "In fact, since it's been a long day, perhaps we should skip supper and go to bed now."

"No." He stepped away and caught her hand between his. "The first time everything happened too quickly. Tonight, let's savor the pleasures of anticipation."

Too much more anticipation, and she would be wild as a panther. But he was right. There was no need to rush, and many reasons to take their time. "That makes sense, though I can't say that I feel very sensible at the moment." She cocked her head. "I have a suggestion. Give me a tour of the house while supper is prepared. Then we can dine informally in our rooms."

"A splendid notion." He kissed her fingertips, then tucked her arm in his elbow. His voice took on the pompous tones of a really superior butler. "This, my dear duchess, is the main hall. The oldest part of the building is believed to date from the early fifteenth century. Pray observe the splendid ornamental plasterwork."

She chuckled, thinking that he really could have had a future as a good comic actor. "Splendid indeed, Your Grace," she said in the role of admiring visitor. "But are fornicating cherubs really proper on the ceiling of a hall?"

"They are not fornicating, madame. Merely great and good friends." He guided her around the ground floor, pointing out interesting features and making similar remarks that kept her laughing.

As in all half-timbered buildings, the floors rose and fell, leaded windows sagged gently askew, and there wasn't a straight line in the place. She loved it. She also loved how they managed to touch in seemingly innocent ways, each encounter another stick of kindling on a growing fire.

As they started up the stairs, she asked, "How often do you come here?"

"Perhaps once a year. I usually stay for a few days when I visit my business interests in the north." He smiled ruefully. "I know. A sad waste, isn't it?"

She shook her head in amazement. "Aren't there any impoverished Kenyon cousins who need a home?"

"Yes, but they all prefer living farther south. Closer to civilization. One cousin stays at my Norfolk estate, where Ellie Warden and her baby went to live." His smile became satiric. "No matter what I might say, Cousin Quintus and his wife will assume the baby is mine, which ensures that the child will be well looked after."

"I'm glad for Ellie and the baby's sake, even if your reputation is impugned." She hugged his arm as he led her down the lamp-lit, irregular hall. Though she'd dreamed of houses for years, none was as fine as this.

She hoped that someday there would be a Kenyon cousin who would have the sense to appreciate it.

When they reached the end of the hall, he said, "The master's room is on the left, the mistress's on the right, with a dressing area and connecting door between." He opened the door on the right.

She stepped inside, and once more caught her breath. The left end of the long room was dominated by a massive, canopied four-poster bed, while the right end was a sitting area with a chaise longue, comfortable chairs, and other furniture. But what riveted her was the roses. Every table and bureau was covered by vases full of fragrant flowers, red and pink and white, the colors glowing in the light of a crackling wood fire. The scent was intoxicating.

Wonderingly she touched a crimson blossom. "Stephen, this is stunning. How on earth did you do it?"

"I'm rather good at arranging things." He kissed her on the incredibly sensitive jointure of throat and shoulder. "The idea was natural: roses for my perfect rose."

She swallowed hard, hoping he would never realize how imperfect she was. "The flowers are exquisite. But they'll be gone so swiftly."

"That is much of why they are beautiful," he said quietly.

Their gazes met for a charged moment. Even now, on their wedding night, it was impossible to escape intimations of mortality. But while he lived, she promised herself fiercely, they would wrench every moment of joy they could from the tempest of time.

CHAPTER 19

Stephen sipped some wine from his goblet, his gaze on Rosalind, who sat on the opposite side of the round table. She'd brushed out her hair and left it hanging loose around her shoulders, the heavy sweep shimmering with dark gold and amber lights whenever she moved her head. Her suggestion to eat in her room had been inspired, for there was an intimacy here they would never have felt in the large dining room.

He'd asked for anticipation, and the fire-lit room was ripe with it. Every bite of food, every sip of wine, was enriched by the knowledge of how the meal would end.

He felt an absurd ambivalence about this wedding night. On the one hand, he wanted her with a fierce, unwavering hunger. He wanted to make love until they were sated, sleep the rest of the night with her in his arms, then wake and do it again.

Yet at the same time, he felt as awkward as a callow boy. Before his first marriage, he'd had the usual experiences of a wealthy young man, bedding several of London's finest courtesans with uncomplicated enjoyment.

That had ceased when he married. Not that Louisa would have reproached him for having mistresses; she had been raised to believe that a well-bred wife should not notice her husband's peccadilloes. But her pride would have been hurt, and there had been so little he could do for Louisa that he could not deny her his fidelity. Nor did he wish to follow in his father's promiscuous footsteps.

It had been difficult, at first, to restrict himself to a cold and unsatisfying marriage bed. On countless lonely, restless nights, he had yearned to lose himself in warm, willing female flesh. But in time he accepted the limits of his life. After all, he was not of a deeply passionate nature, nor did he expect doing the right thing to be easy.

At least, he'd thought he was not particularly passionate. Then he had met Rosalind. Making love to her had been the most intense, satisfying experience of his life. But that had been a swift tempest of sensation, over far too soon. He intended to make sure that it would be different tonight, and whatever other nights they might have.

How well would he be able to please Rosalind? She was a sensual, responsive woman, while he hadn't even seen a naked female body since he'd married Louisa. His first wife had found sex so distasteful that it must be done in the dark under blankets and nightclothes, and she'd recoiled whenever he had attempted anything but the most basic coupling. As a result, he was hardly a master of the subtle carnal arts.

Nor did he have much time to learn them. Though his hopes for a relatively good day had been answered, there was always pain to remind him of his failing body. He was losing strength, too. Only a little so far, but all too soon the day would come when he would be no use to Rosalind as a husband. She would not reproach him; she was too compassionate for that. But he had a powerful desire to leave her with some memories that no other man would be able to obliterate. That meant that he must discipline himself, make love to her slowly rather than with the fevered haste his body craved.

He smiled wryly at the thought of practicing discipline when he was already halfway to being mindless with desire. She still wore the magnificent Ophelia gown, and her cleavage was dazzling whenever she leaned forward. He had seen more of her in the hayloft than of Louisa in all their years of marriage. In fact, he was seeing more of her right now.

Not only was Rosalind irresistibly appealing, she'd been telling wonderful theatrical stories throughout the meal. Laying down her fork, she concluded, "Then the cat, which the stage manager had sworn was perfectly docile, woke up and pushed its head from the basket in the middle of the scene. Mama simply shoved it back and said very firmly, 'Don't be such an ambitious pussy, this isn't *Dick Whittington!*'"

Stephen laughed. "I wish I'd seen that. Is there really a play about Dick Whittington and his cat?"

"Yes." Her eyes sparkled. "It's not very good, but I have fond memories of playing the cat when I was little."

He imagined her as a charming child equipped with tail and whiskers, and laughed again. Setting aside his wine, he sliced several small pieces of cheese from the chunk on the table. "Would you like some of this excellent Cheshire cheese?"

Rosalind gave him a lazy-lidded smile. "Yes, please."

He leaned forward and fed her the piece. Her soft lips closed on his fingertips as she took the crumbly cheese. "Delicious," she murmured. "Would you like some?"

"I believe I would."

She lifted a slice and held it to his lips. Her fingers

were slim and strong. He sucked them into his mouth, his tongue sensuously caressing.

She withdrew her hand slowly. "H-have you noticed how warm it is?"

"Shall I bank the fire?"

"I have a better idea." She got to her feet and turned her back to him. "Since Jessica is not here to be my lady's maid, will you unlace my gown?"

Blood quickening, he stood and untied the bow at the top of the crisscrossed lacing. Even in her stocking feet, the top of her head reached his nose. He liked that she was tall and full-figured, not fragile, like Louisa.

Forget Louisa; comparisons were not fair to either woman. He began pulling the laces through the eyelets. "This is the loveliest wedding gown I've ever seen. Much too fine to be wasted on a watering pot like Ophelia."

She chuckled. "I've always thought this costume fit for a queen. Or a duchess."

As he undid the laces, the back of the gown fell open, revealing the elegant curve of her spine. The skin above her low-cut chemise was satin smooth, like warm cream.

She'd liked it earlier when he'd kissed her shoulder. He bent and lightly nipped her nape through the glossy veil of her hair. She made a small, breathy sigh and arched her neck. Wanting to hear that sound again, he trailed kisses along her throat and traced the rim of her ear with his tongue.

Her whole body quivered. "This . . . this is much nicer than having a lady's maid."

"I aim to please, my dear duchess." He loosened the rest of the laces, then pulled the gown down her arms.

She gave a ravishing shimmy to help free herself. The bodice and sleeves crumpled around her waist. His mouth dried as he drew the heavy silk downward over her ripe hips. The garment fell to the floor with a rich rustling sound, and she stood clad only in chemise, stockings, and the quilted cotton stays required by the clinging gown. He tugged the strap of her stays and the sleeve of her chemise from her right shoulder so that he could kiss the flawless flesh.

"I'm wearing less clothing, but feel even warmer than before," she said with a ghost of laughter.

"Then you're still wearing too much." The laces of her stays unfastened much more easily than those of the gown. He removed the dimity undergarment and caressed the supple arc of her waist. "Ah-h-h. Much better."

She leaned back against him. Her aureoles were tantalizingly visible through the fine lawn fabric of her chemise, and her seductive personal scent twined through the heavier fragrance of the banked roses. God. *God.* Mouth dry, he cupped her breasts in his hands. They were a warm, sumptuous weight against his palms. She gave a shuddering sigh as he caressed them.

"Have we spent enough time anticipating?" she asked throatily, underlining her words by wriggling her round buttocks against him. His groin tightened.

No. There would be so few nights like this. But she was right that the room was too warm. He stepped away and peeled off his coat. He was wondering whether to also remove his embroidered waistcoat when Rosalind turned and began to unbutton it. "My turn, Your Grace," she said with a teasing smile.

She released the last button and removed the garment, tossing it over her shoulder to land on the chaise longue that stood at right angles to the fireplace. Then she skimmed her hands over his shoulders and chest.

His heart quickened and small jolts of sensation followed the track of her touch.

As she began to untie his cravat, her gaze went over him admiringly. "If you hadn't the misfortune to be a duke, you could have had a grand career in the theater playing dashing heroes and causing ladies in the audience to faint with longing." She dropped the length of crumpled fabric and caressed his neck with cool fingers.

He caught her hand and kissed the palm. "I've no desire to impress nameless ladies in a hypothetical audience. It's enough if I interest you."

She looked up at him, her dark eyes hazy with desire. "You do, Stephen. More than anyone I've ever known."

Her lips were luxuriantly full, absurdly erotic. He leaned forward into a kiss. She tasted of the fine French wine they'd drunk. Sweetly tangy. Intoxicating.

His attention concentrated on the endless, drugging kiss, he scarcely noticed as she tugged his shirttails loose and unbuttoned the fall of his breeches. Then she caressed the heavy length of his erection through the fabric of his drawers.

He went rigid, blood pounding through his veins, blinding him to everything but the touch of her hand and his raw need. The bed was too far away, at the opposite end of the room. Urgently he swept her up and carried her the two steps to the chaise longue, laying her on the worn brocade and coming down beside her as he succumbed to madness. How many times would they be together like this? His life and passion were like a candle in the dark, swiftly burning away until nothing would remain. How often would he feel the silk of her tawny hair? Smell her entrancing, mysteriously female scent? Taste the salt of her skin?

How many more times would his blood burn in a red rage that only she could quench?

He pulled her chemise down, and his mouth descended on her left breast. Her choked moan was ambrosia, an aphrodisiac that made him suck harder as the nipple stiffened against his tongue.

"Stephen. Oh, Lord, Stephen." She caught handfuls of his hair with ragged kneading motions that matched the roughness of her breathing.

He lifted the hem of her chemise above her knees. Her stockings were secured by garters embroidered with red rosebuds. He untied the bow of the right one with a jerk of his teeth. The garter fell away, but his mouth stayed. He licked her inner thigh, feeling the pulse of her smooth flesh beneath his tongue.

The soft hair between her thighs was darker than the hair on her head, a demure chestnut. She gave a startled squeak when he exhaled warm breath into the gentle curls. But there was pleasure in that surprise. Pleasure, and eagerness. With a heady sense of power, he kissed the concealed cleft, sliding his tongue into the slick, succulent folds below. She cried out and arched her hips, pushing into the rhythmic strokes of his tongue.

He felt the increasing tremors in her body and was prepared when her hips heaved convulsively. He stayed with her, stimulating her heated flesh until her contractions had faded and her body wilted against the cushioned chaise.

He rested his head on her belly as he caught his breath. Her hand drifted over the disordered waves of his hair. "Oh, my," she whispered. "I had no idea. . . ."

There was a long moment of mutual stillness. Then, shaking with tension, he wrenched his clothing open and mounted her, spreading her legs with his thighs.

His excitement was almost unbearable as he pushed into her. Heat surrounded him, silken and welcoming.

She gasped and her eyes widened. Then she drew her right knee up against the back of the chaise while her left leg dropped to the floor, opening herself as her arms slid around his waist to lock him close. Her hips began moving against him. He thrust into her again and again as pleasure washed over him in hot, mad waves. Rising. Soaring . . .

Crashing in jagged ecstasy. He pressed his cheek to hers, groaning helplessly at the intensity of a climax that came swiftly and lasted long. Death and transfiguration.

He sagged against her, his exhausted body throbbing as he struggled for breath. When he could move, he pushed himself up on one elbow and studied her flushed face. Tawny ringlets clung to her forehead, and her eyes were languorous with satisfaction. The sight gave him equal satisfaction. Though he might not be an expert lover, he had managed to please her while finding shattering ecstasy for himself.

He kissed her temple. "I can't believe that I did that again," he said ruefully. "I had such good intentions of taking my time and celebrating every inch of you."

"Does it count that I celebrated every inch of you?" she said naughtily.

He laughed as he lifted himself away and sat on the edge the chaise. The crumpled folds of chemise did more to reveal than conceal her lovely body. "You are the most deliciously wicked woman I've ever known."

Her face froze, and he realized that he'd made a mistake. She must think his words were an allusion to her actress past. He touched her face, brushing the damp curls from her forehead. "That was entirely a compliment," he said softly. "Having too often been staid, I treasure your openness. Your responsiveness."

Her expression eased, but unselfconsciousness was gone. She tugged at her chemise, covering her breasts and pulling the hem down over her knees.

He extinguished the candles, leaving the room lit only by firelight, then offered his hand. She rose and took his hand, and they crossed the room. When they reached the bed, he turned and put his hands on her shoulders. Though desire was satisfied for now, he still loved looking at her—and would like to see even more.

A gentleman would respect her modesty, but a man who was running out of time could not afford such a luxury. He slid his hands slowly down her arms to her waist, then caught the folds of chemise. "May I?"

A little shyly she nodded. He tugged the garment over her head. Then he knelt and untied her remaining garter—this time with his fingers—and rolled down her stockings. Her calves and ankles were delightfully shapely against his palms.

He stood, feasting his eyes. Freed from the tyranny of clothing, she was magnificent. Made for love, to give and receive pleasure. "You are beautiful," he said huskily. "Terribly, heartbreakingly beautiful."

She swallowed, her smooth throat flexing. "You make me feel as if I really am."

"Never doubt that, Rosalind." He helped her onto the canopied bed. Then he removed his own clothing, very aware that, even though his illness had left no outward marks, he was thinner than he should be. Apparently vanity was another unsuspected vice. Well, his appearance would get no better than it was now, so he'd better bury vanity. He climbed into bed. "I'm tired, but I don't want the day to end so soon."

"I know exactly what you mean." Rosalind took his

hand as he lay down on his side, propping his head up so he could watch her. The room really was warm, so by mutual consent they left the turned-down counterpane at the foot of the bed and relaxed on the cool sheets, their hands loosely clasped.

She loved looking at her new mate, his long bones and the clean definition of muscles. The elegant patterns of dark hair that dusted his chest and arrowed down his torso. The sheer masculinity that had no need to prove anything to anyone.

It had been an evening of surprises, beginning with the revelation of her own capacity for passion. While she and Charles had enjoyed a healthy marital relationship, their couplings had been uncomplicated and ended quickly with him rolling over and going to sleep. While she sometimes found satisfaction, too often she had lain awake and stared into the darkness until her frustrated longings faded away. A single night of marriage had shown her that Stephen was a more generous, and more imaginative, lover.

The companionability of lying together unabashedly nude felt right. Comfortable. "There's an old term for being naked," she murmured. "Sky clad. Isn't that pretty?"

"Sky clad," he repeated. "I like that. It suits you to be bare. A pity you can't be like this all the time, but in the English climate it just isn't practical." His tone became wry. "Nor would I want any other man seeing you like this."

She thought of her unrespectable past. "Do you mind that I've played breeches parts in front of audiences all over the West Midlands?"

"How can I object to what you did before I met you? Although . . ." He hesitated. "It's really none of my business, but was there ever anyone else besides Jordan?"

"Any lovers, you mean? Never." She rolled her eyes. "There was no shortage of men interested in bedding an actress, especially one with a rather overabundant figure. But there's nothing like being grabbed by an ale-scented oaf after a tiring performance to make one lose interest in the local swains."

"You are not overabundant." He pulled a long-stemmed rose from a bedside vase and gently stroked the undercurve of her breast with the blossom. "You are perfect exactly as you are."

She laughed, enjoying the cool slide of the petals against her skin and the subtle fragrance that wafted from the blossom, a scent distinct from the massed floral arrangements. "I'm reasonably attractive, which is useful for an actress, particularly one of no special talent, like me. But perfect? Hardly." Since he'd raised the subject of the past himself, she looked away and asked, "Were there many other women for you?"

She immediately regretted the question. Men with Stephen's power and wealth had access to the most beautiful women in England, both courtesans and the amoral wives of their own rank. From what she knew of the nobility, most would take advantage of such opportunities, and Stephen seemed to be a man of strong appetites.

To her surprise, he replied, "Not since before my first marriage. I had no taste for adultery, and after Louisa's death I . . . I suppose I wasn't in the mood to find a mistress."

So he had loved his first wife that much. Rosalind recognized wryly that she might have preferred for him to admit to a string of dazzling conquests. Lord, she was a fool. He was hers, for now, and she could ask no more. She said simply, "I'm glad."

He trailed the rose silkily to her other breast. "I must have known deep down that something better was waiting. Or rather, someone."

"You have a gift for romantic words," she said, distracted by the way he teased her nipple with the flower, causing it to tighten with tingling pleasure.

He chuckled. "Only if honesty is romantic."

The rose dipped into her navel, then began gliding over her abdomen in lazy patterns. Lulled by the suede-like softness, she murmured, "It's ironic that we would never have married if not for your illness." She stopped abruptly, wondering if she'd committed a horrid faux pas by mentioning his condition, then decided it would be best to continue. "If you'd seen me onstage, you wouldn't have given me a second thought."

"Not true," he protested, tracing the supple angles between abdomen and thigh. "You caught my attention as soon as you removed your Caliban head. I'd have gone to the stage door and joined the ale-scented oafs if we'd been in London, and"—he stopped, then said lamely—"and things were different."

His words hung awkwardly in the air, casting a damper on their mood. Her first impulse was to introduce another subject, but then she realized that this would happen again. Carefully she said, "Your illness is like . . . like having an elephant in the room. Enormous, impossible to forget, always there. I don't know how to talk of it. I'm sure either of us do." She searched his eyes, trying to read his expression. "Do you prefer that I pretend you're not ill, Stephen? Or shall I speak of your condition matter-of-factly, like winter or taxes or some other regrettable subject that can't be ignored?"

His face went very still. It was so silent that she

could hear the brush of rose petals against her skin before he repeated, "An elephant in the room. It's like that, isn't it? Both of us tiptoeing around the fact of my impending death as if we're on eggs." He continued stroking her with the flower as he thought. "I think I prefer honesty. In fact, I know that I do. There isn't enough time to waste even a moment of it watching our words."

Her intense relief made her realize how much she had been unconsciously worried about saying the wrong thing. "You are really a remarkable man."

"Me?" he said with surprise. "The most remarkable thing about me is that I chose my ancestors well."

She laughed. "You actually believe that, don't you? Trust me, as one who has seen men from all stations of life, and not always at their best, I can say with certainty that you would be remarkable no matter what ancestors you'd picked."

He smiled and shook his head. "I'm glad you think so."

The rose rolled along the juncture of her thighs with velvety intimacy. She caught her breath as light enjoyment intensified into something more.

He paused. "Sorry, am I tickling you?"

"Not in an unpleasant way," she said a little breathlessly as the embers of desire stirred deep within her. "But I'm surprised to feel this way again, so soon after . . . after what we just did."

"Interesting. I was thinking the same thing about myself," he murmured. The head of the rose nudged the soft curls between her legs, cool against her warmth.

"This is absurd—who ever heard of being seduced by a flower?" she said with a laugh that was half amusement and half embarrassment.

"If we looked, I'm sure we could find a Greek legend where Zeus took the form of a sunflower in order to pursue a nymph," Stephen said with mock seriousness. "Or perhaps—a turnip?"

"The king of gods, a turnip? Surely not," she protested with a laugh. Her eyes drifted shut, intensifying the effect of his sensual stroking. Her legs separated and the petals danced over her intimately, delicately erotic. Blood began drumming through her most secret places. She pulsed her hips restlessly, wanting a pressure and fullness a flower could not provide.

Then the phantom touch of the rose vanished. Her eyes snapped open. "Wicked man! Or should I say wicked flower? You can't stop now!"

"I don't intend to. But this time, you can do the work."

He drew her close and pulled her on top of him. He was as ready as she. Though she'd never made love like this before, the theory seemed straightforward enough. She raised herself on her knees and clasped him. Then, savoring every fractional inch of movement, she lowered herself on the heated length of his shaft until he filled her. Experimentally she tightened her internal muscles.

He gasped, and his hands went to her hips. "Now who's wicked?"

She laughed aloud and let her head rest on his shoulder as her hips slowly rolled against his. This was different from the frantic need of their earlier encounters, a sensual haze that suffused her entire body rather than concentrating in one spot. She liked that she controlled the tempo. That she could feel the acceleration of his heart when she teased him with a provocative thrust of her hips. Most of all, she loved the mutual awareness between them, a flowing into each other's beings that was very different from the violent passion they had shared earlier, yet equally profound.

Languor slowly became urgency until she was clinging to his shoulders, marking him with her nails as she ground frantically against him. When she cried out, he made a guttural sound, his arms locking around her waist as he surged convulsively inside her.

Their sweat-slicked bodies gradually relaxed. He began caressing her, his palm warm on the small of her back. Neither made a move to separate. She wanted to stay this close, their bodies intertwined, forever.

As she drifted into sleep, she felt tears sting her eyes that this harrowing beauty of love would soon vanish like the rose.

CHAPTER 20

Day Fifty-four

Stephen awoke early, Rosalind curled against him and her arm across his chest. Rain spatted against the window, and pearly dawn light showed the fan of her tangled hair over his shoulder. He petted her head very gently. She sighed and snuggled closer.

Vastly content, he thought about the previous day. It had been almost perfect, apart from one moderate attack of pain, and his wedding night had stunned his senses. Now, selfishly, he wanted another such day.

Another such night. Another such morning of waking with Rosalind in his arms and feeling utter peace. Surely today would be as good as yesterday. Better.

He drowsed, waking again to find the sky lighter and the rain over. Rosalind slept on. The mark of a good conscience, he assumed. He brimmed with energy, too much so to stay in bed. Briefly he thought about waking her so they could make love again, but a considerate man would let his new wife sleep—and gather strength for later.

Deciding to take a walk, he slid carefully from Rosalind's embrace and began to dress. She rolled toward where he had been, her arm going around his indented pillow. She was as relaxed as a kitten, and ten times more charming.

The thought reminded him of Portia, who had happily curled up in her box after being fed the evening before. She was snoozing still, so he picked up the small warm body and laid her beside Rosalind. The kitten yawned hugely, then went back to sleep.

He hadn't taken his medication the night before. Not an accident; he had not wanted to risk drowsiness from opium. From now on he would shift the time of his daily pill from night to morning.

He swallowed a pill and dressed, then jotted a note to Rosalind and left it on the bedside table. Her sleeping face and bare arms were so lovely that he stripped the petals from a pink rose and scattered them over his bride and her kitten. Portia opened her eyes and batted at a falling petal. Then she rolled onto her back with her paws in the air.

Donning his greatcoat, he went downstairs. It was still early and there was no sign of the Nylands. Outside the air was chilly with autumn and the sky overcast, only a few shades lighter than the iron sea. The tide was in, covering most of the sandy estuary, so he stayed on the low bluff that overlooked the water and headed north toward the Irish Sea. His skin tingled from the wind, and he felt intensely alive. Could passion be a cure for his illness? He laughed. That would be a shock for sober George Blackmer.

His exhilaration lasted for a mile or so. Because of the biting sea winds, there were no buildings this close to the shore, except for an ancient stone chapel that had served a long-vanished fishing village. He enjoyed the solitude. It was a new pleasure, one he'd only really discovered since leaving Ashburton Abbey and its army of servants.

He had almost reached the chapel when brutal pain sliced his throat and belly with a suddenness that made him stagger. He lurched to a wind-warped tree and clung to it, retching, his stomach too empty to bring up much. Then he pressed his forehead to the tree trunk, rough bark the sole reality in a world of devouring agony.

Slowly the pain ebbed to endurable levels, leaving him too weak to walk and shaking with cold. He turned and leaned against the trunk, fighting weakness and despair. His hands and feet were numb except for a faint, ominous tingling. Would paralysis render him helpless even before death? *Christ.* How could he have believed, even for a moment, that there was hope?

Unable to face the walk back to Kirby Manor, he lurched the hundred yards to the chapel. Luckily the heavy door was unlocked. He entered the dim sanctuary and slumped into the last of the oak pews. Though the air was stone cold, at least he was out of the wind.

Since the chapel stood on Kirby Manor land, Stephen paid for its maintenance. In fact, he remembered vaguely, he'd recently received a request from a group of Methodists to be allowed to use the chapel for services. It had been merely one of the constant stream of letters and requests that came to the Duke of Ashburton. He'd granted permission readily, for buildings needed to be used, even if only by a group of dissenters. The congregation had sent a letter of surprised, fervent gratitude. He'd been briefly pleased, then promptly forgot the matter.

His gaze went over the ancient leaded glass windows and came to rest on the plain altar, which held only a brass cross. It appeared that the Methodists had cleaned the interior and whitewashed the old stone walls but had not yet started worshiping here. A year from now, the chapel would probably have a welcoming air even when empty. Now it had the bleakness of a tomb.

Every morning his first waking thought was of the number of days he had left, but he was beginning to doubt that he would survive even the ninety Blackmer had originally granted him. How many days would he have after this one? Forty-five? Thirty? God, surely he would have at least another month with Rosalind.

But what kind of month would it be? And why was he invoking the name of God when he had no faith? His mouth twisted with bitterness. Even here, in a church that had probably watched the Viking longboats sail into the Dee, he felt no holy presence, no comfort, no sense of divine plan.

His depression was swept away by a surge of rage. It damned well wasn't fair that he should find happiness for the first time in his life, then be so swiftly jerked away to the loneliness of the grave. *It wasn't fair!*

For the first time in many years, the infamous Kenyon temper scorched through him. He wanted to smash and destroy, punish life's essential injustice. The force of his feelings left him dizzy and gasping for breath. He crossed his arms on the back of the pew in front of him and rested his head as he struggled for control.

And underneath the red rage, he felt the cold, insistent beat of fear.

Rosalind woke when someone punched her in the stomach. Her eyes opened just in time to see a black-and-orange streak bound from the bed. Portia. She grinned as the kitten ricocheted from the chaise toward one of the chairs. Clearly Portia had recovered from the trip and had energy to burn.

But where was Stephen? She pushed herself upright, feeling rather decadent for having slept without a nightgown. There were rose petals all around her, a silent gift from her new husband. She lifted one and brushed it against her cheek, thinking about what he'd done with a rose the night before. That made her feel even more decadent.

Seeing a piece of paper on the bedside table, she reached for it and read, "Gone for a walk. Back soon. Whom shall we have for breakfast? S."

At that she blushed outright and slid from the bed. With the fire burned out, the room was cold, so she washed and dressed swiftly. Then she made her way to the kitchen and begged a cup of tea from a flustered Mrs. Nyland, who wasn't used to duchesses in her domain.

Stephen still hadn't returned by the time Rosalind finished her tea, so she decided to go for a walk herself. She threw on her cloak and went outside. Surely he had decided to walk along the shore, and probably toward the north and the beckoning stretch of open sea. On the other side lay Ireland. Far beyond, the New World and its mysteries. An irresistible prospect.

She enjoyed the walk despite the raw, overcast weather, but there was no sign of Stephen. He must have chosen a different direction. When she reached the small church on the headland, she would turn back to Kirby Manor. He'd probably be waiting for her.

The chapel stood sturdily against the harsh wind, a testament to the skills of its builders. On impulse she tried the door. It opened easily under her hand. She stepped into the austere sanctuary, then stopped at the sight of a dark, familiar figure slumped in the last pew. Her blood froze. Dear God, Stephen couldn't be . . . couldn't be . . .

Before the horrifying thought had fully formed in her mind, he lifted his head and saw her. For a stark moment their gazes held. He must have had another attack, a bad one, for his eyes were a flat, lifeless gray and he looked twenty years older than the night before. Almost worse, she sensed that emotionally he had moved a great distance away, as if he were on the opposite side of a bottomless chasm that she could never cross.

The thought was almost as frightening as her fear when she first entered. Praying that her intuition was wrong, she pushed her hood back on her shoulders and moved forward with a bright smile. "Good morning. I decided to walk, too, in hopes of running into you." She sat in the pew next to him and took his hand.

His gaze went to the altar, and his fingers rested unresponsive in her clasp. Her heart sank. The night before, they had agreed on dealing with each other honestly, and she'd broken that resolve within hours.

Perhaps he'd hardly heard her inane comment, for

when he spoke, it was to ask bleakly, "Rosalind, are you afraid of dying?"

If ever Stephen needed honesty, it was now. "I'm afraid of pain," she said slowly. "And because I enjoy life and don't want to die, I suppose one could say I'm afraid of dying. Yet oddly, I'm not afraid of death itself."

"Why not? Do you believe in heaven and hell? Winged angels and nasty little demons with pitchforks?" he asked, his voice sardonic.

"I . . . I don't know." She sighed, aware that she was failing him. "I wish I had better answers, but I'm afraid that I've never thought too much about religion."

His mouth curved in a humorless smile. "I find myself thinking a great deal about such matters these days."

"It sounds as if your thoughts are not satisfying ones," she said quietly.

"Religion is a fraud, I think. Designed to offer hope to those whose lives are miserable." His lips tightened. "Fool's gold, and fit only for fools."

"I don't agree," she protested. "Many wise men and women have been believers. I think the world is too grand and complicated a place to have occurred by chance."

He raised their joined hands and kissed her knuckles. "Bring me the proof that there is more to life than what we see around us, Rosalind, and I'll be eternally grateful." He smiled faintly. "No pun intended."

She pressed his hand to her cheek, fighting back tears. The night before, the passion between them had been incandescent, so full of life that it had seemed eternal. This morning the mark of death was on him.

He released her hand and got to his feet. "You're

shaking with cold. Time to take you home to a warm fire."

She nodded and slid from the pew. When he started to follow, he lurched and had to grab the back of the pew for balance. Horrified, she said, "You aren't well, Stephen. I'll go to the manor and get the carriage to take you there."

"No!" He straightened, his expression fierce. "I'm fine."

"You're not!" she retorted, not wanting to go against his wishes but painfully aware of his weakness. "Wait here. I'll be back with the coachman in half an hour."

His gaze turned to ice. "Marriage was a mistake," he said harshly. "We had a perfect day together. Go back to your family, and remember me as I was yesterday."

She stared at him, stunned. "You're sending me away the day after our wedding?"

"Don't worry. I shall fulfill the financial promises I made." He flexed his free hand absently, unable to make a tight fist. "Do you want Kirby Manor? You seem to like it. Since it's not part of the Ashburton entail, I can leave it to you outright, along with the income to maintain it."

Rosalind was an expert at suppressing anger, but not this time. "How dare you!" she exploded. "Did you think that I married you only for your damned money? If you ever suggest such a thing again, you'll be meeting your maker much sooner than you planned." Tears began spilling down her cheeks. She wiped at them furiously. "Oh, the devil take you, Stephen. What have I done to make you want to get rid of me?"

After a moment of appalled silence, he stepped forward and wrapped her in his arms so tightly that her ribs hurt. "Damnation. I'm sorry, Rosalind," he said painfully. "The fault is not with you. It's just that . . . I loathe the idea of you seeing me deteriorate. I told myself I could bear that, but the closer the reality comes, the more hateful I find it."

She hid her face against his shoulder. He was so solid. So much a part of her, even though six weeks ago she'd never met him. When she was sure her voice would be steady, she said, "Didn't you listen to the wedding vows we took? For better, for worse, in sickness and in health, till death us do part. I knew what I was doing when I agreed to marry you, just as you did when you asked. Don't let an episode of pain make you forget that." She tilted her head back and glared at him. "Besides, there has to be some kind of rule that says you can't tell a duchess what to do."

"You're taking to the imperious manner very well." A spark of levity showed in his eyes before his expression sobered again. "I want to have you with me. Very much so. But I'm not sure if my pride or sense of justice can stand it."

"What about my pride?" she said with self-mocking humor. "I'll never live it down if I get tossed out by my second husband after a single night. It took my first husband six months to become bored with me." Her voice broke, and suddenly tears were welling up in her eyes. She hid her face again, hoping Stephen wouldn't notice, but he was too perceptive.

"Jordan's infidelity hurt more than you let anyone see, didn't it?" he said softly.

She nodded. "If my parents had realized how upset I was, holy hell would have broken out in the troupe. My father might have murdered Charles. Certainly he would have thrown him out of the troupe, and I'd have had to choose between going with him like a dutiful wife or staying with my family. So I covered up Charles's escapades the best I could and pretended that his behavior didn't bother me. I thought that in time it would become easier to bear. Instead, it became harder and harder. I was relieved when he went to Ireland. Relieved—and then horribly guilty when he was killed."

Stephen stroked her back gently. "Marriage has not been kind to you. One husband who betrayed you, and one who is dying. You deserve better."

She could not let him worry about her, not when his own problems were so much more grave. She reached for composure and found it. "My marriage to Charles is in the past. I'm concerned about now, and I have no complaints about the bargain I've made in marrying you."

She raised her gaze to his, using her acting skill to project sincerity. "We won't have much time together. That's sad, but it also means that we will never grow bored with each other. If either of us truly comes to regret this marriage, at least we won't have to endure the consequences for long. We'll have none of the mundane irritations that gnaw away at the best of marriages. We will have only the cream—the excitement and wonder of discovering another person."

His brows rose, and she noticed that the greenish tone had returned to his eyes. He seemed strong and alert again. He'd made a swift recovery from that horrible attack.

"That's an interesting thought," he said. "You're overlooking the fact that some of that cream will be sour, but it's true that our marriage will never be boring."

"Then let's have no more talk of sending me away." She stepped back and pulled her hood over her hair. "I won't go, you know. I have my reputation to consider."

His laughter was deep and genuine. "You're better for me than that whole bottle of pills. Very well, I promise not to have this fight with you again for at least a fortnight. In the meantime, let's enjoy the cream." He offered his arm. "How can we best use what time we have? I'd like to spend a few days here, then take a leisurely route to London, seeing some sights I've never found the time to visit. Do you have any special requests?"

She took his arm. "I've always wanted to go to York. Would that be possible?"

"Of course." He held the door open and they left the chapel. "I want to see the Lake District myself, though it will have to be a very brief visit."

The sun was beginning to break through the clouds. Rosalind took it as a good omen. Stephen looked almost as well as he had the day before, yet there was still a subtle sense of distance between them. Not as much as when she first found him in the chapel, but enough to make her mourn the loss of the closeness that had existed the night before.

She supposed that a degree of detachment would help him resolve the conflict between wanting her company and despising his weakness. Perhaps that distance would also help her cope with the difficult weeks ahead.

Nonetheless, she hated it.

CHAPTER 21

"Lord Michael Kenyon," the butler intoned.

Michael entered the small drawing room of Bourne Castle on the servant's heels, his companion several steps behind. Seated by the fire over a late afternoon cup of tea were the Duke and Duchess of Candover. Both rose and came toward him with smiles.

"This is an unexpected pleasure, Michael," Rafe said with a powerful handshake. "Well-timed, also. Two days later and we would be on our way to London."

"With the Little Season in full swing, I was afraid that you might be there already." Michael released Rafe's hand and turned to the duchess. "Margot, you're a sight for sore eyes."

She gave him a warm hug. "How are Catherine and the baby?"

"Very well the last time I saw them, which was entirely too long ago." He turned to his companion, who had been hovering uneasily near the drawing-room door. "Rafe, Margot, allow me to present Dr. George Blackmer."

After the introductions, Margot gave Michael a shrewd glance, then said, "You will both spend the night, of course. Dr. Blackmer, I'll take you to your room so you can rest and refresh yourself before dinner. Michael, you'll be in your usual quarters." She ushered the doctor out, giving her husband and his friend a chance to talk privately.

"Have a seat." Without being asked, Rafe poured a cup of tea, produced a bottle of brandy, and laced the tea liberally, then handed the cup to Michael. "Wretchedly rainy out there. You look like you could use this."

"It's not fit for man nor geese." Michael settled in a wing chair, some of his tension easing for the first time since he'd received Blackmer's letter about Stephen. The steaming, brandy-fortified tea brought welcoming warmth.

Rafe resumed his seat. "We've been blessed with a plenitude of Kenyons lately."

Michael came instantly alert. "Have you seen my brother?"

"Ashburton was here a couple of weeks ago." Rafe grinned. "Acting in a play. The Duke of Athens in *A Midsummer Night's Dream,* to be precise, and doing a very decent job."

Michael leaned forward in his chair. "How did he look?"

"Very shaggy. He wore a false beard so that no one would know him, but Margot recognized his voice. I spoke with him after the performance. He seemed to be enjoying himself thoroughly."

"He didn't appear unwell?"

Rafe frowned. "No. Should he have?"

Tensely Michael set down his teacup and got to his feet. "My brother is very ill. Dying, according to Dr. Blackmer. Once Stephen learned how serious his condition was, he left the abbey alone with no word of when he'd be back. Blackmer eventually wrote me, and ever since then I've been trying to trace Stephen across half of England." He began to pace restlessly about the drawing room. "It's like chasing a blasted will-o'-the-wisp. Even Lucien, with all his nefarious connections, hasn't been able to help."

Rafe's expression was grave. "I'm so sorry. Might the doctor be wrong?"

"Who knows? Blackmer doesn't say much, but the mere fact that he insisted on accompanying me doesn't bode well. He's as nervous as a hare on a griddle. I think he's afraid that we won't find Stephen before"– Michael stopped, then forced himself to finish–"before it's too late."

Rafe, who seldom swore, muttered a vehement oath under his breath.

Michael slanted a glance at his friend. "You said that Stephen looked well."

The duke hesitated. "I didn't see him clearly in good light. Now that I think about it, he looked a bit thin and his expression was drawn. I thought nothing of it because his mood was good."

"Do you think he's still traveling with that theater troupe?"

"Perhaps, though he told me that soon he would be returning to his normal life." Rafe's brows drew together. "A day or two after he was here, he sent a message asking for the use of a reliable man to perform some commissions for him in London. I sent him my assistant steward, Gardiner, who was gone for three or four days."

"Do you know what he wanted done in London?"

"I didn't ask because it seemed none of my business, but perhaps the errands will shed some light on your brother's plans. I'll send for Gardiner."

The duke rang for a footman and gave the order to summon the steward. When the men were alone again, he said, "Wouldn't it be easier simply to wait for your brother to return? I've always found him admirably levelheaded. He'll come home in his own good time."

"Will he? He's already been gone for well over a month. Blackmer says it's unlikely that his mind has been affected by his disease, but who can say for sure? His behavior has been so bizarre that I fear the worst." Michael's mouth twisted. "Running away without a servant. Going onstage under an assumed name. He's always been fond of the theater, but even so, that's almost beyond belief."

"Believe it." The duke finished his tea and set the cup aside. "Is there some special reason you need to find Ashburton as soon as possible?"

Michael's pacing brought him to a window. "There are plenty of good practical reasons to find him, but they aren't the important ones." He stared sightlessly at the gray rain. "I . . . I still haven't quite accepted that my brother might be dying. I need to see him with my own eyes. Find out if he's really ill or if Blackmer is only a pessimistic quack. If his condition is serious, I want Ian Kinlock to see him . . . and Catherine, too, of course. It was Ian's medical procedure and Catherine's nursing that saved my life. Maybe they can do the same for Stephen."

"And if he's beyond human help?" Rafe asked quietly.

"Then I want to say good-bye." Michael swallowed hard. "To tell him how much I've come to value him in the last two years. Kenyons are a tough lot—I thought we had thirty or forty years of conversation ahead." He rubbed his neck, which ached from too many days of riding and anxiety. "It's interesting, the different kinds of friendship. You and Luce and Nicholas and I grew up together. We know most of each other's darkest secrets. I would trust any of you with anything.

But Stephen—he's my brother. We're connected by blood and childhood memories and temperament. Sometimes that's uncomfortable. For many years we were estranged. But when he is gone, he'll leave a hole in my life that no one else can ever fill. I . . . I need to tell him that."

"I've always regretted being an only child," Rafe said. "I don't know if what you're saying makes me relieved that my life was simpler, or even more regretful for what I've missed."

Michael hesitated, then said slowly, "Like all kinds of caring, it's better to love and lose than never to love at all. But losing someone you care about is the very devil."

And losing his brother, a vigorous man only two years older than he, brought death very close. Not the swift, random death of battle that Michael had faced so many times, but an insidious, more personal demise. If Stephen could succumb to a mortal disease, so could Michael. So could Catherine or their young son Nicholas, and that knowledge was almost unendurable.

Neither of them spoke again until the assistant steward arrived. Michael turned from the window to see a compact young man with red hair.

Looking a little nervous, the steward said, "You sent for me, Your Grace?"

Rafe nodded. "Gardiner, this is Lord Michael Kenyon, the Duke of Ashburton's brother. He wants to know what commissions you executed for Ashburton in London."

"Well, I took his horse to town and left it at Ashburton House," Gardiner replied. "The housekeeper put together a bundle of his clothing for me to bring

back, and I went to his bankers to cash a draft, and to
Doctors' Commons for the special license."

There was a stunned silence. Then Michael said
incredulously, "Damnation. He sent you for a *marriage*
license?"

"Yes, sir." The steward instinctively retreated a step
when he saw Michael's expression. "That was the main
reason for the trip. The other commissions were merely
because I was going to be in London."

Since Michael was teetering on the verge of explo-
sion, Rafe intervened. "Do you remember the name of
the woman he intended to wed?"

Gardiner's expression clouded. "I'm sorry, sir. I
simply gave the clerk the paper that Ashburton had
written out. I suppose I glanced at it, but I don't
remember the lady's name." He thought, then said
helpfully, "He didn't say it in so many words, but I got
the impression he was going to marry one of the girls
from the Fitzgerald Theater Troupe."

"An actress," Michael spat out. "And you didn't
think twice about that?"

The steward's face pokered up. "It's not my place to
question a duke, my lord."

Rafe gave Michael a swift glance. "If you have no
other information, you're excused, Gardiner. Thank
you."

As soon as the door closed behind the steward,
Michael swore, "My God, if only I'd found Stephen in
time! His mind must be affected by his illness, or he
would never even consider making some round-heeled
doxy the Duchess of Ashburton."

"The fact that he got a license doesn't automatically
mean that there has been a wedding," Rafe pointed out.
"Besides which, if he was hell-bent on marriage, you
couldn't have stopped him."

"I could have tried," Michael said grimly.

Rafe sighed. "The woman isn't necessarily a doxy. Fitzgerald is a very decent sort of fellow, a gentleman by birth. He and his wife run a respectable troupe, as these things go."

" 'As these things go,' " Michael said, his voice caustic. "I don't need Stephen's personal fortune myself, but I'll be damned if I'll stand by and watch while an opportunistic harpy takes advantage of his vulnerability to get her hands on his money."

"Perhaps he fell in love with the woman."

Michael gave an eloquent snort.

"Cynic," Rafe said equably. "Even if it isn't love, if she's making his last days happier, do you have the right to interfere?"

Michael's face tightened. "Stephen is a man of refined tastes. His first wife was a model of propriety. I have trouble believing that a vulgar lightskirt who wants to feather her nest will gladden his final days."

"Ah, yes, his first wife. Do you resent the thought of her being succeeded by a commoner because you were fond of her?"

Michael hesitated. "Because of my years in the army, I never knew Louisa well. She was very lovely. Impeccable manners. She . . . she did beautiful needlework."

Rafe's brows arched. "Did she make her husband happy?"

"I don't know," Michael admitted. "They were very . . . courteous with each other."

"Not exactly the portrait of a dynamic marriage," Rafe said dryly. "In my experience, one can generally tell if a husband and wife truly care for each other, no matter how proper they are in public. If you never saw such a bond between your brother and his late duchess, he might have been merely making the best of an arranged marriage while at heart he preferred a very different kind of woman."

"But an actress with a fourth-rate theater troupe?" Michael protested.

"I married a spy, Nicholas a Methodist school-teacher, Lucien a thief who also had a promising career as a stage comedienne, and you a deceitful widow," Rafe pointed out, his gray eyes gleaming with amusement. "Why shouldn't Stephen marry an actress?"

Knowing that he was being baited, Michael clamped down on his instinctive flash of anger. "That is not a fair description of Catherine or the others. They may be unconventional, but all are ladies."

"Perhaps Stephen's intended wife is, too."

Michael sighed and ran his fingers through his hair. "My wits are dull from travel fatigue. Perhaps you should spell out exactly what you're trying to tell me."

"I know that your protective instincts are in full cry where Stephen is concerned," Rafe said gently. "But you can't save a grown man from folly, if indeed he is being foolish. If you find your brother and go roaring in like the cavalry, accusing his new wife of being a mercenary slut, it could be disastrous. As a gentleman, Ashburton is bound to defend his wife, even to you. If he truly cares for her, your intemperance could cause another estrangement, and there might not be time enough to overcome it before his death. If that were to happen, I doubt you would ever forgive yourself."

The words struck Michael with the force of a hammer. "Lord, I never learn, do I?" he said ruefully. "How many times over the years have you given me good advice?"

"Occasions beyond number."

"How often have I listened?"

Rafe considered. "Perhaps half the time."

"Add today to the 'listened' side of the scales." Michael stared out the window again. The rain had brought an early nightfall. "If and when I meet the new duchess, I shall accord her all due courtesy, whether she deserves it or not." He smiled faintly. "But please—remember that an old infantry officer would never rush in like the cavalry."

Rafe laughed. "I'll bear that in mind the next time you need to be restrained."

And there would be a next time; Michael knew himself and his temper well enough to be sure of that. But thanks to Rafe, he would proceed with more caution. He'd find the Fitzgerald troupe and discover if a marriage had taken place, and if so, who the new duchess was.

And when he eventually found the missing duke, he would remember that what mattered was Stephen, and his wishes for what might be the end of his life. If that meant Michael had to be polite to his brother's doxy, so be it.

CHAPTER 22

Rosalind peered out the carriage window at the teeming streets. "I haven't been in London since I was a child. I thought my memories were exaggerated, but they weren't. The city is even bigger and busier than I remember."

Stephen smiled. "It's impossible to exaggerate London."

"Or the city's smell." She wrinkled her nose, hoping that Mayfair would be less noisome. Then she settled back in her seat, taking his hand again. She had an absurd desire to touch him whenever possible, as if that would keep him by her side forever. Luckily he seemed to enjoy touching as much as she did.

Despite the variable autumn weather, they'd had a wonderful honeymoon. Days of laughter had been followed by nights of stunning passion. Perhaps the poignance of knowing that their time together was limited was responsible for the special intensity. She cried, sometimes, at the knowledge of how quickly the sands were running out. But never in front of Stephen.

He had stoically suffered several more attacks, though none as severe as the first two she had witnessed. For much of the time, it had been possible to pretend that all was well, though after their wedding night there had always been a slight, unbridgeable emotional distance between them.

Such things were never mentioned. Instead, they'd walked the ancient walls of York and visited glorious York Minster, one of the grandest cathedrals in Britain. The Lake District had been as spectacular as its reputation, a fairyland of rugged hills and tranquil bodies of water. They'd hired a boatman to take them out on Windermere, sliding across the glassy surface into the silent mists. Stephen was a marvelous companion. He had the intense interest in the world that Rosalind had seen in young children. Only in his case, he was seeing things for the last time, not the first. He seemed glad to have someone to share his discoveries. She was glad simply to be with him.

The carriage rumbled to a stop. Portia, who had been standing on a door handle with her paws on the window, lost her balance and tumbled to the floor, landing on her feet with a burst of feline acrobatics. She'd grown noticeably in the last fortnight and had adapted to travel with surprising ease.

Stephen expertly caught the kitten, gave her an affectionate pet, and returned her to her box. "Grosvenor Square. We've arrived."

The coachman opened the door, and Stephen helped Rosalind from the muddy vehicle. In the twilight Ashburton House seemed enormous. She mentally girded herself. On their honeymoon they had traveled as Mr. and Mrs. Kenyon. They had been treated with the politeness due a gentleman and his wife, but no special notice had been taken of them. That had suited Rosalind very well. But now they were in London. Stephen was the Duke of Ashburton again, and she felt like a very inadequate duchess.

She put a smile on her face. "The house is very grand."

"Rather oppressively so." Stephen took Portia's box in one hand and Rosalind's arm in the other, and they climbed the broad stairs. "It will be pleasant to be in one place for several nights in a row, but I look forward to returning to the abbey as soon as my business is finished."

He wanted to die at Ashburton Abbey. He had told her that when they were looking at the royal tombs in York Minster.

Stephen's knock was answered eventually by a liveried footman whose face froze when he saw who was on the doorstep. "Your Grace! W-we were not expecting you."

"I know. We shall be here for at least a fortnight,

Milton. Put the knocker up and recall those servants who are on board wages. We shall want a light supper and hot water for bathing as soon as possible." Stephen drew Rosalind forward. "The new Duchess of Ashburton. Obey her in all things."

Then he handed the footman Portia's box. "The duchess's kitten. Please take her up to the state apartments."

Milton almost dropped the box when Portia gave a raucous cry of irritation. Then he darted away to obey, holding the box with great care. Stephen turned and swept Rosalind into his arms. "It's time to cross my second threshold."

She laughed as he carried her inside. "Three more thresholds to go, since I've decided to pass on the hunting box."

"Wise choice." He set her down on the gleaming marble floor and kissed her until her knees were weak. Then he lifted his head and gave her an intimate smile. "Welcome to Ashburton House, Duchess."

She experienced one of her periodic flashes of disbelief that a man so alive could be dying. Instantly she suppressed the thought, for she'd learned that it could quickly bring her to the verge of tears. That would not do when she was with Stephen.

He guided her toward the stairs. "If Edmund Kean is playing at Drury Lane tomorrow night, would you like to see him?"

"That would be wonderful!" She kept her expression bright. But when she surveyed the gilded grandeur around her, she uttered a mental prayer that they would soon go to the abbey. A mansion like this was no place for a provincial actress to make a long run in the role of duchess.

Day Thirty-nine

The first morning in London, Stephen awoke to the sound of autumn rain beating steadily on the bedroom windows. Not that he minded, since Rosalind was curled against him, her back against his chest. He lay still, content to savor her soft warmth and delightfully bare skin. He treasured such moments as much as the mind-destroying passion that they'd shared in the dark of the night. Since they slept together as closely as two spoons, they had soon learned that they had no need of nightclothes for warmth.

He stroked her hair, awed once again that he had found her. Her sunny nature had made the last weeks the happiest of his life. She could not have been more different from his first wife. Not once had he and Louisa shared a bed for an entire night. He thought of his first marriage with regret and some guilt. If he'd tried harder, might he have found hidden passion under Louisa's proper facade? Might a different man have been able to make her happy as he could not? He would never know.

Putting the thought of Louisa aside, he kissed the top of Rosalind's head. Because of his station in life, he'd been raised with a French nurse and spoke the language as fluently as he did English. Perhaps it was the nature of French to be a more emotional tongue, for he found it easier to speak endearments in that language. *"My sweet duchess,"* he whispered. *"You enchant me."*

Her eyelashes fluttered. *"You are my dearest one,"* she murmured in impeccable French.

He came alert and spoke to her in French again. Once more she replied in the same tongue. They exchanged several more sentences before her eyes opened. She gave him a smile of sleepy charm. "Good morning," she said in English.

"Good morning." He twined a lock of her hair around his fingertip. "I didn't know you spoke French."

She laughed. "That's because I don't. Having been raised as a gentleman, Papa does, but we were taught only a few phrases needed in plays."

Thinking that she'd shown a greater command of the language than that, he repeated one of the sentences he'd used earlier.

Her brows drew together. "What does that mean? I feel that I should understand, but I don't quite."

"You answered the same words a minute ago when you were three-quarters asleep." He traced the rim of her ear with his tongue. "Could you be French by birth?"

She considered, then shook her head. "I doubt it. Maria said that I spoke good English when she and Thomas adopted me."

"If you were really appallingly well bred, like me, you might have been taught French in the nursery," he suggested. The topic was interesting but of only theoretical relevance since they were unlikely to learn her true parentage. There was nothing theoretical about her lovely body, though, or his own response to it. He slid his hand under the blanket and began to make circling motions on her midriff with his palm. "I think the reason that marriage is so popular is because it combines a maximum of temptation with a maximum of opportunity."

She laughed and rolled onto her back, her hands also beginning to explore. "I believe you've just codified an important principle. Let's call it Ashburton's Axiom."

He pulled the blanket down and bent to kiss her breast. She sighed rapturously, then gave a small squeak when he tugged her nipple with his lips.

He stopped immediately. "Sorry. I didn't mean to be rough."

"You weren't," she assured him. "I guess I'm just unusually sensitive this morning." She gave him a wicked smile. "Perhaps you're wearing out some of your favorite bits of my anatomy."

"What a terrible thought." He mentally totaled the number of times he'd made love to her since their wedding, then started to move away. "Perhaps I'd better give you a chance to recuperate."

"Don't you dare!" Her hand slid down him until she found what she sought. "That was a joke, my dear. Practice is making me marvelously fit."

He gasped as she slowly caressed him. "My honorable intentions have just gone to hell, Lady Caliban."

Nonetheless, when he began trailing kisses across her belly, he murmured, "Let me know if anything else is in danger of wearing out."

Judging by her quickening breath, his favorite bits were all in good working order. When she began writhing under the stroke of his tongue, he moved between her thighs to welcome the morning in the best possible way.

His last clear thought before he surrendered to passion was that he had been right: marriage was blessed with maximum temptation, and maximum opportunity.

After they made love, Rosalind slept again, coming awake when Stephen kissed her ear. "Sorry, my dear," he murmured. "I must visit my solicitor this morning."

It would be almost the first time he'd been out of her sight since their wedding. She did not consider this an improvement. Still, all honeymoons must end eventually. She covered a yawn. "I may just go back to sleep. It's a very gray morning."

"As long as you're awake for our visit to Drury Lane tonight." He brushed her cheek with the back of his hand, then went into his dressing room.

She dozed and awoke an hour later, feeling groggy. Though being a strolling player had accustomed her to constant travel, she and Stephen had journeyed at much greater speeds and covered far more ground. That must be why she'd felt so tired for the last few days. Yawning, she swung her legs from the bed and started to rise, then sat down again abruptly when a wave of dizziness swept over her.

Her light-headedness soon passed. She stood, this time more slowly, hoping that she wasn't sickening with an autumn cold. She didn't want to waste any precious time with illness. She donned her dressing gown and rang for hot water. A day of pampering should cure what ailed her, for she'd always enjoyed an unladylike robustness of health.

During her bath she noticed again the unusual sensitivity of her breasts. She had to dry them with care after she emerged from the hip bath. Perhaps her courses were about to start. How long had it been since the last time?

The answer struck her like a thunderbolt. Her courses had always been as regular as clockwork, beginning every fourth Friday in the afternoon.

She was a week overdue.

Almost unbearable excitement surged through her. She clamped down on her reaction and tried to be logical. Early in her first marriage, she'd made Maria tell her all the early signs of pregnancy so that she would recognize them as soon as possible. She'd watched for those signs through the three years of her marriage with decreasing hope.

But now she was married to a different man. She dropped her towel and went to the pier glass to study her nude body. Maria had said that changes in the breasts were almost immediate. Were hers larger? Perhaps there was extra fullness, and certainly they were more sensitive than they'd ever been before.

What were some of the other signs? Maria had also mentioned acute sensitivity to smells. Rosalind had noticed that the day before but thought she was merely reacting to London's aggressive odors. Fatigue? Definitely unusual fatigue. And she'd been light-headed, which was almost unheard of for her.

She stared at the image in the mirror, and suddenly she knew. *She knew.* She and Stephen, each of them sure they would never know the joy of having a child, had made a baby together in that loft full of sunshine and kittens.

Stunned by the knowledge, she wrapped her dressing gown around her and sank onto the brocade sofa where Portia was sleeping. The kitten jumped into her lap and scrambled up to her shoulder. Rosalind automatically stroked the silky fur. She'd felt, quite literally, like a different woman since that day in the loft, but thought the cause was love and marriage. Instead there was another, deeper reason. She wanted to throw open the window and exuberantly shout the good tidings to all of London. When Stephen returned home . . .

The thought sobered her. It was far too soon to tell her husband. A physician would probably laugh if she described her subtle symptoms and her intuitive conviction that a new life was growing inside her. And maybe he'd be right to do so.

Dispassionately she made herself consider the possibility that her yearning for a baby had affected her judgment. She truly didn't think so, but if she announced that she was with child and turned out to be wrong, Stephen would be devastated. She must wait.

Dreamily she leaned back on the sofa, cuddling Portia like an infant. Having given logic its due, she turned to intuition again. In her bones she felt that she was carrying a child, and that it would be born hale and hearty. For the sake of the succession, a boy would be nice, and Stephen had said his brother would be delighted at being freed of the burden of the dukedom. But a girl would be equally fine.

A shadow fell across her heart when she realized that unless a miracle took place, Stephen would not be with her to celebrate the birth of their child.

That harsh realization was followed by another. If she bore Stephen's baby, she would be unable to return to her family.

She'd married Stephen in the expectation that she would be his companion until he died, then return to her own kind. But a baby would separate her from her old life with the weight and finality of a prison door. A son would be a duke, a daughter a great heiress. As dowager Duchess of Ashburton, it would be Rosalind's duty to raise Stephen's only child in a manner befitting his or her station in life. That meant she must learn to live among his peers.

And the only chance she had of being accepted was at her husband's side. She would have to take advantage of these weeks in London to meet Stephen's friends. If she was presentable, they would probably continue to receive her for the sake of Stephen and his child, if not for her own.

Even more important, she would have to establish relationships with his family, for as the mother of a Kenyon child she would be one of them. She thought of the haughty older sister, the formidable younger brother, and almost groaned aloud. Even if they grudgingly accepted her, they would probably want her to cut all communications with her insufficiently well-bred family. Of course she would never agree to that, but there would surely be pressure.

She sighed and closed her eyes. She'd worry about that later. For now she would concentrate on establishing a toehold in London society. First some fashionable clothing, flowing garments that would tolerate an expanding waistline. Then she and Stephen must attend some of the social events of the Little Season. She'd have to charm his friends so they would not think of her as "that actress who caught Ashburton when he was dying" but as a woman genteel enough to receive in their homes. Otherwise her child would suffer.

Her hand went to her abdomen again, and a slow smile spread across her face. The future didn't look easy—but if she was right, every scrap of difficulty would be worth it.

CHAPTER 23

Stephen leaned back in his carriage with a sigh, thinking that there was nothing like spending a morning with a solicitor, amending one's last will and testament, to lower a man's mood. And there would be similar sessions in the coming days. Though the majority of the Ashburton inheritance was entailed to Michael, Stephen's considerable personal fortune must be disposed of. Dying was a complicated business.

But at least today's session was over, and Stephen could return to Rosalind and her laughter. When he was with her, he could forget fatigue and the chronic ache in his stomach. As soon as he entered Ashburton House, he handed his damp coat and hat to the footman and prepared to go in search of his wife.

Then the knocker sounded again, and the footman admitted the Countess of Herrington. Stephen mentally braced himself. He would have preferred to defer this meeting, but now he had no choice. Putting on a smile, he said, "Good day, Claudia."

She sailed by the footman, her Kenyon height and chestnut hair polished into elegant hauteur. "I was driving by and saw the knocker was up. I'm glad you've decided to come to London for the Little Season, Ashburton. You'll never find a proper wife down at the abbey."

After brushing a cool, barely perceptible kiss on his cheek, she continued, "I heard the most preposterous story from my maid this morning. She claimed she'd heard from her cousin, who is employed in one of the houses near here, that you arrived yesterday with a new wife. I told her that she'd misunderstood, of course."

Not wanting this discussion to take place in front of the footman, he took his sister's arm and guided her to the small drawing room. "You're looking very fine, Claudia. How are Andrew and the children?"

Her mouth widened in a genuine smile. "Very well, thank you. James is enjoying Cambridge. He's really quite the young scholar."

She gave him other family news while he rang for refreshments. A tray of tea and cakes was brought. When they were private again, Stephen said, "Actually, your maid's information was quite accurate. I did arrive yesterday with my new wife."

Claudia swallowed her tea the wrong way and began to cough. When she could breathe again, she exclaimed, "How extraordinary! Did you marry Chumleigh's daughter? She's the only eligible female of suitable rank within fifty miles of the abbey. A well-enough-looking girl, though I'm not overimpressed with her bloodlines."

"You've never met my wife." Stephen was about to say more when the door opened and Rosalind entered. Smiling, she crossed the room without seeing Claudia, who was seated on the other side of the door.

"Was the solicitor dreadfully boring? I can liven your afternoon if you wish," she said gaily. She raised her face and kissed him thoroughly.

Knowing the fat was in the fire, he kissed her back, then took a firm hold on her hand and turned to face Claudia. "Rosalind, we have the good fortune to receive our first visit from my sister, Lady Herrington. Claudia, my wife, Rosalind."

Claudia stared, startled to speechlessness. Pulling herself together, she said, "You must excuse me. This is quite unexpected."

Rosalind was equally surprised, but she gave a friendly smile. "It's a great pleasure to meet you."

Stephen was proud of her. Though he saw the tightening around her eyes, her manner could not be faulted.

Claudia frowned. "Your face is familiar, but I can't place it. What is your maiden name?"

Wanting to draw as much as possible of the inevitable fire on himself, Stephen said, "Fitzgerald. But Rosalind was widowed, and her married name was Jordan."

There was a moment of silence. Then Claudia shot out of her chair. "Now I know where I saw you! It was in that play at Candover's castle. You're an actress! You played a fairy in a most indecent costume."

"You have a good memory for faces, Lady Herrington," Rosalind said mildly.

Ignoring the comment, Claudia spun to face her brother. "Ashburton, how *could* you marry a common actress?" She stopped, then said almost pleadingly, "This is your idea of a joke, isn't it? She's really your mistress. You always did have a strange sense of humor. It's not at all in good taste to introduce your mistress to your sister."

Stephen took a deep breath. "I'm not joking, Claudia. Rosalind is my wife, and the Duchess of Ashburton."

After a stunned moment, Claudia's hazel eyes filled with fury. "You . . . you disgusting lecher. A gentleman beds his mistress, he doesn't marry her. Have you no sense of decency? Of propriety? What would Father say?" She cast a loathing glance over Rosalind. "It would kill him if he knew what disgrace you have brought to us!"

Rosalind's hand began to tremble within Stephen's clasp. For an instant his own temper flared to white heat. He clamped down on it, remembering that one of his goals before his death was to build a better relationship with his only sister. If he didn't restrain his tongue now, there'd be no hope of that.

"I'm sure the old duke would not have approved," he said dryly. "On the other hand, I didn't always approve of his actions, either, so that's only fair."

Claudia flushed violently. For a moment he thought she was going to hurl her reticule at him. "This is no joking matter! Merciful heaven, I've often wondered how someone with so little sense of decorum could be sired by a real man like Father. Or are you a product of one of Mother's damnable affairs?"

"Enough!" he said sharply. "I know you are shocked. If I'd had the time, I would have broken the news to you more gently. But the fact is that Rosalind is my wife, and I will not allow you to insult her."

"But you don't mind if I insult you?" Claudia asked bitterly. "You're a coward, Stephen, not worthy to carry the Ashburton name."

Rosalind gasped at the vicious comment. Afraid she would say something, Stephen tightened his grip on her hand warningly. "I'm afraid that I can't agree with your definition of worth." He softened his voice. "Claudia, all I ask is that you take the time to become acquainted with Rosalind. When you do, you will realize that she will be a credit to the name she bears." His tone became dry again. "Certainly she is more moral and ladylike than our own mother was."

"If Father were alive, he'd disown you," his sister

said in a shaking voice. "Since he is not, I must do that in his stead." She spun and headed toward the door.

Stephen's anger was tempered by pity. "Claudia, I realize that no one could ever live up to your image of the old duke, and you resent the fact that I don't even try. Nonetheless, the fact remains that I am the fifth Duke of Ashburton and head of the family. An estrangement will benefit no one, and will cause pain to those who are dearest to us. Can't you at least try to accept me and the woman I've chosen as my wife?"

His sister stopped for a moment, her face turning chalk-white. "I can't, Stephen," she whispered. "I can't." She bolted for the door, tears in her eyes.

The silence after the door slammed was deafening. Stephen drew a shaken breath. "I'm sorry you had to witness that, Rosalind."

Though she was struggling to remain calm, her voice was unsteady when she turned to him. "I knew our marriage would cause trouble, but not that it would separate you from your only sister. Oh, Stephen, I'm so sorry to be the cause of that."

He drew her into his arms, as much for his comfort as hers. "The blame belongs to Claudia, not you. She spent most of her life struggling to please a father who could not be pleased. My brother and I, in our separate ways, came to understand that nothing we did would ever be good enough. Michael became an outright rebel, while I suppose I turned quietly subversive. But poor Claudia tried desperately to be the perfect daughter."

He thought sadly of the times when they had played as children, Claudia patiently shortening her steps so that he could keep up. She had been a little mother, a role for which she had more talent than their real mother. One of the earliest memories of his childhood was her calling him to come to her for a hug. He'd always run right into her arms. "As part of her efforts, eventually she took on the worst of his prejudices."

Rosalind hid her face against his shoulder. "Will your brother react as badly?"

"No. Michael will be startled, and possibly disapproving at first. But he, at least, will take the time to know you." Stephen stroked her hair and hoped that he was correct in his analysis. "And when he does, he will understand and accept."

She lifted her head and tried to smile. "Do you know, after you left this morning, I'd quite made up my mind to go into society with you so no one will think your wife is too vulgar to be seen. But now . . ." Her voice broke for an instant. "I'm not sure if I have the courage even to suggest that."

His anger with Claudia turned into resolve. "By God, that's the answer. We'll deck you out in London finery and I'll show you off to everyone. The fashionable world will know that the Duke of Ashburton is proud of his wife." He kissed her, then looked intently into her dark eyes. "What happened with Claudia was the worst. Everything else will be easier. I swear it."

He doubted that she was convinced, but she raised her chin bravely. "I'll do my best not to disgrace you."

"You won't. Even though Claudia is carrying on as if I've committed high treason, I'm hardly the first lord to marry an actress. Elizabeth Farren was the daughter of strolling players, and she starred at both Covent Garden and Drury Lane. Now she's the Countess of Derby, and quite respectable. So you see, there are precedents for our marriage."

Rosalind smiled ruefully. "It sounds as if Miss Farren was a better actress than I. Does that make a difference in being accepted?"

"What matters is your character, not where you performed." He thought a moment. "Since the word of our marriage has gone out on the servants' network, by this time half the beau monde must know. We'll have to start showing you off tonight, at Drury Lane. We can go to a modiste this afternoon, but it will take a couple of days for her to produce any new garments, which won't help us tonight. Let's see if Catherine has left anything suitable." He took Rosalind's hand and led her from the drawing room.

"What do you mean?" she asked warily.

"Michael and his wife use this house as their own, and Catherine keeps some of her most formal clothing here, since she has little need for finery in Wales." His approving gaze went over her. "You're a bit taller, but there's a general similarity in size and shape. One of her gowns should do for you to wear to the theater tonight."

Rosalind gasped and came to a stop, literally digging in her heels. "I can't wear another woman's clothing without permission! That is guaranteed to make an enemy of your sister-in-law, and probably her husband as well."

"Catherine won't mind. Truly, she won't."

Rosalind snorted. "Only a man could say that. Jessica and I shared a room for fifteen years, and I still would hesitate to borrow anything of hers without permission."

"Catherine isn't Jessica," he said cheerfully. "Now come along and we'll see what she's left here."

Rosalind gave in and let him take her to his brother's apartments, largely because it was easier to go and hope there was nothing suitable than to argue with a man who clearly did not have a basic grasp of female nature.

Michael and Catherine's rooms were as splendid as

the ducal chambers. Rosalind entered uneasily, half expecting a man "with a thousand-yard stare," as Michael had been described, to step out and scowl at her. But the apartment was quiet, the furniture under holland covers as the rooms waited for their occupants to return. Stephen led her to a dressing room with wardrobes at both ends. He threw open the doors of one. "What do you think?"

Rosalind's eyes widened. Onstage she'd worn everything from crude rags to aristocratic discards that had been bought and altered into stage costumes. But she'd never seen such a magnificent collection of beautiful garments in one place. Shimmering silks, rich subtle velvets, cascades of intricate lace. Lady Michael had wonderful taste.

Suppressing the urge to touch the fabrics, she said, "Obviously Lady Michael has dark hair. These aren't the right colors for me."

"Her coloring is almost the reverse of yours, brunette with eyes an interesting shade of blue-green," he agreed. "But there have to be a few things that will suit you also." He surveyed the garments, then pulled out a silk evening gown in a beautiful shade of blue. "This, for example."

He draped the dress across her, then turned her to face the pier-glass mirror. She caught her breath. The man had a damnably good eye for color. The blue-green fabric looked wonderful with her fair hair and complexion. "The gown is pretty, but it might not fit," she said weakly. "There's rather a lot of me."

He grinned. "You have a gloriously feminine figure, a trait shared by Catherine. Try the gown on."

She still hesitated. "This is terribly presumptuous."

He shook his head. "Catherine was an army wife who followed the drum across Spain. She's been threatened by French soldiers, searched for the wounded on battlefields, and nursed dying men in hellish emergency hospitals. As a result, she has a firm grasp of what matters most, and it isn't clothing. She will not be disturbed to learn that you had need of one of her gowns for an evening."

Stephen's explanation was convincing in a way that his glib assurances hadn't been. Silently she turned so that he could unfasten her morning dress. He'd become very adept at taking off her clothing during their honeymoon. The thought made her smile.

And he was right about the gown, too. The simple, high-waisted style suited her very well, though it revealed a rather spectacular amount of cleavage. She glanced down at the crystal-studded bodice dubiously. "Are you sure this will convince society that I'm respectable? It's as low as anything I've ever worn onstage."

He laughed and came to stand behind her, sliding his arms around her waist. "You're the height of fashion. Men will be dazzled and women envious. All you have to do is act gracious and regal, as when you played Hippolyta."

She looked at his reflection in the mirror, his affectionate embrace and handsome face, and knew the image was one she would never forget. Every day she stored up more pictures to carry in her heart through the long years without him.

Hiding her sadness, she said lightly, "Can I carry Hippolyta's weapons to defend myself? Since she was Queen of the Amazons, I'm entitled to at least a bow and arrows."

"I have better weapons than that."

He linked his arm through hers and took her downstairs to the study. "Watch. You'll need to know how to do this."

He went to the desk and demonstrated how to open a secret drawer. Inside was a key. After showing her a second secret drawer containing another key, he removed the painting of a landscape from the wall to reveal a safe. Both keys were needed to open it. She was touched, and a little awed, at his complete trust in her.

Inside the safe was a neat stack of papers and boxes. He selected the largest box. "The most important family jewelry is at the abbey, but there are some nice pieces here."

He set the box on a table and flipped up the lid. "Your choice."

She gasped at the glittering contents and wondered if she would ever take such riches for granted. Probably not.

After careful consideration she lifted out a necklace composed of elaborate openwork medallions in the form of a gold and cloisonné floral garland. In the center of each enameled plaque was a small, brilliant diamond. The gems would complement her crystal-studded bodice, and the bluish-green enameled leaves would pick up the color of the gown. "This should do nicely." She lifted one of the matching earrings and held it to her ear as she glanced in a mirror.

He nodded. "The Hapsburg wedding collar and earrings. Very appropriate."

"Are you serious?" She stared at the earring. "This was worn by royalty?"

"Only a minor princess," he assured her. "There were a lot of Hapsburgs."

She laid the jewelry back in the box, feeling suddenly depressed. Stephen had accepted her, but he had a degree of tolerance rare in any class. Could a foundling and actress really live among people who considered Hapsburg jewels to be among the less important family possessions?

The contrast in their stations produced a sudden, terrifying thought. If she bore a child after Stephen was gone, would his sister try to take the baby away from its "unworthy" mother? Alone, Lady Herrington could probably not manage that, but with the support of Michael, she might. If the new duke did not approve of his brother's wife, Rosalind would be at the mercy of the Kenyons.

She took a deep breath, telling herself to rein in her imagination. That probably wouldn't happen. And if there were any attempts to take her baby—well, she would run away to America and support her child by whatever means available.

Stephen touched her shoulder. "You're very quiet."

A thought took form in Rosalind's mind, surprising but somehow right. For as long as she could remember, she had deliberately tried to blot out everything that had happened before the day the Fitzgeralds had found her. But if she was going to have a child, it was time to force herself to look at the past. Slowly she said, "I was thinking that I'd like to visit the waterfront someday soon."

He understood immediately. "You mean where Thomas and Maria found you?"

She nodded.

He frowned. "Five or six miles of the Thames are used for shipping. Do you have any idea where we should start to look?"

She tried to recall anything that might help. "They'd gone to visit the Tower of London, then decided to explore the area a little. To the east, I think Papa said once."

"That area is called St. Katherine's, after a religious foundation that's been there for centuries. It's a warren of crooked streets and bad housing, which fits what you said about your scavenging." He stroked her arm with one large hand. "We'll go tomorrow. What do you hope to find?"

She hesitated. "I'm not sure. My roots, I suppose."

"It doesn't matter to me who your natural parents were," he said quietly. "Any more than it mattered to Thomas and Maria."

"I know," she said in an almost inaudible voice. "But it matters to me."

She looked at the Hapsburg necklace and felt a bleak, surprising stab of sympathy for Claudia. Neither of them would ever feel that she was good enough.

CHAPTER 24

Rosalind heard the murmurs begin as soon as she and Stephen entered the boxholders' lobby at Drury Lane. As she held his arm and he greeted friends, she heard comments such as, "So there really is a new duchess," "Does anyone know who her people are?" "The wretched female; I had hopes of Ashburton," and one masculine voice murmuring, "It's not fair that dukes get the most beddable women."

Ignoring the remarks, Rosalind kept her head high and concentrated on the introductions Stephen made. To her relief, no one reacted like Lady Herrington. Everyone was polite, and most were genuinely friendly. That was because of Stephen; it was clear that he was held in high esteem and that his absence from society while mourning his first wife had been regretted.

Still, it was a relief to go up to their box. It had been a tiring day. They had spent the afternoon at the shop of London's finest modiste ordering a wardrobe fit for a duchess. Stephen had been an active participant in deciding what his wife should buy. He'd pointed out, with perfect truth, that left to her own devices she would never spend enough money to be fashionable.

When they reached the Ashburton box, she looked around eagerly. Drury Lane was the largest, most splendid theater she had ever seen. Thank heaven Stephen had persuaded her to wear Lady Michael's magnificent gown. Rosalind would have felt like a drab wren in anything from her own wardrobe. "It's beautiful. How many people does the theater hold?"

"A full house is well over three thousand. After the old theater burned down nine or ten years ago, it was rebuilt to be the largest playhouse in London."

She settled in one of the comfortable seats, spreading her skirts carefully. "I could become accustomed to such luxury."

He smiled as he sat beside her and took her hand. "Good. I want you to." His thumb provocatively stroked her gloved palm. "But my favorite theater will always be the barn in Bury St. James."

"We didn't perform there," she pointed out.

"Didn't we?"

The wicked gleam in his eyes made her blush. She lifted her fan to hide her smile and slowly wafted cool air over her heated face. Fans were convenient accessories for a woman onstage, and Rosalind was very good at using one. Elegant fanning was a vital skill when so many curious eyes were on the mysterious new duchess.

The play began, and at least some of the audience turned their attention to the stage instead of her. She leaned forward with excitement at Kean's first entrance.

He was a small man with an oversize head, but his flashing dark eyes and stage presence were riveting. Tonight he was to do *Othello*, one of his most famous roles. He played the tragic, jealousy-ridden Moor with murderous intensity. Rosalind was so caught up by the performance that she forgot everything else, until Stephen's hand clenched convulsively on hers.

She turned and saw that his eyes were squeezed shut and his body rigid with pain. "Stephen!" she whispered with alarm.

She started to rise, but his grip on her hand tightened and he gave an infinitesimal shake of his head. Of course he would despise having his weakness made public, and the theater was so well lit that any unusual activity would draw unwelcome attention.

She forced herself to turn her gaze to the stage again, though she continued to watch him from the corner of her eye. Perspiration glazed his face, and his hand became chilly. Her whole awareness was attuned to him, to the point where his every labored breath resonated through her and she heard none of Kean's thundering words.

Acutely aware that this attack was lasting longer than previous ones she had witnessed, she said urgently, "We should leave. Let me call a porter to help you."

His eyes opened, flashing with real anger. *"No."*

Reluctantly she obeyed, her sightless gaze going back to the stage. Gradually Stephen's grip on her hand relaxed. It happened none too soon. The first interval had arrived, and with it a knock on the door of the Ashburton box. She gave her husband an agonized glance. "Stephen . . . ?"

He opened his eyes, and she saw the flat gray color of pain. "I'm fine." After a visible effort to collect himself, he raised his voice. "Come in."

Rosalind released his hand and swiftly changed chairs so that she was between Stephen and the door. That way visitors wouldn't see him quite so clearly.

She wanted to shriek at everyone to leave. Instead, she smiled and acknowledged introductions, deliberately drawing most of the attention to herself. She was not beautiful, but she knew enough of acting to give the illusion of vivacious beauty.

As she played the belle, Stephen slipped into the role of fond, indulgent husband, saying little and not moving from his chair. For someone watching as closely as she, it was obvious that he was not well, but no one else seemed to notice.

It was a relief when the next act began. Several people lingered, as if hoping to be invited to stay, but she gave them Maria's most aristocratic glance and they left.

As the next act began, Stephen said with humor lacing his strained voice, "You're taking to this duchess business with remarkable speed."

She took his hand again. "I will play whatever role you wish of me."

"The only role I want is that of wife," he said softly.

She smiled and lifted his hand to her cheek. "That is not a role, but the reality."

The rest of *Othello* passed without incident. She managed to persuade Stephen to leave before the farce began, but only by claiming she was tired, which was true. Even though her husband was gray with fatigue, he would not have left for his own sake.

On the ride home, he asked, "What did you think of Edmund Kean?"

"He's a very powerful actor. I can see why he's

earned such a reputation." She hesitated. "No doubt it's daughterly prejudice, but I think that Papa is his equal."

"I agree." He took her hand. "You were a great success. I trust that allays your fears of how society will see you?"

"Most of them." She returned the squeeze of his hand. "As long as you're with me, I'm safe. Everyone likes you."

"I haven't been duke long enough to make many enemies," he said dismissively.

She noticed, not for the first time, how he brushed off compliments. Perhaps that was because he, too, had been raised to believe that he could never be good enough.

They made the rest of the trip in silence and retired as soon as they reached Ashburton House. For the first time since their marriage, they did not go to bed and make love. Instead, Stephen fell asleep in her arms, his head on her breast.

Tenderly she stroked his back and shoulders. The role of wife had dimensions she had not expected. She must be not only his lover and friend and companion but his conspirator, for she was not the only one with something to prove.

Though she could not save his life, she made a vow to do everything within her power to help him save his pride.

Day Thirty-eight

The next day dawned with a pale autumn sun. Since their destination was miles to the east, Stephen had hired a six-oared wherry, one of the long rowboats that carried passengers along the river. Not only would a boat be smoother than a carriage but faster.

He also took some precautions because the neighborhood they were going to visit was not a particularly safe one. One of the precautions was asking two of his footmen, both veterans of the late war who had served under his brother, to accompany them in normal clothing instead of their usual aristocratic livery. It was all very well to risk his own rather worthless life, but it wouldn't do for Rosalind to be endangered.

Rosalind was enthralled by the trip, studying the sculls, lighters, and barges that glided over the water in all directions. "I had no idea the river was so busy,"

"London would not exist without the river. If you think it's busy here, wait until we get below London Bridge, into the Pool of London. That's where the great seagoing ships are moored. Since you were found in that area, you probably came to London on either a coastal or cross-channel vessel."

She nodded, her gaze going up to Blackfriars Bridge as the wherry shot through one of the arches. Stephen studied her rapt profile, enjoying her pleasure in new sights. He wondered if she would remarry among the nobility. She had entranced every man she'd met the night before at the theater. Granted, high sticklers would not approve of her actress past, but soon she would be a rich and lovely widow. She could have almost any man she wanted.

He considered who might be good enough for her, then decided that he was not ready for such an exercise in self-torture. He'd ask his brother to look out for her and keep the fortune hunters away.

The Pool of London was jammed with sailing ships at anchor and the swarming lighters that carried the cargo to the quays. The wherry slowed as the oarsmen chose their route carefully. Soon they passed the massive, forbidding walls of the Tower of London.

Stephen told the boatmen to moor at the first set of water stairs to the east of the Tower. That would put them in the St. Katherine's area. If Rosalind remembered correctly, the Fitzgeralds had found her there. After giving his footmen orders to follow at a distance, he helped his wife from the boat.

She stepped onto the dank stone water stairs, then swayed, her face pale. "That smell!" she exclaimed. "I've never forgotten that. We must be close."

The odor was a distinctive combination of the filth of crowded humanity combined with the stench of rotting fish on the mudflats, the tang of hops, and a faint, exotic trace of cargoes from foreign lands. Interesting, but hardly pleasant.

He frowned at her pallor. "Are you sure this is a good idea?"

She took a firm grip on his arm. "No. But I want to do it anyhow."

They climbed the steps to the bank and chose one of the narrow streets at random. The dilapidated houses on each side were darkened by coal smoke and age. After they had walked two blocks, he asked, "Do you recognize anything?"

She looked around, pulling her cloak more closely even though the morning was not cold. "No, but the look is right. There was a church, and a brewery."

"St. Katherine's church is nearby, and there is certainly a brewery—I can smell the hops now." He guided her around a pile of unidentifiable trash. "There's talk of tearing down the whole neighborhood to build another enclosed dock like the ones used by the East India Company. None of this would be much of a loss."

They went deeper into the maze of filthy streets. Rosalind scanned the neighborhood with restless eyes. "It's quieter than I remember."

"I thought it best to come early in the day." He caught a quick, furtive movement from the corner of his eye. A rat. "Those who have jobs are at work, and with luck the ungodly aren't up yet."

She smiled, but it didn't reach her eyes. Stephen had the incongruous thought that she was like a flower growing in a byre.

A filthy, ragged man was coming toward them, his ferretlike gaze curious. Even though Stephen and his wife wore their plainest clothing, they stood out in such mean streets. The man studied Rosalind with insulting thoroughness as he passed.

Her fingers clamped on Stephen's arm. "That man . . ." Her words caught.

"Do you know him?" He looked over his shoulder, but the man was already gone.

"No, he wouldn't be old enough. B-but he reminded me of someone from then." She wiped the back of her hand across her mouth.

Grimly preparing for the worst, Stephen asked, "Did that other man hurt you?"

"He . . . he offered me something to eat," she said haltingly. "A sausage, I think. I didn't like the way he looked at me, but I was so hungry I took the food. He caught me, and, oh, God, he kissed me and . . . and put his hand under my skirt. He stank, and his tongue . . . I thought he was trying to eat me." She wiped her mouth again, hand shaking.

Feeling homicidal, Stephen said, "He molested you?"

"Only to a point. I bit his tongue until it bled, then ran away when he screamed and dropped me." She made an effort to collect herself. "I managed to keep the sausage. As I recall, I hid in a mound of trash and ate it there."

Stephen felt a terrible combination of helplessness and rage as what she had endured came to vivid, horrifying life. "How did you survive? Where did you sleep?"

She began walking again, her steps quick and tense. "There are plenty of small corners that a child can squeeze into. Of course, other things hide there." She tugged her left sleeve up, revealing a small, almost invisible scar under the elbow. "That's from a rat bite."

He wanted to take her in his arms and carry her away from this place, back to the wherry and the safety of Mayfair. But she wanted this, so he controlled himself. "Does anything bring back memories of your life before you were orphaned?"

"The boat that brought me to London," she said slowly. "It was a rough voyage." She paused, then said with surprise, "We sailed from a place where they spoke French, and I understood it. At least, I understood as much as a child that age understands anything."

"With whom were you traveling?"

"A woman." Rosalind came to a halt, her eyes unfocused. "I wasn't sick, but she was. I remember bringing her something to eat. She groaned and told me to go away. I couldn't understand why she was so unwell."

"Was the woman your mother?"

"No!" Rosalind said sharply. "Not my mother."

He wondered what caused her vehement denial. But now was not the time or place to probe more deeply. He tucked her arm in his and started walking again, turning a corner into another street. As Rosalind had said, it was quiet. Several times he sensed someone watching from a grimy window, but the few people they passed on the streets regarded them with indifference.

As he warily avoided a thin, slinking dog, he said, "Now that I see the place, it's easier to understand why no one bothered to help an orphaned child."

She smiled bleakly. "How much I owe the Fitzgeralds. I trusted Maria immediately. I . . . I think she reminded me of my mother. When she picked me up and asked me if I wanted a new mama and papa, I remember very clearly vowing to myself that I'd never, ever cause her any trouble."

"And you didn't. Thomas said that you were the perfect child." Stephen smiled a little. "Unnaturally so."

"I was afraid that if I was bad, they'd bring me back here." She nervously brushed her hair away from her face. "Nonsense, of course, but I could never put the idea entirely out of my mind."

Stephen's stomach clenched with pain at the thought of the terror Rosalind must have lived with for years after her adoption. "No wonder you were unnaturally good."

They turned another corner. In the middle of the block, an ancient woman sat on the steps of a decaying house, a clay pipe clamped between her gums. Rosalind gasped. "I recognize her! Or at least, there was a woman who would sit outside like that every day. Old Molly. I . . . I think that she was married to a sailor, so she spent much of the time when he was at sea watching what happened in the neighborhood."

"Could this be the same woman?" Stephen asked.

Rosalind bit her lower lip as she thought. "Molly seemed very old then, but her hair was dark. This woman looks just the same, except that her hair is white and she has more wrinkles. I think it really is her." Rosalind scanned the dingy buildings. "Because this is the street where she lived. I remember the odd shape of those building facades."

"The style is Dutch." Stephen tried to imagine how the street had appeared to a small, frightened child. It wasn't a happy thought. "Is there any particular reason why you remember her after so many years?"

Rosalind nodded. "Thomas and Maria found me right here, and Molly was watching when it happened."

"Then let's see if she remembers that day, too." Keeping a steady hand on Rosalind's elbow, Stephen approached the old woman. She drew in on herself but didn't attempt to flee. Her face was so lined and weathered that she might well have spent a good part of the last few decades sitting outdoors.

"Good day," he said politely. "My wife would like to ask you a question."

The old woman removed her clay pipe. "Aye?"

"A long time ago—twenty-four years—there was an orphaned child in this neighborhood who lived by scavenging scraps," Rosalind said. "Do you remember that?"

The old woman shrugged. "Lots of orphans."

"This one was a very small girl."

The old woman drew on her unlit pipe reflectively. "Oh, aye, her. Not many little girls on the streets. They worth more in a whorehouse. Dark-haired man and woman took 'er. Didn't look like whoremongers, though mebbe they were." She looked up at Rosalind, and her gaze narrowed. "Be you that girl? Not be many with blond hair and brown eyes."

Rosalind nodded.

The old woman's gaze went to Stephen. "If this be your husband, you done well for yourself, girl."

"Believe me, I'm very aware of that," Rosalind

agreed. "You were good to me, too. You gave me bread once."

"Not *give*." The crone cackled. "Old Molly don't give food away for nothin'."

"That's right, I traded you something," Rosalind said slowly. "But I can't remember what I had to trade."

"Handkerchief," Molly announced. "Fine stuff, pretty stitching. Kept it for a long time, then sold it for two shillings."

Rosalind caught her breath, her eyes widening. "A handkerchief. Can you remember what it looked like?"

Molly screwed her face up. "Flowers. Some kind of animal, and a letter. *M*, it was, like my name." She cackled. "Almost kept it 'cause of that."

Rosalind said tensely, "Stephen, do you have paper and a pencil?"

He produced a pencil and a folded letter. Rosalind swiftly sketched a small square with a stylized lion in one corner and an elaborate initial *M* in the other, with a scattering of flowers around both. Showing the drawing to Molly, she asked, "Did the embroidery look like this?"

The old woman squinted at the sketch. "Aye, that's it. 'Twas yours, then."

Stephen took Rosalind's free hand. It was trembling. To Molly he said, "Do you remember anything else about how my wife came to be on the streets?"

Molly shrugged. " 'Twas said a wherry brought 'er and an old woman from a sailin' ship. Woman had some sort of fit soon as she stepped onto the quay. As she was dyin', a guard tried to catch the girl and she run off. So 'twas said."

An old woman. That confirmed Rosalind's belief that she hadn't been traveling with her mother. "How long was my wife on the streets before she was adopted?"

"Two months mebbe. Don't remember."

So Rosalind had spent perhaps eight or nine weeks living in filth, dodging rats and perverts, scrounging food scraps whenever possible. Sixty days, maybe more. The thought made him almost physically ill and redoubled his resolve to do something for Thomas and Maria. He inclined his head to Molly. "Thank you, madame."

She gave him a toothless smile. "A fine gent like you must have somethin' for old Molly's help."

He pulled a gold coin from his pocket—a year's salary for a housemaid—and gave it to the old woman. Cackling gleefully, she went inside with her gold before he could change his mind and take it back.

Stephen examined Rosalind's sketch. "This lion looks like it might be from a coat of arms. Do you remember anything more about it?"

Rosalind shook her head. "The image just jumped into my mind."

He traced the elaborate initial. "I wonder if your real name begins with *M*. Mary? Margaret?"

Rosalind gasped and backed away from him, her face going dead white. "Oh, God. This was a mistake. I shouldn't have come here."

Wondering what dark memories had been stirred by his words, Stephen put his arm around her shoulders. "We'll go home now," he said soothingly. "It's all right, Rosalind. Whatever happened then, it's all right now."

She looked up at him with dazed eyes. "It will never be all right again." And she spoke in French.

He'd been a damned fool to agree to bring her here. Taking Rosalind's arm, he turned back toward the waterfront. "We'll be on the river soon, and then home. You don't ever have to come back here, little rose. Never again."

She walked blindly, stumbling sometimes on the rough ground. His concentration on her made him less watchful. Then they turned a corner and almost walked into a burly man with a wickedly gleaming knife held low and menacing in one hand.

"Give me the gold, guv," the thief said menacingly. He was tall and flabby and stank of whiskey. "I saw you give some to old Molly, but I bet there's plenty more for me." His mouth stretched in a gap-toothed smile. "Be quick about it, and I won't cut you or the lady." But his gaze went to Rosalind and lingered speculatively.

She shrank back against Stephen and gasped, "No. *No.*"

The rage that had been building since they'd stepped ashore exploded into swift, lethal violence. Stephen kicked the hand holding the knife, sending it spinning through the air. Then he moved in with a hard right fist that knocked the man to the ground.

The thief bellowed an obscenity. Stephen whipped out his pocket pistol, cocked it, and aimed it between the man's eyes. His finger was squeezing the trigger when he saw the terror in the bloodshot eyes. Poor bloody bastard.

Reminding himself that if one goes into a snake pit, one should not be surprised to find snakes, he eased off on the trigger. "Find an honest line of work," he said icily.

His two footmen, who had been told to stay well behind, came around the corner. Seeing trouble, they barrelled down the street to Stephen's side. "Your Grace, are you and the duchess all right?" the taller one exclaimed, his face ashen.

"No harm done. But take this fellow's knife." Stephen flicked the barrel of the pistol toward the fallen weapon. "A defanged serpent can't cause much damage."

He uncocked the pistol and put it back under his coat, then turned to Rosalind. Drawing her into his arms again, he said, "Shall we leave this place to the rats?"

She didn't reply at first. Her whole body was trembling, and she seemed almost fragile despite her height. He stroked her silky hair and murmured soothing words, feeling a confusing blend of protectiveness and desire.

Then she looked up, and her face was eerily serene. "You keep showing unexpected new talents, Stephen. If you had been the younger son who went into the army, you'd have made a good job of it."

He realized that he was witnessing an almost supernatural ability to detach from fear and distress. That must be how she had managed to survive the horrors she had suffered. Releasing her from his embrace, he said, "It never hurts for a man to know how to defend himself."

He kept his arm around her shoulders as they returned to the water stairs and the waiting wherry. The footmen stayed much closer this time.

But though they could leave the filthy neighborhood, Stephen doubted that the dark memories aroused in Rosalind would be put so easily to rest.

CHAPTER 25

For the first part of the ride back, Rosalind drifted in the mental place where she'd learned to hide when she was a small child. Her mind was full of light, obscuring the terrifying world. Nothing could hurt her there. Gradually she emerged, remembering what had happened but safely separated from the crippling emotions she had experienced.

When she realized that Stephen was watching her with sharp concern, she smiled and took his hand. "Tell me about the ships moored over there by the Customs House."

He relaxed and began a running commentary on the sights. After the wherry had picked its way through the heaviest concentration of lighters and barges, he said, "If you're not too tired, there's a place I'd like to show you near Covent Garden."

Welcoming a distraction, she assured him, "I'm not tired."

Stephen should be, perhaps, but he looked fine. Vanquishing villains seemed to agree with him. They disembarked by the new Waterloo Bridge, with Stephen sending his servants the rest of the way in the wherry. Then he hailed a hackney cab, and they set off for Covent Garden.

Just past the bustling market, Stephen signaled for the hackney to stop and paid the driver to wait for them. Rosalind stepped from the cab and found herself in front of a small playhouse. "The Athenaeum Theater? I've never heard of it."

"It's been closed for years. I thought you might like to see the place because of its historical interest. It's the last remaining example of the London playhouses that were built after Charles II was restored to the throne and lifted the Puritan ban on theaters. The others have burned or been torn down and replaced." Stephen went to a small door at the right of the main entrance and knocked hard.

While they waited for a response, a flower girl from the market came by carrying a basket heaped with warm-toned autumn blossoms. Sizing up Stephen with a glance, she said, "Flowers for the lovely lady, sir?" She held out a nosegay temptingly.

She'd chosen her mark well. Stephen paid a generous price for the flowers, then presented them to Rosalind with a smile. "No roses here, I'm afraid."

"A world with only roses would be less interesting." She buried her nose in the autumn blossoms. "Thank you, Stephen. You take such good care of me."

His mouth twisted. "If that were true, I'd never have taken you to that slum."

She shivered as something dark and menacing stirred under her carefully constructed calm. Nonetheless, she shook her head. "It was good that I went." Her mouth curved into a rueful smile. "But like so many things that are good for us, it was not a pleasant experience."

The theater door opened then, revealing an elderly man with a piece of cheese in his hand and a sad-eyed hound by his side. "Yes?"

"I'm Ashburton," Stephen said. "Sorry to disturb your luncheon. If you're Mr. Farley, the caretaker, you should have been informed that I would call soon."

"Oh. Aye." Farley stepped aside so Stephen and Rosalind could enter the shabby lobby. Stephen waited gravely for the hound to give him a sniff of approval before asking, "Do you mind if we explore on our own?"

"Suit yourself, sir. I'll be back in the greenroom." Farley took a bite of cheese and headed down the side corridor, the dog ambling lazily by his side.

Rosalind went through the lobby doors into the auditorium. It was dimly lit from clerestory windows high above. "What a nice theater," she said, running an experienced eye over the stage and seating. "Large enough for a good-size audience, but small enough so that an actor can be subtle instead of having to shout. Not at all like Drury Lane, which is beautiful but makes most barns look cozy."

"Because the Athenaeum wasn't a royal patent house, it's had a checkered past. Many managers and different kinds of entertainment." Stephen strolled down the left aisle past the rows of backless benches. "Lack of prosperity saved it from being rebuilt into a huge playhouse like Covent Garden or Drury Lane. I always liked coming to performances here, and was sorry when it closed."

She sneezed as she followed him. "It's in dire need of refurbishing."

"Very true." He reached the orchestra pit. Against the wall a narrow set of stairs went up to the stage. Turning, he extended one hand. "Hippolyta, will you join me?"

Life had been much simpler when he was Mr. Ashe and she a strolling player. Wanting to return to that, if only for a few minutes, she flipped her cloak back like a royal cape, donned the character of Queen of the Amazons, and took her husband's hand. "My pleasure, dearest Theseus."

They climbed onto the stage as if they were making their grand entrance in *A Midsummer Night's Dream*. Stephen changed roles, sweeping her into the absurdly histrionic kiss he'd performed when playing the wicked duke in *The False Lover*. Except that in an empty auditorium, the kiss was quite genuine. Clearly her husband had recovered from his attack the night before.

She emerged from the kiss laughing, a stir of passion warming the inner chill left by the morning's trip into her past. His hand cupped her breast and slowly stroked the tip with his thumb. She sucked in her breath. "Sir, you are too bold. Have you forgotten that we have an audience?"

He smiled, his tanned skin crinkling around his eyes. "Only mice and spiders."

"Not true." She twirled from his embrace into the middle of the forestage. "The house is full of the ghosts of old audiences, ready to laugh and weep or throw rotten oranges if they aren't pleased." She made an elegant curtsy to the unseen watchers, holding her skirts with her left hand and her nosegay with her right.

He said with interest, "Does that mean we should practice our kissing to ensure that it is competently done?"

She gave him a naughty smile but shook her head. "You know where that would lead, my lord husband. We'd frighten the spiders to death."

Chuckling, he strolled past the proscenium into the shadowy depths of the stage. "From the looks of the set, the last thing performed here was a gloomy Gothic melodrama." He pushed at a canvas flat that portrayed a distant, menacing castle. It slid sluggishly back along the grooved runners. Behind was another flat showing a sunny, idealized pastoral scene that must have been used for the happy ending.

Rosalind watched his smooth, athletic movements, recording the moment as another image for her private gallery. Mentally she labeled it "Stephen, looking handsome and heroic." He would be a sensation in the black costume traditionally worn by Hamlet. The dark doublet and trunk hose would emphasize his long, muscular legs and broad shoulders. And the codpiece . . .

The direction of her thoughts made her blush. She was tempted to suggest that they return to Ashburton House immediately, but that would seem ungrateful when Stephen had arranged a visit to this charming theater just because he'd thought it would please her. Besides, anticipation would enhance eventual fulfillment.

She sniffed her nosegay, feeling cherished. Though Stephen's love might be reserved for his first wife, his second wife had no cause to complain.

He glanced upward. "I suppose those ropes and walkways above are used for flying effects?"

She nodded. "And I've counted no less than three trapdoors for ghosts and other creatures to leap from. Brian would love this place."

Stephen grinned. "One doesn't need elaborate rigging to get flying effects. At Bourne Castle, even Maria was swinging through the trees like a monkey."

She laughed at the memory. Saint Katherine's and old Molly seemed years away. "Shall we explore the rest of the Athenaeum?" She tucked her flowers provocatively into her bodice. "Then, alas, I shall need to go home and take to my bed for a time. The rigors of the day, you know."

"Ah, so that is what will happen." He nodded sagely as he opened a door that led behind the stage. "Rigors."

Laughing, she sailed through the door. Stephen really would have made a good comic actor; when he wished, he could inflect even the simplest of statements with wicked meaning.

The Athenaeum was a warren of dressing rooms and workshops. Having grown up in the theater, Rosalind had a store of trenchantly amusing comments that kept Stephen chuckling. The tour was enhanced by the fact that the two of them slid into a delicate duet of glance and touch that gave a foretaste of what would happen when they returned home. She would pass him closely when he held open a door, her skirts brushing him provocatively. He used any excuse, such as helping her over a rough floorboard, to take her hand, caressing her palm when he did.

Maximum temptation and maximum opportunity.

After exploring the main floor, they ascended to the level above. Much of the floor was taken up by the scenery construction shop. "This is downright eerie," Rosalind commented when she saw a partially constructed set sitting in the middle of the room. "The theater must have closed very suddenly."

"It did. The principal financial backer went bankrupt. The theater owner held on to the property but was unable to find a new backer willing to pay off the existing debts. Everything is pretty much the way it was the day the theater closed." Stephen left the scenery shop and began opening other doors. Most led to storage rooms packed with jumbled furniture and set pieces.

The last door led to the costume department. Shelves contained hats and false royal regalia and similar props, while silent costumes hung on wall pegs. Rosalind went to the nearest and lifted the protective fabric covering. "Ah, if it isn't King Henry the

Eighth. He's always dressed exactly as in the portrait by Holbein."

Stephen smiled as he recognized the slashed and padded sleeves and rich materials. "Thomas would look splendid in that. Very regal." He raised the next holland cover. "This costume has a ruff and Cavalier boots. Falstaff, I presume?"

"Probably—that's how he's usually dressed. Lately there has been more interest in historically accurate costumes, but we have a long way to go." Rosalind lifted a tawdrily glittering crown in both hands. "This would suit Papa. He's planning on doing *King Lear* next season. He says no man should play Lear unless he's at least fifty."

Stephen picked up a prop sword from a pile by the wall and hefted it thoughtfully. "Thomas is right. Youth believes it's immortal. Could a young actor really understand the vanities and desperate folly of age, when death is inescapable?" He winced when he heard the elegiac note in his voice. It came perilously close to self-pity.

Experimentally he cut the air with his blade to test the balance. "This sword isn't fit for slicing cheese."

Rosalind watched him with sultry admiration. "I assume that swordplay is one of those aristocratic skills that you learned early."

He nodded. "I was fairly good at it. In my melodramatic youth, I occasionally hoped to be challenged to a duel so I'd have the pick of weapons and could choose blades over pistols." He lunged forward, his blade skewering an invisible opponent.

"How bloodthirsty young men are." Rosalind set down the large crown and lifted a smaller one. "I'll have to find a theatrical costumer so I can buy Papa a new crown. The old one is in sad shape."

"You'd better get a queen's crown for Maria at the same time."

"Actually, I was thinking of a really sumptuous, ermine-trimmed cloak." Her gaze went around the room with some sadness. "Do you think the Athenaeum will ever come alive again?"

"It's quite possible." He set the prop sword on top of the pile of weapons. Thinking that the time was right, he continued, "Would your parents like the Athenaeum?"

"They would adore it. Imagine Mama lying on a sofa as the dying Isabella, the audience weeping hysterically." Rosalind smiled fondly. "Or Papa as Lear, staggering blindly about the stage with Jessica guiding him as Cordelia."

"Shall I buy this theater for them?" Stephen asked in a conversational tone.

Lost in her imaginings, it took Rosalind a moment to register his words. Then she lowered the crown, her eyes round as saucers. "You're joking."

"Not at all. I've been weighing how to give your parents security for the future. What better way than if they have their own theater? As owner-manager, your father can do exactly as he wishes. Together they can finally find the success they deserve." He studied a plaster pillar that held a battered bust of Julius Caesar. "Since I remembered the Athenaeum fondly, I had my solicitor look into its current status."

Voice hushed, Rosalind said, "The lease is available?"

"Actually, the theater, all the contents, and a modest house behind this building are for sale outright. I thought I'd give the property to your parents freehold and pay for the refurbishing and a fund to cover two years of operating expenses." He took the crown from Rosalind's limp clasp and set it jauntily on Caesar's head. "Since they won't have to pay rent, they should be able to operate the theater very profitably even though it's small by modern standards. Luckily the rules for unlicensed theaters have relaxed quite a bit in the last few years, and a good thing. London entertainment needs fresh blood."

Rosalind's elegant jaw dropped. "Buying and redecorating this place would cost a fortune!"

"I have a fortune," he pointed out. "Several of them, in fact, and I can't take any of it with me."

She ran a dazed hand through her hair. "Papa is very independent. He might not accept such a gift."

"From his son-in-law? Why not? He's independent, but not a fool." Stephen grinned. "Think of the Athenaeum as your bride price. I could have paid in cows or camels, but I thought a theater would be more appropriate."

Rosalind's eyes began glowing as the possibilities began to sink in. "If they come to London, Jessica won't have to leave the troupe in order to achieve success. Nor Brian, either, when the time comes."

"And if your sister marries Simon Kent, or another actor, they can carry the Athenaeum into the middle of the century. Perhaps have children who will follow them." He smiled a little wistfully. "Even though I won't be here to see it, I like the idea of helping to establish a Fitzgerald theatrical dynasty."

"Oh, Stephen, this is the most wonderful idea I've ever heard, and you're the most wonderful man. And not only because of your financial generosity." She came into his arms, hugging him tightly. "You looked at Thomas and Maria and didn't see just a pair of provincial strolling players who lived hand-to-mouth. You saw their goodness, their talent, their dreams." She looked up at him, tears in her eyes. "And you're taking those dreams seriously enough to help them come true."

He looked at her glossy hair and lithe, womanly figure, and thought of the terrified child she had been. "They saved your life. If you hadn't been rescued from that slum, you would have died in some horrible way. Maria and Thomas were young, they had little money and no security. Yet they took you in and made a loving home for you." Tenderly he cupped her face between his hands. "For that, I would happily give them every penny I have."

"A theater will be quite enough." Laughing through her tears, she raised her face and kissed him, her lips saying more than words ever could. He kissed her back. The desire that had been slowly building between them flared into a hot, fierce need to possess her so deeply that she would never again know fear.

She broke the kiss, saying huskily, "Let's go home." Her eyes had darkened to nearly black and her lips were ripe with sensual promise.

"Later." He wanted her *now*. The night before, he'd been too drained by pain for intimacy. Every day he felt the advance of his disease. How many more times would he have the strength to make love to her? Should he start counting down the potential couplings as well as the days until doom?

Urgently he set her against the wall among the costumes. King Henry's knee-length velvet gown tumbled from its peg to the floor. As he captured her mouth again, his body imprisoned hers, his chest crushing the nosegay in her bodice into bittersweet scent. She exhaled, startled, but her tongue touched his with eagerness and her hips rocked against his groin.

He put his hand on her full breast. Feminine ripeness, both erotic and nurturing.

She might have died of starvation or disease. Or of horrible abuse at the hands of some adult monster. Christ, he might never have known her. The thought was unbearable.

A fragment of Andrew Marvell's poetry flitted through his mind: *"Had we but world enough, and time . . ."*

But they didn't have time. The days and hours were spilling away. He slid his hand between them to the juncture of her thighs, caressing. She moaned, and her hands slid under his coat, making restless circles on his back.

"But at my back I always hear / Time's winged chariot hurrying near." He raised her skirt, delving through layered undergarments until he found intimate heat. The pulse of life. Her eyes closed, and her head went back into the rich fabric of the royal costume as his hand moved rhythmically against her slick, secret flesh.

"The grave's a fine and private place, / But none, I think, do there embrace." But now he was alive. Blood and bone and sinew, alive.

He wrenched his breeches open. Raising her left leg and wrapping it around him, he thrust forward into searing welcome, burying himself inside her.

Mind and heart and sex, alive.

She inhaled sharply. He stilled for an instant, ashamed of his rough haste.

"A fine and private place . . ." His control fractured, for with Rosalind he was wholly, desperately alive. He surged into her again, impaling her against the costume-padded wall.

She made a harsh sound deep in her throat, her hands clawing into his back. As he drove forward again and again, her raised leg locked around him, her supple body writhing within the cage of his.

"None, I think, do there embrace." But here and now, they

did embrace, melded by a savagely primal bond. His wife, his mate, imprinted on his soul, if he had one. Passion rising, building into all-consuming fire. Alive. *Alive.*

She gave a shuddering cry. He buried his face against her hair and ground his hips against her yielding body. Her teeth sank into his shoulder, and she convulsed around him. Her climax triggered his own explosive release. Life spilling into her, mysterious and profligate. The little death, annihilating his being and blending it briefly, profoundly, with hers. Life beyond life.

Then, too soon, alone. Two separate beings instead of one.

He clung to her, his breath coming in harsh pants. Her raised leg slid along his calf to the floor, but otherwise they didn't move. She was molded against him, so womanly soft. His closed eyes intensified the intimate heat and musky scents that hung suspended in the silent air.

So little time left, he mourned. So little time . . .

Distantly he heard a clicking sound. Then something pushed against his calf.

Startled, he opened his eyes and looked down. Farley's hound gazed up at him with mild interest. The dog had come upstairs and wandered through the open door.

Stephen smiled wryly. "Reality returns." Keeping one hand on Rosalind's arm for balance—he wasn't sure which of them needed it more—he stepped away and used his other hand to restore himself to decency.

Looking wonderfully, sinfully desirable, Rosalind straightened her skirts and made a futile attempt to tame her rioting hair. "I think that was a lovely way to

celebrate the rebirth of the Athenaeum." She adjusted
her cloak demurely over her morning gown.

A kind of peace settled over him, replacing the
frantic urgency he'd felt. Yes, his death was imminent,
but life would go on, with new births, new crises and
triumphs.

He only wished that he could be present to celebrate
more of them.

CHAPTER 26

Their social life began as soon as Rosalind and her husband returned from the Athenaeum theater to find a
small mountain of invitation cards. Apparently she had
passed the preliminary test at Drury Lane.

Ignoring the cards, they went straight to bed, though
not to make love. The shattering encounter in the costume room had left both of them mentally and physically drained, so they slept in each other's arms.
Rosalind tired rather easily these days. Stephen's sta-
mina was also failing, but that was not mentioned.
Though they had agreed on honesty about his illness,
she'd soon realized that many subjects were best
avoided.

They slept all afternoon. After a quiet supper,
Stephen went through the pile of invitations while they
drank coffee in his study. He sorted the cards with
the speed of long practice. "Barnham, no. Wigler, no.

Manningham, no. Strathmore, yes. Hillingford, no. Devonshire, maybe."

Rosalind watched with fascination, her elbow on his desk and her chin propped on her hand. "What are your criteria for accepting and rejecting?"

"Since we want to present you socially, only the most prestigious of hosts and events." He discarded three more cards.

"Do you take any account of what the event actually is?"

"A little." He glanced at the next card. "For example, this is for a Venetian breakfast. Too cold at this time of year, and only a second-rank hostess. It joins the goats, not the sheep."

She laughed. "And here I thought you weren't a snob."

"Fashionable society is largely a game. If one is going to play it, one should know the rules, and play to win." After discarding four more cards, he paused. "St. Aubyn, yes. He and his wife are particular friends of mine. In with the sheep."

She shook her head dolefully. "All these eager hostesses would be heartbroken if they saw how cavalier you are about their invitations."

"*Au contraire.* Most would admire my ruthlessly high standards and scheme to find a way to join the sheep."

She took a swallow of coffee. "In the game of society, being a duke must be like holding a hand full of face cards."

He flashed a quick smile. "And as my duchess, you play with the same hand."

Not quite, but close enough. At least for as long as he was by her side. "Don't accept too many. While I wish to meet people, I prefer spending time alone with you." She stopped, realizing that the fashionable world was his natural milieu and that he probably wanted to see as many of his friends as possible before . . . before it was too late.

Stephen didn't seem annoyed by her presumption. "I like that, too, but it's important for you to meet some of my close friends. That way you can call on them later if you ever wish to move in society."

"Won't the grander ones assign me to the goats?"

"Not those who are real friends." Absently he squared the pile of discarded invitations. "I used to take social obligations more seriously because I thought the heir to a dukedom had to. It never really occurred to me that I had a choice. In the last weeks I've learned that there is very little worth taking seriously."

The somewhat awkward pause was broken when Portia came tearing into the room like a small black-and-orange rocket. She stopped abruptly, gave her owners a crazed glare, then executed a wild combination of sideways hops and a backward somersault. Rosalind and Stephen both laughed as the kitten streaked away again. "Given a choice between laughter and high seriousness, I'll take laughter any day," she said. "After all, I've spent most of my life in the business of entertainment."

Stephen nodded. "The first night I saw you, in Fletchfield, I noticed two elderly sisters waiting to attend the performance. It was obvious that seeing a play was a rare and special occasion for them, one they would discuss and remember fondly for years. Bringing such pleasure is a task worth taking seriously." He lifted another invitation, then tossed it over his shoulder. "Going to an assembly given by the most socially ambitious man in England is not."

He opened the next missive and scanned it. "This is from Cousin Quintus in Norfolk. He informs me that

Mrs. Reese—that's Ellie Warden's official name—and her baby have settled in nicely, and that the head groom is courting her. The groom is a fine fellow and the chit seems to fancy him. Would I object to such a match?"

Rosalind smiled ruefully. "You're right. Your cousin assumes Ellie was your mistress and her son your by-blow. I imagine you have no objection to her marrying."

"None whatsoever. The groom is indeed a good fellow. They should deal very well together." He opened the last card. "Lady Cassell is having a musicale. I don't know her well, but I do like music, and she always engages excellent performers."

"A sheep," she declared. "I like music, too. We might as well do something simply because we want to."

Stephen chuckled and added that card to the acceptance pile. "If I sent a carriage, would your parents be able to come to London for a day or two? I want to broach the idea about the Athenaeum, since I won't buy the place if they aren't interested."

She liked the fact that he didn't automatically assume that the Fitzgeralds would jump to accept his gift. "They should be able to slip away, though their absence will limit the plays the troupe can perform. Shall I book a room at one of the inns near here?"

His brows rose. "Will they refuse to stay under my roof?"

She hesitated, then decided on the truth. "They would not want you to have the embarrassment of housing two players."

Stephen looked pained. "I know you think I'm a snob, but I would be a very poor sort of gentleman if I didn't acknowledge my own in-laws. Besides, I want to have Thomas and Maria here. I've missed them."

"Very well," she said, glad that London had not

made him too conventional. "The carriage can bring them directly to Ashburton House so they have no choice."

He reached for a quill pen. "I'll also summon my secretary and valet from the abbey. They must be wondering what happened to me."

She stared at him. "In all these weeks, you've never written to let your household know your whereabouts and welfare?"

"No," he said simply. "I quite liked escaping. Though I won't mind having the services of my valet again. I learned that I can manage alone if I must, but now that I've proved it to my satisfaction, I shall cheerfully hand such chores back to Hubble."

She shook her head, smiling. Different worlds.

"No smug smiles," he said sternly. "We must engage a lady's maid for you. You'll need one."

She groaned but agreed. After all, her foray into society was not for her own sake but for Stephen and the child she carried. For them she would give the performance of her life.

They quickly fell into a routine where Stephen attended to business in the mornings. Afternoons they spent together, talking or reading or laughing at Portia's antics, and in the evenings they went out. Every day was different, and as Rosalind had pointed out after their wedding, they were tasting only the cream. There was painful irony in that fact. Most newly married couples soon began laying the foundation for their future lives. Rosalind's marriage would be over before the honeymoon ended.

And they were still on their honeymoon, with all the romance that implied. Every morning, she found a perfect red rose in a crystal vase on her dressing table. A red rose for the passion that thrummed and sang between them.

Her new wardrobe started to arrive, several garments every day. There was nothing like stunning clothing to make a woman feel capable of anything. Stephen's friends made her very welcome. As a bonus, the events Stephen had chosen were uniformly enjoyable. Despite his flippant remarks about playing the social game, clearly he had decided not to waste his limited time on anything he didn't like.

One of the subjects they didn't discuss was Stephen's first wife. When Rosalind admired the exquisitely embroidered fire screen in her sitting room, Stephen said tersely that it had been done by Louisa. After that, Rosalind started taking note of the superb needlework scattered about the house. Pillows and chair seats, a lovely hanging, a bookmark sewn with graceful flowers.

Rosalind studied the bookmark when she found it in a Bible, tracing the stitches of the delicate blossoms with her fingertips. A framed pastel sketch of the late duchess had shown Rosalind what her predecessor had looked like. Louisa had been truly beautiful, with an otherworldly quality and small skillful hands.

Sometimes Rosalind wondered if Stephen's illness was rooted in grief over Louisa's death. She had seen cases where the loss of a beloved spouse had been soon followed by the passing of the survivor. In fact, she suspected that when one of her parents died, the other would not last long. It was impossible to imagine Thomas and Maria separated.

She returned the embroidered strip of fabric to Louisa's Bible, where it marked the Twenty-third Psalm. *"Yea, though I walk through the valley of the shadow of death, I will fear no evil: for thou art with me."*

Her throat tightened. Stephen knew fear. He never spoke of it, but she could sense its dank presence, perhaps because she had lived with fear herself. Without faith in something greater, how could he not be afraid? She had many small fears, but she also had an underlying faith that had always been part of her. It was a mark of Stephen's courage that he carried on so calmly, finding intense enjoyment in life when possible, enduring the increasingly corrosive pain without complaint.

Resolutely she put aside both the thought and the Bible. Then she lay back on the sofa and closed her eyes. Soon it would be time to dress for the Cassell musicale. As always before a social event, she called on one of Maria's tricks and spent a few minutes mentally preparing herself to be very charming and very beautiful.

There was so little she could do for Stephen. At least she could try her best to ensure that he was proud of her.

Day Thirty-one

As the carriage took them to the Cassell musicale, Stephen wondered darkly about the accuracy of the thirty-one days left in his mental count. He'd thought three months was a minimum and that he would probably live longer. Now he was beginning to seriously doubt that he would survive the third month. In health he'd taken his body for granted. Now he was acutely aware of his internal rhythms and functions, and of his inexorable physical decline.

Soon he would pass some invisible boundary and become so ill that he would no longer be able to maintain the illusion of normal life. And if the pain continued to increase, death would eventually come to feel like a mercy.

But he didn't want to die. *He didn't want to die.* He looked at Rosalind's clear-cut profile silhouetted against the window. There was so much more that he wanted to learn about her. More that he wanted to do with her and for her. His day started with her drowsy smile in the morning and ended with her gentle sigh as she settled against him in their bed. There had been shadows in her eyes since the visit to St. Katharine's, but she always had a smile for him. She was always giving, always warm. His perfect rose.

Thirty-one days, more or less. *Please, God, if you exist, more.*

The carriage pulled to a halt in front of Cassell House. They were late, and a harpsichord was playing when the butler admitted them. The earl and countess had finished receiving and were heading toward the salon where the concert was beginning, but they returned to greet the newcomers graciously.

Lord Cassell introduced himself to Rosalind while his wife, a tall, distinguished woman in her fifties, extended her hand to Stephen. "Ashburton, I'm so glad you could come." Her voice dropped with mock secrecy. "I'm perishing to meet the new duchess. Everyone is talking about her loveliness and charm."

"Every word is true." He bowed over her ladyship's hand. "Sorry we're late. A lame horse. Will we be forgiven and admitted?"

"A duke may be late almost anywhere except the sacred precincts of Almack's," the countess said with wry humor.

"True, but tardiness is so ill-bred." He turned to

Rosalind, who was laughing at a remark by Cassell. "Come meet our hostess, my dear."

She turned with a smile. Garbed in amber silk, she looked particularly radiant this evening. "It's a pleasure to be here, Lady Cassell. The harpsichordist sounds heavenly."

Lady Cassell started to extend her hand, then dropped it. Her face went dead white as she stared at Rosalind. Then, shockingly, she crumpled in a faint.

Only a step away, Stephen was able to catch the countess so that she didn't injure herself on the marble floor. Lord Cassell exclaimed, "Anne!" and dived to his wife's side, taking most of her weight from Stephen.

Her lids fluttered open. "I'm . . . all right, Roger," she whispered. "Help me to the library. Ashburton, you come, too." She looked at Rosalind, and a shiver went through her. "And your wife."

Stephen exchanged a startled glance with Rosalind, then helped Cassell take the stricken woman to the library, which opened off the foyer. As her husband settled her on the sofa, the butler poured a glass of brandy, then withdrew at a signal from the earl.

Lady Cassell swallowed a mouthful of brandy, and color returned to her face. "Sorry to frighten you all." Her gaze went to Rosalind. "It's just that you bear a resemblance—an *uncanny* resemblance—to my younger sister, Sophia. My maiden name was Westley. Can we possibly be related?"

Rosalind stiffened. "I . . . I don't know. I was a foundling, adopted when I was about three years old."

The countess said sharply, "When? Where?"

Rosalind folded into a chair, her hands gripping the arms. "I was found near the waterfront here in London in the summer of 1794." In the silence that followed, the chime-sweet notes of a Mozart sonata could be heard clearly from the salon.

"Dear God." Lady Cassell pressed a hand to the center of her chest and looked up at her husband. "Do you suppose it's possible, Roger?"

Rosalind's stillness made Stephen think of a rabbit trying to avoid a fox. He went to stand by her chair, laying a quiet hand on her shoulder. To the countess he said, "Tell us about your sister."

"Sophia married a Frenchman, Philippe St. Cyr, the Count du Lac. They both died in the Reign of Terror. She had a daughter, Marguerite, who was about three and a half then. We assumed that the child must have died, too." Lady Cassell leaned forward urgently. "You look very like Sophia, Duchess, except that you have brown eyes, just like her husband, Philippe. Do you remember how you came to be in London?"

"No." Rosalind shrank back, her face ashen and her head slowly shaking back and forth. The tempo of the distant harpsichord increased, the notes swift and edged.

His worried gaze on his wife, Stephen said, "She apparently was brought across the Channel by an elderly woman who died as soon as they disembarked in London. Rosalind lived by scavenging for some weeks before she was adopted by a couple named Thomas and Maria Fitzgerald. And I've recently learned that she speaks some French when she's half-asleep, though she has never formally learned it."

Lady Cassell set her brandy aside, her hand unsteady. "Even though she had trouble with her heart, our old nurse, Mrs. Standish, went to France with Sophia because my sister wanted her children to speak English." Her voice broke. "In the last letter I received, Sophia wrote that her daughter was speaking both

French and English very well. She . . . she was so proud of the girl's cleverness."

"It could be a coincidence, Anne," Lord Cassell said, his gaze searching Rosalind's face. "It's been almost thirty years since you saw your sister. Perhaps you exaggerate the resemblance."

Perhaps, but Stephen could see a likeness between Rosalind and the countess, who was of similar build, and whose hair was a blend of silver and tawny light brown.

His hand tightened on Rosalind's shoulder as he answered for her. "My wife remembers very little before her adoption. But she did recall a child's handkerchief embroidered with flowers, and the initial *M* and a stylized lion in opposite corners."

"The lion from the St. Cyr arms! My mother embroidered two handkerchiefs like that for Sophia's baby." Tears in her eyes, Lady Cassell extended her hand. "My dear girl, you are my niece. Mrs. Standish must have saved you and brought you home to England. Marguerite—"

Rosalind's stillness shattered. "Don't call me that!"

"Why not?" Stephen asked quietly.

As the music built to a crescendo, Rosalind stood and began moving about the room anxiously. "When we ran away, the soldiers came after us. I . . . I was warned to never say my real name. Never."

"Were you running away from the Palais du Lac?" Lady Cassell asked. "That was your family's home outside of Paris. It was a huge palace built of white stone, with towers and a lake with swans."

"Swans. Oh, God, I remember the swans. I loved feeding them." Rosalind stopped in her tracks as if she'd been struck. Then she bent her head and pressed her fingers to the middle of her forehead. "I . . . I remember running up to the nursery to find Standy. I was screaming, and she slapped my face to stop me. She said I mustn't make a sound. Yet she was crying. I'd never seen her cry."

Lady Cassell said hesitantly, "What happened to make you scream? Were the soldiers hurting people?"

Not answering the questions, Rosalind said tightly, "Standy took me down the back stairs. It was dusk. There were servants' cloaks by the back door. She took two. We went by the lake as we were leaving. The soldiers had shot the swans, and the bodies were floating in the water." Rosalind drew a shuddering breath. "We ran and ran until my side hurt and I couldn't run anymore. But we could still hear men shouting, so Standy picked me up and carried me. She said again that I mustn't tell anyone my real name. I must be very, very good so no one would notice us on the way home to England. B-but she couldn't stop crying."

"The girl must have seen other horrible sights, Anne," Lord Cassell said in a voice so low that Rosalind couldn't hear the words. "Don't ask her more."

Silently agreeing, Stephen went to Rosalind and put his arm around her rigid shoulders. Then he guided her to a sofa and sat beside her. She hid her face against his chest and began to weep with utter desolation.

"I wonder exactly what happened to Sophia and Philippe," the countess murmured, her face gray.

"Something swift and terrible," her husband said grimly. "We can be grateful for the swiftness, at least."

Stephen held Rosalind close, wondering what other horrors were still locked in her mind. No wonder she'd fled from a uniformed guard who looked like a soldier on the London quay. No wonder she had become so good at detaching from pain, and had made herself into a perfect adoptive daughter, a perfect wife.

He'd accepted her generous nature willingly because it made everything so easy for him. Gad, he was selfish for not looking more closely at the hints of pain he'd seen in her whenever the subject of her origins came up. He should buy the Fitzgeralds every damned theater in London in gratitude for what they'd done for Rosalind. Not only for the fact of the adoption but for the constant love that had healed many, if not all, of her emotional wounds.

In the salon there was a burst of applause as the harpsichord piece ended. The applause faded, and a new selection began, the fluid notes incongruously happy.

Rosalind's sobs began to abate. Stephen placed his handkerchief in her hand and said softly, "Shall I take you home, my dear?"

"Not quite yet." She sat up and blew her nose. Her expression was stark, but her eyes calm. "I'm sorry, Lady Cassell. I wish I could remember more."

"My dear girl, I should apologize to you for bringing up such ghastly memories." Her aunt gave her a crooked smile. "We have found you, and that is a great blessing."

Gently Stephen brushed the damp strands of Rosalind's hair back from her face. "So Rosalind is the Countess du Lac. Does she have many relatives on the French side of her family?"

"Some cousins, I believe." Lord Cassell's eyes narrowed thoughtfully. "Now that Bonaparte is gone and the French king is back on the throne, your wife is probably a considerable heiress."

Perhaps. But Stephen doubted that there was enough money in the whole of France to compensate Rosalind for what she had endured.

CHAPTER 27

For years Rosalind had wondered who might have been waiting in London for a little girl who had never completed her journey, but she had never imagined that someone like the aristocratic Lady Cassell would be her own mother's sister. "Please tell me about your family, Lady Cassell," she asked her newfound aunt. "Or rather, my family."

"Call me Aunt Anne," the countess said, looking grateful to turn from past to present. "There's my younger brother, Lord Westley, and his wife and four children. The family seat is in Leicestershire. Roger and I have two sons and a daughter, and three grand-children, too. Our seat is in Suffolk." She patted her husband's knee absently, a display of intimacy that would ordinarily never have been made in public. "Lots of cousins. And of course my mother, the dowager Lady Westley. She lives in Richmond, and her health is very delicate. You must visit her very soon, Marguerite."

"I'm Rosalind," she said vehemently, feeling sharp revulsion at the French name. "That is what I've been called most of my life, and I do not wish to change."

"As you wish, my dear," her aunt said peaceably. "Now tell me about the people who adopted you. Fitzgerald, I believe Ashburton said. Is that the noble Irish family?"

"My parents are strolling players," Rosalind said

bluntly. "I was raised in the theater, traveling the West Midlands circuit."

"Oh, my," Lady Cassell said rather faintly. "I'd heard rumors, but . . . Well, I'm sure the Fitzgeralds must be very good sorts of people."

"They are my *family,* Lady Cassell." Hearing the defensive note in her voice, Rosalind continued more mildly, "When I recover from the shock, I shall be very glad to have found you. I've often wondered about my kin. But it was Thomas and Maria who raised me, for no other reason than the goodness of their hearts."

"I'm proud to have them as family," Stephen interjected.

"Then I shall be, too." Lady Cassell leaned forward in her chair. "It will mean so much to my mother to know that Sophia's daughter is alive. Tomorrow I shall go tell Mama myself so that she will not be overcome by the news. Will you come to Richmond the next day? I'd like to invite my children and my brother's family as well."

Rosalind looked to Stephen, feeling incapable of a decision. His hand tightened protectively as he said, "We'll be there, but please keep the gathering small."

She was relieved that he understood without having to be told. Heavens, she had a grandmother. Aunts, uncles, cousins, family seats. It was more than Rosalind could absorb. She whispered, "Can we go home now, Stephen?"

"Of course." He helped her to her feet. To their hosts, he said, "Please excuse us. Rosalind needs to rest. Let me know the time and place in Richmond."

Lady Cassell nodded, then rose and approached Rosalind. "My little sister was very dear to me," she said softly. "I can't tell you how glad I am that part of her has survived in you." She gave Rosalind a light kiss on the cheek, her lips warm.

Rosalind managed a smile in return but was too numb for anything more. Later she would probably be glad for what had happened tonight, but not yet.

Not yet.

Mercifully Stephen maintained silence as he summoned the carriage, took Rosalind home, and efficiently stripped off all her clothing. After removing his own garments, he snuffed the candles and slid into the bed beside her. She burrowed into his embrace, finding a primal comfort in the touch of his skin against hers.

Holding her close, he murmured, "How do you feel?"

Groping for an honest answer helped focus her chaotic thoughts. "Stunned. Hollow. Who am I? I'm not really Rosalind Fitzgerald, but Marguerite St. Cyr died many years ago."

"But you are most certainly the Duchess of Ashburton." His warm hand drifted down her spine. "And my wife."

How lucky she was to have him. The terror of being hunted still clung to her like a bad dream, but in Stephen's arms, she was safe. She wondered briefly what other memories were locked in her mind, then determinedly shut the thought away. "What an extraordinary coincidence to meet my aunt as I did."

"Not really," he said matter-of-factly. "If you were not of aristocratic birth, you would not have had to flee France. Given your strong resemblance to your mother, being identified was only a matter of time once you entered fashionable society."

And she had decided to do that because of the child

she carried. Her hand went to her stomach. Very soon, enough time would have passed that she would be able to tell Stephen. An ironic thought struck her. "If I'm really a French countess, you didn't make such a bad match after all. That's almost amusing."

"I knew that I'd made a good marriage long before tonight." He caressed her from shoulders to hips with a gentle, undemanding hand. "I hope that knowing your origins will cure your belief that you are unworthy to be my wife. That idea was always nonsense, you know."

Mere knowledge of her parentage would not instantly overcome the effect of the snubs and sneers she'd endured as an actress. But it was a start. She smiled faintly into the darkness. "A countess in my own right. It will take time to become accustomed. What will my family . . . ?" She stopped, then said, "What will the Fitzgeralds think?"

"They're still your family, little rose," he said quietly. "You're fortunate to have several families now. The one of your birth. The one of your adoption. The one of your marriage."

Her new status should make her more acceptable to the Kenyons. A cheering thought. Would Claudia relent? Rosalind sighed. That was too much to hope for.

Misinterpreting her sigh, Stephen said, "It must be hard to discover who your parents are and at the same time know that they must have died violently. But it happened many years ago." He pressed a kiss against her temple. "Your parents are at peace now. It's right for you to mourn, but the best memorial you can make for them is your own life and happiness."

She knew he was right. Yet in the darkness, the raw pain of her new memories merged with the knowledge of Stephen's imminent demise into an unendurable whole. She wrapped her arms around him. He was warm and powerful and very much alive. But he was too thin, his ribs distinct, hard ridges against her breasts. How much longer would they have?

She could not speak of that, but neither could she prevent herself from the aching whisper, "I don't want to be alone."

He kissed the pulse in her throat, his mouth gentle and familiar. "I can't be with you always. But I'm with you now." His lips moved to hers, soothing, not demanding.

She recognized that he was weaving a cocoon of protection around her, using the primitive power of touch to reach her in ways that words never could. Merciful heaven, what would she do without him?

Her mouth opened under his in a silent plea for comfort. Tomorrow, God willing, she would be stronger. But tonight she needed him with shameless desperation.

Understanding, he deepened his kisses and caresses, no longer her protector but her lover. The slow heat of passion began to warm the chill in her bones. The past faded, not forgotten, but decently dimmed by the urgency of growing desire.

From the beginning their bodies had recognized each other as perfect mates. Tonight he used his intimate knowledge of her like a virtuoso musician playing a cherished instrument, creating an exquisitely sensual song that built by slow degrees into a crescendo of need.

And when her breath became swift and harsh, he filled her emptiness, possessing her with a fierce tenderness so profound that she could almost believe it was love. The joining of their bodies began to heal the newly slashed wounds in her spirit. Stephen, her husband. The father of her child. Her beloved.

The eternal dance ended in a climax that was long and deep, suffusing every fiber of her being with warmth. Ah, God, how many more times would she hold him like this, sharing the madness of fulfillment and the peace that followed? How often would she taste the salt tang of his skin and feel the rough power of his passion?

She suppressed tears as ragged breathing slowed and tense bodies softened into a gentle embrace. Sufficient unto the day were the evils thereof. For now, when she needed Stephen so desperately, he was here.

"Sleep well, little Marguerite," he murmured.

The words should have been soothing, but instead they sliced through her contentment into another level of buried memories. She heard the same words spoken by an old Englishwoman, voice hushed as woman and child took refuge in a barn. Images began racing through her mind, scalding like lava. "Merciful heaven," she gasped, horror-struck. "I . . . I can see now how my parents died."

"You were there?" Stephen said sharply. His arms tightened around her.

She nodded, her whole body chilling. "The soldiers came, filthy brutes carrying wine bottles. They burst into the drawing room, where Mama and Papa were having coffee after dinner. I should have been in the nursery, but I was hiding in the minstrel's gallery with my doll Minette. I did that often."

"What did the soldiers want?" he asked, his voice quiet and steady.

She twisted restlessly within his embrace. "They . . . they said it would be Madame Guillotine for all aristos. Papa protested, saying he'd always been a friend to the

Revolution, but a soldier hit him and he fell. Mama screamed and tried to go to him, but the soldiers caught her. One said, *'Trés belle aristo putain.'* They began to laugh.

"Another said, 'Why waste such a one on Madame Guillotine when we can do for her here?'" Rosalind's heart was pounding with a harsh, driving beat that drowned out the world and isolated her with her memories. "They . . . they threw my mother to the floor and began ripping at her clothing."

Stephen sucked in his breath. "How damnable that you were there to see such a thing!"

The horror that had been trapped inside Rosalind for so many years rushed out in staccato bursts. "The soldiers had forgotten Papa. He stumbled up and went to a table. He'd put a gun in the drawer because he was concerned about the street riots. He took it out and said . . ." She began writhing frantically, like a caged animal. "He said, 'May God forgive me, Sophie.' Then . . . then . . ."

Her voice broke and she could not speak until Stephen whispered, "Don't be afraid, my darling. No matter what happened then, you're safe now."

She squeezed her eyes shut, wanting to block out the scene burned on her brain. "He . . . he shot Mama in the heart," she said in an agonized voice. "The gun was loud, so loud, and the smoke hurt my eyes. I didn't really understand, even when she went limp and stopped resisting. Her face was . . . peaceful. But the soldiers were furious. One yelled, 'This swine killed the whore before we could have her.' "

Rosalind drew a shuddering breath. "The soldier pulled out his sword and . . . and he cut my father's throat."

Stephen swore under his breath again, then cradled

her head against him, his warm body a shelter against the terror inside her own mind.

Dimly aware that she could not have remembered all this if she didn't feel so safe with Stephen, she whispered, "There was blood everywhere. Rivers of blood. I started to scream. The leader looked up and saw me and shouted, 'The aristo child is called Marguerite. Bring her to me. She'll do in her mother's place.' Two soldiers began looking for the way up to the gallery. One of them called, 'Here we come, Marguerite.' There was something so horrible in his voice . . . ."

She took another shuddering breath. "I ran and found Standy, and . . . and you know the rest." She was clinging to Stephen so hard that she could feel the hammering of his heart, or perhaps it was hers.

"It's a terrible tale, little rose," Stephen said, his soft voice a balm. "My heart breaks for the fact that you witnessed it. Yet—it was over quickly. Your father had the courage and resolution to save your mother from unspeakable suffering." He caressed the damp tangle of her hair. "He must have loved her very, very much."

Rosalind thought about the swift and terrible decision her father had been forced to make. "Not only did he spare her, but he also earned a quick end for himself," she said unsteadily.

"Your father was a brave man," Stephen murmured. "I don't know if I would have had the courage to pull the trigger."

"You doubt your courage when you face death every day with composure and dignity?" she asked softly. "You're the bravest man I've ever known."

"Not the bravest, but one of the luckiest." He kissed her temple. "To think that of all the places in England where I might have wandered, I found you."

His tenderness was even greater than during their earlier lovemaking. Slowly she began to relax. "I'm glad that I remembered," she said, thinking aloud and surprised by her own feelings of relief. "My whole life I've known there were monsters hiding in the darkest corners of my mind. Now I know what they are."

"Monsters can't survive the power of the light." He turned her around and cradled her against himself spoon fashion. "Sleep, little rose, and know that you're safe."

Secure in the strength of his caring, she fell into an exhausted, dreamless slumber.

CHAPTER 28

Soft, heavy flakes of snow whirled through the air, adding to the bleakness of the north county landscape. Winter came early in Scotland. Michael gazed out the window at the snow, taking an occasional sip from his tankard of scalding hot whiskey punch.

Someone joined him at the window carrying a matching tankard. Without looking, he knew it was George Blackmer. Their travels through England had produced an odd camaraderie that was, if not friendship, at least familiarity.

Blackmer said, "Do you think we'll be snowed in here?"

"Probably for a day or two, no more." Michael

sighed, weary to the bone. "But the storm is a sign that it's time to give up and head south."

"I didn't think you believed in surrender," the physician said dryly.

"Sometimes one must. Call it a soldier's superstition, but this whole expedition has been cursed. We've been searching for weeks, always in the wrong place at the wrong time." Michael swallowed more punch, craving the warmth. "The crowning folly was following a carriage with the right description but the wrong travelers all the way to bloody Scotland. I should have behaved like a sensible man and waited for my brother to return in his own time."

"Why didn't you?"

Their weeks of travel together had made Michael even less inclined to say that he wanted to get Stephen to a different physician. He settled for saying, "The need to be doing something. Anything. A rather primitive form of magic, I suppose. As if putting effort into searching will prolong my brother's life." Saying the words aloud made him realize how foolish that instinctive hope had been. He glanced at his companion, tired enough to give in to rude curiosity. "Why did you come all this way? Ashburton may be your most prominent patient, but you're neglecting the rest of your practice."

"A sense of responsibility. Or perhaps guilt." The physician's face twisted. "If . . . if I had done things differently, the duke would not have run away."

"If my brother's dying, there won't be much you can do about it." Michael gazed into the steaming depths of his drink. "And if your diagnosis was wrong and he is prospering, he won't need you."

"Perhaps not." Blackmer shook his head. "The more

time that elapses since I last saw him, the harder it is to predict his current condition. I simply don't know."

"You're very honest for a physician. Most of your breed prefer obfuscation."

"You don't like physicians much," Blackmer said bluntly. "Why not?"

Michael shrugged. "Pills and potions and complicated schedules for dosing. Most of it designed, I think, to impress patients so they'll fill the doctor's purse. My dealings have mostly been with surgeons." He thought of Ian Kinlock and almost smiled. "The ones I've known are cheerful bloodthirsty sorts who approach the world with a knife and a smile. I can understand that sort of directness much more easily."

There was extended silence while they watched the blowing snow and the rapidly falling night. Then Blackmer said, "I treated the old duke when he was at the abbey, but I never really knew him. What was it like to have him for a father?"

Michael smiled without humor, glad that the physician couldn't know how ironic that question was. "Difficult."

"Better a difficult father than none at all."

Michael thought about the vicious beatings he'd endured, the scathing lectures that were even worse, the humiliating sneers, and knew that Blackmer was wrong. Being raised by a man who hated one's very existence was far worse than being alone. But he supposed it was only natural for a foundling to romanticize what he'd never had. "Families can be heaven or hell. You were spared both."

The family Michael was raised in had been hell. With Catherine he'd found heaven. He supposed that was preferable to the opposite order.

Catherine. The chronic ache of missing her flared

into overpowering urgency. He needed to be with her. To lose some of his grief about Stephen in her arms. And, of course, to make love to her until they were both senseless. Just before he received Blackmer's letter and went haring off on this mad chase, she'd said that it was time to think about another child. He was willing. More than willing.

He'd written Catherine several days earlier, asking her to meet him in London. If Stephen wasn't at Ashburton House, they could go on to the abbey together. Stephen loved the blasted place and would probably choose to die there.

Stephen, dying . . . . Michael drew a deep, slow breath, then turned from the window. It was time to go home.

CHAPTER 29

Day Twenty-nine

A stab of pain brought Stephen from drowsing to full wakefulness. He lay still for a moment, gauging the strength of the attack. He'd taken two pills the night before and they'd helped him sleep a little, but the effect had worn off.

Rosalind, bless her, still enjoyed the sleep of the pure in heart, her arm over his chest and her face tucked into the angle between his shoulder and neck. Slowly he extricated himself, sliding a pillow into her embrace.

He'd learned over the course of numerous bad nights how to leave without waking her.

The bedroom was cold, more like winter than autumn. He fumbled in the dark to locate the woolen robe thrown over a chair. Then he made his way to his dressing room by touch. When the door was safely closed, he used flint and steel to strike a light.

The dressing room had become his refuge in the dark watches of the night when his body betrayed him and he wanted to conceal the evidence. Besides two armoires and a washstand with a pitcher and basin, the room held his favorite wing chair, a decanter of milk on the table beside it. The milk had startled Hubble, who had arrived from Ashburton Abbey several days before. The valet had scolded like a mother hen because Stephen had escaped his ministrations for so long.

Stephen took another opium pill, washing it down with a glass of the milk. Some days milk was the only nourishment he could keep down. Sipping the cool liquid, he drew aside the curtain that covered the small window. Almost dawn.

In a few hours, he would take Rosalind to Richmond to meet her grandmother and other relatives. She had recovered somewhat from the exhausting revelations of her evening at Cassell House. Though her eyes were shadowed, he sensed a new peace in her. The past might be tragic, but it was no longer a mystery.

Knowing he would be unable to sleep until the pill took effect, he stretched out in the chair and mentally tallied the amount of business remaining. His last will and testament was complete. All debts paid, his charities funded, Kirby Manor placed in Rosalind's name. Everything was shipshape for his successor. Within a few days, he'd be free to return home to settle estate matters there.

He'd already written Michael in Wales, asking his brother to meet him at the abbey. Some business should be done face to face with his heir. He also wanted to see his brother once more, though it would be a miserably painful business for them both. In fact, he'd seriously considered not letting Michael know of his impending death. It would spare them both a wrenching scene. But he knew his brother well enough to realize that Michael would not thank him, or forgive him, for taking the easy way.

Was there any chance of a rapprochement with Claudia? He'd sent her a letter, and it had been returned unopened. He would try again, but he was not optimistic. His sister was not known for changing her mind once it was made up.

The gnawing internal pain turned virulent with shattering suddenness. He gasped, and the glass slid from his nerveless fingers. Lurching from the chair, he staggered toward the washstand, hoping to reach the basin in time. He failed and crumpled to the floor, conscious but helpless in the grip of wracking pain and violent sickness as his near-empty stomach tried to lacerate itself with futile heaving.

Gradually the sickness receded, but the paralyzing weakness remained. *It's happened. The balance has shifted irrevocably from health to disease.* He closed his eyes in despair. Instead of being a reasonably healthy man with episodes of illness, he was now a dying man whose periods of apparent normality would be hard-won, requiring enormous energy and impossible to sustain for long.

Would he be able to go to Richmond? He must, for

Rosalind would need him on this first encounter with her mother's family. Concentrating on that, he slowly collected his strength until he could roll onto all fours. He crouched, shaking with effort, until he was able to pull himself to his feet by clutching the chair. Then he sank into the upholstered depths, hoping the weakness would ebb.

Death was closer now, almost near enough to take a chair and strike up a conversation. What would death be like? Heaven and harps? Hell and flames? Or simply oblivion? It was the great mystery, along with the equally great mystery of what was the purpose of living in the first place.

The day before he'd visited his banker in the City of London. On the way his carriage passed St. Bartholomew's Hospital, a vast, untidy establishment that had been founded in the twelfth century. He'd stared at the sprawling buildings, struck by the knowledge that those old walls must contain many patients on the brink of death. The desire to order his coachman to stop was almost overpowering. He wanted to go inside and find a dying man and demand to know what the poor devil saw. Perhaps someone in Bart's would have the answer—would know the reality of death and be willing to share the secret.

He would have done exactly that if he'd thought there was a chance of learning the truth. But he suspected that the only ones who really knew were beyond answering.

His body had recovered a little while his thoughts wandered. Even so, the only thing that got him to his feet was knowing that making a supreme effort would take him back to his bed, and Rosalind's arms.

• • •

It seemed a good omen that the day was sunny. Rosalind held Stephen's hand as the carriage took them to Richmond, a community on the Thames just west of London. He looked distinctly unwell today. She knew he'd risen in the night, because she'd woken when he returned, shaking with cold. Wordlessly she'd wrapped herself around him, and gradually he had warmed again.

But it would no longer be possible to conceal his state of health. Anyone who knew him well would immediately notice his gauntness and the bleakness in his eyes. She clamped down on the rage in her heart at the bitter unfairness of it. If she ever allowed that anger to break loose, she might never be able to control it again.

The carriage swung between a pair of open iron gates into a driveway that circled in front of an elegant Palladian villa. "What a pretty house," Rosalind said as Stephen helped her from the carriage.

"Charming," he agreed as they climbed the front stairs.

The door opened before Stephen could lift the knocker. An elderly butler bowed. "Welcome, Your Graces," he said, expression sober but eyes bright with excitement.

Rosalind mentally braced herself. One of her stage parts had been as a long-lost prodigal daughter. She could play that role again.

They stepped into the foyer and were immediately greeted by a small, fragile-looking woman with pure white hair and a fine-boned face wreathed with smiles. "I'm your grandmother, child," the old woman said. "Let me look at you."

Lady Westley clasped Rosalind's hand with thin fingers as she made her examination. Rosalind looked back with equal interest, though she felt large and clumsy. Obviously her height hadn't come from her grandmother.

Her study completed, Lady Westley gave a sigh of satisfaction. "Anne was right. You are very like Sophia. But you aren't her, of course. You are Rosalind."

Rosalind bent and kissed the pale, parchmentlike cheek. "I've never had a grandmother before," she said. "I'm not quite sure what to do."

Lady Westley laughed. "Just indulge me. I've ruthlessly used my age and general infirmity to spend a few minutes alone with you. After all, it isn't every day that I get a new grandchild, much less a lovely, full-grown one."

She turned to Stephen. "We've met a time or two, Ashburton, though it's been a good few years. I knew your mother. A wild girl, but a good heart. I'm so glad that you're now a member of the family."

A satiric glint showed in his eyes at the mention of his mother, but Stephen's bow was impeccable. "The pleasure is mutual, Lady Westley."

"We'd best go to the others before all of my descendants coming boiling forth to meet their new cousin. The younger ones think your story most romantic." Lady Westley made a face as she led the way to the salon. "They haven't yet learned that romantic tales are deucedly uncomfortable."

Rosalind laughed, liking her grandmother. Stephen opened the door to the salon, and in an instant the three of them were surrounded by people. Clearly these unknown relatives really were delighted to meet a long-lost member of the family.

As Lady Cassell efficiently took charge of the introductions, Rosalind realized that for the first time since she was a tiny child, she had no need to prove anything. Here she belonged by right of birth. That right was visible in the faces of the people around her, in their coloring and height and bones. She went from one new relation to another, looking for signs of kinship. Her uncle, Lord Westley, was a large, mellow man. Was that easy disposition a Westley trait that had come to Rosalind through her mother? And that pretty girl, Cassandra, who was just out of the schoolroom. She might almost have been Rosalind at seventeen.

As Rosalind laughed and talked and tried to remember names, the pain of her parents' death slipped further into the past. She'd experienced the misery of a family lost. Today she was discovering the joy of a family found.

Stephen stayed in the background throughout the introductions and the luncheon that followed. This was Rosalind's day, which was fortunate because he would not have had the energy to share center stage. Instead, he sipped wine and moved his food around his plate while keeping an eye on his radiant wife. Here were more people who would offer support when the time came. As a countess by birth and a duchess by marriage, she would be secure in every sense of the word.

He thought again of her likely remarriage. Her cousin James, Westley's heir, looked so dazzled that he might have offered on the spot if Rosalind didn't already have a husband. Young Westley was about her age and seemed a good sort. She could do worse.

The topic was not one Stephen wished to dwell on. He scanned the rest of the group. Rosalind's grandmother sat opposite. When their gazes met, the dowager said, "As soon as we rise from the table, you must escort me to the garden, Ashburton." Her faded blue eyes twinkled. "A prerogative of age is that I can order the handsomest man present to bear me company, and he daren't refuse."

Stephen laughed. "I have no desire to refuse." Which was the truth. The exuberant family party was tiring him. He would welcome a walk in the garden.

Young Cassandra dashed upstairs to get her grandmother a shawl, returning also with a cane and the dowager's elderly dog, a small beast with massive amounts of fur and dignity. Stephen exchanged a smile with Rosalind across the room. Then he and the old woman went outside, the dog walking sedately beside his mistress. It was a lovely October day, with golden sunshine burnishing the changing leaves and autumn flowers.

One hand on her cane and the other on Stephen's arm, Lady Westley guided him into the garden, a rich landscaped area that sloped down to the Thames. Cleverly winding paths made the garden seem much larger than it was. Despite the lateness of the season, masses of blossoms were everywhere. Admiring a bank of roses planted before a sun-baked brick wall, he said, "Your garden is very lovely."

"Autumn is its peak, I think. Soon a frost will kill most of my flowers. The leaves will fall and the bitter winter winds will blow off the river." She stooped to pick a golden chrysanthemum and absently rolled the stem between her fingers. "I'm sorry I won't be here to see the spring. I've lived in this house for half my life, and every spring the flowers are more beautiful than the year before."

"Will you be moving in with one of your children?"

"Oh, no. I'll be dead," she said in a calm voice.

A jolt ran through him. "Surely you can't know that."

"I can." She glanced at him. "I do."

Thinking she must be in a similar situation to himself, he asked, "Are you ill?"

"Age," she said simply. "My body is wearing out, and swiftly now. I would have died earlier, I think, but perhaps on some level I knew that Rosalind was coming."

They came to a clearing with a weathered stone fountain in the center. Lady Westley regarded the laughing cherub whose vase spilled water into a moss-edged pool. "There is no pain like that of losing a child," she said softly. "One never gets over it. Never. Meeting Rosalind is a little like having Sophia back again." She touched the chrysanthemum to her lips, then dropped it into the water by the cherub's plump toes.

As they continued along the path, he said, "I gather that the resemblance is strong, but Rosalind has lived a very different life from that of her mother."

"When I think of that sweet little infant digging for food in the rubbish, it makes my blood curdle." Lady Westley shook her head, then said in a lighter tone, "And imagine, a Westley on the stage! I wish I could have seen her."

"Rosalind is quite a good actress, though she hasn't the passionate need to perform that many players do." He smiled, thinking of her as Caliban. "Since the mere idea didn't shock you senseless, you would have been well pleased with her skill."

"It's hard to shock someone my age," the dowager said with a laugh. "For all that the girl has had a difficult life, she's still much like her mother. I knew the moment we met that she had Sophia's sweetness of disposition."

"No one knows that better than I," he agreed.

The next clearing held a sunny bench with a good view of the river. "Let's stay here a bit," she said. "This is my favorite spot. I like to watch the boats and barges." They sat down side by side, the little dog curling up by the dowager's feet.

"Sophia was my youngest, you know," the dowager said. "I almost died giving birth to her. Perhaps that created a special bond. Though truth to say, there is a special bond with each of my children. With Anne, my eldest, who fusses over me like a mother hen. With Richard, my only son. I've been fortunate in my children."

Stephen felt the familiar ache of regret for the children he'd never had. "And they have been fortunate in you."

He hesitated, weighing whether to proceed. Lady Westley had a faith and serenity that he wanted desperately to understand. It was scarcely proper to ask a woman who was a near stranger about such matters, but there was no one else he could ask. "How can you be so calm about your approaching death?"

She gave him a look of mild surprise. "Death is a natural consequence of life. Something that comes to us all, and no bad thing."

"I'm dying, too," he said harshly. "But I lack your philosophical calm."

"I see," she said. "I wondered a little at what I saw in your face during luncheon. You watched as if you were a step away from all of the others. How advanced is your illness?"

He appreciated her matter-of-factness. Many people would have been struck speechless with embarrassment at his announcement. "Quite advanced. I have weeks, at best. Every day I feel as if I've drifted farther away from the normal run of mankind."

"Does Rosalind know?"

He nodded. "I told her before we married. She might not have accepted my proposal if it meant putting up with me for years, but she was willing to bear me company for the little time remaining."

"Nonsense. It's quite clear that yours is not a mere marriage of convenience." Her expression became troubled. "Death is much harder for a young person like you who isn't ready. And it will be very hard on her. But death is not the end, you know. You shall see each other again."

He searched her face. "You really believe that?"

"Not believe." She gave him a tranquil smile. "Know."

"How?" he asked intensely. "What gives you such faith?"

"You may not believe my answer."

"Perhaps not, but I'd like to hear it."

She clasped her arthritically gnarled hands on the gold head of her cane as she considered her answer. "As I said earlier, I almost died of childbed fever after Sophia was born. The pain was dreadful, and I was terrified because I could feel my life ebbing away. Then suddenly I found that I was no longer in my body but floating by the ceiling. I remember looking down at myself and feeling very sorry for the poor miserable young woman in the bed.

"Then I heard someone call my name. I turned, and there was my mother, who had died five years before. I couldn't believe it, until she hugged me." Lady Westley pursed her lips. "It's hard to explain, since I didn't have a body, but it was still a very satisfactory hug. I had missed her terribly. She took my hand and led me into a garden of light. The most beautiful garden I'd ever seen." The dowager gestured at their surroundings. "Ever since, I've tried to re-create that garden, but this is only a pale shadow of what I saw there."

Fascinated without quite believing, Stephen said, "What happened then?"

"There were other people I knew, all of whom had died. They'd come to make me feel welcome and to help if I was confused." She smiled. "It was rather like the best soirée of one's life, only a thousand times better. As I looked around, I saw that in the center of the garden was a sort of temple of crystal that glowed with the brightest light of all. I wanted so much to go there, because I could feel the love radiating from it." Her expression became distant, yearning visible in her eyes.

"Did you go into the temple?"

She blinked, brought back to the present. "No. I heard a child crying, and knew it was my new baby. Suddenly I was in the nursery with the wet nurse, who was holding my shrieking daughter." The dowager smiled. "She wasn't very pretty then, all red face and squalls. But I was troubled by the idea that she would grow up never knowing her mother. I drifted through a wall into the next room and found Anne and Richard curled up in a corner. She was patting him on the back and saying that surely Mama would be all right. But she was crying, too."

The dog whimpered, and the dowager bent to stroke his head until he was silent again. "Then I found myself back in my own room, still on the ceiling, mind you. My husband, James, was there by the bed, holding my hand. He didn't say a word, but there were tears running down his face. I'd never seen him cry."

She glanced at Stephen. "We'd had an arranged marriage, you know. It turned out better than most. We got on well." She flashed a suddenly mischievous smile. "Both in bed and out of it. But I never knew until then that James loved me. He wasn't the sort to quote poetry or speak romantic words. Yet I could see the love inside him. He was glowing like a lantern with the same light that had been in the garden I'd just left."

Her brows drew together. "That was when I realized that I had a choice. I could go back to the garden or return to my family."

He studied her expression, trying to understand. "Surely remaining with your husband and children wasn't a difficult choice."

"Believe it or not, it *was* difficult," she said slowly. "I'd never felt so happy, so at peace, as in that garden. There were people I loved, and so much to learn. But I knew that my family needed me, and that the garden would always be waiting. I reached out to touch James. The next thing I knew, I was back in my bed, sweaty and feverish, and the physician telling me that I'd been unconscious for three days."

Stephen felt a crash of disappointment. "So it was all a dream."

"I said you wouldn't believe me." She shrugged. "It makes no sense, of course, but in that garden our kind of sense doesn't apply. For what it's worth, I later asked my husband if he'd sat by my bed, holding my hand and crying. He blushed the color of port wine but admitted it. Hard to see how I could have known that if I was unconscious, unless I really was floating up on the ceiling."

She could have been delirious and forgotten later that she had seen her husband. Still, it was a lovely story, and it gave her comfort. He asked, "Did you ever regret returning to your body?"

"Not really. Except, perhaps, when we lost Sophia, and again ten years ago, when James died, too." She gave a luminous smile. "But I'll be with them soon."

Perhaps she really would rejoin her lost loved ones. But if faith was the key to that heavenly garden, Stephen was doomed to eternal darkness.

A bank of clouds slid over the sun, and the air was suddenly cold. "I'd better take you in before you catch a chill," he said. "Your assembled progeny will toss me in the river if I don't take good care of you."

She gazed at him with a perception that seemed to slice to the center of his being. "You don't have to believe me. You will still find existence beyond this life."

He felt an aching desire for such certainty, but desire was not enough to create faith. Bleakly he said, "I hope you're right."

He got to his feet, then bent and kissed her cheek. "Even if you aren't, it's been a pleasure to make your acquaintance, Lady Westley. I don't know if Rosalind is like her mother, but she is surely like you, which is a great compliment to you both."

All of which was true. But as he helped the dowager to her feet and adjusted her shawl over her thin shoulders, he knew that he was no closer to the answers for his questions.

CHAPTER 30

Luncheon with the Westleys ran well into the afternoon. Rosalind might have stayed all night, except that she looked across the room and saw Stephen talking with her uncle Richard. Her husband looked very tired. Immediately remorseful about her lack of consideration, she said her farewells and soon they were on their way back to London.

Tired herself, Rosalind settled into her carriage seat and took her husband's hand. "That was much nicer than I expected. You were right, Stephen. I'm lucky to have so many families. Perhaps someday I'll have a chance to meet some of my French kin."

"I talked to Lord Westley about them," Stephen said. "He said that your first cousin, another Philippe St. Cyr, fought with the royalists and reclaimed the du Lac title and property after the Bourbons were restored to the throne. Apparently the estate is in poor shape, but your cousin is slowly restoring the place to its former glory." He glanced at her. "Of course, by rights it's yours."

"Heavens," she said blankly. "I'm entitled to an estate in France?"

"I don't think it will be hard to prove that you're the rightful heir."

She thought a moment, wondering if her French cousin had brown eyes like hers, then shook her head. "I may be the direct heir, but it sounds as if the estate belongs to my cousin by right of blood and sweat.

Besides, I don't want to live in France. Let Cousin Philippe have it."

Stephen smiled at her. "I thought you'd say that. You're very generous."

She laughed. "I can afford to be, when you take such good care of me."

"I'll tell my solicitor to write your cousin. He should know of your existence, and it would be best if you formally renounced your rights in his favor." He squeezed her hand. "In return, perhaps he might be willing to give you some pieces of family furniture or jewelry as a reminder of your French heritage."

She had a sudden, vivid memory of a bedroom furnished in graceful, un-English furniture. Her mother's dressing table . . .

"I'd like that." She smiled. "A whole new family to discover! I wonder if they are as nice as my mother's family."

"The Westleys remind me a bit of the Fitzgeralds," he observed. "I hadn't realized that members of aristocratic families could be so fond of one another."

His family certainly wasn't a model of mutual affection. "My grandmother said that your mother was wild but had a good heart," she said hesitantly. "Was that true? You've never really spoken of your mother."

"Wild was a polite way of saying promiscuous," he said dryly. "She was very beautiful, and my father was obsessed with her. Their marriage was a strange, unwholesome struggle for power. My father hated the fact that he could not control his lust for her, while my mother disliked self-control on general principle. I used to give thanks that I hadn't inherited my parents' passionate dispositions. Michael did, and it has cost him dearly, though he has mastered it now." A shadow touched his eyes. "And yet it's true that my mother had a generous heart. I've wondered sometimes what she would have been like if she'd been born to less wealth or made a different marriage. She died when I was fifteen."

Strange that he did not consider himself passionate. She'd seen the passion in him the first time they met, and nothing that happened since had changed her opinion.

He covered a yawn with one hand. "Sorry. I didn't sleep well last night. If you'll excuse me, I think I'll nap."

Yawns are contagious. Rosalind covered one of her own. "An excellent idea."

Stephen closed his eyes and relaxed back in his seat. With his features in repose, she was acutely aware of the changes that had taken place gradually over the last weeks. His weight loss emphasized the lines and planes of his face, making him look twenty years older than his real age. And, to her dismay, she saw that there was a faint yellowish cast to his skin. The disease was attacking his liver. Her heart clenched at the knowledge of how quickly time was running out.

She laid her head against his shoulder, and his arm came around her. So right, so natural. Yet she could not rest, despite her fatigue. A day where she had laid the foundations for new family relationships underlined the fact that Stephen had not been so fortunate with his relatives. As she closed her eyes, she made a silent vow to do what she could to change that.

Rosalind stepped from the Ashburton carriage and climbed the steps of Herrington House. After wielding the knocker, she waited for a response with no visible sign of nerves even though her stomach was in knots.

Wryly she thought that thespian training was excellent for someone wishing to swim in the treacherous waters of polite society. Maria had taught her daughter to mimic manners and accents, wear clothes well, and conceal her emotions. No aspiring lady could ask for more.

A footman opened the door, and Rosalind breezed by him as if there could be no question of admittance. "I am the Duchess of Ashburton." She handed the footman one of her newly engraved cards. "I wish to see my sister-in-law."

The footman hesitated. "Lady Herrington does not usually receive this early."

Rosalind narrowed her eyes in the expression Maria used when playing Queen Elizabeth as she regarded the Spanish Armada. The footman flinched.

"Of course, you are family," he said hastily. "Pray take a seat in the drawing room, Your Grace. I shall inform her ladyship that you've arrived."

Rosalind went where he directed, but preferred to pace rather than sit. The drawing room was beautifully furnished, immaculately kept, and about as welcoming as the average tomb. Not unlike Claudia.

Speak of the devil . . . The door opened, and Lady Herrington marched in, her expression coldly furious. "How dare you come to my house when you know how I regard you! I suppose you think that propriety will prevent me from having you thrown out. Well, you're wrong. If you do not leave within one minute, I shall have my servants pitch you into the gutter, where you belong."

This was even worse than Rosalind had expected. "Believe me, it's not my habit to force myself where I'm not wanted," she said in her most reasonable tone. "But I have something of the greatest urgency to discuss with you. Will you give me five minutes to explain? If you do, I promise never to trouble you again."

Claudia's expression became even colder, but she said grudgingly, "Very well. It's worth five minutes of my time on the chance that I'll be permanently rid of you, though I doubt your word is to be trusted." She stationed herself behind a wing chair, as if protecting herself from possible assault.

Rosalind took a deep breath. "Perhaps it will make you more tolerant to know that we have just learned that my mother was Sophia Westley, sister of the present Lord Westley and Lady Cassell."

Claudia shook her head with disgust. "You're nothing if not a bold liar. I knew Sophia Westley. She married a Frenchman and died many years ago in the Reign of Terror. I've never heard that she left children."

Rosalind felt a flicker of pain as the image of that death crossed her mind. "She had one daughter. Me. By birth, Marguerite St. Cyr, Countess du Lac," she said calmly. "My English nurse brought me to London but died before we could reach my mother's family. I was adopted by the Fitzgeralds, and you know the rest. I shall not apologize for either them or myself. However, given your obsession with breeding, you should be pleased to hear that the Westleys have accepted me as Sophia's daughter. If you doubt it, ask any member of the family. For that matter, if you knew my mother, just look at me. Apparently I am the image of her."

Claudia's eyes narrowed as she studied her visitor. Rosalind guessed that the other woman wanted to dispute the resemblance but couldn't.

"It's true you look much like I remember Sophia," she said reluctantly. "But even if you are her legitimate daughter, it takes more than good birth to make a lady.

Being raised among some of the coarsest elements of society has left its mark. Look how you used your actress wiles to seduce my brother and turn him from his duty."

"You overestimate my wiles, and underestimate Stephen's intelligence," Rosalind said with real amusement. "Obviously nothing will change your opinion of me. Still, you must at least be grateful that in the eyes of your world, Stephen will be seen as having made a match worthy of the Duke of Ashburton."

Claudia's lips thinned. "The world may approve. My father would not have."

Guided by what she had gleaned about the Kenyons from Stephen, Rosalind said quietly, "Your father is dead. No matter how hard you try, nothing you do now will earn you his approval, or his love."

Claudia turned white. "Leave this house instantly!"

Mentally kicking herself for straying from her purpose, Rosalind said swiftly, "I have a minute left to tell you why I came." She hesitated, then decided on bluntness. "Stephen is dying. He is unlikely to survive more than a few weeks longer. Scorn me as much as you like, but please go to him before it's too late."

The other woman's eyes widened with shock. "Stephen dying? That's impossible. Kenyons always live to a ripe old age."

"Not Stephen. He has some sort of horrible internal disease," Rosalind said, unable to keep the bleakness from her voice. "Clear proof that only the good die young, because he's the best man I've ever known. He cares for you deeply, and your repudiation hurts him. If he dies when you are estranged, I think that fact will hurt you even more than it does him."

"Dear God, not Stephen," Claudia whispered, her expression agonized. She closed her eyes with a shudder. When they reopened, they were full of bitterness. "You've done very well for yourself, haven't you? Since my brother is generous to a fault, a few weeks of acting the role of a devoted wife will allow you to spend the rest of your life with wealth and status."

Even though Rosalind knew protest was futile, she said coldly, "I didn't marry him for his money."

"No?" Claudia's mouth twisted. "Is he really dying of natural causes? Or did you turn Borgia after deciding that you would prefer the freedom of being a rich widow?"

Rosalind gasped as if she had been struck physically. Even though it was clear that Claudia didn't mean the charge, that she was lashing out from shock and grief, the words were scalding. "It's hard to understand how a man like Stephen could have a sister as vicious as you," she said, voice shaking. "He was already mortally ill when we met. If you doubt that, ask the Ashburton physician, Dr. Blackmer."

Unable to bear Claudia's malice a moment longer, she stalked across the drawing room to the door. Her hand was on the knob when she decided, for Stephen's sake, to make one last plea. "Within a few days, we will be going to Ashburton Abbey. I suggest that before we leave, you search your conscience to decide what means more—your damned pride, or the brother who loves you."

Then she left, temples pounding. She would like to think that her words had softened Claudia's heart. But she couldn't.

During the ride back to Ashburton House, Rosalind invoked all her actress's discipline to get her emotions under control again. Stephen was working at home this morning, and she did not want him to see her distress. Certainly she would not tell him of her disastrous visit to his sister.

Growing up in the same household that had produced the poisonous Claudia, how had Stephen become so kind? So fair-minded? She remembered him saying that he and his brother had learned that it was impossible to meet their father's standards, but Claudia hadn't. The thought produced a flicker of compassion for her sister-in-law. Trying to please a dead man was a game that couldn't be won.

Her carriage halted at Ashburton House, pulling up behind a large traveling coach. Rosalind stepped out and found that her parents had just arrived. As a footman brought out the Fitzgeralds' modest baggage, her mother was surveying the imposing facade of the house doubtfully.

With a burst of gladness, she cried out, "Mama! Papa!" She flew to greet them as if she were five years old again. Thomas was closer, and she almost bowled him over when she hurled herself into his arms.

He hugged her back enthusiastically. "It's good to see you, lassie, but it's only been weeks, you know, not years."

"It's felt like years." She turned and embraced Maria, though what she really wanted was to crawl into Maria's lap and be rocked to sleep. "Before I married Stephen, I hadn't been away from you for twenty-four years."

"True, but you do make a lovely duchess, my dear." Laughing, Maria stepped back and waved a hand at Ashburton House. "The coachman insisted on bringing us here, but really, we'd be just as happy at an inn. Happier."

"Stephen wouldn't hear of it, and neither will I."

Rosalind linked her arms through her parents' and escorted them up the steps, leaving the footman to bring the baggage. "You made good time."

"Easy to do when one has a luxurious traveling coach at one's disposal," her father said genially. "Now, my girl, what is this pressing business of Ashburton's? He wouldn't say in his letter, but surely you know what he has in mind."

"Yes, but I'll let Stephen explain." They entered the foyer together. To the butler she said, "Please bring refreshments to the salon. When the duke's solicitor leaves, tell him that my parents have arrived and that I hope he may join us."

Then she led her parents to the salon. Portia was snoozing there, and the kitten instantly reduced Thomas's susceptible heart to mush when she jumped on his lap and began to purr. The next few minutes were spent exchanging news. Jessica and Simon Kent were not yet betrothed, but an announcement was expected. Brian missed his tutor, and had made no visible progress in Latin since Stephen had left. Mary Kent had taken over Rosalind's duties as stage manager, and was handling them very efficiently.

After the first rush of talk, Rosalind decided to reveal the only important piece of news that she was free to discuss: the story of her newly discovered identity. Making it clear that she considered her adoptive parents to be her real family, she described how she'd met the Westleys. Thomas and Maria were startled and intrigued. When Rosalind finished speaking, Thomas said, "To think, the cuckoo in our nest was a countess!"

"No. Just a baby chick badly in need of tending." The refreshments arrived, so Rosalind put on her best performance of a gracious hostess. As she poured tea, she suddenly realized how she should have answered when her husband had asked where her spiritual faith came from. She believed because surely a benevolent God had sent the Fitzgeralds down that street in St. Katherine's so many years before.

Day Twenty-seven

Stephen's session with the family solicitor was draining because he had finally revealed the reason behind his flurry of recent business. The solicitor had been shocked and uncomfortable with the news. The poor devil had barely had a chance to adjust to the old duke's death, and now he'd have to accustom himself to still another Kenyon.

It was a relief to emerge from the meeting and learn that the Fitzgeralds had arrived. Spirits rising, Stephen went to greet his guests. The Fitzgeralds and Rosalind were chattering like magpies when he entered. His wife rose and came to give him a kiss.

Under her breath, she said, "Papa is perishing to know why you asked them to come. I've done an admirable job of not telling him."

"You're always admirable." He hugged her for a moment, his fatigue diminishing at her touch. Then he turned to his guests. "It's good to see you both. Maria, you look beautiful." He kissed his mother-in-law, then shook Thomas's hand. "How long can you stay?"

"Only a night, two at the most," his father-in-law said. "The troupe can manage without us, but fewer players drastically limits what can be performed." He gave a wicked smile. "I'm hoping we can see Kean tonight, so I can make catcalls."

Knowing his in-laws would want to see a play, Stephen had checked the schedules. "Tonight Kean is performing as Sir Giles Overreach in *A New Way to Pay Old Debts*. My box at Drury Lane is only a short toss of a rotten orange from the stage."

"My husband will give neither catcalls nor rotten fruit." Maria gave Thomas a steely stare. "Will he?"

"No," he admitted. "But I can dream, can't I?"

"Dreaming is permitted," she conceded.

"Speaking of dreams . . ." Stephen took a seat and accepted a cup of tea from Rosalind. "Are either of you familiar with the old Athenaeum playhouse near Covent Garden?"

Maria nodded. "We saw *The Way of the World* there once many years ago. Decent Mirabell, terrible Millamant."

"But she had good ankles," her husband said, eyes twinkling.

"Not better than mine," Maria informed him coldly.

"Perhaps I'd better check." Thomas leaned toward his wife with the apparent intention of raising her skirt a few inches.

As Maria swatted at his hand, Rosalind said in perfect mimicry of Jessica, "The Parents are at it again!"

Everyone burst into laughter. After the amusement died down, Stephen said with studied casualness, "Would you two like to have the Athenaeum for your troupe?"

"It would be a fine place to perform, and no mistake." Thomas took a sip of his tea. "A pity we can't take it on the road with us."

"Actually, I was thinking in terms of giving you the theater so the troupe can be moved to London permanently."

There was a moment of incredulous silence. Then Thomas banged his cup down on the saucer. "The devil you say!"

"The devil would have nothing to do with it. The Athenaeum is available freehold at a reasonable price with all properties and costumes, and a modest house nearby for you to live in." Stephen smiled a little. "There are no strings attached. As owner-manager, you'll answer to no one except Maria, so I have every confidence that the two of you will make a great success of it."

"But . . . but . . ." Stunned, Thomas looked at his wife. Her gaze met his in wordless communion.

If Stephen and Rosalind had spent so many years together, would they have developed that profound an understanding? The currents were so intense that Stephen could feel them. Thomas, startled and too independent to want to owe anyone anything. Maria silently reminding her husband of too many years of financial insecurity, the sacrifices that had been made, the dreams that had been put aside.

"How can we possibly accept such a gift?" Thomas said uncertainly.

"Very easily," Maria said, her gaze still on her husband. "We're too old to be traipsing around the Midlands ten months a year." For all of the years of their marriage, she had subordinated her brilliant talents for the good of her husband and family. Now she wanted the Athenaeum, and she expected Thomas to bend enough to accept it.

Thomas gave a faint nod and turned to his son-in-law. "Why?"

"For what you did for Rosalind," Stephen said quietly. "And for me, and for others. In short, for being good. Why shouldn't goodness sometimes be rewarded?"

"Just accept, Thomas," Maria said. "Plenty of plays have a deus ex machina. Why can't we have one in our lives?" She rose and gave Stephen a kiss. "Bless you,

Stephen. I don't have to tell you what this means because you already know."

She turned to her husband. "What play shall we put on first? It needs to be one with good strong roles for you, me, Jessica, and Simon."

Thomas's lingering doubts vanished as the vision of opening in London took hold of his mind. "We must start with Shakespeare, of course. How about *The Winter's Tale*? Meaty roles for you and me, and the young people as well."

Maria nodded approvingly. "Excellent choice. Jessica and Simon will make poignant young lovers, you'll stun the audience with your kingliness, and I shall reduce all the females to torrents of tears as your unjustly accused wife."

"All that, plus a happy ending to send everyone home smiling." With a sudden whoop, Thomas swept Maria up in his arms and spun her in a circle. "Be damned to seeing Kean tonight. Let's go visit the Athenaeum right now!"

Laughing, the four of them did just that. Stephen spent the afternoon with Rosalind by his side and her parents darting around the playhouse like swallows, making plans, discussing how many new people would have to be hired, and cheerfully squabbling about the refurbishing. The Fitzgeralds also treated the younger couple to a dazzling segment from *The Way of the World*, with Maria showing how she thought Millamant should be played.

For years after Stephen was gone, Thomas and Maria would be bringing joy and tears to London audiences. Wealth had many advantages. But one of the very best was the way it could make dreams come true.

CHAPTER 31

It had been a tiring day, so Rosalind was grateful that her parents had decided not to go to Drury Lane. Within two months they'd be living in London and able to go to the theater whenever they pleased, at least until the Athenaeum reopened. Probably that would be sometime in late winter, after the refurbishing and suitable public notices.

Following dinner the men were left to talk business over port while Rosalind withdrew to the salon with Maria. She was grateful for the opportunity to be alone with her mother, since the Fitzgeralds would be staying for only two nights.

"I can hardly wait to finish our season so we can come to London for good," Maria said as she paced the salon, looking as young as on the day when she'd rescued Rosalind from the slums. "A house of my own, Rose! A theater in London that we can run as we choose! And the money to keep us going long enough to become established. Stephen isn't a deus ex machina, he's our guardian angel."

Relaxing on the sofa, Rosalind smiled indulgently, feeling as if she were the elder.

Maria turned toward her, eyes dancing mischievously. "You're going to have to be a little easier on your husband, though. You're blossoming, while he looks burnt to the socket. You must remember that men are frail creatures, unable to match female endurance in the bedroom."

Rosalind's pleasure in her parents' company burst like a punctured bubble as she was brought face to face with the stark reality of Stephen's condition. The tears that were very near the surface these days erupted into shuddering sobs.

"What's wrong, sweetheart?" Maria said with alarm. "Surely you and Stephen are getting along well. I can see it in the way you look at each other."

"He . . . he's dying." Rosalind tried to collect herself. "I knew before we married, but . . . oh, Mama, I didn't expect it to be so hard." Her tears became worse.

"Dear God," Maria whispered. She put her arms around Rosalind, cradling her to her breast as she had in the early years when her adoptive daughter woke screaming in the night. "What a terrible, terrible thing. Such a young man, and such a fine one."

Rosalind cried as she had been longing to do ever since learning of Stephen's illness. Even though there was nothing her mother could do, it was a comfort to tell her the truth. When her tears ran out, she said in a rusty voice, "There is one piece of good news. I think I'm with child."

"Oh, Rose, how wonderful! That must be a great comfort to you both."

"I haven't told Stephen yet. I wanted to be sure."

"Tell me what your body has been doing," her mother ordered.

Rosalind obediently listed all of the definable changes, as well as her own inward conviction. At the end Maria gave a nod of satisfaction. "You're definitely breeding. God willing, you'll have a fine, healthy child to take your mind from its sorrow."

A thought struck her. "Heavens, a boy would be the next duke from the moment he first draws breath." She shook her head. "To think, my first grandchild a duke!

It's a good thing you've discovered your grand relations, Rose. With Stephen gone, you'll need their support, for you'll have to be at ease in society for the child's sake."

Maria had deduced that much more quickly than Rosalind had. "The Westleys have been all that is kind." She took Maria's hand in hers and said, trying not to sound plaintive, "But you're still my mother, aren't you?"

"Always, Rose." Maria smiled with a warmth that briefly alleviated Rosalind's underlying sorrow. "Always."

Day Twenty-five

Much as he enjoyed the Fitzgeralds' visit, Stephen was glad to see them go. Their exuberance was tiring, and he was very aware of having to husband his strength. As he stood with Rosalind, waving good-bye to her parents, he was struck with the sorrow of knowing he would not see them again. Every day brought new losses.

After the coach rumbled away, Rosalind turned to him with a smile. "I'm going to Cassell House to have luncheon with my two new aunts." She stretched up for a kiss. "And tonight I have something special to tell you."

He held her close for a moment. Though passion was ebbing, he still craved her nearness and regretted that she would be away for several hours. But he had work to do.

After Rosalind left he went to his study, giving orders not to be disturbed. It was time to deal with his public responsibilities. He was Lord-Lieutenant of the County of Somersetshire, governor of two different schools, a trustee of the British Museum, and a dozen other things. One of the advantages of a slow death rather than a swift, unexpected one was that he had time to tie up neatly the loose ends of his life. And the sooner these ends were tied, the sooner they could return to the abbey.

The pain was bad today. Weighing it against the need for a clear head, he took two opium pills. Then he set to work on the small mountain of papers prepared by his secretary. With everything laid out so neatly, he should be finished by the end of the day.

The attack, as always, came swiftly, between one document and the next. He froze as agony seared through his esophagus and stomach. His hand spasmed shut, and the quill pen snapped as he doubled over, retching violently. A good thing he'd asked not to be disturbed. No one would come for hours. That would give him time to recover.

He levered himself upright with one hand on the desk, intending to go from his desk to the sofa on the other side of his study. But his head spun and his limbs were numb, incapable of support or balance. He pitched to the floor and scarcely felt the impact when he hit.

He lay dizzily on his side, unable to move, pain racking his internal organs. Even so, it was a shock to begin to lose consciousness. As the world blackened around the edges, he thought with astonished fury that surely he couldn't be dying now, today. He had more than three weeks until Blackmer's allotted time was up.

It was his last thought before darkness vanquished him.

"Stephen!"

Rosalind's voice pulled him from the dark, swirling mists. She was kneeling beside him, face white.

The intimate rustle of her petticoat. Warm fingers on his wrist as she felt for a pulse. Her scent, sweetly floral. He managed to say, "Not . . . gone yet."

"Thank God! When I came in and found you lying here . . ." She stopped, tears glinting in her eyes. "If I help, can you get upstairs to the bedroom?"

He thought about it and realized bleakly that the boundaries of his world had just contracted to the walls of this house. He could no longer maintain even a pretense of normality. He'd never see the abbey again. *Christ.* He'd probably never make love to Rosalind again. He hadn't known that the last time was . . . the last time.

After absorbing that blow, he said in a rasping whisper, "No. Bring . . . two of the footmen."

She stood and went to the bellpull, jerking it hard. Then she returned to kneel beside him, gently wiping the perspiration from his face with her handkerchief.

When the footmen came, she gave orders to take him upstairs. Her voice was calm on the surface, though he could hear the brittle edge.

The footmen were young, and shocked and alarmed to see their master in such a state. They handled him gently. Dizzily Stephen thought that in moments like these, a man was rewarded for treating his servants well.

He maintained a tenuous thread on consciousness as he was taken upstairs and put to bed. In a nightshirt, the first he'd worn since marrying Rosalind. For warmth, he guessed, since he was shaking with cold.

Rosalind sat by the bed and took his hand in her warm clasp. "Can you hear me, Stephen?" When he nodded, she continued, "I'm going to call a physician now. I should have insisted on that when we first reached London." She started to rise.

He caught her wrist, stopping her. "No! I've seen

what physicians do when a rich man is dying. My father was bled and purged and blistered and put through every kind of hell. The beasts in the fields die with more dignity than he did. I swore then that when my time came, I would not let that happen to me." He caught Rosalind's gaze with his to emphasize his seriousness. "I can face death. After all, I have no choice. But I see no reason to let a collection of damned butchers loose on my body."

"But what if a doctor can help?" she said pleadingly. "You've only had the opinion of Blackmer. What if he was wrong and your disease is curable?"

"If I believed that, I would have been willing to try every quack in Britain." He exhaled roughly. "But the body doesn't lie. I'm dying. Promise that you'll let me do it in my own way, Rosalind. Please."

She bit her lip, on the verge of tears, then nodded. "I promise. Shall I get your opium pills for the pain?"

"On my dressing table. Bring me three." A strong dose, but it should be enough to ease the agony, at least a little.

Rosalind went into his dressing room and returned with the jar. "This one?"

He nodded. "I thought the pills would run out before the end, but it appears that Blackmer's calculations erred on the side of generosity," he said with the blackest of humor. "The medicine will outlast me."

She raised his head and put the pills in his mouth, then gave him water to wash them down. Even the small effort of swallowing exhausted him.

Tenderly Rosalind laid his head back among the pillows. Strands of tawny hair had come loose to curl around her face, and her eyes were great dark pools of pain. Though his physical body was numbed, his emotional sensitivity was heightened to the point where he could feel her fear and devastation almost as if they were his own. In some ways that was harder to bear than the physical pain that was chewing at his vitals.

He wanted to tell her how much she meant to him. How precious their weeks together had been. But he didn't have the words. He'd never had such words.

As darkness flowed through him again, he watched her face, hoping desperately that this would not be the last time he would ever see it.

Rosalind held Stephen's hand as he drifted to sleep. What to do next? Unless he made a remarkable recovery, he would be unable to return to Ashburton Abbey. She must tell his secretary to summon Lord Michael, who might be waiting at the abbey now. Or perhaps he was still at his home in Wales. Fyfield would have to send express messages to both places.

What of herself? Should she ask her mother or Jessica to come stay with her? The company would be welcome, but it would inconvenience the troupe. She must think about that, and at the moment she was not thinking at all well.

Stephen's breathing was very slow but even. She hoped that meant the opium pills had reduced the pain. She rose and went to tell Fyfield to send for Lord Michael and take care of any other business needing attention. Luckily the staff had accepted her from the beginning and obeyed her orders without question.

Then she spoke with Hubble, Stephen's valet. Like her, his first instinct was to call a physician, until she explained why Stephen did not want one. Hubble had been part of the household when the old duke had died. Memory of the medical torture that had taken place then made him agree to abide by Stephen's wishes.

The valet wanted to sit with Stephen, so she gave permission. He'd known Stephen far longer than she, and had earned the right. Besides, she would not be able to do everything, much as she wanted to.

After the valet went in to his master, Rosalind hovered indecisively in the hall outside the bedroom. She wanted desperately to hide where she could break down without being overheard. Unfortunately privacy was hard to come by in a mansion full of servants.

Then she remembered the other suite, the one used by Lord Michael and his wife. Apart from a weekly cleaning, the rooms were left undisturbed. Numbly she went down the hall to their apartment.

The furniture was covered with holland covers, but that didn't matter. She went into the bedroom. There, aching as if her heart were being torn from her body, she threw herself onto the massive bed and gave in to her grief.

CHAPTER 32

It was good to be back at the abbey again. Stephen walked along the path that ran diagonally across the cloister garden, enjoying the crunch of gravel beneath his boots. The garden was perhaps his favorite spot on the estate. Some of his earliest memories were of playing here. He'd never seen it more beautiful than today. The flowers were at their peak, scents intoxicating and brilliant blossoms swaying languidly in the sun.

Yet how could he be at Ashburton in summer? He was in London, and the season was autumn. Frowning, he halted to survey his surroundings. Everything seemed quite normal, including his own body, dressed in his usual country garb of riding boots, dark blue coat, and buff breeches.

Except that he felt no pain. That was no longer normal.

Puzzled, he began to walk again. The garden had been the private courtyard of the original religious foundation. All four sides were bounded by an open arcade of ancient stone arches. Long ago the nuns of Ashburton Abbey had taken their exercise here. The modern inhabitants of the abbey still did the same. He'd always particularly enjoyed the covered walkways on stormy days, when he could be protected by the old stones while rain poured down a few feet away.

Louisa had also been very fond of the place. She would spend hours in the garden on fine days, or sheltered in the cloisters during inclement weather.

In fact, there she was now, sitting on a stone bench and embroidering with her usual meticulous care. The sight was so natural that it took him a moment to realize that there was not usually a bench in that spot.

And an instant longer to remember that Louisa was dead.

Was this a dream? It must be. Yet he'd never had a dream that seemed so real.

"Louisa?" he said doubtfully. He walked toward her.

She looked up and smiled with a serenity he'd never seen before. Though she didn't speak aloud, he sensed her greeting in his head. *Stephen. I've been expecting you.*

He went down on one knee on the grass in front of her so that their eyes were level. Louisa was as petite and beautiful as ever, but her expression was different from what he remembered. She looked—*accessible* was the best word he could find. The invisible wall that had always separated them had vanished. "Where am I?" he asked. "And why am I here?"

She laid her needlework on her lap and regarded him with tranquil blue eyes. *This is a sort of anteroom to heaven.*

He stared at her. "So there really is life after death?"

The word death has such finality. In truth, there is only life. What is called death is merely . . . transition. She smiled faintly. *Admittedly, it's a drastic one.*

He remembered Lady Westley's garden of light. "A few days ago, I met a woman who told me of an experience rather like what is happening now. Have I died and you're here to help me make that transition?"

You are not dead. However, you are so near that the veil between the seen and the unseen has become very thin. That is why you can be here. She gave him a rueful smile. *As for me—it's true that I've come to help you, but also to make amends.*

"Make amends? For what?" he asked with surprise. "You never harmed me. You always behaved with grace and courtesy. It is no one's fault that . . . that our marriage was not a closer one."

You're wrong. The fault was mine. Her expression showed deep regret. *I always knew, even when I was a small child, that I should not marry. But I let myself be persuaded that it was my duty because I desperately wanted to return to Ashburton Abbey. So I agreed to be your wife. By serving my own selfish needs, I deprived you of the warmth you deserved, because it was not in me to give. You are a good and loving man. Though I made you deeply unhappy, you always treated me with consideration and respect.*

Few men would have done as much. Can you forgive what I did to you?

He rocked back on his heels, puzzled and shocked. Him, loving? No one had ever suggested that before. He was cool. Detached. A gentleman, even of temper and committed to justice. A good friend. But those mild virtues were certainly not love. He didn't really know what love was.

Then he thought of the aching silences of his first marriage. The physical and emotional despair that had sometimes overwhelmed him, and the banked anger that had burned deep inside. Perhaps those things were all signs of love that had never had a chance to be expressed. The idea was novel, and rather disturbing, for it meant that he was not the man he thought he was. Yet he could not deny that the passionate intensity of his feelings for Rosalind were not those of a cool, detached gentleman.

He raised his eyes to Louisa's, seeing the regret in the clear blue depths. "There is nothing to forgive, my dear. I also had doubts about marrying you, and let myself be coerced into going against my instincts. But— didn't we both try our best? If there wasn't love or passion between us, at least there was civility." He hesitated, then added, "And surely, kindness?"

Her delicate face became luminous. *Yes, there was kindness, especially on your part. Thank you, Stephen.*

Deep within him he felt a sense of release as the guilt and remorse over his first marriage dissolved. They had both done their best. One could do no more.

Louisa bent her head over her needlework again, and they sat in friendly silence. He had never felt more at ease with her. The garden was so tranquil that one of the exquisitely colored butterflies floated down to perch on his hand for a moment.

But he wasn't ready for ultimate peace. Remembering her earlier remark, he said, "You told me that you accepted my proposal because you wanted so much to return to Ashburton Abbey. Why? You'd never even seen the place before we married."

She set one last stitch and knotted the shimmering thread. Then she raised the embroidered panel to reveal an exquisitely wrought tapestry of the cloister garden. But not as it was in the present. The stone arches were not worn, the plantings were different, and the square shape of a chapel bell tower rose in the background. He recognized the scene from an old etching from before the dissolution of the monasteries. This was how Ashburton Abbey had looked in its days as a religious foundation.

Louisa gave the tapestry a little shake, and suddenly it came alive and surrounded them, as if they had stepped back in time. They were both standing on velvety grass, and Louisa now wore a dark nun's habit.

She raised her calm gaze to his. *Long ago, in another life, I lived at the abbey and was at peace. In this life I was drawn to the abbey again because I instinctively sought what my heart desired. But when I married you and came here to live, I learned that it wasn't the stones that called to me. What my heart truly yearned for was the community of faith I had lost.*

The bell began to ring in the tower above, a deep, solemn call to prayer. She inclined her head for a moment. *Good-bye, Stephen. May grace be with you.*

She turned and walked away, her long robes gliding silently over the grass. He saw that a line of similarly dressed women were walking in the west cloister. Louisa joined the procession at the end, her head bowed, the veil obscuring her face as she moved in stately time to the tolling bell.

The first nun turned into the door that led to the

chapel. One by one the women disappeared from sight. After Louisa, the door silently closed, and Stephen was alone.

In the same wordless way as Louisa had communicated with him, he realized that once she had been part of the spiritual sisterhood that had lived and prayed here for centuries. Celibate and devout, she had been whole. Because she had not found that wholeness in her life with him, there had been a deep sadness in her that separated them more thoroughly than stone walls would have.

Now she was whole again. He closed his eyes and gave a prayer of thanks on her behalf. The first true prayer of his life.

If he really was alive. Life was Rosalind, not an empty courtyard that had again become the garden he knew and loved.

He glanced around restlessly. His heart leaped when he saw Rosalind coming toward him along one of the diagonal paths, her hand tucked under the elbow of the man beside her. His wife and her companion were dressed in the sumptuous, elaborate clothing of a quarter century before.

And yet—the woman was not Rosalind. Her eyes were blue, not brown, her height a little less, the shape of her spirit different. With eerily calm acceptance, he realized that he was seeing Sophia Westley and her husband, Philippe St. Cyr. The Count and Countess du Lac.

Sophia gave him a smile as if she'd known him all his life, and offered her hand. It was warm and firm and very real. He bowed over it. When he straightened, he realized with a small shock that she was younger than Rosalind was now, and her husband only a few years older. Younger than Stephen.

She continued to hold Stephen's hand, and vivid images began to run swiftly through his mind. He saw an elderly woman stumbling through the woods holding a terrified child. Hiding from soldiers, using her small stock of coins to buy coarse peasant food and rides in farm wagons. Finally, on reaching a seaport— France? Belgium?—buying passage to London. Stephen had the uncanny sense that Sophia and Philippe had traveled with the nurse and her charge, guiding and protecting as best they could.

But they could not save the old woman when her badly strained heart finally failed on the London quay. Stephen saw the uniformed guard reach for Rosalind, saw her run in terror, her small legs taking her into the stinking maze of streets behind the quay.

Sophia and Philippe stayed with the child, using what small power they had to protect her. Sophia also searched for someone who might take her daughter and keep her safe, but without success. She had been only a ghost, and a new, confused one at that.

Then came the day when Sophia found Thomas and Maria leaving the Tower of London, laughing and talking about their visit to the crown jewels. There had been a kinship of spirit in Maria that Sophia had been able to reach. Silently she urged Maria to walk through the mean streets of St. Katherine's.

Sophia brought the Fitzgeralds to the right place. It was Philippe who gave his small daughter the invisible nudge that had sent her into Maria's arms. Then, finally, the Count and Countess du Lac had been free to seek their own Garden of Light.

"I understand." Stephen bent and kissed the smooth cheek of his mother-in-law. Then Philippe clasped his hand, shaking it firmly. He was a dark, handsome man with warm brown eyes. Rosalind's eyes. Stephen continued, "You both did your work well."

Not us alone. Philippe made a gesture, and Stephen was looking into a walled garden. An elderly woman with a serene face was watching over several children who danced around in the sun. *Madame Standish, Marguerite's brave nurse.*

The old woman raised her head and smiled at Stephen, then turned her attention to her charges again. He realized that in this place that was not earth and not quite heaven, she was caring for children who had died young.

Stephen glanced back to Sophia and Philippe. "Thank you," he said quietly. "I know that you didn't save your daughter for my sake, but I have benefited from your actions. She has been the greatest joy of my life."

In his head Stephen heard the joint words, *Tell Marguerite how much we love her. And that we look forward to the day when we shall see her again.* Then they turned and walked away, toward the sun, until they disappeared into the light.

Throat tight with raw, newly discovered feelings, Stephen watched them go, feeling the light burning through him, searing every fiber of his being.

And the light was love. He sank down onto the bench that Louisa had used, shaking from the force of the emotions surging through him as internal barriers burned away.

He could see quite clearly how he had built a wall to protect himself from the pain of caring. Construction had begun when he was an infant. His earliest memories were of being punished for being too free with his emotions. Bricks had been laid when his father scolded him for weeping over the death of a pet, or beat him for playing with lowborn estate children. Whole courses had been laid when he first discovered his mother's promiscuity. Fear, anger, shame, and betrayal, brick by brick the wall had risen until it separated him from the pain of living.

And also, of course, from the joy. By the time the wall was completed, he was the very model of an English gentleman. Cool, detached, fair-minded, never too passionate for decorum. Never risking the heights and depths of love.

The shock and painful flashes of emotion made him feel as if he were made of ice cracking in a spring thaw. But the light surrounding him was warm, healing his wounded spirit with love. There had always been love in his life, he realized, though he had not dared call it by that name. He'd loved his mother, for all her failings, and his sister, who was better able to give than receive. He'd always loved Michael, even though the emotion was twisted together with complicated strands of competitiveness and the scorn he had felt in an unrecognized desire to win approval from his father.

Most of all, he loved Rosalind. Her warmth and understanding had illuminated the dark places of his spirit from the beginning, and the passion they shared was the closest thing to paradise he'd ever known. The fact that he'd found her, against all the odds, was clear evidence that there must be some kind of a divine plan underlying life.

He closed his eyes, letting the blessed light flow through him. Rosalind. His wife, his beloved. He felt a deep sense of awe, and of gratitude, that in the shadow of death he had discovered the nature of love.

And he would never fear death again.

CHAPTER 33

Long after she had run out of tears, Rosalind lay sprawled on the bed, chilled from the autumn cold but too drained to move. Stephen's illness was progressing with terrifying speed, far swifter than her ability to deal with it emotionally.

But she had no choice. He was her husband, and she must do her best to be a perfect wife, whether that meant coaxing him to eat or keeping the doctors away. What she could not be was weak and crippled by her own grief.

The light was fading. She'd been here for hours. Soon she must get up and relieve Hubble in Stephen's room.

Portia, who lay beside her in a small black-and-orange ball, stirred and opened her great green eyes. The kitten had a genius for darting through doors, and she'd followed Rosalind into Lord Michael's suite. Then she'd flopped down on the bed and tucked her miniature nose under her tail, keeping her mistress silent company all afternoon.

Rosalind smiled faintly and scratched the kitten's neck with one finger. Stephen's wedding gift, chosen to give pleasure at even the darkest hour. A successful choice, too. It was impossible to see the kitten's antics, or feel the rasp of her tiny abrasive tongue, and not feel a little better.

Vaguely Rosalind heard sounds downstairs. Visitors, perhaps. She really must rise and wash her face and become presentable. She was an actress. She could master her emotions and play the role of strong, dignified mistress of the house. And she would, in a few more minutes, when she had gathered her strength.

The door to the sitting room opened, and crisp footsteps sounded. A moment later the door to the bedroom swung open.

Feeling horribly vulnerable, Rosalind pushed herself to a sitting position and found that she was facing the most beautiful woman she'd ever seen. The newcomer had dark hair, a perfect heart-shaped face, and looked supremely elegant even in a plain traveling costume.

Rosalind groaned inside. Painfully conscious of the tear stains on her face, she slid from the bed and stood with a hand on one of the tall bedposts. "Good day. You must be Lady Michael. I . . . I'm sorry to be in your room."

"No need to apologize. I wasn't expected. And you must be . . ." Lady Michael cocked her head to one side. "Stephen's new wife?"

Rosalind nodded. "My name is Rosalind."

Lady Michael glanced over her shoulder and said to her lady's maid, who had been following, "You may go, Molly." Then she crossed the room with a smile. "It's a pleasure to meet you, Rosalind. Call me Catherine."

As Rosalind accepted the proffered hand, she found herself blurting out, "I wore one of your gowns my second night in London. Stephen swore it would be all right, but I'm not sure I believe him."

Catherine laughed. "By all means, believe him. Stephen is invariably right." She turned and removed her hat, then her cloak. "Is he at home now?"

She must be ignorant of her brother-in-law's condition. Rosalind took a deep breath as she mastered her emotions. "He's here, but very ill. He had a bad episode earlier this afternoon and is probably still sleeping."

Catherine spun around, expression dismayed. "So it's true? His doctor, Blackmer, wrote my husband some weeks ago, saying that Stephen was unwell and had run off without so much as a single servant. Michael immediately went after him. He's been looking ever since." She bit her lip. "Since Stephen was getting married and leading Michael on such a merry chase, I convinced myself that Blackmer must be wrong. I . . . I didn't want to believe he was really seriously ill."

"Lord Michael has been searching for his brother?" Rosalind said, surprised. "Stephen didn't think anyone would be so concerned about his absence. He merely wanted to get away from his usual life for a while."

"Which he did very effectively." Catherine rolled her eyes. "My husband, never noted for his patience, has become quite exasperated. He finally wrote from Scotland to say that he was giving up, and to meet him here in London."

"Scotland?" Rosalind said incredulously.

"Apparently he and Dr. Blackmer, who is with him, followed a carriage carrying a couple who fit your description almost all the way to Edinburgh."

Rosalind blinked. "Oh dear. I'm not sure whether to commiserate or laugh."

"You might as well laugh," Catherine said pragmatically. "It feels better."

She was right, but there was little laughter in Rosalind at the moment. "When should your husband reach London?"

"Tomorrow or the next day, I think." Catherine sighed as she lit a lamp against the gathering dusk. "It seems as if he's been gone forever."

"The sooner Lord Michael comes, the better," Rosalind said. "Even two days might be too long."

Catherine looked up from the lamp with shock. "Stephen's condition is that bad?"

Rosalind sank down on the foot of the bed. "Critical. He almost died earlier today, I think. I . . . I'm afraid that he could go at any time."

Catherine sucked in her breath. "What does the doctor say?"

"Stephen won't let me call one. Apparently his father suffered terribly from the treatments of various physicians when he was dying, and Stephen doesn't want the same to happen to him."

"That's hard to argue with," Catherine agreed. "May I see him? I would want to anyhow, but I also have considerable nursing experience. That might be useful now."

"Of course." Rosalind led the way from Lord Michael's suite into the hall, then to the duke's rooms at the other end of the hall. The bedroom was cozy, warmed by a fire and lit by a branch of candles. A somber Hubble sat by the bed.

Stephen was so still that Rosalind had a swift, terrible jolt of fear before she saw that he was breathing. Catherine also flinched at the sight of her brother-in-law. His gauntness and sunken features were clearly those of a man on the verge of death.

Rosalind went to his side and said softly, "Are you awake, my dear?"

Stephen's eyes flickered open. "Death be not proud, though some have called thee mighty and dreadful, for thou art not so," he murmured. "One short sleep past, and we wake eternally."

For an instant Rosalind's heart sank, for she thought he must be delirious. But his eyes were warm and lucid.

She smiled with relief. "You must be feeling better if you can quote John Donne."

"I am. Sorry to upset you earlier." He smiled with great sweetness. "I must talk to you, but . . . I haven't much energy at the moment."

"Why not rest a little longer?" she suggested. "You look far better now than you did before. More sleep should bring even more improvement." And not only was he stronger but also different in a way she could not define.

He nodded faintly. "Later, then."

She realized that what she saw in his gray-green eyes was peace. Even a kind of happiness. The hidden fear and anger at his fate that had been part of him since they met were gone. For that she was deeply thankful. Yet she realized sadly that his acceptance of dying was another step away from her.

Burying the thought, she said with a smile, "You have a visitor."

His sister-in-law came up on the other side of the bed. "Hello, Stephen."

"Catherine." His face brightened. "Is Michael here, too?"

"No, but he will be soon." She bent and kissed Stephen's cheek. "It was very bad of you to become so ill. I don't approve."

"I don't either. Damned careless of me," he said wryly. "I gather that you and my wife have introduced yourselves."

Catherine laughed. "Oh, yes. I intend to split a bottle of wine with Rosalind and compare notes on the subject of living with a Kenyon man."

He gave an exaggerated wince. "A good thing I won't hear that."

"It would just increase your lordly arrogance,"

Rosalind said, a catch in her voice from the fact that he could still joke.

He glanced at the dark window. "You two should take yourselves off for some food. Catherine must be hungry if she's been traveling."

"Very well." Rosalind lifted the jar of pills from the table. "More medicine?"

He nodded. "Two, please."

She shook the pills into her palm, then used a glass of the omnipresent milk to help him wash them down. After he swallowed she kissed him, pressing her cheek against his for a moment. His skin was cool, but without the clamminess of earlier.

Rosalind told Hubble that she would have dinner sent up and relieve him later. Then she and Catherine left. When they reached the ground floor, her sister-in-law said, "Michael's letters gave all sorts of tantalizing tidbits about his search, and left me perishing of curiosity. I gather that you're an actress, and Stephen joined your family troupe for a time? I'd love to hear the full story, if you don't mind telling me."

Rosalind sighed, wondering if Catherine was going to be like Stephen's sister. "I didn't marry him for his money."

Catherine's elegant brows rose. "That's obvious from seeing you together."

Rosalind relaxed. "I'm glad you see that. Claudia certainly doesn't."

"Ah, Claudia," Catherine said dryly. "She's never given me the cut direct. Quite. But that's mostly because she can barely tolerate being in the same room with Michael, and assumes that he deserves a coarse, vulgar creature like me."

"She disapproves of *you*?"

"Claudia can disapprove of anyone, and I gave her

an abundance of material." Catherine's eyes danced. "A widow encumbered with a daughter, a woman who'd nursed naked men who were not her husband, and who had followed the drum through the Peninsula—dreadful! No really well-bred lady would have survived such a life."

Rosalind actually laughed. "I think we have a great deal in common, Catherine."

"We certainly do." Catherine linked arms with her new sister-in-law. "Now let's go raid the kitchen, and you can tell me all."

Rosalind did exactly that. In the breakfast room, over the simple meal of soup, bread, and cheese that was all either of them wanted, she spoke of how Stephen had rescued Brian from drowning. How "Mr. Ashe" had become part of the troupe, and the meadow marriage. Then she described her own background. Being able to say that she was a French countess added a certain cachet to the recital.

In return, she learned about Catherine's adored children and home in Wales. It was clear that she also adored her husband, which Rosalind found a relief. Any man loved by a woman like Catherine couldn't be too terrifying.

After they finished a pot of coffee between them, Rosalind said, "I'm going to go up now and relieve Hubble for the night. I would try to be a good hostess, but I imagine that you know more about the household than I do."

"Probably. Don't worry; I'll be fine." Catherine covered a yawn. "I'm ready to go to bed. It was a swift and tiring trip. But one last question." She hesitated, then asked, "Are you by any chance with child?"

Rosalind gaped at her. "You must have been a wonderful nurse."

"There is a look some women get." Catherine explained. "So it's true?"

Rosalind nodded. "I'm almost certain."

"Hallelujah!" Catherine beamed. "I'm so glad. Stephen must be delighted."

"I haven't told him yet. I intend to tonight, if he's awake."

"Now let's pray that it's a boy."

"Stephen said that Michael didn't want to be duke, but as a mother, don't you want that for your son?" Rosalind asked curiously.

"Not really. I have no doubt that my little Nicholas will grow up to be equal to anything, but Michael would hate being duke, and I don't want to see him miserable." She smiled. "Or too busy to have time for me."

Rosalind suspected that no man would ever be too busy for Catherine Kenyon. Still curious, she asked, "Why does Lord Michael so dislike the idea of inheriting?"

Catherine hesitated, weighing her words. "I never met the old duke, but I know that he treated Michael abominably. Except for some boyhood occasions with Stephen, my husband has no good memories of Ashburton Abbey. He doesn't mind visiting there, but he wants no part of the title or estates."

Rosalind nodded, able to understand that. Getting to her feet, she laid a gentle hand on her abdomen. "I'll do my best for you both."

Catherine stood and gave her a swift hug. "I'm so glad that Stephen found you."

Rosalind relaxed for a moment in the other woman's embrace, realizing that part of what she liked in Catherine was a maternal quality reminiscent of Maria.

"So am I," she replied softly. "Despite everything, so am I."

Stephen awakened from his dreamy haze to find Rosalind sitting quietly by the bed, circles under her eyes. "Why on earth are you in a chair," he murmured, "when there is a perfectly good bed available?"

She blinked sleepily. "Do you really want me in it? I don't want to hurt you."

"I don't think this kind of pain will get any worse if I sleep with my wife. In fact, I imagine I'll feel better." He hesitated. "Unless you don't want to be that close to someone in my condition."

Her eyes widened. "Idiot. How can you imagine that I would not want to be with you?" Yawning, she left the room. "I'll join you as soon as I change into a nightgown."

He sighed, not liking the idea of the nightgown. They would both be overdressed. But some earnest, well-meaning soul might come in to check his condition. He'd already learned that reduced privacy was one of the many small costs of dying.

A few minutes later, Rosalind reentered the bedroom wearing a delicately embroidered chemise and with her long hair in a braid down her back. After reducing the light to a single candle on the dresser, she came to the bed. "More medication?"

"No. Just you." He didn't want to waste precious time in drugged sleep.

She slid in beside him. He drew her soft body into his arms, feeling a pleasure so great that it was almost pain. Paradoxically, holding her reduced the internal pain, or at least made him notice it less. "You feel marvelous," he murmured.

"Mmm. I can say the same for you." She exhaled, her breath warming his throat.

They lay quietly together for a few minutes. Then she said shyly, "I have some good news. I've been waiting to be sure. It . . . it seems that I'm going to have a baby."

He caught his breath, afraid to believe. Then joy blossomed in his heart, bubbling through him like champagne. "That's wonderful!" A surge of energy allowed him to push up on his elbow. In the faint light, Rosalind's face had the sweet satisfaction of every woman since Eve who had just announced that she was presenting her husband with a child. He smoothed back her tawny hair. "What a very clever girl you are."

"You had something to do with it, too." She laughed and placed his hand on her abdomen, where the gentle curve did not reveal its secret. "I think it happened the first time we made love, in the hayloft."

"It's a miracle, Rosalind." He settled down again, keeping his hand on her. "Each of us thinking ourselves barren. Yet together, we've created a new life." One that he would not be here to see. It was bitter knowledge. Perhaps, like Sophia and Philippe, he would be able to visit at least once. But it would not be the same as holding a baby in his arms, or looking for signs of Rosalind in its face. . . .

He cut off the thoughts as unprofitable. He was here, now, with Rosalind, and he'd been given joyous news. In return, he must deliver the message he'd been given for her. "Earlier today, after that attack," he began, "the most extraordinary thing happened."

He went on to describe his nonphysical visit to the abbey. He did not mention what Louisa had said about their marriage, for that seemed a private matter, but he did say how she had explained death as a mere transition. He also talked of his meeting with Rosalind's parents, and how they had watched out for their child.

He ended by saying softly, "Your parents said to say they love you very much."

In the silence that followed, he wondered if Rosalind was trying to decide whether to consign him to the precincts of the mental patients at Bedlam Hospital. Then she made a choked sound, and he realized that she was crying against his shoulder. "Rosalind? I'm really not mad, you know." He kissed her temple. "Probably I just had a very realistic dream."

"Blame it on pregnancy. Everything seems to make me cry now." She wiped her eyes with the edge of the sheet. "If it was a dream, it was a true one. When you spoke of my parents being together and watching over me, the words sang in my heart."

She rubbed her cheek against his, making him glad he'd been shaved by Hubble. "You asked once why I believed there was more to life than the world we see around us, and I couldn't answer. But you've just explained why. I had my parents for guardian angels. I recognized that as soon as you said the words."

And if Sophia and Philippe were together, surely he and Rosalind would be someday, too. He stroked her back, feeling as close to her emotionally as physically. The devil of it was that he wanted to be closer still. He wanted to enter her body, hear her rapturous cry, feel the shattering pleasure. . . .

He bit off an oath. "Before now, I never realized the extent to which desire comes from the mind, not the body. I want so much to make love to you. But I can't." His lips twisted. "I simply am not capable of it."

"It's all right, Stephen," she whispered. Her warm hand moved down his body, coming to rest on his genitals in a gesture of infinite tenderness. "I . . . I don't know if I could bear to be intimate knowing that it might be the last time."

He felt a lump in his own throat. More losses, and this a very large one. Would there be physical union in the Garden of Light? He'd read once that in heaven there was a spiritual joining that was better than sexual congress. He'd questioned then how the writer could have known that. Now, having made love to Rosalind many times, he doubted that anything could ever be better.

But at least the possibility gave him something to hope for.

Rosalind lay awake long after Stephen slid into sleep. The experience he had related to her had seemed utterly right and true. Her natural parents had been with her and had given her into the arms of her adoptive parents. She had been doubly blessed. And yet, she had lived her whole life with fear.

The recognition made her furious with herself. Then images of her parents' deaths flashed through her mind. Yes, they had died swiftly, but the horror of that night had imprinted her very soul. The tragedy had been followed by weeks of terror, culminating in the sight of her beloved nurse dying. After that there had been cold and hunger and paralyzing fear as she struggled to survive.

No wonder she had felt unsafe ever since, even though she had been miraculously rescued. She had buried the terror and concentrated on being the perfect daughter so that Thomas and Maria would keep her.

Through the years fear had been a shadow companion. She'd been afraid of the unknown, afraid of leaving her adoptive family, afraid of caring for any one person too much. In numbers were safety, so she had loved many people. She'd married Charles because he was safe, part of her familiar world. Even marrying Stephen had seemed safe, because his illness meant she would soon be able to return to the life she knew.

But loving him was not safe, because that exposed her to the risk of loss, like the loss that had haunted her since her parents' deaths. So she had not admitted to love. Liking, yes. Passion, certainly. But not love.

It was humorous, really. She'd always thought herself calm and sensible, yet even in the privacy of her own mind she hadn't been honest about how much she cared for Stephen. Loving him had never been "safe," and losing him would be like having her heart sliced in half.

But someday they would be together again. She believed that now. And the knowledge was enough to finally send her into an exhausted sleep.

Chapter 34

Day Twenty-four

Stephen awoke the next morning feeling surprisingly refreshed. Probably that was because Rosalind still slept in his arms. Even Portia had sneaked in and spent the night curled up on the bed. For a kitten she was a good sleeper.

By the time Rosalind awoke, the pain was chewing

at Stephen again, but it diminished after she gave him two more opium pills. Then she coaxed him into drinking an eggnog, saying that the egg and honey beaten into the milk would give him some much needed strength. He sipped cautiously, but the drink went down and stayed down.

Walking across the room would have been so far beyond his capabilities that he didn't even consider it, but he did feel strong enough to sit up in bed. Catherine joined them by invitation, and they spent a pleasant morning together. He relaxed against the mound of pillows Rosalind had piled against the headboard while the women did most of the talking. It was enough that he was with two of his favorite people.

He wondered, with detachment, how much longer his body would survive. A day, perhaps two. His chief remaining wish was that his brother would arrive before the end.

Then Hubble entered the room, his expression dismayed. "Your Grace, Lord and Lady Herrington are here. She insists on seeing you."

Rosalind gasped and Catherine, seated on the other side of the bed, almost dropped her cup of tea. Equally surprised, Stephen said, "Bring them in."

Claudia and her husband, Andrew, entered a few moments later. His sister stiffened when she saw him. He guessed that she had been told of his illness but was still shocked by the reality.

Face set, Claudia came across the room to the bed. "I had to come, Stephen."

"I'm glad to see you. And you also, Andrew." His quiet brother-in-law's handshake was brief but heartfelt. He'd always been a good fellow.

Rosalind regarded the visitors like a lioness guarding

a sick cub, but Catherine said politely, "Good day, Claudia. I trust that you and your children are well?"

Claudia's face softened as it always did when the subject of her children came up. "Very well, thank you. And your son and daughter?"

"Also well."

The conversation languished until Stephen added, "You may also offer Rosalind and me congratulations."

"Why . . . how splendid." Claudia looked startled but genuinely pleased. Babies had always been the quickest way to her well-defended heart. "You must take very good care of yourself, Rosalind."

"I intend to," Rosalind said, looking surprised again.

Not having the strength for idle conversation, Stephen said, "Rosalind, if you don't mind, perhaps Claudia would like to see me alone."

"Yes, but first . . ." His sister gave her husband an agonized glance. He touched her elbow lightly. Apparently drawing strength from that, she continued in a halting voice, "Rosalind, Catherine. I . . . I want to apologize for my past behavior to you both."

Now looking downright stunned, Rosalind said, "Apology accepted. It is natural that you were concerned about your brother's marriage."

Though there was an ironic glint in her eyes, Catherine also murmured a few words of acceptance.

Claudia's mouth twisted. "You are both more generous than I deserve."

"I don't want to be at odds with you, Lady Herrington," Rosalind said with quiet dignity. "I never did." She collected Catherine with a glance, introducing herself to Lord Herrington as the three left the room together.

Instead of sitting, Claudia paced the room restlessly.

It was tiring just to watch. "I'm glad you came," Stephen said. "I didn't think I would see you again."

"You almost didn't." His sister didn't meet his gaze. "Your wife came to tell me of your illness, and I was absolutely horrid to her."

He winced, easily able to imagine the scene. "You've always had a wicked tongue when you were upset. What changed your mind and brought you here?"

She went to the window and gazed out. Her unyielding profile was a feminine version of the old duke's. "After your wife left, Andrew came into the drawing room and found me crying. I . . . I don't think he's ever seen me cry before. Naturally he wanted to know why. I explained, expecting him to say that of course I was right to condemn your marriage. That no actress could possibly be worthy of being Duchess of Ashburton."

"He didn't agree?"

She shook her head. "He frowned and said that I was letting my obsession with the Ashburton line get quite out of hand. Then he said something very like what your Rosalind had just told me: that nothing I could do now would win me Father's approval." Tears glistened in her eyes without falling. "That I must respect your choice of a wife, and stop blaming you and Michael for being men when I wasn't."

It had never occurred to Stephen that Claudia had resented him and Michael for their gender, but it made perfect sense. Very perceptive of Andrew. "If life were just, you would have been a son, Claudie," he said, using his childhood nickname for her. "You were the child who would have come closest to Father's ideal of what the Duke of Ashburton should be."

He sighed, thinking of the many times he'd suffered the lash of his father's contempt. "But he was unfair to all of us, you know. Because you were female, he did not give you the attention you needed and deserved. He disliked me for not having the arrogance he respected, and his behavior to Michael was truly abusive." The reason for that Claudia did not need to know. "I have trouble forgiving him for what he did to Michael. Yet from what I understand, he was very like his own father. He was raised to believe that his way was always the only way."

"And as you said, I am very like him." Claudia bent her head, her expression bleak in the pale sunshine. "I didn't know how much I depended on Andrew's support until I lost it. I know I'm a difficult woman, but Andrew has always been there, despite my flaws." She swallowed hard. "I don't much like who I am, Stephen, but I don't know how to be different. If I'm not my father's daughter, who am I?"

"You are also a wife, a mother, a sister," he said quietly. "Not to mention the Countess of Herrington. As for Andrew—obviously your husband understands you very well. Do you really think he's going to stop loving you over this when, as you said, he's always been aware of your imperfections?"

"He doesn't love me. How could anyone love me?" she cried out with despair. Terrible, silent tears began running down her cheeks.

It hurt to see her misery. Remembering how when he was very small she would call him to her for a hug, Stephen said, "I can't walk across the room, Claudie, so you'll have to come here if you want to be hugged."

Whenever she'd called him to her, he'd gone straight into her arms. She smiled through her tears when she heard the familiar invitation from him, and came to sit on the edge of the bed. "I'm sorry, Stephen," she said, wiping her eyes. "You're the one who is dreadfully ill. I should be offering you comfort, not asking for it myself."

He patted her hand. "Actually, I'm finding that dying is a rather simple business. Nowhere near as complicated as living."

Tears began flowing from her hazel eyes again. "I can't bear the thought of losing you, Stephen," she whispered. "I'm older than you—it's not right that I'm hale and hearty and bad-tempered, while you, who are a much better person, are dying."

He smiled. "Maybe it's true that only the good die young?"

She pressed her hand to her mouth. "Rosalind said that when she called on me. Oh, Stephen, I've gotten everything wrong my whole life."

He took her hand and tugged, pulling her down beside him so that he could put an arm around her shoulders. She buried her face in the counterpane and wept. Only partly for him, he knew. Most of those tears were of regret—for the father she had adored but could never please, for her failures to live up to impossible standards.

"Don't be so terribly hard on yourself, Claudie. During my childhood, you were my favorite person, you know. You listened to me. Made me feel cared for. You were always wonderful with smaller children." He smiled. "If you weren't a countess, you would make a really good nursery maid." She would have been like Mrs. Standish, risking her life to protect any child in her charge.

She gave a watery chuckle. "And probably would have done more good."

He had a sense that if he said the right thing, it would help her, but he wasn't sure what the right thing was. Then a thought struck him. "Why did you marry

Andrew? You had better offers. You could have been a marchioness rather than a mere countess."

"Why, because I liked him the best, of course. When I was with Andrew, I always felt pretty and clever. Wanted." She sighed. "It was wonderful to be wanted, even though I've never understood why he did."

"Have you ever regretted marrying him?"

"Never." The answer was immediate.

"In other words, you love him and always have. Do you ever tell him that?"

She stood up and began to smooth the wrinkles from her morning gown. "He knows that I . . . I care about him."

Stephen was not surprised to hear that she could not use the word *love*. He'd been the same way for most of his life. Until the day before, in fact, when he had stepped outside of life.

Knowing now what his sister needed to hear, he said, "The old duke taught us his version of the cardinal virtues, Claudie. Pride and propriety were at the top of the list. Love wasn't there at all. In fact, without a single word on the subject being said, we learned that wanting to give or receive love was a sign of weakness. Despicable, in fact."

He paused, needing to rest before he could continue. "Father had things backward. Love is the ultimate virtue, the one that makes life worth living when pride and propriety are only ashes. For your sake as well as his, tell Andrew that you love him, Claudie. And while you're at it, tell your children, too." He smiled faintly. "Even if it feels as if your tongue will fall off if you try to say the word."

She looked at him uncertainly. "Do you think they would want to hear that?"

"I believe it highly likely. Don't dislike all that you are, Claudie, because so much of your character is admirable. You have courage and integrity, and you've usually been loving in your deeds if not always your words."

"Loving? Me?" she said in amazement.

She sounded as surprised at the idea as he had been when it was suggested to him. "Yes, you. You've always had a good heart behind that caustic tongue." He sank deeper into the pillows, too tired to sit upright any longer. "Just remember the next time you feel tempted to lash out, or get on your Kenyon high horse, to bite your tongue instead."

"I . . . I'll try." She gazed at him, her expression somber. "Good-bye, Stephen. I never realized just how much I'm going to miss you until now, when it's too late."

He gave her a tired smile. "We'll see each other again."

Her brows drew together. "You really believe that?"

"I know it," he said, and heard echoes of Lady Westley in his voice.

"I hope to heaven that you're right." She bent and kissed his cheek. "I . . . I love you, Stephen." She smiled crookedly. "My tongue didn't fall out."

He laughed a little. "I love you, too, Claudie." The words were so easy to say. Why had they been so unthinkable for most of his life?

As his sister left the bedroom, he rolled onto his side with a tired sigh. Now that he thought about it, he realized that he hadn't yet told Rosalind that he loved her. Looking back, it was quite obvious that he'd been in love with her almost from the time they met. What a damned fool he'd been not to realize. But he was a Kenyon, and love had never been part of his vocabulary. The night before, when his tongue had finally been unlocked, there had been too many other things that needed saying.

As he fell into exhausted sleep, he reminded himself forcibly that telling Rosalind how he felt about her was the one thing that absolutely must be done before he died.

Tick tock. Tick tock. Tick tock. The clock on the bedroom mantel sounded abnormally loud in the silence. Straw had been laid down in front of Ashburton House to muffle the sounds of traffic, and it was working too well.

Rosalind ran a restless hand over the counterpane of Stephen's bed. It was late afternoon, and he'd been sleeping since Claudia's departure. She found herself resenting that his sister had used up so much of his precious energy.

Still, the tear-stained Claudia had been positively cordial when she left, clinging to her husband's arm. Hard to believe she was the same woman who had practically hissed when she first met Rosalind. Stephen must have cast a spell on her. If so, Rosalind hoped it was permanent.

Catherine was sharing the vigil, quietly sitting nearby and working on a pile of mending. The butler had been horrified that Lady Michael wished to do such a humble task, but Catherine wanted to keep her hands busy.

Rosalind preferred watching Stephen's sleeping face. He looked far more peaceful than either his wife or his sister-in-law.

Tick tock. Tick tock. Tick tock. Every click measuring out Stephen's life.

Suddenly unable to bear the sound a second longer, Rosalind rose and stalked to the fireplace. Smashing the ormolu clock onto the brick hearth would have been very satisfying, but the blasted thing was worth a small fortune and probably a family heirloom as well. She settled for opening the back and stopping the pendulum.

Blessed silence. She went to the window and looked out into the street. It was dusk, and a fine, steady rain was falling. A suitably wretched day.

Would Stephen still be here at dawn? Or the dawn after?

Catherine murmured from behind her, "I'm glad you stopped that clock. It was definitely getting on my nerves."

"Really? I thought you were nerveless. You're so good in a sickroom."

"I've had plenty of practice, but it's harder when the patient is someone you care about." She sighed and rubbed her temple. "And I care about Stephen a great deal. He has always been a friend to me, and to my daughter, too. Amy is going to be devastated."

"It's selfish of me, but I'm glad you're here." Rosalind gave a faint, wry smile. "I considered asking my mother or sister to come. However, they both tend to get queasy when anyone is ill. That's why I was the one who got the job of tending the cuts and bruises of everyone in the troupe."

"I gather that you took on every task that your temperamental colleagues couldn't be trusted with," Catherine said with amusement. "I've always been the same way. Talent is all very well, but someone must mend the socks."

Rosalind's brief smile faded. She leaned her forehead against the cool window glass. "Catherine, I'm so ashamed of myself, but part of me just wants this to be *over*. Yet how will I bear it when he's gone?"

"Wanting an end to suffering, for both Stephen and yourself, is normal," Catherine said softly. "As to how you will bear it—you'll do that minute by minute, because you must. For your sake, and the sake of your child."

Remembering that Catherine had buried two parents and one husband, Rosalind straightened, feeling ashamed of herself for her weakness. She must be strong for the sake of the baby who would be Stephen's greatest legacy.

From behind them Stephen's voice said faintly, "Rosalind?"

She turned swiftly and went to the bed. "How are you feeling?"

He shrugged. "Well enough."

In other words, he was in pain but not about to complain. How could he be so calm, so composed? She'd thought him a hero when he saved Brian, but that courage was nothing compared to this.

Silently she gave him two more opium pills. After he'd swallowed them, she kissed his forehead. "Would you like some more eggnog? Or perhaps some broth?"

"The eggnog sounds good."

She turned to the decanter that the cook had prepared earlier in the afternoon and set in a basin of crushed ice. As she poured a glass, he said softly, "There's been something I've been meaning to tell you."

She glanced up with a smile, just in time to see him gasp, "Damnation!"

Then he convulsed on the bed, face white and eyes closed as he suffered the most violent attack Rosalind had witnessed since the one in the hayloft. She gripped his hand, raging inwardly because there was nothing she could do to help him.

The episode passed quickly, for even illness took more strength than he could spare. Within minutes he was still and unconscious again. Wordlessly Rosalind and Catherine worked together to replace the soiled bedding.

When that was done and Rosalind began to sponge Stephen's face with a moist cloth, Catherine said urgently, "Let me call a doctor I know."

Rosalind glanced up. "You know I promised him not to allow that."

"Ian Kinlock isn't like other doctors," Catherine said. "I knew him in the army. He's brilliant and unconventional, with qualifications as both physician and surgeon. He saved Michael's life when other surgeons wouldn't even bother to try. In fact, one of the principal reasons Michael went searching for Stephen was the wish to take him to Ian."

Rosalind hesitated, torn between her promise and the desperate desire to grasp at any hope, no matter how slim. Seeing that she was wavering, Catherine continued, "At least let Ian perform an examination. He'll respect your wishes if you forbid any treatments that would increase Stephen's suffering." Catherine closed her eyes and pressed her wrist to her forehead. "Please, let me call him. We must do *something*."

Rosalind capitulated with an exhausted sigh. "Very well. Send for your friend."

Catherine left the room at a pace that was almost a run. Rosalind finished sponging Stephen's face. Then she straightened the covers and kissed him. "I love you, Stephen," she whispered. "I always will."

He might not want to hear that. But the words were ones she had to say.

• • •

Hubble, grateful for something to do, was dispatched to find Ian Kinlock. It took several hours to locate the surgeon and bring him to Ashburton House. By then, Stephen was breathing more easily and showing signs of returning consciousness. Rosalind sat beside him and held his hand, watching his face as if sheer concentration would keep him alive.

The door opened, and Catherine got to her feet. "Ian, thank heaven you've come."

Rosalind looked up to see her sister-in-law hug a broad-shouldered man with an unruly shock of white hair who had just entered the bedroom. Then she brought him to the sickbed, her arm through his. "Rosalind, my friend and miracle worker, Ian Kinlock. Ian, the Duchess of Ashburton."

He said with a distinct Scottish burr, "Flattery will not get you a miracle, Catherine. Those are dispensed only by God, and he's almighty sparing of them." He nodded to Rosalind and set his instrument bag by the bed. "Tell me about your husband's illness, Duchess."

The surgeon was younger than she'd thought at first, no more than forty despite the white hair. He also radiated intelligence and imperturbable calm. Glad she'd agreed to call him, she replied, "I believe the pains started in late spring or early summer. He said his physician diagnosed the disease as a tumefaction of the stomach and liver."

"That's more of a description than a diagnosis," Kinlock grunted. "What are the symptoms?"

Wishing she'd asked Stephen more questions, she answered the surgeon as best she could while Catherine withdrew. Kinlock began his examination. After a thorough palpation of Stephen's abdomen, he muttered, "A tumefaction can be either a hard mass or a swelling. I don't feel either, though there's obviously sensitivity."

All too true. Even semiconscious, Stephen was groaning from the surgeon's probing. Rosalind flinched along with him. "Does that mean he's less ill than we thought?" she asked hopefully.

"Ashburton is in a critical condition and no mistake." Frowning, Kinlock dug into his case and pulled out a needle. "But I must admit to being puzzled about what he's suffering from."

She bit her lip when he lifted Stephen's hand and stuck the needle into the middle of the palm. Stephen hardly reacted at all, which was more than could be said of Rosalind.

He hadn't wanted to suffer from medical abuse. But as she tensely watched the surgeon's tests, she reminded herself that Stephen had once said that he'd have tried every quack in England if there had been a chance for a cure.

Any chance, no matter how slender, was better than none at all.

CHAPTER 35

Saturated by the chilly rain, Michael and Blackmer rode the last short distance through Mayfair in silence. It was a night as dismal as Michael's mood.

His spirits lifted when they turned into Grosvenor Square and he saw Ashburton House. "Look at the lighted windows and the straw on the street. Stephen is here, and, God willing, Catherine as well."

Blackmer straightened in the saddle, his dull expression becoming alert. "I hope to heaven you're right. I'd almost begun to think this search would never end."

Michael understood the feeling perfectly.

In the stables the groom confirmed that the duke and his new wife had been in London for a fortnight or so, and that Lady Michael had arrived the day before. The servant's voice dropped to a whisper when he continued that the duke was very ill. Not expected to last more than another few days at most, they said.

Face like granite, Michael used his key to let them into the house. Giving his younger brother that key was one of many things Stephen had done to make Michael feel as if he were really part of the Kenyon family instead of a despised outcast. And now Stephen was—Harshly Michael cut off the thought. Not much caring if Blackmer followed or not, he cut through the public rooms to the bottom of the sweeping staircase that led to the private quarters. There he glanced up and saw his wife sitting on a bench in the hall outside Stephen's apartments. Her dark head was tilted against the wall, and her expression was as weary as his own.

Instinctively keeping his voice down, he called her name. Catherine lifted her head as if startled from a doze. Then her face lit up. "Michael!"

She leaped to her feet and raced down the stairs as Michael bounded upward three steps at a time. They met on the landing where the ascending staircase split in two, coming together like striking cymbals.

"God, Catherine, I've missed you!" He swept her off her feet in a fierce embrace. Home. At last.

"The feeling is entirely mutual." Oblivious to his

cold, wet clothing, Catherine locked her arms around his neck and raised her face. Her kiss almost made him forget the last maddening weeks.

Ending the embrace with reluctance, he set her down. "How is Stephen?"

She sighed and rested her forehead on his cheek. "Alive. He's just woken up, but his condition is very grave. He . . . he won't last much longer."

Blackmer, who had been waiting a discreet distance away, came up the steps to join them. "Take me to him," he said urgently. "Perhaps I can do something."

The physician looked almost wild-eyed, poor devil. He must be hoping to work a miracle that would justify all the time and effort he'd expended on the search.

"Ten minutes shouldn't make a difference. I want to see him first, since he's conscious. Use the time to find some food or change into dry clothing." Michael started up the remaining steps, one arm around his wife, not giving a damn how improper his behavior was.

"But I'm his doctor," Blackmer said vehemently. "I must see him immediately."

Michael turned and said in the voice that could make a hard-bitten sergeant blanch, *"Later."*

Catherine interjected hastily, "There's a surgeon with him now, Dr. Blackmer. A friend of ours, Ian Kinlock." Her brow furrowed. "Ian seems puzzled, though he hasn't said why. Perhaps the two of you can confer while Michael visits with Stephen."

Blackmer opened his mouth to protest, then closed it again, looking almost ill. "I'll change and be up in a few minutes." He turned and went down the steps, flagging down a footman who'd appeared with the new arrivals' baggage.

Michael resumed his ascent, savoring the feel of his wife's soft, familiar body next to his. Quietly he said, "I'm glad you called Kinlock. It was my intention to do so the moment I got here. If anyone can help, it's Ian."

"He says he can't supply miracles," Catherine said soberly.

That didn't mean Michael couldn't hope for one. "What do you think of Stephen's provincial actress?"

Catherine gave him The Look that any married person recognized. "Let go of your preconceptions, my dear. Rosalind is wonderful. She and Stephen are thoroughly in love with each other, and I wish they'd met ten years earlier." Her eyes twinkled. "She's also so attractive that I'm glad I got to you first."

He laughed a little and buried his face in her hair. Her scent was sweet and fresh and irresistible. "There will be time enough to fish for compliments later, shameless wench."

Her hand caressed his unshaven chin for a brief moment of promise before she resumed climbing the steps again. "Rosalind has also very efficiently managed to get herself in the family way, so I suggest you pray as hard as you can for a boy."

He felt like a prisoner who'd just glimpsed an open door. "That's marvelous! Stephen must be delighted."

A shadow crossed Catherine's face. "He is."

Michael understood what she wasn't saying, because he knew how he would have felt if he'd become mortally ill when Catherine was carrying Nicholas. A combination of gladness that something of him would survive, and fury that he wouldn't be there to raise his child.

His pleasure in the reunion with his wife faded at the reminder of why he had come. He paused to peel off his wet cloak and toss it over the railing. Then, face grim, he opened his brother's bedroom door.

• • •

Stephen woke under Ian Kinlock's examination. Though obviously in pain, he was stoic and didn't reproach Rosalind for calling in the surgeon. Nonetheless, she felt twinges of guilt as she moved away from the bed so the men could talk privately.

She settled in the window seat, her gaze on Stephen, and remembered something she'd told Jessica in simpler days. Dignity was so much a part of Stephen that nothing, not even death, could rob him of it. She had spoken more truly than she had known.

Then the door opened, and a man with a thousand-yard stare came into the room. Lord Michael Kenyon, of course. Even travel-stained and weary, he had the air of predatory alertness that Rosalind had seen in other soldiers. He also had a strong family resemblance to Stephen, and Catherine tucked under his arm like a favorite cloak.

Since Stephen was talking with Kinlock and hadn't yet noticed his brother, Rosalind decided to get the introductions out of the way. With luck, Lord Michael would be so concerned with his brother that he would hardly notice her.

She stepped forward and said quietly, "Lord Michael, I'm glad you've come. Dr. Kinlock is almost finished with his examination."

He turned his gaze on her. Piercing green eyes, not like Stephen's more peaceful gray-green. She felt like a mouse being regarded by a cat.

Then, amazingly, he smiled. The predator vanished and his resemblance to Stephen became even stronger. "Rosalind. Catherine has told me about you." He clasped her hand briefly, since bowing would have meant letting go of his wife.

Good heavens, how could this meeting she'd been dreading go so easily? "I'm almost afraid to ask what she told you," Rosalind said truthfully.

"She said that you are wonderful and must be treated with all due courtesy." His arm tightened around Catherine's shoulders. "And I always do what my wife tells me."

Catherine rolled her eyes in an elaborate show of disbelief. "And the moon is made of Cornish clotted cream."

Their laughter caught Stephen's attention. He turned his head toward the door and gave a tired smile. "Michael. In the nick of time."

There was death in Stephen's drawn face. The recognition caused Michael's lungs to constrict with a faint early warning of the asthma that he'd never entirely outgrown. Forcing himself to breathe evenly, he broke away from his wife and went to the bed. "No thanks to you. Did Catherine explain how Blackmer and I have spent weeks chasing you around Great Britain?"

Though his face was drawn and his voice hardly more than a whisper, Stephen said lightly, "I must be cleverer than I thought to evade you for so long."

Ian Kinlock glanced over. He'd patched up Michael twice during the wars, and he had the interested expression of a carpenter checking to see how one of his tables was wearing. "Good to see you, Colonel."

"My pleasure." Michael gave the surgeon a brief, firm handshake. "Are you through with your poking and prodding?"

"For the moment. Go ahead and talk. I've got to think about this." Brows furrowed, Kinlock went across the room and stared broodingly into the fire. Catherine and the new duchess also tactfully withdrew to the far end of the room, out of earshot.

Michael sank onto a chair by the bed, feeling a little awkward. How the devil does one speak to one's dying brother? There were a thousand things he might say, and none seemed important enough.

Stephen made it easy for him. "I'd best take care of business first. I thought I wouldn't leave any loose ends, but I ran out of time sooner than I expected. Also, last night Rosalind told me there will be a baby, which is another complication."

"A good one," Michael interjected.

"Very, but I literally never expected that I might leave an heir. I . . . I'd long since given up hoping." Stephen closed his eyes for a moment. "I had assumed you would inherit immediately. Instead, there will be months of waiting to find out if the child is a boy or girl, which leaves my careful plans in limbo. My secretary is with the solicitor right now. They're drawing up papers that designate you and Rosalind as joint trustees of the Ashburton property for the time being. If the child is a girl, of course you'll take over then. If it's a boy, you'll remain as guardian until he's twenty-one." A glint of humor showed in his eyes. "In other words, you'll get all the work without the title."

"Believe me, I'd prefer it that way," Michael said feelingly.

"Please—look out for Rosalind." Stephen's gaze shifted to the bed hangings. "Not that she isn't perfectly capable of taking care of herself. I expect she'll marry again. Don't be too indignant on my behalf if she does."

"You're more generous than I," Michael said with wry self-mockery. "If I were to die, I'd much prefer to think that Catherine would never look at another man and would spend the rest of her life in sackcloth and ashes."

Stephen raised an ironic brow. "Would you really?"

Even as a child, Michael had never been able to fool his brother. "No," he admitted. "I'd want her to be happy. Just not as happy as she was with me."

"Admirably honest," Stephen said with a glimmer of humor. "When I left the abbey and went north, I considered going into Wales to see you. I wanted to ask what it was like to face death, since you know so much about the subject. But I didn't. Too much pride to ask my younger brother how to deal with fear." The lines in his face deepened. "Pride seems rather trivial now."

"You appear to have found your answers without my help." Michael studied his brother's face, recognizing the bone-deep acceptance that he himself had experienced when on the verge of death. "You seem to be at peace."

"I am." Stephen's gaze went to Rosalind at the far end of the room. "God knows, I don't want to die. But I've known more happiness in the last weeks than most men find in a lifetime. I never would have had that if not for my illness."

And Rosalind, the "provincial actress," was the reason for that happiness. Michael should have had more faith in Stephen's judgment. When he remembered Rafe's admonition not to assume the worst, he wanted to kick himself for his damned aristocratic reaction to the news of his brother's marriage. Sometimes he was appallingly like the old duke. Not often, luckily.

His gaze still on his wife, Stephen said softly, "I think that if we knew the world was about to end, the streets would be full of people running to find the ones they love, so they could tell them of that love." He turned his head back to his brother. "I love you, Michael. I wish we'd been better friends through the years."

The grief that had been pulsing below the surface erupted with a force that seared Michael's heart. He laid his hand over Stephen's and bowed his head. "I love you, too," he said haltingly. "We wouldn't be friends now if you hadn't reached out to me at the worst time of my life. That's a debt I can never repay."

"There's no debt, since I benefited equally." Stephen drew a labored breath. "Claudia was here earlier, and in a mood to make amends for past follies. If she extends the olive branch to you—and I think she will—please, for my sake, don't throw it into the nearest fire."

"I won't," Michael promised. For Stephen's sake. He could feel the slow pulse in his brother's hand. How much longer? Christ, how much longer? He drew an unsteady breath. "If we don't change the subject, I'm going to have an asthma attack."

"Can't have that." Stephen closed his eyes again, collecting his strength. "Let me go over the other outstanding business. For one thing, I'm in the process of buying the Athenaeum Theater for Rosalind's parents. See that the transaction is completed quickly. Rosalind knows the financial arrangements I intended."

He was buying his in-laws a theater? Well, Stephen had never been one to stint. "I'll see that it's done."

His brother tersely listed other unfinished business in an implicit display of confidence that Michael found almost as moving as the explicit declaration of love. Three years ago this conversation, this unquestioning trust, would have been unthinkable.

Stephen was clearly tiring, his sentences getting shorter, his pauses to rest more frequent. Michael hoped the blasted secretary and solicitor would arrive with the trusteeship papers soon. It would relieve

Stephen's mind, and simplify the legal situation, to have them safely signed.

Ian Kinlock turned abruptly from his contemplation of the fire. "Catherine, Duchess, come over here. I want to talk to all of you."

The women came to join Michael by Stephen's bed. Seeing her husband's drawn face, Rosalind lifted a jar on the bedside table and gave him a questioning look. Stephen gave a faint, exhausted nod, so she shook two pills into her hand and poured a glass of water. Michael liked her gentle attentiveness to Stephen. In that she was very like Catherine, and he could think of no higher praise.

Catherine asked, "Have you come up with a different diagnosis, Ian?"

"Aye. I've been wondering whether I dare mention it, because my idea is so incredible, and I don't want to raise false hope. Yet it fits the facts as nothing else does." The surgeon ran tense fingers through his white hair, tangling it hopelessly. "If I'm right, Ashburton, it changes the prognosis entirely. And yet, I can't understand how it could be true." He fell silent, his expression troubled.

Stephen might live? Michael said sharply, "For God's sake, Kinlock, what are you thinking?"

The surgeon hesitated for another long moment, then said slowly, "I believe the duke is being poisoned."

CHAPTER 36

Ian Kinlock's statement produced a stunned silence in the people gathered around the bed. Poison? Shocked to alertness, Stephen waved off the opium pills Rosalind had been about to give him. If Kinlock was right, he could not afford to dull the pain at the price of his wits. "How can that be?"

"Absurd!" Michael snapped at the same time. "Who could possibly want to poison my brother?"

"It may not be deliberate. The symptoms are of arsenic, which has many uses in medicine and household materials such as wallpaper, so the poisoning could be accidental." The surgeon regarded Stephen soberly. "If I'm right about your condition, you could make a complete recovery."

Michael gasped, and Catherine breathed, "My God!" Her gaze went to Stephen.

Recovery. The possibility was a shock more profound even than the suggestion that he was being poisoned. Stephen felt a curious numbness at the thought. Perhaps he had gone so far toward death that life no longer seemed possible. Then Rosalind's hand locked around his. He turned his gaze to her and saw unbearable hope in her expressive eyes. If Kinlock was wrong, her disappointment would be crushing.

Stephen took a deep breath, praying that Kinlock was right for Rosalind's sake even more than his own. "What is the treatment for arsenic poisoning?"

"Actually, drinking milk was the best thing you

could have done. Not only does milk soothe the esophagus and stomach, but it binds the arsenic and reduces the likelihood of permanent damage." Kinlock gave a troubled sigh. "*If* I'm correct in my diagnosis, and *if* the source of poisoning can be located and removed, you would start recovering immediately."

Catherine, the former nurse, frowned. "Stephen could have some form of gastric fever. What makes you think it's arsenic poisoning?"

"Because I've treated two cases, and the similarities to Ashburton's are unmistakable. One was acute poisoning, when a young Spanish wife decided to get rid of her rich old husband."

Rosalind made a choked sound. Stephen said in a warning tone, "If you so much as look at my wife, Kinlock, I swear I'll get up from this bed and throw you out of the house." When a stab of familiar pain lanced through him, he added wryly, "Or at least, I'll tell Michael to do it."

Kinlock made a dismissive gesture. "By your own account, you were ill long before you met your wife. You've had some acute episodes, but most of your symptoms are those of chronic poisoning, which is usually accidental."

Catherine asked, "How could that happen?"

"The case of chronic poisoning I treated was a child sickened by arsenic vapors given off by new wallpaper in his bedroom. There are other kinds of contact that could produce a similar result." Kinlock regarded Stephen narrowly. "But I don't see how you could be suffering from accidental poisoning. If the poison source was on your estate, you should have recovered when you left."

"The same argument applies to deliberate poisoning," Catherine said slowly. "Stephen hasn't been with any one person through the course of his illness. After he left the abbey, he spent weeks traveling under an assumed name with no one knowing where he was. Michael couldn't find him, so I doubt that a murderer could."

Stephen thought back over the course of his illness. There was no consistent environment or person. Which must mean that Kinlock's colorful theory was wrong, and Stephen was suffering from a mortal illness after all.

Then Rosalind broke the baffled silence. "Your medicine, Stephen," she said with horror. "The opium mixture."

She opened her other hand to reveal the two pills she'd almost given him. "You've been taking at least one a day for months. Lately, more than that."

Kinlock said sharply, "Where did the pills come from?"

Stephen stared at the small, innocuous disks on Rosalind's palm. A sick chill went through him. "My physician made them up for me. George Blackmer."

The faint squeak of the door sounded loud in the shocked hush that followed his words. Then Blackmer entered the room. Stephen wondered if he was hallucinating, until he remembered that the physician had accompanied Michael on the ill-fated search.

Blackmer halted, feeling the weight of watching eyes. "The duke. Is he . . . ?" His voice broke and his face paled.

"No, he's not dead." Michael exploded across the room like a panther and grabbed Blackmer in a furious grip. "Stephen is being poisoned by the arsenic you gave him. You *bastard!*" He slammed the physician against the wall.

"Wait!" Kinlock protested. "Perhaps the pills aren't the source."

But Blackmer made no attempt to deny the charge. He simply stared at his attacker, horror and guilt vivid on his haggard face. Everyone in the room recognized the wordless admission.

Michael said in a low, lethal voice, "Say your prayers, Blackmer, because I'm going to kill you." Suddenly there was a pistol in his hand, and it was aimed at the physician's skull.

Before Michael could shoot, Stephen snapped, "No!" His voice was scarcely more than a whisper, but the authority in it sliced through the room. "Don't kill him, at least not yet."

His brother hesitated, then reluctantly released the physician and stepped back. Though he tucked the pistol back under his coat, he kept a dangerous gaze on his quarry.

Poison, not a lethal illness. He was going to live. *To live.* Stephen could barely get his tired mind around the fact. This crisis must be dealt with first. Dredging strength from some unknown reserve, he said to Rosalind, "Help me sit up."

"You're not going to die!" she whispered, her face radiant. She raised him with an arm behind his back, then shoved pillows into a solid support. "Thank God!"

Stephen pulled her down to sit on the edge of the bed before turning his attention to the man who had nearly killed him. "Since my life was the one threatened, I claim the right to question him. Blackmer, do you admit that you've been trying to murder me?"

"I . . . I didn't mean you to die." The physician drew a shuddering breath. "It started with the medication I gave you when you had food poisoning in the spring. Only about a quarter of the pills contained arsenic, and the amount varied from pill to pill. The chances of you taking a lethal dose at one time were very remote."

"But taking the pills over time gave him chronic poisoning, with acute episodes whenever he ingested a particularly large dose," Kinlock said grimly. "Diabolical. The more pills he took, the closer he came to death."

"Good God, these might have been the ones that would have killed him!" Aghast, Rosalind hurled the pills into the fire, then wiped her palm on her gown with revulsion.

Michael glanced at Stephen. "The swine has admitted his guilt," he said conversationally. "May I kill him now?"

"Control your bloodthirsty tendencies a little longer. We still don't know why he did it." Looking back, Stephen saw how the first moderate pains had indeed begun as he was recovering from food poisoning. And the attacks had always come shortly after he took some of the pills. As Kinlock had said, it was diabolical. Voice like ice, he asked, "Blackmer, what the devil have I ever done to deserve such treatment at your hands?"

"I never meant for it to go this far." Blackmer sagged back against the wall, visibly shaking. "I . . . I was going to wait until you'd had several bad episodes. Then I would miraculously 'cure' you."

"So you damned near killed a man to cater to your ambitions," Kinlock said incredulously. "How could any physician stoop so low? Don't shoot him, Colonel. He deserves to have his liver sliced out with a dull lancet."

Stephen frowned, trying to understand. Surely there had to be more to it. "You still haven't said why. You're a successful physician with a respected position in the community. Prosperous. You've been keeping company with the vicar's widowed sister for years. You

didn't need miracles to improve your standing." A horrific thought struck him. "Or have you been poisoning
other patients in the guise of healing? Christ, you were
attending Louisa when she died!"

"No!" Blackmer said vehemently. "I swear, I have
never deliberately harmed another patient. Certainly
not the duchess."

Oddly enough, Stephen believed him. If Blackmer
was capable of telling such convincing lies, he would
have denied the poisoning. "Which once again leads
me to wonder why I was uniquely blessed. Are you a
republican who despises the nobility in general? Or was
it simply because you despise me?"

Blackmer hung his head, his chest rising and falling,
and didn't answer.

The heavy silence was broken by a swift intake of
breath from Rosalind. She said sharply, "Blackmer, my
husband said once that you were a foundling raised by
the parish. Who was your father?"

His head jerked up and he stared at her, his face
gray. "You . . . you've guessed."

"Look at him closely." Rosalind's piercing gaze went
from Blackmer to Michael to Stephen, then back to
Blackmer. "The shape of his face, his height and coloring, Stephen's gray-green eyes. The resemblance isn't
as strong as between Stephen and Michael, but it's
there. Blackmer was fathered by the old duke."

Her words caused a shocked silence. Then Michael
said with loathing, "This swine is no brother of mine!"

"Michael." Stephen stilled his younger brother with
a glance. Then he shifted his gaze to Blackmer, who
was still in the shadows by the wall. "Come here."

Walking as if to the scaffold, Blackmer approached
the bed. Michael followed him, ready to strike if the
man made a wrong move.

Stephen studied the physician's face, seeing the resemblance. As Rosalind had said, it was less pronounced than the likeness between him and Michael, but it was certainly there. This man who had almost killed him was blood kin. "What did you hope to gain by poisoning me? Revenge for the fact that I was legitimate and you aren't? That wasn't my fault. Hurting me would not change the circumstances of your birth."

When Blackmer didn't answer, Rosalind said, "It wasn't revenge he wanted, but recognition. Who was your mother?"

"A dairymaid who died when I was born. She had no family and had never named the father of her child, so I was turned over to the parish." Blackmer closed his eyes wearily. "One day when I was eight, the old duke rode by the field where I was digging weeds. He called me over and said I was his son, and that he would see that I got an education and a respectable trade. He also said that when I grew up, he would acknowledge me publicly, but he never did. After he died without naming me as his son, I was furious. Bitterly resentful. Eventually it became a . . . a kind of madness. I didn't understand how mad I'd become until you left the abbey, and I realized that I could not stop what I had set in motion."

His eyes opened, the gray-green leached to slate. "I wanted to . . . to matter to you. If I couldn't be a Kenyon, at least I could be the brilliant doctor who had saved your life."

"He wanted a connection that went beyond professional service," Rosalind said tersely. "To be treated as a friend."

Blackmer's puzzled gaze went to her. "Why do you understand me better than I understood myself, Duchess?"

"I was a foundling myself," she replied. "A more fortunate one than you. But I understand that desperate hunger to belong. To be part of a family."

"Very touching," Michael said caustically. "Nonetheless, Blackmer very nearly murdered Stephen."

"As God is my witness, I never intended the duke to be seriously harmed," Blackmer said vehemently. "Why do you think I was so determined to find him? I wanted to stop the poisoning before it was too late."

"Or make sure that he was really dead," Michael growled. "And if Stephen still lived, you were hell-bent on treating him because you knew a different doctor might realize that he was being poisoned."

Blackmer sighed and rubbed his forehead. "There is no way I can prove what was in my mind. But you can look at the rest of my career as a physician. There have never been any suspicious deaths. As Ashburton said, I've always been well regarded."

Stephen thought back to his first wife's final illness. "When Louisa was dying, he was with her almost day and night until the end. He has a reputation for treating everyone in the parish, whether they can afford to pay or not."

Michael said with reluctant honesty, "In the Midlands, we were on the scene when a tree crushed a house with a man and child inside. Blackmer risked his life to crawl into the wreckage to prevent the man from bleeding to death before he could be rescued." He scowled. "I'll grant that he's brave. But courage is a common virtue among criminals."

"Perhaps. But it's also true that he was wronged by the old duke," Stephen said soberly. "You of all people should understand that, Michael. Being raised by the parish in my father's time means he would have been fostered with different families, treated like an unpaid servant more often than not."

"Rags, beatings, and cold gruel," Blackmer said starkly. "And . . . and sometimes other things that were far worse. It wasn't until you succeeded to the title that the vicar was charged with seeing that orphans were well treated and given a basic education. I was relieved when you did that."

"You picked a very poor way of showing it," Catherine said, her expression stony.

"I'm sorry for what you had to endure—no child should be treated so badly." Stephen shifted position, fatigue weighing on him like a boulder. "But why poison me to get my attention? All you had to do was tell me of our relationship."

The physician stared at him. "Would you have believed me?"

"Probably. The physical resemblance is there, and I'm well aware of my father's lecherous habits," Stephen said dryly.

"It never occurred to me that there would be any point in talking to you." Blackmer's mouth twisted. "I did not expect justice from the Kenyons."

So the old duke's arrogance and promiscuity had reached beyond the grave and almost caused the death of his heir. There was ironic humor in that.

Wearily Stephen rubbed at the pain in his belly. Hard to remember when it hadn't been part of him. "What the devil am I to do with you, Blackmer?"

There was a pause until Catherine said, "The obvious answer is to turn him over to the magistrates for trial and probable hanging. If you don't want to do that, how about sending him someplace like the Australian colonies? They could use physicians there."

"Assuming that he could be trusted not to kill

someone else." Kinlock's expression was as flinty as Michael's. "The man's a disgrace to the oath he took."

Stephen glanced at Rosalind, who still stood to his right. "What do you think?"

"Part of me wants him to suffer as you did. After he'd experienced a year or two of excruciating pain, I might consider clemency. And yet . . ." She paused, her expression troubled. "Which of us has not made a mistake that might have had disastrous consequences? When Jessica was little, she once helpfully tried to bathe Brian and almost drowned him. What Blackmer has done was not an innocent accident. But I believe him when he says that he didn't mean to kill you."

In his years as a magistrate, Stephen had often administered justice and done it well, but he had never judged a matter that concerned him so closely. He scrutinized Blackmer's haggard face. His brother, who waited stoically for judgment.

Once Blackmer learned who his father was, the knowledge must have been like an open wound. Every time he saw Stephen or Michael ride by, he would have resented the fact that his half brothers lived with wealth and privilege while he was starved and abused. In fact, since he was a year or two older than Stephen, he would have had the additional torment of knowing that if he'd been legitimate, he would have been the next Duke of Ashburton. Poor bastard, in every sense of the word.

Yet by and large, he'd made the best of his situation. He'd taken advantage of his education and done well enough to be sent to study medicine. He'd become a first-rate physician, generous with his time, caring of those less fortunate. The very model of a self-made man—until bitterness turned him into a poisoner.

Stephen glanced at his younger brother. Michael had

also been treated abominably by the old duke, but he had been raised with the advantages of wealth. He had been able to escape the abbey by going to Eton and the homes of his friends. Even so, the emotional and physical abuses of his childhood had caused Michael to behave in difficult, destructive ways until he had made peace with his demons.

In fact, all of the duke's children had suffered from the old man's harsh treatment. Claudia had grown caustic and bitter, while Stephen, the favored son and heir, had become so detached that he'd cut himself off from what mattered most in life. Should Blackmer, who had suffered the most of all, be destroyed because his anger had erupted in such an appalling way?

Blackmer broke the tense, waiting silence by saying flatly, "Lord Michael is right. Though my intent was not murderous, the results nearly were. You have every right to send me to the gallows." The physician's mouth twisted. "I don't expect forgiveness. But I must, for my own sake, say how sorry I am. To you, Ashburton, for putting you through hell." He looked at Rosalind. "To you, Duchess, for clearly you have also suffered. In some ways, perhaps, more than your husband."

His gaze went to Michael. "And to you, Lord Michael. I caused you great grief and separated you from your family. There was not a moment of time during our journey when I did not regret that."

Stephen thought suddenly of *The Tempest,* the play performed by the Fitzgerald Troupe the first time he saw them. One thing he'd always liked about the story was the way Prospero forgave his brother Antonio for a murder attempt a dozen years before. Stephen had always thought of the play in terms of himself and

Michael. But between them there had been no real crimes to forgive, only a history of wariness.

Stephen drew a deep breath, his whole body aching, his stomach burning with agony. He'd suffered months of savage pain because of what Blackmer had done. He should be furious, except that anger would take more strength than he could afford.

He'd always thought of himself as a man committed to justice for all. Where did justice lie in this case?

The key fact was that Blackmer hadn't intended murder. Being a magistrate had taught Stephen to tell the difference between true and false repentance. The physician's remorse was genuine, as was his statement that he had never intended serious harm.

As head of the Kenyon family, it was Stephen's responsibility to rectify the crimes of his father. "If I pack him off to Australia, Great Ashburton will be without a physician, and Blackmer is a good one. I prefer a different approach." Face stern, Stephen caught his half brother's gaze. "Will you give me your word, as a Kenyon, never to deliberately harm anyone again?"

Blackmer blinked with shock, then stammered, "I–I will."

"Then return to your home and your medical practice." Stephen's voice turned dry. "While I don't believe you'll ever commit another crime, I imagine you'll understand that I prefer to find a different physician for myself and my household."

"You . . . you're going to let me go?" Blackmer said incredulously. "After what I've done?"

Stephen laid his hand on Rosalind's. Her touch revived his flagging strength and made him understand why he felt so little anger. "While being poisoned is not something I would have chosen, I've done very well from it." He glanced up at his wife, who was regarding him with grave, dark eyes. "I would never have met Rosalind if not for what you did."

Nor would he have discovered the spiritual faith that was now part of him and that gave his life a profound new dimension. Having found joy as a result of disaster made compassion surprisingly easy.

His gaze went back to Blackmer. "I will acknowledge you as the old duke's son. If you wish to take the name Kenyon, I will not object. Someday I will be ready to become better acquainted with you. But not quite yet."

Blackmer's stoicism shattered. "Dear God. Your generosity makes what I did seem even worse." He covered his eyes as he struggled to compose himself, then dropped his hand and said in a low voice, "I swear to . . . to go forth and sin no more."

Stephen looked at Michael. "Will you accept my judgment? I'm not asking you to become friends with Blackmer. Just not to kill him."

Michael sighed. "Rosalind's remark about how we all make mistakes reminded me of the monumental errors I've made. Having benefited by the forgiveness of my friends, I'm in no position to complain if you choose to be lenient." He put his arm around Catherine and drew her to his side. "What matters most is that you will recover. But I think I'll leave sainthood to you and my wife. It will never be my style."

Too tired to move anything more than his eyes, Stephen glanced at Ian Kinlock. "You are the only one here who is not a member of the family. Are you willing to keep silent about what has happened?"

"I suppose so." Kinlock scowled at Blackmer. "But why couldn't you have been a lawyer? Then wickedness wouldn't have been a shock. I expect better of a doctor."

"You can take comfort in the fact that I will never forgive myself for breaking my oath," Blackmer said starkly. "The punishment might seem light compared to my crime. But I assure you, it will be punishment."

Kinlock studied the other man's face, then gave a nod of grim satisfaction.

Rosalind sent a stern gaze to the people around the bed. "If everything essential has been said, it's time for everyone to leave so Stephen can rest."

"Everyone but you," Stephen murmured, his voice barely audible now that the crisis had passed.

Kinlock looked at Stephen. "Plenty of rest, plenty of milk, and no more arsenic. I'll come by in a couple of days." He collected his medical bag and left the room.

Catherine glanced at Blackmer. "I'll order a room to be prepared for you," she said without enthusiasm.

He inclined his head. "You're very gracious, Lady Michael, but I think it would be best if I went to an inn."

She nodded and kissed Stephen's cheek. "Ian said he couldn't provide a miracle, but he did," she whispered. "God be thanked."

Michael laid a hand on Stephen's shoulder, his feelings evident in the brief, wordless touch. Then he and his wife left the room arm in arm. Blackmer started to follow, looking broken and tragically alone.

Reminded of Michael's appearance when his younger brother was at the shattering point, Stephen summoned the strength for one last effort. "You can't change your past, Blackmer, but you can change your future. Since your father failed you, create a family of your own that will be more satisfying."

The physician paused. "I've wanted to, but I felt . . .

unworthy. That it would be wrong to offer marriage to Jane when she's the daughter and sister of clerics, and I'm a bastard whose own father would not acknowledge him."

"Marry her, Blackmer. Though I've never met the woman, your Jane must have already accepted your illegitimacy or she wouldn't be keeping company with you," Rosalind said crisply. "Stephen is giving you a second chance. Use it well."

There was a faint lightening of the physician's features. "Perhaps . . . I will." He left, closing the door gently behind him.

The exhaustion that had been hovering over Stephen descended like a London fog. He rolled over, his grip on his wife's hand bringing her down onto the bed. "Oh, Rosalind," he whispered, barely coherent. He wanted to tell her how much he loved her, but he had used every last iota of strength. "Rose . . ."

Tears shining in her eyes, she stretched out beside him on top of the covers and drew him into her arms, cradling his head to her breasts. "Sleep, my love," she murmured. "Sleep, and be well."

Releasing his breath in a ragged sigh of contentment, he sank into the blessed welcome of her embrace and let the darkness take him.

Rosalind woke when Stephen kissed her under her ear. She opened her eyes and gave him a shining smile. It was morning, the room was full of light, and they were lying face to face wrapped around each other like ivy. As soon as she saw his expression, she knew that his escape from the valley of death had not been a dream born of her desperation. He was going to live. *He was going to live.* "I won't ask if you slept well," she said lazily, "because I don't think you moved all night."

"Probably not." He patted her breast with interest. "That being the case, how did you get into this fetching shift? Or were you wearing it last night during all the melodrama, and I simply failed to notice?"

She smiled. "I got up in the middle of the night and changed, then came back. You never stirred."

"You could have marched a regiment through here and I wouldn't have noticed. It's the best night's sleep I've had in months." He flexed his fingers. "I feel better already. The numbness in my hands and feet is lessening, and the ache in my stomach is almost bearable."

"Wonderful!" She stretched joyously. "I'm so happy that I'd be turning somersaults if it weren't so much nicer being in bed. You must feel even happier."

"Oddly, last night when I learned that I wasn't going to die, I felt . . . numb. I guess I had adjusted so well to the prospect of death that it took time to absorb the idea of continued life." He grinned. "This morning is a different story. I no longer fear death, but I'm amazingly glad that it's not yet my time to shuffle off this mortal coil." He ran a slow hand along her side from shoulder to hip. "However, the change in prospects means we must now renegotiate our marriage."

She stared at him, her heart seeming to freeze. "What do you mean?"

"If you'll recall, when I proposed I made the point that even if we didn't suit, you'd be safe because I wouldn't be around to plague you for more than a few months. As you said, we'd have only the cream." His hand came to rest on her hip, his palm warm through the thin fabric of her shift. "Now you're stuck with me indefinitely, which means milk and cheese and other mundane things along with cream."

"You beast!" she exclaimed as her heart started again. "I should push you out of bed. I thought you meant that now that you have the time to take a good look around the Marriage Mart, you'd like to put me aside in favor of a more suitable wife."

He looked startled. "Quite apart from the fact that it's almost impossible to put aside a wife, even if I wanted to, which I most certainly don't, what kind of wife do you think would be more suitable than you?"

She shouldn't have spoken, but now she must continue. "One more like Louisa." She swallowed. "A wife you could love."

After a moment of stillness, he said gravely, "I didn't love Louisa, and she didn't love me. In fact, our marriage made us both wretched, though we tried our best."

"I . . . I guess I misinterpreted what you said, or didn't say, about your first marriage," Rosalind said, startled. "I thought you loved her so much that no other woman could ever be more than a bedmate."

"You think that I only regard you as a bedmate? I owe George Blackmer and the valley of the shadow even more than I thought for the forced lessons on life." He smoothed back her hair with one warm hand. "As a Kenyon, love was not part of my view of the world, until I had that dream or visit to heaven or whatever it was. I realized then that love was the essence of being."

His eyes darkened with the force of his feelings. "I desired you the moment I saw you. I liked you as soon as we spoke, and knew that I must have you with me after we became intimate. But only when I neared death and was beyond desire did I fully realize how much you mean to me." He bridged the few inches between them for a kiss of exquisite tenderness. "I love your body, love your mind, love your soul. I was incapable of saying that earlier, so now I'll make it official. I love you, Rosalind. I've never said that to a woman before."

Her eyes widened. "Never?"

"Well, I said it to Claudia yesterday." He smiled. "But the meaning isn't quite the same with one's sister."

She felt a glow of warmth that started in her heart and swiftly spread through her whole being, driving out pockets of cold shadow that she had not recognized herself. "I love you, too," she whispered. "At first I didn't dare admit it to myself, and then I didn't speak because I didn't think it was right to burden you more. But the truth was always in my heart. I love you now, and I will forever."

He kissed her again. "You are my heart and my beloved," he said softly. "It was worth going to the brink of death to find you, my perfect rose."

Even as she luxuriated in the warmth of his love, her conscience prodded her. "Since it's truth-telling time, I have a confession to make—I'm not perfect, though heaven knows that I've tried. I did my best to be the perfect daughter, the perfect stage manager. I wanted to be the perfect wife to you, always warm, loving, and reasonable." She regarded him a little anxiously, feeling foolish but needing reassurance. "I think I could have maintained the illusion if we were only going to be married for a few months, but I can't do it for years on end. I have a temper and I'm selfish and I'll never be perfect. I thought I'd better warn you before your expectations get too high."

He laughed and hugged her closer so that her soft curves molded against him. A pity that his body wasn't strong enough to express the fierce passions of his mind and soul. How long would it be until he recovered enough to make love to her?

Not long, judging by the way he was feeling now. "I shall modify my statement. You aren't perfect. I'm sure that if I think for a week or two, I shall be able to come up with at least five or six examples of imperfect behavior on your part." His voice dropped to a whisper. "But you are the perfect woman for me."

EPILOGUE

London, 1819

Naturally the Duke and Duchess of Ashburton had the best box in the Athenaeum Theater. Rosalind was bubbling with excitement when she and Stephen arrived for the Fitzgerald Theater Troupe's grand opening production of *The Winter's Tale*. Five months of refurbishing had transformed the company's new home into an extravaganza of rich colors, ornate moldings, and glittering chandeliers.

Before taking her seat, she paused by the railing and surveyed the auditorium. Men and women in brilliant evening dress were entering the boxes and milling about in the galleries, laughing and talking over the lively strains of the orchestra. In the opposite box, an assortment of Cassells and Westleys were taking their seats. She waved to her relatives, then to the Duke and Duchess of Candover, who had come to see the troupe that had been their personal discovery.

There were other friends, too, for society had proved very welcoming to an actress who was a French countess by birth and a duchess by marriage. She picked out the Strathmores, the Aberdares, the St. Aubyns, and knew that other couples were in seats not visible to her. "It's a full house, Stephen. With all of your grand friends taking boxes, this has become the most desirable location in London tonight."

He laughed and put his arm around her waist. "This

time there will be no need to go out into Covent Garden during the interval to bring people back."

She leaned against him contentedly and looked up into his face. It was hard to believe that he had been at death's door five months earlier. Now he was strong and whole, better-looking than any man had a right to be, and—since it was in the privacy of her mind, she could admit it—marvelously virile. Inventive, too, which was useful considering her ever expanding figure.

His pas de deux with death had left another legacy, for both of them had found that every day, every hour, every minute was charged with a special sense of life's preciousness. They had discussed that more than once, grateful and determined never to take each other and their love for granted. She smiled into her husband's eyes. "You're looking particularly handsome tonight, my love."

"And you are ravishingly beautiful." He looked as if he wanted to kiss her, but restrained himself since half of fashionable London was watching.

She laughed as she settled, carefully, into her chair. "I'm the size of a cart horse."

"Yes," he said equably. "But still beautiful." He sat on her right and unobtrusively put his hand on her swelling belly, receiving a kick for his reward. "She's active tonight. It must be the Fitzgerald in her responding to an upcoming performance."

Rosalind chuckled. "*He* is being quite aristocratic and demanding the attention which is his due, like a Kenyon or a St. Cyr."

The door to the box opened, and Lord and Lady Herrington stepped in. Claudia looked both younger and softer than she had five months before. "Good evening, Stephen, Rosalind." Claudia gave her sister-in-law a light kiss. "Congratulations. Your family's theater is going to be a great success."

Amazingly enough, Rosalind and Claudia had become friends. Not that Claudia couldn't still be caustic, but she was amazingly more relaxed and tolerant than she'd been before. Stephen's doing, from what Claudia had confided to her sister-in-law.

Taciturn as always, Andrew bowed to Rosalind and shook hands with Stephen, then helped Claudia into a chair as tenderly as if she were made of porcelain. His wife gave him a glance that was positively sultry.

Rosalind hid her smile behind her fan. The visible warmth between Claudia and Andrew was another result of the way Stephen had transformed his sister's life.

Stephen murmured in her ear, "I like seeing a couple who have been married for two decades acting like newlyweds. Will we be like that in twenty years?"

"Without question." Wearing her most demure expression, Rosalind used her fan to mask touching her husband in an exceedingly improper way.

Stephen caught his breath, his eyes going green. "Do you have any plans for later, Duchess?"

"I intend to go backstage to celebrate the night's triumph with the Fitzgerald Theater Troupe." She gave Stephen a slanting glance. "Then I want to go home and seduce my husband."

He gave her an intimate smile. "You won't have to work very hard to achieve that."

Rosalind glanced at the stage and saw that Maria, costumed as Hermione, was peeking out from the wings, her expression blazing with excitement. Seeing that Rosalind was looking her way, she waved, then ducked out of sight.

All was probably chaos backstage at the moment, but Rosalind had perfect faith that by the time the curtain rose, the troupe would be ready to create magic. Mary Kent, Simon's sister, had stepped capably into Rosalind's shoes as a competent actress and an excellent stage manager. She and Jeremiah Jones were planning to marry in May, a week after the wedding of Jessica and Simon.

Stephen asked, "Do you wish you were backstage, waiting to step out and create magic for all of these people?"

"Not at all," she said with complete sincerity. "How could I be happier than I am now?"

The last guests for the Ashburton box arrived: Lord and Lady Michael Kenyon and Catherine's beautiful fourteen-year-old daughter, Amy, who was shimmering with excitement at attending an adult event.

There was a flutter of greetings. Claudia and Michael were unlikely ever to be close, but now they were at least civil to each other. Rosalind had become very fond of Michael, who was in some ways very like Stephen, and in others completely different.

Her gaze went back to Stephen. He was the linchpin of the Kenyons, the head of the family both in terms of custom and natural authority. It was a tribute to the largeness of his spirit that he had even become friends with his illegitimate half brother, who now went by the name George Blackmer-Kenyon. The physician had followed Stephen's advice and married his gentle widow. Rosalind had seen the two together, and knew the marriage would in time heal the wounds on Blackmer's spirit.

In a flurry of laughter and silk skirts, Catherine kissed Rosalind's cheek, then settled into the chair on her left. She was also pregnant and expected to deliver several weeks after Rosalind. Clearly she and her husband had enjoyed a very satisfactory reunion after he joined her in London.

The musicians in the orchestra pit went silent for a moment. Then they struck up a stirring triumphal march. Conversation died and all eyes turned to the stage.

With a roll of drums, the curtain began to rise, revealing the grandeur of a royal palace. Rosalind leaned back in her chair and clasped Stephen's hand. His fingers tightened around hers, and he raised her hand to press a kiss on her wrist. He murmured, "Let the magic begin."

She smiled into his eyes. "It already has, my love. It already has."

NOW IN PAPERBACK

The *New York Times* hardcover bestseller

SOMEONE LIKE YOU
by Elaine Coffman

"An emotionally satiating work that is
an instant keeper . . ."
—*Affaire de Coeur*

"An intensely moving tale of emotional growth
and discovery. Once again, Mrs. Coffman spins
a complex tapestry of the human heart,
a vivid portrayal of life and
the grace and redemption of love."
—*Romantic Times*

In this stirring romance set in nineteeth-century
Texas, a mystery man who appears to be a down-on-
his-luck cowboy and a beautiful young "spinster" hiding a secret past of her own dare to reach for love.
Hailed for the richness and complexity of her work,
Elaine Coffman demonstrates yet again why she is one
of the most beloved romance writers.

On sale June 2